D0468688

BROADVIEW LIBRARY

THE NINE

NO LONGER PROPERTY OF
SEATTLE PUBLIC LIBRARY

Tracy Townsend

The Nine

an imprint of Prometheus Books
Amherst, NY

Published 2017 by Pyr®, an imprint of Prometheus Books

The Nine. Copyright © 2017 by Tracy Townsend. All rights reserved. No part of this publication may be reproduced, stored in a retrieval system, or transmitted in any form or by any means, digital, electronic, mechanical, photocopying, recording, or otherwise, or conveyed via the Internet or a website without prior written permission of the publisher, except in the case of brief quotations embodied in critical articles and reviews.

Cover illustration © Adam S. Doyle
Cover design by Jacqueline Nasso Cooke
Cover design © Prometheus Books

This is a work of fiction. Characters, organizations, products, locales, and events portrayed in this novel are either products of the author's imagination or used fictitiously.

Inquiries should be addressed to
Pyr
59 John Glenn Drive
Amherst, New York 14228
VOICE: 716-691-0133
FAX: 716-691-0137
WWW.PYRSF.COM

21 20 19 18 17   5 4 3 2 1

Library of Congress Cataloging-in-Publication Data

Names: Townsend, Tracy, 1979- author.
Title: The nine / Tracy Townsend.
Description: Amherst, NY : Pyr, an imprint of Prometheus Books, [2017] | Series: Thieves of fate ; 1
Identifiers: LCCN 2017011546 (print) | LCCN 2017027054 (ebook) | ISBN 9781633883420 (ebook) | ISBN 9781633883413 (softcover)
Subjects: | BISAC: FICTION / Fairy Tales, Folk Tales, Legends & Mythology. | GSAFD: Fantasy fiction.
Classification: LCC PS3620.O975 (ebook) | LCC PS3620.O975 N56 2017 (print) | DDC 813/.6--dc23
LC record available at https://lccn.loc.gov/2017011546

Printed in the United States of America

For my mother.

I never found my tears for you. I wrote a book, instead.

DAY ONE

1st Elevenmonth

1.

For years, Ivor Ruenichnov had run New Vraska Imports with the glass-eyed hunger of a shark. He wasn't a man prone to sentiment or waste, and so it was scarcely a surprise to Rowena Downshire to find the old man waiting for her up in the warehouse's courier loft when she returned from the Shipman's Bazaar.

"You saw Sticks?" he asked by way of greeting. "Gave it that damned monkey-rat it wanted so much?"

Rowena nodded. Her hands still ached from the dozen half-moon cuts the little beast had taken out of them as she'd carried it, stuffed into the smallest cage she could manage, down to the lanyani merchant's sad curiosities booth. The damned thing had gone half-mad when she hauled it free for Sticks's inspection. Then again, Rowena hadn't exactly found the lanyani's rutted face of old oak or its white, iris-less eyes soothing, either.

Every kind of animal, it seemed, knew better than to trust the walking trees.

Ivor thrust out his hand, fingers flexing greedily.

Rowena passed her purse on. She was glad she'd thought to nick the spare halfer out of it before coming back to the warehouse. If there was anything the old man could do fast, it was count. He'd know an extra half-piece would mean she'd been engaging in . . . What was his phrase? *Extracurricular profiteering.*

"Get caught stealing while you're my bird," Ivor had snarled the day he bought Rowena up from Oldtemple, *"and I'll buy you back from the gendarme so I can slit your neck myself, savvy? I have a* reputation *to uphold."*

Rowena looked down at Bess's foot chest on the loft floor between them.

A reputation, she thought. *He certainly has that.*

Ivor grunted approvingly at the bag before stowing it away. "Now, business. Been days since we've seen Bess, poor bird. She en't coming back. Let's see what we can make of this lot."

Ivor unlocked the chest and shoved it toward Rowena with a hob-nailed boot. It was large enough she could have curled up in it and shut the lid. She had, actually, in the days when she and Bess were small and playing their games in the loft above Ivor's stocking rooms and offices. Rowena still recalled the wallop of his false hand when he'd discovered their muddy footprints on the fine clothes inside. Since then, the key had rattled from the remoteness of Ivor's belt, hidden among half a hundred others of every length and heft a locksmith could craft.

It had been a little better than two weeks since Bess went out on delivery to Smallduchess Avergnon. The smallduchess had offered Ivor only a shrug and her apologies when he came calling the day after Bess's scheduled delivery. *"But really,"* the smallduchess tutted, *"could one be surprised by a street lark taking leave of her work and her senses to go back to the rough life whence she'd come? It happens all the time. A pity."*

Mick's familiar laugh jolted Rowena to attention. The boy was her age but big and craggy-looking with a broad, flat nose. He could have passed for eighteen, and it was well for him he often did. His delivery routes ran along the rough wharves of Oceanside. Rowena had started keeping the knife in her boot on Mick's sage advice. Bess had kept her own knife ready for Mick himself.

Mick sat on his pallet by the coal brazier, warming his hands. He winked. "G'wan, Rowie. Give us a look, eh?"

"You turn your back, Mick, or I'll sock you in the neck," she snapped.

"Enough," Ivor growled. His iron gray moustache hunkered down like some burrowing creature. "I'm not your bloody ladies' maid, Downshire. Try the fit in your own time." Ivor threw open the chest, then put a hand on a gouty knee, rising with an effort. "Last of the ladies now. Need you to pretty up for the gentry's goods."

Rowena lifted a muslin skirt and tucked it against herself. Bess had been tall. Pretty, too—a favorite among customers for discreet, sensitive jobs, with clothes that were nearly costumes. The chest was full to bursting with blouses, chemises, and skirts; little fitted jackets, broad sun hats, and tidy bonnets; even a decent fur muff and wool shawl. There were two pairs of walking slippers and a lovely pair of ankle boots the color of cream, laced with silk ribbons wound around polished brass frogs. Everything would need hemming, but Rowena knew the trick of it and could work at it on slow days.

Ivor snatched the skirt from Rowena's hands, hissing like a kettle. "Look at your hands! You'll get this filthy." His hands were scarcely better, the right stained with tobacco and ink, the left an ever-changing array of filthy prosthetics. Today, it was a rough brass replica of a hand, its digits stiff and brutish. But it might have been worse. Some days, it was a rust-flecked gaff hook. Others, Ivor attached his "experiment," a sharp, scissoring riot of gear teeth and cranks bought from a Nipponese tinker with too little language to keep from getting skinned down to his britches. Today, the false fist merely punched about Rowena, as if it could attach the clothes to her frame by main force. He paused and held the skirt out, squinting at Rowena eclipsed behind it.

"Bah. You haven't any hips."

The old man dropped the skirt and pulled out a high-collared blue day dress. Rowena felt him clamp down on her chest with a metal thumb and forefinger, pinching through her clothes. She stared down at his hands. The fleshy one drifted a bit lower than was needed to mimic a fit.

"No tits, either, damn you," Ivor spat, casting the dress back into the trunk. "How old are you now, Downshire?"

"Thirteen."

The reply was a long, indigestive noise peculiar to Ivor. Rowena had been running for him for nearly seven years and still wasn't certain if the sound meant agreement, or displeasure, or thoughtfulness.

Probably *not* thoughtfulness.

"Not *so* bad," he decided. "Thought you were fifteen. You're a hopeless-looking girl, but at least not a hopeless woman. You've time yet."

He picked up his braided hawthorn walking stick, all knots and lacquered thorns, and stumped toward the long ladder stretching down to the warehouse floor.

Ivor tucked his stick under his false arm, easing his bulk through the square cut around the ladder. "Stuff the brassieres until you've grown something of your own," he advised. "Folks in Bess's districts like a girl who *looks* like one. Makes 'em charitable. Some even tip."

Rowena listened to the ladder moan as Ivor descended. These days, by the time he reached top or bottom on a visit to his bird's nest, he was flushed and snorting like an ox. The stick had once been a weapon; now it was a prop for his gouty constitution. Still, under his straining belt, that barrel body was as much muscle as fat, and all it took was one crack to remind you of it.

Rowena looked down at the chest. She tucked a lace apron back inside. She folded the muslins and damasks and little tartan lovelies. Then she shut the lid. On his pallet, Mick snored like a steel grinder.

"Some even tip."

Rowena sat with her feet dangling over the railed edge of the loft. Casting a furtive glance to be sure Ivor was well out of sight, she reached for the leather strap hidden up her right sleeve. It was where she tucked all her "extracurriculars." So far, it had outmatched the old man in half a hundred friskings. She dug for the halfer she'd pinched off the pudding man just an hour before. There'd been no time to go to Oldtemple and put it against her mother's ledger before she was due back at the warehouse. Rowena ran her thumb down the coin's imperfect edge. A bad break, really more of a third-piece than a half, but if she was lucky, the prison accountant wouldn't be bastard enough to take out his scales. She leaned against Bess's chest and felt its latch dig into her back, nagging.

I'll probably have to learn how to act ladylike, too. At least until Ivor gets a new bird.

If he got a new bird. Three years before, the courier staff had been Rowena's older brother Jorrie, and Bess, and Mick, and of course Rowena herself. But consumption had taken Jorrie, and none of the birds Ivor had sprung from the debtors' prison of Oldtemple or the workhouse of Brixton since had worked out. One he'd clouted so hard the poor girl took a brain fever and never awoke again. The other tried to steal from the office strongbox. In her darker moments, Rowena still wondered where that boy's bones lay. Now with Bess swallowed up by the streets, the little aerie of couriers had grown spacious and the routes long. Enough of Ivor's business was aboveboard he could carry on moving the illicits with a small staff, but not for very long. There were always new clients, and Corma's districts were forever swelling.

Bess had been careful. So very careful.

Rowena recalled Bess's knife and how quickly the older girl could make it appear. The blade had only been as long as her thumb, but its edge was ground to a faint, blue blur. It looked like a serpent's tooth, full of menace and purpose. Now, it seemed very small in Rowena's memory.

Rowena shivered. She might have looked down at the ground floor of Ivor Ruenichnov's warehouse shop. But there was no point. It always looked the same. Desks with busy clerks. Pallets of goods. Instead, she gazed out the windows running along the wall of the space between floor and ceiling she called home.

In the distance, Rowena could see smokestacks and steeples, clock towers, jail towers, and the low, rude walls surrounding them. The city was the gray of pigeon wing and granite here, the black of soot and brackish mold there; the rust stains on the teeth of gargoyles; and the faint smells of charring meat and alley fires and sour ale. The cracking whips of carters driving loads and the screams of balking horses making reply echoed down the cobblestone streets.

New Vraska Imports was near enough Dockside that she could spy a little knot of squints from the Ecclesiastical Commission prowling around a new pump design some lay engineer had been tinkering with for weeks. Rumor was he meant to do away with old, heavy crank handles—the aigamuxa bars that drove clockwork ships and owed their name to the burly ogres employed turning them. Only they could wind the massive mainsprings to which the bars were linked. But the aiga had been damned hard to employ on the up and up since the workhouse laws changed three years before. If this loon could replace manual pumping on ships with a pressure engine, he'd cut the size of crews at sea by nearly half.

Rowena leaned close to the glass, peering suspiciously. If the pumping crews lost their work, she knew all too well where they'd end up.

"I hope your engine's a pile of goat pellets," she whispered.

Moments later, the acrid tang of scalded gears wafted down the alley. Now, the tinker was scurrying about, throwing one sloshing bucket after another on the contraption while his reverend audience staggered back, batting at the smoke with their long, embroidered sleeves. The whole scene disappeared in a cloud of spilling steam.

Stupid idea anyway, Rowena thought. *Bess would've liked it.* Bess had liked anything new and odd. *Modern.*

"It's by the Grace of the Unity that we live in a city," Bess had declared once with a solemnity that belied her comment's obviousness. They'd been walking a delivery together, Bess carrying the real goods in a daintily covered grocer's basket, Rowena pushing a load of decoy parcels with a grouchy old handcart, dressed every inch the good serving girl. Bess loved looking the proper lady. Loved talking like one even more.

"We should be happy to have people inventing new conveniences," she'd gone on, *"and happy to live civilly because of them."*

And Bess had punctuated the statement by slipping a bag of chestnuts nicked from a roasting cart into her muff.

Rowena had a suspicion of clockworks, let alone standing engines. They could snap a man's arm up in gear teeth and grind him down to a paste. The coke sellers and coal men had a notion of trying to supplant them with mobile engines, but their designs were little better than giant samovars with wheels. And they left their own messes. An engineer from the Ecclesiastical Commission had debuted a hulking, awkward platform affixed to an old lightning rail undercarriage just a month earlier, trying to begin the Decadal Conference season with an inventive bang. He drew quite a crowd down by the Cathedral Commons and, in the end, had his bang. Not half an hour in, the street filled with the screams of his coaling boy, cooked like a piece of meat plunged in a kettle.

Yet Bess seemed to love the city's danger as much as its elegance. She was perfect, or so Ivor had told Rowena when she was new to the trade and brought out to shadow her.

"Bess is a natural, little bird," the old man had whispered in Rowena's ear, *"because she was born to look clean and proper. Look how she smiles at the*

woman selling scarves. Bad thieves and couriers sulk and stalk. Good ones stuff the payoff in their handbag, all smiles, and you'll never look twice. And there she goes, beautiful thing. See? A natural."

And Rowena had seen. Two weeks ago, looking more like a wealthy merchant's daughter than a courier minx, Bess took her last package and disappeared like fog on a hot morning.

Rowena looked below. She could almost see Bess's phantom claiming that tiny bundle, small enough to tuck in a brocade purse. Ivor had pulled her in close, his flesh hand straying low, tracing the laces of her corset. His lips almost touched her ear, whispering something. Rowena remembered the point of Ivor's hook tangled in her skirts. Bess stiffened just slightly, and her smile became porcelain—painted on, brittle.

And then Bess threw a wave and a kiss up at Rowena and swirled away, skirts bustling about her. Gone.

Rowena wondered if she could ever make Bess's clothes fit. She knew in an instant she didn't want to.

She pressed the half-clink coin under her leather strap again. She knew something of getting *tips*, all right. But she had her own ways of scoring them.

Rowena Downshire had never been to so much as an EC free school, let alone had tutors, but she knew numbers because numbers *mattered.* Numbers told her if she'd been cheated and would get Ivor's hawthorn, or if she'd saved enough to mark against the Oldtemple clerk's ledger. Whether she had nipped away at her mother's debt or only shaved the always-climbing keeping fees. Rowena had a number in mind. She knew it down to the quarter-clink.

Five hundred fourteen and a half more.

Ivor Ruenichnov slammed the door of his ground-floor office with enough bile to impress upon the clerk half-asleep outside that he did not wish to be disturbed. The room was hot and noisome, choked by a dense, gray smoke from his private stove. Anyone else found the heat oppressive. Ivor thrived in it. It loosened the pain in his legs and made the room feel close, tight—private.

He pushed around the papers stacked on his desk until he found the letter pouch he sought. The clerk, Albert, had attached a scribe's ciphering of a galvano-graph spark to it—something from the Coventry Passage rectory, inquiring after a delivery long expected.

Ordinary folk kept their correspondences to posted letters and galvano-grams. The public post came twice daily, but its letters were lost near as often as delivered, eaten up by sorting gins and postage-punchers. And some messages were too long for galvano-graph. And so, there was still a brisk business in letter-carrying for Ivor's New Vraska Imports, a legitimate way to earn coin outside smuggling off the quaysides.

The Reverend Doctor Nora Pierce of the Ecclesiastical Commission and her colleague, the Reverend Doctor Phillip Chalmers, had relied on Ivor for their correspondence for the better part of a year. Ivor liked long-standing customers.

The longer they employed his services, the more of their letters he could steam open.

The packet Ivor now held was late—*very* late—because he had found its contents interesting. It would need to be carried soon, if only because the mailing pouch refused to hold any more. Ivor had been scowling at Pierce's letters to Chalmers for nearly a month now. He was troubled both by how much and how little of them made any sense. There had been research. Apparently it promised to be big, though in what way was beyond Ivor. That didn't trouble him. Indeed, he prided himself on being obtuse where matters of theosophical science were concerned. No, what bothered Ivor Ruenichnov about Nora Pierce's letters was how much of them seemed to be written in plain language and *still didn't make sense.*

Ivor was, at bottom, a thug, and though he had a spy's ambition for gathering useful secrets, he lacked the discernment to make anything of them. He ground his teeth and resisted the urge to fling the letters at the coal stove in disgust. He had only a prickly feeling about Chalmers and Pierce's business that foretold both danger and profit—but for whom? The woman's last flock of letters said little about the research. The scientific scrawl had grown sparser and sparser, finally giving way to a desperate change of tone.

Ivor unfolded the most recent piece, dated a week earlier.

The sooner you can destroy our notes, the better, Phillip. They will be following not far behind these letters.

It was that last phrase that most bothered Ivor—*They will be following not far behind these letters.* "They" could mean more notes. But why warn Chalmers of that? No. "They" were people of some kind. People who Pierce seemed to think would make things hot for— Ivor frowned. For whom? Surely whoever "they" might be, they'd seek the *recipient* of the letters, Reverend Chalmers.

Ivor chewed his lip and stuffed the letter back into the pouch with little regard for the illusion of it being unmolested. He *was*, he supposed, technically a recipient of the letters, too. But what could Pierce have been afraid of? Some rival scholar in the Ecclesiastical Commission? Ivor snorted. As if reverend doctors and bishop professors hired guns to menace one another or steal research.

And he paused.

They didn't, Ivor knew. Not exactly. They hired people whose *job it was* to hire those others. Middlemen. Go-betweens. He should know. Ivor had not always been a smuggler.

The thought that he had been sitting for a week on documents that could embroil him in something more hazardous than his retainer compensated loomed suddenly large. The sooner he was rid of the lot, the better.

Rowena needed to start picking up Bess's routes. There was no time like the present to be about it.

2.

Smallduke Abraham Regenzi's clockwork carriage clamored down the cobblestone streets of Westgate Bridge, throwing up a racket like an ill-tuned piano tumbling downhill. The carriage crew had hammered relentlessly at its signal bells, as if the power of sound waves might part the sea of people through which it had just recently passed. Now, they seemed to keep on making the racket for sport. The smallduke tapped a hand restlessly on the head of his walking stick. He had to speak quite loudly to be heard over the ringing outside, close to shouting words Bess was certain were meant in confidence.

"When we get to the shop, keep well away from the old man. I've business to transact of a most sensitive nature." He fixed her with a stern look, his pursed lips nearly lost in a tawny bristle of moustache and side whiskers.

Bess nodded. Regenzi seemed satisfied.

Bess had always made a show of liking the style of a clockwork carriage and four winding men. Truthfully, she'd never actually ridden in one before. Now that she had, she longed for the familiar, quiet jouncing of an ordinary hackney. She sat looking to the quayside, watching barrow men lift their wobbly loads and make for the workhouses lining the riverbank.

None of this, she thought gloomily, *is going to plan.*

Three weeks ago, the idea seemed like simplicity itself. After only a few subtle inquiries to the maids of her finer clients, Bess received a note by way of a mute girl working for the Smallduchess Avergnon. Her ladyship's good friend, the Smallduke Abraham Regenzi, wished to employ a courtesan. Bess was no trained companion, but her mother had been the matron of a rather fine brothel. She fancied she knew a bit about how to look at a man and move her hips. Odds on, she could convince him of her aptitude without any formal papers. Smallduchess Avergnon agreed to meet Bess, interviewed her briefly—most of the conference conducted without the bothersome imposition of clothing—and recommended her to Regenzi with many compliments.

And until just now, things had been quite lovely. The smallduke asked very few bedroom favors and rewarded Bess with jewels and little pets and sweets. That morning had been pleasant. Abraham had let her sleep late, then met her in the breakfast parlor with instructions to wear a good hat and bring along a parasol. There would be a ball at his city manor that evening; she would need to dress well for it—very well, in fact. He'd flourished the invitation roll before her, as if the cascade of long, layered titles running down the page should mean anything to Bess at all. *"Smalldukes and the governor's cabinet and bishop professors, and even Reverends Pierce and Chalmers, the keynote speakers for the Decadal Conference,"* he'd boasted. *"Nothing less than the finest will do, poppet."*

And so, they had journeyed to the shops and spent hours choosing, trying, returning, rejecting, tailoring, cinching, lacing, unlacing, and fitting over and over again. Now, hours later, the carriage's parcel platform was loaded down with tissue-lined boxes of petticoats and gowns, with high-lacing boots and teetering ivory heels: a freight worth two working men's yearly salaries at one of the Regenzi family's textile mills.

Yet, Smallduke Regenzi had grown stiff and commanding. They were traveling to the edge of the Old Town, toward Westgate Bridge. It was such an ancient quarter that this neighborhood, once farthest west in all of Corma, was now very nearly its easternmost appendage, the rest of the city swollen up against the seaside to the true west. The people of quality did not come to Westgate Bridge—a rumpled borough of fulleries and fisheries and pubs and common greengrocers—for any reason save one: they came for the Alchemist at the Stone Scales.

Bess supposed Corma had dozens of alchemists, being a city of better than a hundred thousand souls, and that excluding the aigamuxa in their shanty villages of fire escapes and rope ladders in the south river quays, and the lanyani in their traveling wains and secret hothouses. The quality might secure a reverend doctor to act as chemist and physick, but for the everyday citizen, an alchemist was Rational enough. Most were immigrants from lands far south and east of Corma, where the Divine Unity had never quite taken hold—women and men the color of ochre or ebony, with exotic accents and an eye for good clink. A few were castoffs from the many Amidonian seminaries, fourth- or fifth-year students who couldn't afford the final examinations required for a doctorate of theosophical sciences. Couldn't afford or, perhaps, couldn't pass.

But there was only one man called "the Alchemist." His shop sold a bit of everything. Rumor was he had never been asked a question he couldn't answer with authority. His goods always worked, even when they promised unlikely results. Old men and women, recalling the superstitions of their ancestors, called him a sorcerer. Or a witch. The terms varied, but the implication was the same: what he was and what he sold were very real and not to be trifled with.

Bess felt a sharp rap against her knee and flinched from the window. Smallduke Regenzi leaned toward her, all but bellowing over the sound of drive-train chimes and scrambling feet.

"You don't scare easily, I hope? Just hold your tongue and don't dawdle about his things. He has a beastly temper. The folk around these parts think the devil of him. But he'll give you no trouble while I'm around."

Regenzi offered her a wink and a salute with his crystal-headed cane, the picture of gentlemanly confidence.

Bess smiled, all beatitude, and thought, *I already know him, you silly bastard.*

Of course she knew him. The common alchemist needed supplies that were damnably hard to find, and so import and a bit of smuggling was an assumed professional overhead. But *the* Alchemist? He needed all these things and more. Since she was a pretty, proper thing of twelve, Bess had made Ivor's monthly deliveries to Westgate Bridge and the infamous Stone Scales. There might not be a soul who had seen the Alchemist more regularly than Bess or knew his shop better. She knew very well the local people didn't think the devil of him. He was, if anything, something like a talisman—held at a careful, superstitious distance, a human ward against whatever bugbears they imagined still lurked in the world.

Still, Bess was terrified of him, and with good reason.

For two weeks, she'd been protected from Ivor by dissolving into thin air. She hoped fervently the old bastard believed her dead. But now, the Alchemist would see her. If she were unlucky, he would recognize her as the mannerly young woman who had passed him his tight-wrapped parcels so many times before. If she were as miserably unlucky as she feared, he would assume her a runaway and contact Ivor with the news, and that would make an end of it. And why shouldn't the Alchemist turn her in? Out from under Ivor's boot, she could do anything—turn to the constabulary and testify about his operations, implicate the Alchemist in years of illegal trafficking. No. At large, she was a threat, and one didn't become a fearsome legend by turning a blind eye to one's own weaknesses.

A fortnight ago, Bess's life began anew. The clench in her stomach warned it might soon be ending.

The carriage jangled to a halt in front of a familiar block of cross-framed buildings. Bess felt sick and dizzy.

"Abraham," she said, smiling as sweetly as she could, "I feel a little under the weather. Might I just stay in the carriage? Please?"

Regenzi frowned. "What a pity, poppet. Still—" he stepped down to the curb and reached back to her with a gloved hand, "—if you're feeling green, we're sure to find a remedy here."

Oh, Bess, you're such a fool.

The color must have drained from Bess's face, for Regenzi stepped toward her quickly, lifting her in a sweeping gesture about the waist. "Come, darling," he said. "Be easy about the stairs." His hand closed on her waist and squeezed, the grip sudden and fierce. "And remember what I said," he hissed into her ear.

The road leading directly to the Stone Scales was too narrow to admit carriages, and so Smallduke Regenzi's driver had parked one street below. Regenzi and Bess walked up a curving stone staircase, stubborn lichens making each step treacherous. The stairs led to the highstreets of Westgate Bridge, lanes so old they had no names and no need of them.

The Stone Scales was a tall, slender building with a wide, leaded glass window, its deep sill displaying a menagerie of goods and décor. There was the dog, Bess saw, curled up on a battered, old cushion just inside the door. It was a shaggy hound, russet apart from its gray muzzle.

Bess tried not to flinch as the little silver bell over the door sang out. She peeled free of the smallduke's arm to imitate a careful examination of some well-dusted books. She kept as close to the door as she might and put her back to the shop counter far down the center aisle. The dog raised its head and thumped its tail, a little nasal trill begging attention. Bess glared at it, shooing. The beast tucked its nose back under its tail and sighed.

Regenzi turned over a price tag dangling from some chemical apparatus with the head of his stick. He snorted and looked around again. "Hullo? I say, anyone here?"

"There in a moment," Bess heard the familiar voice reply. The dog uncurled itself and trotted toward its master's voice.

It sounded close by—off to her right. That way lay more and taller bookshelves. Bess could see the Alchemist's left shoulder and part of his backside around the edge of a display case. He was up on one of the rolling ladders, nudging a sheaf of papers back into place before climbing down. The dog got no warmer a reception from the Alchemist than his customers and slunk under the front counter with its tail low.

Bess cut up the center aisle between a chemicals rack and a shelf of folded canvas smocks. They might hide her and still leave gap enough to watch Regenzi's "private transaction."

Knowing what she did of the Alchemist, Bess supposed Smallduke Regenzi could not have done a worse job of introductions had he been given lessons.

A handsome, dandyish young man in a robin's-egg-blue tailcoat and high, black boots, Abraham Regenzi regarded the Alchemist and his rolled shirtsleeves and bracers—his canvas apron tied off around the front and his spectacles hanging from the button hole of his shirt—as one beholds a shoe shiner in a half-kept hotel. Regenzi removed his hat but did not offer his hand or his name. The Alchemist was a tradesman, and a gentleman gives a tradesman nothing more than his card. That was the proper order of things.

Abraham Regenzi believed quite strongly in the proper order of things.

The Alchemist took the card wordlessly, slipped on his spectacles to read it, then studied the smallduke over their rims. He was at least a hand taller than Regenzi and might have been twice his age. Bess found it very hard to guess ages, particularly men's, who were so often much fussier about concealing them than any woman she knew. Then again, Bess supposed the Alchemist probably was not the sort to care what anyone thought of his age—or anything else about him.

"What may I do for you, my lord?" he asked at last. His voice was deep, perfectly unaccented. Practiced. He folded his glasses and returned the card.

Regenzi held the slip of pasteboard, dumbfounded at having his imprint spurned. "I've come for something quite . . . specific."

He looked around furtively. Bess realized it must have been for her. Regenzi reached for the Alchemist's arm, meaning to turn him toward the back of the shop.

The older man saw the approaching hand and turned before it reached him, walking back to the counter. Regenzi spoke quietly, hurriedly, stalking beside the Alchemist.

Bess chewed her lip and watched. The sales counter was at the back of the shop on a raised step. The Alchemist lifted its hinged flap and walked to the other side. He stooped behind the counter, only half-listening to his murmuring customer. Bess heard a muffled response. Regenzi scoffed. The Alchemist straightened and shrugged. Leaving the counter, he shouldered past the smallduke, carrying a wooden crate well packed with straw and glass beakers, which he began arranging on a shelf so near Bess she could have plucked at his sleeve.

Regenzi stood stubbornly by. "If you can make it, say your price. There's no figure you could name I can't answer."

"One thousand sovereigns."

"For a *dram*?"

"Be happy you don't require more."

Regenzi tugged at his whiskers. He paced a tight path up and down the aisle, cutting in between Bess's hiding place and the Alchemist's perfectly disinterested backside. Finally, he cursed.

"And it *will* work?"

The Alchemist turned a gaze on Abraham Regenzi that made Bess's heart stall. There was a tightening in his jaw, as if he had a response he'd closed his teeth on and needed to savage till he could be quite sure of its being dead.

"Yes, my lord," he said quietly. "It will work."

"Fine," Regenzi spat, marching back to the counter. He reached in his breast pocket for his bankbook and counted paper notes in curt, snapping motions. "One thousand. Can it be made now, or shall it be sent along?"

The Alchemist set the last of the glassware in its place and returned behind the counter. He dropped the raised leaf with an absent gesture and began drawing items from the decades of potions and ethers and powders filling his workroom.

"It doesn't take long," the Alchemist said, never looking up from his work. Bess saw several old catalogues and references shelved nearby. He never reached for them. Whatever had been ordered, he seemed to have its recipe committed to memory.

"Excellent. Good. Fine. Yes." It was the smallduke's peculiar habit to revise his assessments downward in quick succession. He turned and, as if he'd forgotten her entirely, startled upon seeing Bess half-hidden among the shelves. "Beatrice, darling!" He reached out both hands and smiled. "Look at you, trembling like a leaf! You're feverish. There's something here to see to that, isn't there, my good man?"

No, no, no, no, no, no, no—

The Alchemist had been massing something grainy on a set of balances. He looked up over the rims of his spectacles as Regenzi produced Bess like a conjuror drawing a scarf from his sleeve. Bess felt the flash of recognition in the old man's eyes like a physical blow. Her knees buckled. She leaned into Regenzi, shuddering.

The room swam. She felt herself bundled up in the smallduke's arms, carried to a little wooden chair beside the front counter. She shivered with cold and sweated with heat, the morning's toast and clotted cream threatening to find its way back up again. Regenzi fanned her with a folded gazette.

"She's sick. Fainting."

"Give her air," Bess heard the Alchemist say, his voice very close. "Your fussing all over the girl won't help."

Bess stared at the floor, trying to fix her gaze to something steady. Regenzi's polished shoes retreated, and she saw the Alchemist's scuffed boots take their place. He crouched before her, lifting her chin with a bent finger.

The Alchemist was dark—of skin, and eye, and expression. Bess had always imagined his eyes to be as black as the rest of him, but this close, she could see a shadow of color, like the green gloss on an opal. They were watchful eyes, deeply creased at the corners. The spectacles hung at his shirt front again.

"If I'm to diagnose something," the Alchemist said rather loudly, glancing back at the smallduke, "I'll need to ask some questions for which the lady might wish her privacy."

Regenzi nodded and backed away, sketching a little bow to Bess. He retreated near the shop's front door and examined a collection of microscopes and crucibles with exaggerated interest.

The Alchemist held Bess's wrist, two fingers over the pulse. He drew out his chronometer, glanced at it long enough to suggest he might be working figures, and returned it to a fold behind his apron. Bess made a study of breathing—slowly in, slowly out, striving to master the art of her lungs filling and emptying. She could not pull her gaze from the old man.

When he spoke at last, it was in an undertone Regenzi would not have heard had he been packed into her corset.

"Beatrice. Well. I never knew your name."

Stupidly, Bess realized she didn't know his, either—apparently no one did, or no one ever troubled to use it. She tried to interpret his tone.

He might have said "Raining today" or "Time to close shop" in the same voice. Factual. Disinterested.

"I expected you a week ago," he continued. "Ivor sent some boy a day late. He dropped the package taking the stairs up from the lowstreet and broke half my goods." He pinched the pad of her thumb and watched the nail turn colors. "I'm sure your master has been wondering what became of you."

"Please," Bess whispered. Without thinking, she closed her hands around his, squeezing as hard as she could through her shaking. "Please. You *can't*."

Two weeks before, Bess would never have dreamed of grabbing the Alchemist's hands. There was some kind of wall around him, deflecting the foolishness of other men, their little courtesies and intimacies. Now, she clung to those hands and felt her arms quaking. He studied her a long, inscrutable time.

"Well?" Smallduke Regenzi's impatient voice cut the air. "What's the story, eh?"

The Alchemist's hands returned Bess's grasp for an instant so brief she thought she'd imagined it. And then he pulled away as easily as if she'd no grip on them at all.

"A minor hysteria," the old man answered. He turned and stepped behind the counter again. "There are half a dozen tonics to treat it. I'll have one prepared in a moment."

Bess stared at the Alchemist as he resumed working, hands moving automatically among his instruments, measuring and combining. If it were not for the slow steadying of her heartbeat to prove otherwise, she might have sworn their conversation had never taken place. It was as if he had forgotten her entirely.

Soon, the Alchemist had a tiny aluminum flask sealed with a gasket-lined screw top and a dainty glass philter bottle wrapped up together in a paper parcel. He laid the order beside the stack of untouched sovereign bills and began tidying up his workspace.

Smallduke Regenzi took the package and donned his four-cornered hat once more. "A pleasure doing business. Good day to you."

The Alchemist was busy stuffing a beech pipe. He nodded, as much to it as to his customer.

Bess stood and slipped her arm into Regenzi's.

They were passing through the door when the old man called.

"Madam, a word."

They turned.

The Alchemist set his pipe beside the till.

"There are some instructions for your medicine." He began scratching on a pad of paper.

Regenzi nudged Bess with a reassuring smile and stayed outside on the stoop, searching about the pockets of his tailcoat for his cigarette case. The bell rang as the door closed between them.

Bess stepped up to the high counter. The Alchemist pushed the pad and pen aside. The pipe smoldering by his elbow smelled sweetly of marjoram and fennel.

"The philter is nothing more than distilled water and some ginger tonic," he said. "And you're not an hysteric, in any case."

Bess tried to look at him squarely. "I know."

He snorted and looked to the front window. Regenzi stood under the awning, wreathed by fog and cigarette smoke.

"Stay with that one and we'll see how long your nerves last." The old man folded the note and offered it between two fingers. "I have a customer in Oldtemple Down who keeps a ladies' garment shop. She complains sometimes how hard it is to find a good clerk."

Bess frowned and took the note. Through the ecru-colored fiber, she could see the digits of an address written in a precise hand.

"Thank you." Somehow, the words sounded more like a question than a statement. She slipped the note into her bodice.

The Alchemist had taken up his pipe again, speaking around its stem. "Your lover has need of rather dangerous things. Be mindful what that might mean for you."

And then he turned, shrugging past the heavy curtain separating the counter room and the storerooms beyond, as if she were already gone.

"Thank you," Bess repeated, louder.

There was no response. As she turned, Bess heard a trilling sound, something like a whine, near her ankles.

The dog. It thrust its head out from a perch on the cash counter step, tail beating a trench in the floor. Bess bent low and smoothed one ragged ear, and for a moment, the creature was the soul of joy.

Outside, the air smelled cool and damp, promising rain. Regenzi dropped his cigarette on the stoop. Bess blinked at him. He seemed suddenly strange—a man half again her age, whiskered and groomed and full of self-assurance. He looked at her solicitously, and something in the look—so sincere and yet so false—struck her like a blow. She felt herself inch away. Regenzi raised an eyebrow and frowned.

Bess straightened. She gave him her most perfect, painted smile.

A few minutes later, he was helping her climb the stairs back into his carriage.

"Not so bad, was it, my dear?" the smallduke asked. "I told you: he may be shyster enough to frighten the locals, but put a man of means and spine in his way and it's plain he's just a common shopkeep."

Bess nodded absently. She tried to recall just what Abraham had said about the Alchemist earlier. It didn't seem to have quite been that. But things were disordered in the attic of her thoughts; she did not think much on his boasts or anything else he said the rest of the ride. She did look down at the paper parcel on the seat beside them, though.

As they entered the foyer of Smallduke Regenzi's manor house, Bess excused herself for a headache's sake, claimed her philter, and retreated to her rooms.

She kept the blinds drawn. She unsealed the bottle, smelled it, and considered. It *did* smell of ginger. She couldn't tell anything more than that, but still—there was prudence, and then there was caution. She set the bottle aside and reached into her bodice, withdrawing the note.

Gooddame Audrea Carringer, 108th on Lower Hillside, Street 19.

It seemed a credible sort of name. Perhaps Audrea Carringer was even a real person.

But still.

Bess returned to her sitting chamber and searched its smoking box for a packet of lucifers. In the lavatory, she dropped the note into the copper basin and pressed a lucifer onto its face, watching the paper curl and cinder. Once there was just a ghost of ash left, she poured the tonic over it and pumped the tap handle to flush the basin clean.

Slowly, she undressed, shrugging and unlacing and unbracing down to her underthings. Bess curled up to sleep, knowing she would turn the kitchen maid away when she came with an afternoon cordial. Her stomach would be unsettled a long while yet. She tried to fill herself with thoughts of the ball—the gentry and peerage and even the Decadal keynotes smiling and taking her daintily proffered hand. But there was no room left inside for their silks and frippery, only a brown parcel dug deep in her guts and words of warning still sounding in her ears.

3.

It might have been the heat of the lecture hall or the swirling light of alchemical globes, shaded to accommodate the lamp film projector. Or it might have been the susurrus of conversation slithering among the auditorium seats. It very likely *was* the presenter's Trimeeni accent, a syrupy drawl spooning out a lengthy paper on conceptualizations of the Golden Mean as demonstrated through the flora of the upper Hebrides. Whatever the cause, though he had scarcely been out of bed three hours, the young Reverend Doctor Phillip Chalmers was left fending off drowsiness barehanded. He shifted about, leaned forward, rested his chin in his palm. He affected a thoughtful, sober expression that involved drawing his lips into a tight purse and his brow down to his knees, looking—for all that effort—like a nearsighted monkey in the robe of a decorated scholar.

His imagination for socially apt contortions exhausted, Chalmers stifled a yawn and checked his chronometer.

Quarter of eleven. The lecture would not end for another half hour.

The published abstract on the session scarcely resembled the business this Trimeeni deacon was carrying on about now. A sham. A trumped-up bit of buggery. Gloomily, Chalmers wondered if he were within his rights to show his contempt by sleeping the rest of the way through.

Certainly, Chalmers thought, *you're entitled not to have your time wasted. You're the bloody keynote.*

The keynote. The drowsiness left him in a rush at the thought. Chalmers checked the date window on his timepiece, though of course he knew well what it would say. Three days from now. Well, properly, two days, one hour, and fifty-one minutes. The *keynote*. Chalmers tried a slow, composing breath.

It did little to help.

For him, the Reverend Doctor Phillip Chalmers—late of the seminary of Rimmerston some three thousand miles east, a gangly tradesman's son from a plantation town—to have found himself a project of such moment, and a partner of such repute as the Reverend Doctor Nora Pierce, was still an unaccountable miracle. They were better than two decades younger than any keynote speakers the Council Bishopric had selected in ages. Chalmers lived in constant fear of some archdeacon coming up from the back of the hall to tap him on the shoulder and show him, *so very sorry*, that there *had* been a mistake in arranging the Ecclesiastical Commission's Decadal Conference program, and he was, indeed, *not in any way suited* to being the keynote.

Probably, the Decadal Committee had chosen his project with Pierce strictly for its provocative title. They had debated a long time over it. Chalmers had wanted something rather straightforward. Say, "On the Movement and Accumulation of God Particles in Statistically Significant Zones: A Case Study." The colon and subtitle had been his little creative flair. He'd been quite proud of them.

But Nora Pierce had a vision and daring quite apart from Phillip Chalmers's. She revised the final copy of the proposal and sent it away. As first author, it had been her right. When the acceptance of the proposal was quickly followed by an invitation to keynote the once-a-decade grand conference, he'd been so pleased he'd scarcely even read the handpress-printed copy of the letter past its first laudatory sentences. He'd seen the new presentation title for the first time only a fortnight before, published as a banner on the conference packet sent by post.

It was the title that sent his fame rolling downhill, skirting the sheer edge of notoriety:

> "God Is With Us: A Seven-Year Communion with the Conscious Divinity, Featuring Mathematical and Material Proofs."

Since then, Chalmers had spent his nights pacing the floors of his rectory apartments and his days reviewing his copies of the notes Pierce had been sending by courier from Lemarcke over the summer. There *was* a sort of truth in that title. But it seemed a mud trap, too, sucking inexorably at his heels. A title like that *promised things*—not explicitly but *implicitly*, which was far, far worse to Chalmers's way of thinking. His colleagues of the EC were no ruffians at a cabaret, but any audience that felt itself shorted on a spectacular premise was likely to turn sour. Chalmers spent days living on a bottle of paregoric and his jangling nerves, searching all his drawers for the evidence to exonerate himself if Nora's presumption earned them both the boot off the EC's rolls.

And yet, the first morning of the conference had nearly passed, and Phillip Chalmers had collected only a gracious tip of a hat while walking the Cathedral campus between lecture sessions, and polite queries after his health and rising fortunes. The fearful tap on his shoulder had not yet come.

Well. At the dinner hour, he would meet Pierce in the Commons and they would retire to his rectory apartments. They could take a meal and discuss the presentation. Perhaps, very gently, he could suggest some kind of opening remarks regarding the title—something to soften its edge. The Council Bishopric would attend the keynote, of course, and who could know whether they would share the Decadal Committee's enthusiasm for such an audacious project? Science and theology had merged generations before those grand old men and dames were born, but for some the word "God" was still a talisman, not a synonym for the ordered processes of creation. Chalmers liked to imagine that science had the better end of things now, with conservative theology pared down to trappings and titles. But that was not an opinion on which one should wager a career. There were still women and men who crossed themselves or blessed themselves or said little prayers when they should be working figures or studying theory. It was like a race memory, the young reverend thought, something in the marrow of bone and stitching of sinew.

Perhaps it was not all bad. Science and the superstitious character of Old Religion had made their peace, in most respects. The cathedrals had been kept, for they were marvels of the forces that gave shape to God's creation, tabernacles of physics and mathematics. Indeed, more of the massive structures had been built, though the modern versions lacked the Gothic opulence of their forbears. Their stained glass windows portrayed the fractal design of the snowflake, the nervous system of the human body, the orbital paths of comets spied at the furthest reaches of a telescope's lens. No more virgins and shepherds giving watch in the night. To be taken seriously as a person of education, one had to see in the cosmos the hand of God—a hand that shaped and cast the first die and now studied with perfect dispassion the restless action of creation.

Chalmers had thought that, for a time. *Believed it* with a fervor once reserved for the Old Religion itself. Now, he was less certain.

Two days more would decide whether he was right to look with doubt on what he thought he knew.

The Reverend Phillip Chalmers felt a pressure on his shoulder.

He snapped forward in his seat with a yelp, sending his note papers shooting out from under a propped elbow. Two sheets filled with idle curlicues fell into the seats before him. A woman with a black bonnet and a pinched face glared back. She wore the brooch of an archdeaconess on the shoulder of her bodice.

"*Sorry*," Chalmers said in an imploring undertone.

He looked from where the touch had come.

A page boy in the stark, clean black-and-gold collar of the EC stood by. He offered the reverend a folded note and a curt bow before departing the lecture hall.

Chalmers's face burned as he felt the weight of many eyes. He looked to the note—long for a galvano-gram, folded twice over.

He read . . . and wished he had not.

To the Reverend Doctor Phillip Chalmers
Lemarcke, 1st Elevenmonth, 0800

The galleon from Lemarcke has turned back to port after a malfunction in one of its sweeps. It is under repair but cannot be expected to sail again sooner than Third-day. There is steerage passage on a freighter that departs on the morrow, though the captain has made buying the berths very dear. I am told it will attain the Port of Corma by Fifth-day, which means I shall miss our keynote. Please use the notes I have sent along to plan the last of it. We shall have much to discuss when I arrive.

Regrets,

Nora Pierce, ThD, PhD, Order of the Physical Sciences, Ecclesiastical Commission

With the stiff composure of a mannequin, Phillip Chalmers rose and began gathering his papers, muttering, "Excuse me, I beg your pardon, so sorry . . ." as he walked up the aisle to the back of the auditorium, addressing no one in particular.

He stepped out into the hall.

He stood at the brass doors in the vestibule.

He put on his tricorn hat.

His nerves did not begin to inform him that he should be afraid until he stepped from the building onto the evergreen paths lacing the Cathedral campus. The terror crept up very slowly, quite unlike the flushed and defibrillated worry he had felt back in his seat. He walked with his hands thrust into his tailcoat pockets and shoulders shrugged up to his ears, all his grave composure carefully ordered.

It was not to last.

Nora is not coming.

Chalmers tried reframing the statement as a thought experiment, something merely theoretical. *What if* Nora didn't come?

But no. That wasn't it.

Nora *was not* coming.

It was cold out—far colder than an early Elevenmonth morning ought to be. His hands were already tingling, even in the depths of his pockets. Chalmers's right fist clenched the galvano-gram. It most assuredly *was* real, and it *was* First-day of the month, and the ship from Lemarcke would not come until *Fifth-day*.

And then, at last, the little winding spring in his head tightened a turn too far, and Phillip Chalmers found himself running down the hill of the Cathedral campus, dodging between strolling ladies departing a laity lecture, passing parsons and deacons and reverends, leaping a squat topiary globe, and tearing around the corner of the great iron gates toward Coventry Passage. He threw a hand up to save his hat from skirling away and did not stop running until he reached the rectory.

The landlady, Mrs. Gilleyen, was dusting the foyer art. She scarcely had time to greet the reverend before the scrabbling young man was up the marble curve of stairs, taking them two at a go, his smooth-soled shoes sliding out from underneath him as he barreled into his study and slammed the door.

Inside, it was as it always had been: woody and paneled and busy with papers and instruments, a wreckage of pedantry and bachelorhood.

Use the notes I have sent along, Chalmers recalled. He found his writing desk, pulled its drawers, and dumped them. The rectory's very fine Aubusson rug disappeared in a cloud of dusty mail and forgotten parcels.

The study door opened, spilling daylight over the riot of stationary in which Chalmers knelt, desperately burrowing. Vast as a prison hulk, Mrs. Gilleyen loomed in the threshold.

"Doctor Chalmers, have you lost your senses?"

"The post, Mrs. Gilleyen. Has it come already?"

The old woman frowned. "Post? Yes, sir, it's all there. Smallduke Regenzi sent a footman by with an invitation to a welcome ball for the conference attendees, as well. Not half an hour ago. Quite a sudden thing."

"No, no, *no*. I don't care about *balls* or *footmen*. I want *the other post*," he said, dragging himself into the chair behind his escritoire. "The girl—what's her name who brings all the letters from Reverend Doctor Pierce?"

"*Ohhh*," Mrs. Gilleyen said. It was a very long word in her vocabulary, a statement of not less than three syllables. "Well, that en't any proper post, sir. Not what she brings."

Phillip Chalmers buried his face in his hands. He was imagining the Old Cathedral of Corma two days hence, the only place big enough to hold all six thousand of the Ecclesiastical Commission's attending members, and himself standing there in the pulpit, about to give the keynote with only half—no, with *less* than half—of the presentation in hand.

"I need *the other* post," he moaned and dropped his head onto the blotter.

"It's First-day," Mrs. Gilleyen said. "That's near when she comes 'round. Shall I have a boy send a spark, check for it coming soon?"

"*Yes*. Yes. Do."

"Very good, sir."

"And, Mrs. Gilleyen?" Chalmers lifted his head. In the reflection of a brass lamp teetering at the desk's edge, he spied a blue bruise of ink smeared up to his hairline. "A little gin, please."

She frowned. "'S'not even dinner hour, sir. Are you sure?"

He didn't manage a word—just a squeak and a feeble nod.

4.

Ivor lifted Rowena's chin with the butt of his hawthorn. She stood at the foot of the courier loft's ladder, turning her head as he raked her with a customary scowl.

"Shall I wash up?"

"Nah." Ivor's flesh hand offered a leather letter pouch, stuffed full to bursting. "You'll pass muster this time. Bring this to Reverend Chalmers, Coventry Passage."

She took the package. Coventry Passage had been one of Bess's routes. An old neighborhood, monied and clean. She was less sure than Ivor about skipping a turn at the washbasin.

"Any return goods?"

He took a long time figuring the reply.

"No," the old man said, brows knitting. "Just be quick about it."

New Vraska Imports squatted at the foot of Blackbottom End, less than a quarter mile from the docks of Misery Bay. The street ran steeply down toward the sea, and so the climb back up it was slow going, especially with the fishmongers driving their carts all around. With the weather turned unseasonably cold, the streets and markets should have winnowed down to the maids-of-all-work doing shopping, or the odd pair of young lovers looking for the novelty of privacy in a crowd. But the Decadal Conference was back in Corma. What exactly that meant was a mystery to Rowena, apart from the glut of high-collared reverends, sober deaconesses, and other squints of the EC taking up near every room in the Upper Districts. Like rats jumping a scuttled ship, the city natives had moved out of doors in search of air. That had made a riot of Rowena's usual haunts. Beyond Blackbottom, Corma's streets transformed into a maze of people. There was a dance to staying arm's length from the cutpurses, eyes down from the beggars. Rowena knew its moves as well as she knew the city's cobbled streets.

Coventry Passage sat snugged in the middle north of Corma, beyond the hue and cry of fisheries and coal barges and marketplaces. The alehouses traded places with row houses, each with narrow front gardens and tidy iron wickets. There were dozens of sober, black hansoms parked hereabouts—evidence of the EC philogians making social calls between the sessions of the conference, no doubt. Perhaps that accounted for the well-swept dooryards looking tidier than usual.

Rowena found herself regretting time unspent at the wash. The monkey-rat's musk still clung all about her.

The Reverend Doctor Phillip Chalmers lived at 16 North Lamplighter Circle, Coventry Passage, in a vertiginous row house shadowed by the Old Cathedral on the High Hill. Most row houses had a bellpull to announce arrivals. The rope for number 16 seemed stuck, or perhaps the bell was off its mooring. Rowena all but swung herself from its rope before it finally sang out.

When the front door opened a half minute later, the wind had long since chewed its way through Rowena's gloves.

An old woman with arms like rolling pins glared down at her. "No alms here. Shove off."

"Delivery." Rowena patted the bulging letter pouch. "For the Reverend Doctor Chalmers, if it please milady."

"I'm not a lady. Give it here."

Old bitch.

Rowena smiled innocently and passed the pouch over.

The old woman opened it, thumbed through the sheaves of paper crammed within, and sucked her teeth.

"Madam?"

The landlady peered at Rowena as if she'd left a shit on the stoop. "You," the woman said, "are *late.*"

Rowena blinked. "I—what?"

Until that moment, Rowena Downshire thought only kittens' and puppies' necks had scruffs. But the landlady found Rowena's all the same and dragged her, ankles swinging, through the rectory's threshold.

"Two weeks, at least—no. *Three* weeks since we've had even *one* letter parcel, and the keynote speech just two days off! What does he pay you for?"

Rowena's mouth opened to answer, but the woman shook her like a rag doll and pitched her toward the stairs to the second floor. "You'll explain yourself to him, that's what. Now up, you! No dawdling, and keep your hands close. I've no use for light fingers."

The rectory's vestibule opened to an array of great roll-armed chairs and overstuffed divans. It had, Rowena thought, something of a gentleman's society air, though she'd seen about as much of those places in her life as she'd seen of square meals. Pushed and prodded like a calf to the charnel, Rowena took the stairs that rose up about a dozen steps before splitting right and left into a balcony circling the entry floor below. The landlady guided Rowena to the right and hissed like a kettle when she looked too long at a gilded urn sitting in a wall nook.

They paused at the door of a study. Rowena had seen a "study" once before at the end of the job with Bess's picnic basket and the grouchy handcart. She supposed they were all the same, apart from small details. Imposing furniture, oddments and certificates and awards, looming bookcases bursting with leathery old tomes. There would be a little bar stocked with bottles of this and that, lots of leaded crystal stacked in presumptuous little arrangements by a fastidious maid. The only thing that varied was whether the help was some blushing minx or a sour old spinster. Clearly, the Reverend Doctor Chalmers favored the snarling sort. From the look of it, he also favored gin.

When the landlady appeared in her honorable tenant's doorway with the packet of letters and a bedraggled Rowena, the reverend doctor scuttled toward her and snatched the parcel up as if it had just been conjured out of the air and was likely to disappear in a moment.

"I assumed you'd want a word with this little louse," the landlady announced proudly. "Here. Explain yourself, then."

"I—that is, milady—or, your honor—" There didn't seem much use in trying to finish the apology, if that was really what was expected of her. Rowena fancied she could blow a crate of New Year crackers up in the room and Chalmers wouldn't notice.

The reverend doctor paced a rut in the floor, reading unfolded letters and tossing them over his shoulder as they were finished. He seemed to be hunting for something in particular. Mouthing words, he walked back over his groove, trampling letters dropped moments before.

"Come in," he said, flapping papers. "Come in. Have a seat."

The landlady stiffened and pulled back her shoulders, as if she were about to let an objection fly like an arrow. Rowena thought better of noting she'd already come in, and trotted forward before the old woman's temper could spoil a chance at a tip—or at the tea tray. It sat on a low table amid more game-lodge sorts of chairs, laden with six lemon buns and a crown of lovely strawberries.

Rowena chose the maroon chair with golden fringe. The cakes smelled warm and wonderfully sticky. Her stomach groaned.

"Um, sir?"

The young reverend looked up. He had pale eyes of some dishwater shade. "Hm?" Something in Rowena's hopeful smile must have explained the gist of it. "Oh! Oh, yes. Yes, if you like. I'll only be a moment." He waved absently at the landlady. "Thank you, Mrs. Gilleyen. That'll be all."

"But, sir. The lateness. Don't you want to send her back with a message for—"

"No, no, no. Everything's splendid now. Thank you, Gilleyen." Another wave, all dainty fingertips, painting dismissal.

Rowena smirked at the old woman and twiddled her own fingers in farewell. "Bye, missus."

Mrs. Gilleyen's face was a storm cloud as she whirled back into the hall and shut the study door with a good bit more force than Rowena imagined necessary. *Well.* There was no sense pretending at good breeding. Rowena tore off her gloves, claiming three cakes for her plate and the better part of the strawberries, licking her fingers after touching each. She was on her second cup of tea—perilously full, with as much milk as could be crowded in—when the reverend finally fell into a seat across from her.

"I can't begin to say how relieved I am to see you," he began, sugaring his tea and stirring the cup with a little too much enthusiasm. It swam in his saucer, balanced above a jogging knee. "So many new conclusions have been sent along. Nora must be longing to discuss them face-to-face. . . ." He stopped, as if finally seeing Rowena in earnest. "I'm sorry. You're . . . not the usual girl."

"No, sir."

"Well." Chalmers set down his cup and clapped his hands, as if that was all it took to do away with that little inconsistency. "Welcome to the dawn of a new era, Miss . . . ?"

"Rowena Downshire."

"Downshire. I suppose it's not every day you're able to play a part in something so monumental!"

Rowena stared at him. She was working at another tea cake, chewing slowly. "Sir?"

"The Commission has been *looking* for this kind of information for years—years!" He laughed at himself, a sudden yipping noise that seemed to surprise him, too. "What a foolishly small unit of time. For *centuries*. This research is a breakthrough. An historical moment! It *almost* didn't happen at all. Two hours ago, I was in despair, abandoned by my partner. *This close* to giving it up altogether, and now you've brought us right back into it!"

Whoever "us" was, Rowena had a fair notion she wasn't properly a member.

The young man tore into his lemon cake with shocking abandon. He was supposed to be a learned type, a savant. Rowena frowned. He seemed more like one of the nervous, rodent page boys darting about Ivor's warehouses, always eager for scraps to snatch.

"Um, your honor . . . sir," Rowena began, "I'm just the legs here." The young man turned his puzzled eyes on her. She tried it another way. "I'm the courier. I don't know what's in the packages. Actually, I don't much want to know. Better that way for all of us. And you give a fine spread. It's really jake of you. I'm obliged. But . . ."

The reverend sat back and reached for his napkin, patting the tray blindly for a moment before finding it. His gaze did not come loose from Rowena's face for a long while. "But," he supplied finally, "you've no idea what I'm talking about."

She nodded.

"Oh. Dear." Now the reverend didn't look jocular or ravenous. He looked green. "I suppose when you say it's better that you *don't* know these things, there's a reason for that?"

"You used to take deliveries from another girl—Bess?"

Chalmers waited expectantly.

"Well, she won't be working for us anymore. Something happened, and . . . Well, it's just that way sometimes. When people send things through a courier, it's often because it's better not to have hands on it themselves."

"Your work is . . . dangerous?"

Rowena shrugged. She stuffed the last strawberry in her mouth. "En't everything?"

"Well, no. I'm afraid I don't go in very much for danger."

That, Rowena supposed, *I can believe.*

"Why use Ivor, then?"

Chalmers frowned. "I don't follow."

Rowena had lived so long in a world of miscreants and thieves, the thought that anyone else didn't—that anyone could be so positively out of touch—was completely baffling.

Rowena bit her lip. "Maybe . . . I'm sorry. I think I've gone a bit far."

The young reverend shook his head vigorously. "No, now, now, wait—wait a moment. I don't *know* your Ivor." He looked down at the scattered letters on the floor, still somewhere in the green range of pallor. "I suppose the Reverend Doctor Pierce chose your employer for a reason. I've always relied on her discretion. In that she has it. And that, I suppose, I don't." The reverend stood up again. "And Nora's been . . . delayed." Something dawned in his eyes. "You say you deliver *dangerous* things?"

"*Some*times," Rowena said cautiously. "Dangerous if you don't know what you're doing, savvy?"

The look on the reverend's face was painfully eloquent: *Do I look like I know what I'm doing?*

Rowena knew the answer instantly.

Chalmers stood frozen behind his chair. Something was clearly going on between his ears—some quick calculation of details. "*Delayed.* . . . And, I suppose that in dealing with you, I might be doing something dangerous?"

"Um . . . maybe?" Rowena attempted a heartening smile. Seeing the reverend's dishwater eyes widen, she knew it hadn't been very convincing. "Do you have something to send back? If you do, that's probably the bad bit, and it's only bad for me, because I'm the one holding it."

The young scholar flew at his desk. He pulled a drawer from its track and dumped it over his feet, releasing a puff of dust and a bomb of loosely bound papers that exploded around his ankles. He crouched in the detritus and after a few moments' hunting emerged with something resembling a thick journal. He threw it on the desk and began wrapping it into a brown-papered package, knotted with a length of sisal.

"Brilliant idea. *Here*," Chalmers said, breathless, and rushed toward Rowena. He held the packaged book at arm's length, as if it might at any instant burst free of the wrapping and open its covers like snapping jaws. "Take this. Take it to your Ivor, whoever he is, and tell him to send it *back*."

Rowena took the package. It was lighter than she expected, perhaps only half the mass her eyes told her it should be. "'Send it *back*'?"

"Nora hired him to send the letters and notes to me. So he'll know what that means—won't he? Of course he will. Just send it back to her. That's all I want."

"All right," Rowena said, hesitating. Ivor had said there'd be no return delivery. Then again, he might be glad of the chance for a surplus on the retainer. She was doing her job well—better, even, than had been asked of her.

"All right," she repeated. "See, usually, there's a gratui—"

She hadn't time to finish the thought. The reverend stuffed the last two lemon cakes in Rowena's jacket pockets and all but shoved her out the door, the package in her arms, her heels skidding as he pushed her along and hiked her down the stairs with all the speed of a seasoned bouncer. All the while, he spluttered courtesies.

"I thank you very kindly for your services—You will be remembered fondly for your part in all this, I'm certain, but I am quite afraid our time is up, and there are urgent matters—urgent!—that require my immediate attention, not least of them conveying to those individuals concerned the need to make some important adjustments to the itinerary—"

The heavy front door of the rectory thumped shut again, this time nearly nipping Rowena in the rear. When she turned to look back, her eyes passed over the bundle in her arms, and she realized she was still clutching the silver sugar spoon. She could hear the reverend's reedy voice piping some set of orders as he thundered back up the stairs, calling the landlady's name over and over.

For a guilty moment, Rowena considered the spoon. She crouched down to set it on the mat.

She heard the landlady answer the reverend's calls in a few brisk barks. Rowena paused, her spoon-bearing hand hovering midmotion.

Almost certainly the landlady owned the rectory's housekeeping effects. There was a dull ache in Rowena's shoulder from the woman dragging her about—nothing to one of Ivor's blows but there all the same. And there was a return delivery, too, and no added clink for that added hustle.

Rowena slipped the spoon into one of her pockets, trading it for a lemon cake.

Strange man, she thought as she ate. She turned back down the street, brown paper package tucked under her arm, belly full, and the delivery run still a quarter hour ahead of schedule.

Between here and the warehouse was a maze of shops and stalls and public houses, and nearly any of them would be happy to change out a real silver spoon for a bit of minted coin. She had plans for that coin and time enough to drop it into Mama's coffer in Oldtemple.

5.

When the hothouse of Crystal Hill came into view, gleaming in the midday sun, Rare caught herself truly admiring it. Her wonder lasted half a heartbeat—then, tossing her hair, she loosened her knife in its strap.

Rare had left Maeve and the portmanteau of goods at the crossing a half block down from the hill. She approached the hothouse alone, carrying one of the bundles from Maeve's precious luggage under her cloak, wondering if there really was a useful place to put a blade into a lanyani, should business turn ugly. Knives were made to kill creatures with blood coursing through a proper circulatory system—things with veins and muscles and tendons to cut. Long ago, the Old Bear had shown her a sample of the lanyani's fibrous flesh under a microscope. She'd been small enough to need a stool to see through the eyepiece. The sample showed cells diffusing the fuel of photosynthesis through a dense lattice. No. The knife would do little good. Rare doubted the alley pistol belted beside it would prove much better.

The best strategy is to avoid needing either.

The hothouse doors steamed in the autumn air. There was no need to knock. The housekeeper was on duty.

The Crystal Hill's housekeeper was an aigamuxa female with shoulders as broad as Rare was tall, and dugs little more than fists of flesh on a knotted, seal-gray chest. It opened the great glass doors and loped up to her, its saw-toothed, eyeless face tilting to the side. It sniffed. Breath like turned earth hung in the air.

Then the aiga swung into its pedestal position, heel-mounted eyes glaring suspicion. Watching an aigamuxa's hulking body twist into that strange shape—hands on the ground between its legs, crouched low, legs swung behind and over the shoulders so that the pink eyes winked like shards of spinel in the mountings of their heels—always left Rare's stomach in a tumult. The creature's lips parted over jagged teeth, ready to pronounce the human visitor unwelcome.

"I've come to see the Pit Masters," Rare said, as if her call were altogether ordinary.

A snort. The pink eyes narrowed. "What do you know of the masters?"

"Enough to make them an offer."

"And you are?" The aigamuxa's voice was surprisingly expressive, even feminine, under its heavy timbre.

Rare smiled sweetly. "A friend, perhaps. Here." She reached under her cloak and offered the aiga a leather-wrapped parcel the size of a small brick.

For ogrish beasts, the aigamuxa had exquisite balance. In a blur of motion, it lifted one arm from the ground, took the parcel, and swung back to its feet without so much as a wobble. Its four-jointed fingers lingered over the parcel, exploring it carefully. It inhaled, pressing the object to its eyeless face. Then the aigamuxa leaned close, breath flaring against Rare's cheek. Its face wrinkled as it sniffed for traces of lye or turpentine or chlorine, poisons that could harm its masters and pollute the house's soils. A few vials of the right substances could wither an entire copse in mere days.

The fact that it did not paw Rare over to find the knife or the pistol whose powder it must have smelled, or snatch the hand-length, steel-tipped hairpin from her bun, or slip the strangling wire braided innocently about her wrist, said how much good those weapons might do here.

"I'm clean," Rare promised.

The housekeeper tilted its head, considering. Then it nodded, thrusting the parcel back into Rare's hands. "I will ask if they will see you."

The aigamuxa leapt straight into the air, grasping the vines woven through the hothouse's thick canopy. "Follow."

It swung steadily along, heel eyes blinking down at Rare.

The hothouse was nearly a hundred yards long, glass roofed and walled, its panels tempered as strong as steel. The outer walls and inner walkway's dense foliage offered all the privacy of slate and limestone. Sensible humans dared not trespass here. Every soul in Corma had heard stories of folk gone off in the company of the wandering trees, never to return.

The stories, Rare knew, were seasoned with more than a little truth.

Rare spied movement amid a clutch of rhododendrons. She didn't turn her head. Good eyes spotted everything they needed, even in fleeting glimpses, and Rare had very good eyes.

Lanyani children. They were small, willowy things, with limbs scarcely thicker than her thumbs, their roots freshly raised from the loam. *Seedlings, they're called. Or cuttings.* There was a difference. Rare had known it once, but the nuance was lost under all the years since the Old Bear shared his stories.

Rare followed the aigamuxa's shadow, speaking as if it were quite a regular thing for her interlocutor to swing in the branches overhead.

"Do the Pit Masters speak Amidonian?"

"They speak not at all, in this season. I will translate."

"And I can trust that you'll represent the masters' intentions honestly?"

There was a straining sound, the groan of a bough bearing weight. The aigamuxa vaulted to the ground, landing hands-first to protect its eyes.

"You came here speaking of the Pits. You must know something of them." There was a note to the aiga's voice—something almost like sympathy. From an aigamuxa, sympathy was almost as menacing as its double-rowed teeth. "You forget that I have as much to fear from them as you."

The light from the glass ceiling seemed very far away. The aigamuxa turned, speaking into the heavy, moss-bearded trees all around.

"There is an offering for the Pits, Old Ones."

Two of the largest trees stirred and lurched slowly forward. Rare held her breath and straightened her back.

The lanyani Rare had seen in the city were lithe, supple creatures in the summer and spring, and silent, creaking shades come autumn. They disappeared on winter winds into the households that could afford to take on exotic servants, or otherwise to the hothouses of their copse clans. They did not grow large, and they always kept a human shape, their limbs and digits moving like Men's.

The Pit Masters were altogether different—hunched, knotted giants crawling with lichens and long robes of moss. They kept the hothouses rich in resources, secure against outsiders. Dwelling in that fertile clime all their lives made them vast. Strong. Monstrous.

The bark of one Pit Master split near to the top, where the eyes of a more human creature might have been. Two white slits gleamed fiercely down at Rare. The masters' backs were quilled with leafy branches bristling with thorns. They shivered all at once. It was the sound of a thousand locusts thrumming.

The aigamuxa listened. "They wish to see this package," she said at last.

Rare lifted the parcel in her hands into clear view and parted her skirts to fetch her knife. *She*, Rare realized as she slit open the brick's wrappings. *I thought of the aiga as a she.*

The lanyani ancients were too little like humans for her to give them whatever gender they might once have owned. Were those knots the shadows of breasts? Was that bulge at the trunk's fork the shape of its forgotten sex? Or did the lanyani ever have such structures in the first place? Rare had thought so, but perhaps she was wrong. *You left too much of what the Old Bear taught you behind, when he left you.* Everywhere, the Pit Masters sprouted things and smelled of soil. One loomed over her, waiting, a spider dangling from its slash of an eye like a hideous tear.

You're more cousin to the aiga ape than these creatures, Rare reminded herself. *That's what makes this deal possible.*

She unfolded the leather, revealing a tarry brick. Heated, it would burn with a heady, sweet perfume, all sticky buns and poppy seeds and sins.

The lanyani giant drew a gnarled finger slowly down the opium block.

The other master's leaves trembled, its eyes wide.

Rare pretended distraction as she scanned the hothouse's wild interior. She spotted a space between the honeybushes. It was too tight for the giants to pass without trampling and lacked any hanging limbs from which the aiga might pursue. *Yes.* That would be her way out, if she needed one.

The housekeeper's brow furrowed. "What need do the lanyani have of your human concoctions?"

Rare smirked. "You feign innocence badly." She addressed the Pit Master directly, then. "We had the hottest summer in almost a tenyear. But I'm sure you know that. The EC's Meteorological Society predicts this will be the earliest winter in many years, too—and one of the longest. Harsh climes make for hard use of the hothouses, don't they?"

One Pit Master's gnarled head tilted toward the other. A moment of uncertainty.

Rare pounced upon it.

"I've lived in Corma most of my life. There are four hothouses in the upper eastern districts, this the largest, home to seven copse clans. Eleven volunteer tribes wander through between seasons. This summer, you've had more lanyani coming here to use your soil and water and warmth than in the last four seedling cycles combined. The soil is nearly exhausted. Your composting Pits must be, too."

A rattle in the branches, brief and brittle. Rare did not wait for a translation. She knew assent in any language.

"Some of the copse clans are due to plant their cuttings. Clan Mossdown was already told to wait for the spring, and they're not happy. Clan Rootwater will ask next, and if they are deferred, too, you may see an uprising. The volunteer tribes will take advantage of the unrest to insinuate themselves into Crystal Hill. They could even claim a place in the Grove. Propose one of their own to grow into a new Pit Master." She dropped the parcel of opium with a thud and picked at her fingers daintily. The looming creatures seemed a little wilted. "Perhaps I'm wrong, though. After all, it's none of my affair."

Silence. Rare smiled down at her hands, plucking tarry blackness away. She was *not* wrong. She'd spoken to every walking tree she could corner, from the exotic housemaids to the buskers on the streets. Sounding the politics out, confirming, denying, exploring. It had taken three weeks, and she'd been exquisitely thorough. Even the Old Bear would have been proud of her prudence. She'd earned her way to a coup of knowledge, a confirmation of those nightmare stories, and now she could turn it all into a tidy profit.

The aigamuxa bitch was right. The Pits meant something very different to the flesh-born than the tree-born. Rare had been counting on that.

The Pit Masters began rattling and hissing at one another, the aigamuxa's head turning rapidly, taking in the argument.

Rare found a mossy stone and sat, smoothing her skirts. The Pit Masters had much to consider, and the lanyani were not known for acting swiftly. As she listened to the susurrus of debate, she imagined its progress.

Of course the Pits were depleted. The lanyani survived by photosynthesis, and the city offered their people precious little on which to survive. The hothouses were the lanyani's alehouses, inns, and common spaces—the place they could come to settle into good loam and find warmth and wetness, no matter the season. A hothouse was the difference between life and death for city-dwelling lanyani.

An *overused* hothouse meant death closing in on the copse clans.

The Pits that enriched the hothouse soil needed to be replenished—needed organic matter, and heat, and time. The lanyani were plants, after all. Sentient and mobile, they needed all the things their dumb, still cousins did, but in far greater shares. Brutal weather demanded even more nutrients to ensure survival. Bad climates drove the migrant volunteer tribes out of the battered wilds and into the cities, seeking safe haven in the hothouses. The lanyani needed strong soil, and strong soil needed strong matter to enrich it.

Blood and bone meal were powerful amendments. Powerful and, in a city ruled by humans, hard to come by, without a little ingenuity.

The Pit Masters studied Rare, their eyes gleaming with hunger and distrust. She maintained a theatrical interest in her nails, made perhaps less than ladylike by the application of her blade to her cuticles.

"If it helps you make your decision," she offered, "the constabulary knows about the opium shipment from which this was taken. They've already done the accounting on the bust. It's clean. All of it." Rare sheathed her knife slowly, revealing a long leg and the buckles of her hose. "I know your arrangement with the law is a delicate thing. Cleverly made, though. Bravo."

It was the aiga housekeeper who asked the question this time. "And what do *you* know of the arrangements?"

Rare rolled her eyes. "*Please*. The masters send the lesser clansmen out to kidnap people, slit their throats, and bleed them into the hothouse composting Pits. You bury the rest under that mound." She waggled a fine-fingered hand toward the shadowy copse from which the masters had emerged. "The worms strip away the flesh, and then the bones are ground back in with the rest. The constabulary gives you no grief over the disappearances as long as you confine yourself to orphans and vagrants and convicts released from the hulks. They prefer you picking off human refuse over animals, in any case. Even the greenest gendarme draws a deal more clink a week than a dogcatcher." The silence continued, damp and heavy. Rare looked up at the towering Pit Masters. Their shadows fell over her. She rose to shrug off the fear that threatened to pin her in place. "You can't afford your fertilizers making a fuss, so you drug them. But it has to be with something that won't harm the soil. So, opiates. Perfectly natural. Half your marks are addicted to opium already. The rest would happily take it to escape their lives for a moment."

The Pit Master with the spider hanging from its eye slit rustled softly.

"How much?" the aigamuxa translated.

"I have a dead stone's worth in four packets. The other three are being held against my safe return."

The Pit Masters hissed among themselves. Rare thought it might have been more than her ego hearing a certain admiration in their discourse.

"And how much for the lot?" the aigamuxa asked.

"Seven thousand sovereigns."

By rights, the lanyani should have been in the early stages of their winter torpor—slow and silent, leaning on their translator. But the Pit Masters exploded in a frenzy of rustling, jerking limbs, showering leaves broad as dinner plates. Rare took a step back, darting a wary look between the thorny figures.

"That," the aigamuxa hissed, shark teeth smiling, "is too much."

"I gathered that. Call it six thousand, if you like."

The Pit Master with shoulders like a cantilevered roof creaked round so fast Rare could hear the fibers of its body groan and tear. Strange words crackled from its branches.

"That is also—"

"Unacceptable," Rare finished. "I gathered that, as well."

"You will leave here alive. *That* is something," the aigamuxa volunteered. It seemed that she was making an inference, though—not a promise on her masters' behalf.

"Fifty-five hundred," Rare countered. "Or nothing."

The Pit Masters seemed to settle, the locust hiss of their animate limbs dying down. They conferred in brief crackles, and then, Rare saw the spider-eyed master nod.

"Fifty-five hundred and a *gift*."

Rare raised an eyebrow. "A *gift*?"

"Yes." The housekeeper had uncoiled from her pedestal position, obscuring her eyes. Even so, Rare could read her expression.

She smiled. "Of course. A gift."

Maeve waited, folded in the shadows of an alley at the bottom of Crystal Hill. Rare let the heels of her dress boots *click-click* on the cobbles, announcing her arrival. The fox-faced woman slackened at Rare's approach, finger uncoiling from her alley pistol's trigger.

"Bless me, Rare, I thought you were filling one of their Pits by now," she breathed. "What news?"

"Never hold the trigger while you stand guard," Rare snapped. "If you'd pulled a shot at some passing carter out of nerves, we'd have had a deal of trouble."

Maeve looked hurt. She reached under her muslin skirts, fumbling the gun back into its holster. "This is *your* sort of business, not mine. And you wouldn't have gotten this far if I hadn't slipped into Brietney's bed while you slipped into his shipyards."

Rare looked up and down the street. "That may be." She smiled. "Ready to hear your cut? You'll be pleased."

Maeve's eyes glittered. "G'wan."

"*Five hundred.*"

The eager spark snuffed. "Five *hundred*? You told me you lifted about two *thousand's* worth."

"Negotiations," Rare said, spreading her hands. "We need to get rid of the goods as badly as they need to buy them. It's five hundred you didn't have before. It's a *gift*, really."

Maeve stepped over the portmanteau on the ground behind her. Her hand was back at her skirts, reaching for the pistol.

That decided matters.

Rare pulled the steel-tipped pin from her hair, thick around as her little finger. She lunged inside Maeve's reach and drove the pin into her throat. For an instant, there was resistance and a gurgling cry. Rare twisted the needle. Then there was only the blood running down her hand.

Maeve blinked at Rare, glass-eyed. Her hands drifted up, fingers plucking the hairpin's gilded tip. She sagged to her knees. Pink bubbles frothed her wordless mouth. Maeve's body pitched forward, twitching. Then it fell still.

A shadow dropped into the alley from the gangways between apartments.

Rare tugged the portmanteau from under Maeve's body. She flung it to the housekeeper, who snatched it midair and tucked it under one massive shoulder. How the beasts did such things with their eyes planted on the ground, Rare didn't know—and didn't want to.

"A gift," she announced, gesturing to Maeve's body. Rare tossed back one of the coin purses newly filling her cloak pockets. "And this, too. Her share."

"The lady is most generous."

Rare smiled sweetly. "I hope we can do business again."

"Perhaps. Perhaps soon, even."

"I'm listening."

"The clansmen bring the masters news of the conference your people have called."

"The Ecclesiastical Commission," Rare corrected. "Not really my people. What should it concern you?"

"You find things. The copse clans can find buyers for them. Eager buyers."

A fencing operation. Well. It should be no surprise that the lanyani had carved such a niche for themselves.

Rare tugged a handkerchief from Maeve's bodice. She wiped the blood from her hands. *Monogrammed. On this sort of errand, she brought her damned monogram.* Maeve had been a woodcock bumbling into a snare. Thinking back on it, Rare was amazed she'd suffered her so long.

"Eager buyers of EC goods," she mused. "I'll remember that."

Rare swept her skirts away from the puddle of blood. She cast the handkerchief down on Maeve's frozen face.

As she walked off, Rare heard the aigamuxa hefting the body, and the clink of coin, and all her other gifts making their way back up the hill.

She hailed a hackney cab four streets down, lightening one purse by a quarter clink. Regency Square wasn't so far off, and she felt a powerful need for a bath and a bed.

It was nearly past noon dinner. And, really, it had already been a very long day.

6.

Anselm Meteron lifted his chin, watching the reflection in the gold-tinted shaving glass carefully. Rare leaned close behind him, the straight razor's edge just under his Adam's apple. Her hand scraped upward with expert care. Still, the wry twist in her lips at moments like these gave him pause.

"What?" Rare wondered aloud. She wiped the blade on a cloth beside the basin. Anselm could feel her bare chest pressed between his shoulder blades, the graze of her nipples against his skin. "Don't trust me, love?"

"I have a mark under my right ear that remembers the first time you did this."

She kissed his earlobe, then nipped it sharply. Anselm winced. A moment later he felt himself stirring—a surprise, given how little rest he'd had since they'd finished, but then again, Rare could do that. It was her particular gift.

"I was practically a baby then," she purred. She lifted his chin and tilted his face toward hers. "Seventeen, maybe."

"Damned if I remember."

They were in his master bedroom suite at the top of Regency Square. It was not the tallest of the apartment buildings that shared the skyline of Corma with the spires and bell tower of the Old Cathedral and the Custom House, but it was doubtless the most extravagant. A smallduke and two smallduchesses called it home and probably glared up from their lower balconies with some resentment at the shadow cast by Anselm's penthouse. To have their station surmounted by a scarcely retired criminal—the owner of a gambling house and, if rumor held true, financier of more than a few brothels and gentlemen's clubs—was galling in the extreme.

Keeping a suite in the Regency was costly, but Anselm could afford it—one look around his apartments and their gold-chased refinements, the deep-piled carpets and burnished cherry floors, confirmed his means. He lived alone, apart from Rare, who came and went with the entitlement of a well-stroked alley cat, lingering a few days or weeks before disappearing on a whim. He never asked where she went, or why, and she never asked who occupied his sheets between her comings and goings.

Anselm's day had begun late, as ever. He kept the calendar his business demanded, which meant rarely rising before one in the afternoon. At dawn, he had gone to sleep alone, awaking after the dinner hour to find Rare perched above him, shimmying free of her skirts and running a hand under the satin sheets and between his legs. Her hair smelled of soil and sweat, the perfume of some recent sideline.

Anselm had been especially slow to quit his bed that day, and then only to share a long bath and a leisurely accounting of human anatomy. Afterward, Rare had moved the washstand to the foot of the four-poster, Anselm sitting on the bed's edge. She knelt on the mattress behind him, shaving his cheeks and jaw and trimming sideburns to the narrow strips he preferred. Anselm studied her reflection, reading the lines of her smooth, ivory body, the pillars of her thighs as she leaned around him. He had never tried his hand in an artist's studio. His sister had been the one with a gift for visualizing and sketching. She could draw up almost anything in staggering detail. Still, the curves of Rare's body made him wish for the skill to mold her in clay.

"You should let me shave the moustache," she said suddenly. "It's going white, just like your temples."

Anselm sighed and policed the urge to shake his head. The blade grazed just past the corner of his mouth. "Leave it."

"But why?"

"*I* like it, and it's my face."

A few more strokes. She did leave the moustache. At times, Anselm supposed, the girl *would* listen.

"Why white?" Rare mused. "Even pale blondes like you usually go gray first, don't they?"

"I've always been precocious. Shouldn't you be saying it makes me look distinguished?"

"Makes you look *old*."

"Bitch."

Rare laughed and finished with a snapping motion that cut a cleft just under his chin. Anselm hissed and snared her wrist, twisting in place and turning her hand back, hard. She gave a little shriek of pain and delight and hooked a leg around his waist, pulling him over. In a moment, Anselm was on top of her, pinning her hands above her head. The razor lay forgotten on the coverlet.

Rare pressed her hips against him and smiled. "*Hello*. I feel that. Ready again?"

Anselm kissed her forehead, her nose, her lips, her chin, and dwelled over the thumbprint of her collarbone. "No time," he sighed into her throat. "Gammon's been waiting a quarter of an hour."

Rare's ice-blue eyes flashed. Her hair was still wet from the bath, looking more golden than usual in its damp, tousled state. "So *keep* her waiting. Make her remember who's in charge."

Anselm rolled away and snapped the towel off the basin. Frowning, he dabbed at his bloodied chin. "*No one*'s in charge, kitten. That's the reason the system works."

He threw the towel over the back of a settee, walked to the armoire, and began the search for something expedient in the way of clothes.

The Regency's entire penthouse level belonged to Anselm, though he cared little how badly it was wasted on his bachelorhood. Indeed, the master bedchamber could have contained both the guest rooms with space to spare. The bed at center was draped with curtains Anselm never bothered to close, though the north wall was almost entirely windows and balustrade, the rest of the room studded with furniture of white-lacquered wood and golden marble. He stepped into black silk lounging trousers and slid into a dressing gown, pausing at the armoire's mirrored door to see if he'd need a plaster.

Rare had cut a neat little "V" just under his sharply tapered chin. Scowling, he licked a thumb and dabbed at it. She'd been right, of course. There were a few white hairs in his thin moustache, cousins to ones at his temples. Only a woman who came as close to his face as Rare was likely to notice, and those sorts of women had very few illusions, regarding Anselm with an appetite that had little to do with aesthetics. He rolled his neck along his shoulders, cracked his knuckles—all nine, without an option for his shortened right forefinger but to curl its scarred stump toward his palm. Somehow, though he knew it was impossible, he was sure he felt a crack. He looked down at his hand ruefully. It had been years since the injury, and still he felt an ache right where the fingertip should be, never quite done haunting him.

In the armoire mirror, Anselm saw Rare sprawled on his bed, regarding him languidly. She rolled onto her back and stretched a leg in the air, turning her ankle idly.

Anselm watched her in earnest. *The most damnably frustrating part*, he thought, *is that she* knows *how perfect she is.*

"I don't understand why you don't just *buy* her, Ann," Rare sighed.

"I already have—with information. It's the best coin for both of us."

"She could still sell you out."

Anselm glanced at an elaborate water clock on the nightstand. *Nearly five. A half hour late now.*

"Be a good girl," he said. "Stay here while the grown people talk."

"Go to hell."

"Later. I want to take you to the club tonight. Make sure you wear something striking."

City Inspector Haadiyaa Gammon was slender as a riding crop and half again as stiff, her hawkish nose raised against Anselm's arrival as if it carried in a whiff of brimstone. Among her own kind—the gendarmes and clerks and pages of the constabulary—she was rumored to be quite amiable, but putting the roof of Regency Square overhead snapped her tight as a sail in a gale. She was on her feet as Anselm entered the solar, the jacket with the insignia of her office draped over her arm, its epaulets as heavy as the look she offered her host.

"Haadi." Anselm smiled innocently. "Leaving so soon?"

Gammon did not consult a chronometer. She seemed to have her own, mysterious internal mechanism, wound to the second.

"*Soon*," she sniffed. "It's five o' the clock. We were to meet at half past four."

"The clock in my chamber is badly off." Anselm stopped by the mahogany sideboard and poured himself a whisky. There was a silver chaser resting beside it with a folded galvano-gram. He opened and scanned it, then tucked it into the pocket of his dressing gown. "You'll take a drink, I hope?"

"No."

"It's quite charming that after all these years, you still refuse even the least hospitality."

"If hospitality matters so much, do me the courtesy of dressing properly when we meet."

Anselm tsked, feigning woundedness. "I don't offer sartorial advice when I come to the constabulary, do I?"

Gammon's unpainted lips pressed in a hard line. "I'm never in my nightclothes there."

"You might consider it."

She turned on her heel, making for the door.

"Haadi, for Reason's sake, sit down and at least *look* at a glass of whisky while we talk. It's only civil."

Gammon eyed Anselm, stonily silent, and finally returned to her seat. Anselm slipped the galvano-gram into one of his escritoire's lower drawers before sweeping back to the sitting area, armed with a second drink for his guest. He nudged a smoking box at the inspector. Gammon snapped the box open and lit a cigarette from it with one of her own lucifers.

"I saw in yesterday's gazette you collared Brietney," Anselm began. "Brava, Inspector."

Anselm enjoyed watching Gammon's guarded expression sift through layers of hostility, color rising along the copper of her throat right up to the steep angle of her short, glossy hair. A trifle masculine, that cut; still, it suited her, apart from that unfortunate nose.

"It went well enough, though your estimates were overgenerous. The transaction was for ten thousand sovereigns of opium, not twelve."

The difference caught in Anselm's ear. *Ten thousand.* He tapped his own cigarette in the ash stand to cover a momentary hesitation. Then he shrugged.

"The information was less complete than I would have liked. Everyone has an off day."

Gammon snorted. She glanced down at the whisky glass. Anselm smiled crookedly. With a sigh, the chief constable raised it to her lips.

"Tell me what you know about the Reverend Doctor Nora Pierce."

Anselm studied the ceiling. "Pierce. . . . Oh. Yes. Rather tiresome woman, but supposed to be brilliant in her field. Sharp eye for figures, does business in the harder sciences. I heard she's going to keynote the Decadal Conference this weekend."

"Nothing *else* of interest?"

"Nothing, unless . . . wait." Anselm tapped his temple in a gesture suggesting he'd nearly forgotten something. "She spent a deal of last fall at the club. For a while, things were going well by her—breaking even, then coming out ahead. I was starting to think she was running numbers, and then the streak broke. She's in my red book now for fourteen thousand, give or take."

Gammon's eyebrows climbed. "And that almost slipped your mind?"

"There are a lot of people in my red book, Haadi." Anselm sighed. "If I'm remembering right, she was trying to scare up funds for her research. The junior scholars don't fare well in the scrap for grants. I put a stay on collecting through this winter and drew the debt up as a private note."

"Very kind of you."

"At twenty percent interest."

"I take it back, then."

Anselm stubbed his cigarette out with a fatalistic flourish. "It seems she might avoid paying out after all."

Gammon's dark eyes were expectant.

"Haadi, you're asking me the sort of questions you *always* ask before I learn someone is missing or dead. Which is it this time?"

"Missing. The Council Bishopric contacted the constabulary late this morning. Pierce's research partner got a spark from Lemarcke saying she would miss the keynote. Some kind of travel mishap."

"Happens often enough. Any reason not to believe it?"

"It's the Decadal Conference *keynote.* And her home district's bishop finds it out of character that she'd have traveled so far afield so close to the conference."

"Haadi, you must forgive me." Anselm offered the inspector a sympathetic look. "I think I've missed something. Is this a case of a missing person in *Corma* or somewhere *else?* It doesn't seem to me you have jurisdiction."

Gammon smiled. "You'd have made a good lawman if you weren't such a moral degenerate."

"Turpitude is my problem, not degeneracy. A law-abiding life was out of the question from the start."

Gammon finished her drink and walked toward the balcony windows that gave the solar its name. She watched the skyline chuff smoke against a sinking sun.

"I agreed to look into the matter as a courtesy," she said at last. "It's procedural. She hasn't yet overstayed her amended itinerary. Still, there is a lot of competition for the keynote address, and shared research doesn't usually earn that showcase. Perhaps Chalmers decided to put her aside to secure an exclusive billing. Such things happen."

"Hmm. No." Anselm shook his head. "I've heard a little of this Chalmers. There are some old books on my shelves with more spine than he has. And, for the record?"

The city inspector turned. Anselm Meteron leaned forward, nine and a half fingers steepled.

"I've been called many things, but never a bad banker. Corpses don't repay notes. I hope you remember that if the Reverend Doctor Pierce should turn up in ill repair."

Gammon pursed her lips. "I'll try."

"Good."

The inspector returned to her seat, donning her coat and hat. "I intend to take Chalmers in for questioning, just to be certain. If I find out anything that sheds light on whether your note will be repaid . . ." She let the sentence trail.

"Of course. Assuming nothing comes of that, what's the rate of exchange for today's conversation?" A moment passed, utterly silent. Anselm smiled innocently at the furrow in Gammon's brow. "It's not that I don't love our time together for its own sake, you understand."

"I had thought conveniently ignoring the two thousand sovereigns of opium missing in the Brietney deal would settle matters. I'm surprised, Anselm. I hadn't thought you the type to expand into the chemical trade."

Anselm gestured vaguely and rose. "I'm a hobbyist. Always seeking new diversions."

He offered Gammon his hand.

Most people, Anselm Meteron had learned, found shaking a hand missing its most critical digit rather too disconcerting an experience to repeat. The vacancy in his grip was but one of many things that might make a person uncomfortable shaking Anselm's hand. He considered it a credit to Inspector Gammon's resolve that she had never refused the gesture.

Anselm saw Gammon out the suite's main door. He lingered long after it closed, running a thumb over the stump of his finger in small, irritable sweeps.

"Are the grown-ups done talking now?"

Anselm turned toward Rare's voice, behind him at the solar door. Her hair was dry and done up in a loose, piled affair, ash blond strands falling into her face. She wore one of his white dress shirts, its lower hem barely covering her buttocks.

"When I told you to put on something striking," Anselm said dryly, "that wasn't quite what I had in mind."

Rare sauntered into the solar and swung herself into the chair Anselm had just vacated, draping crossed legs over one arm. "Either Gammon is a worse copper than I took her for, or she's lying."

Anselm studied Rare from the doorway, his arms folded. She began fishing in a sweet bowl and, the silence stretching on, glanced up absently.

"You look cross, love."

"I've just realized you're right. I must be getting old." Anselm's right hand ached, this time from clenching it too hard. "Sentimental, at least. I had actually persuaded myself that you came here to roll in my sheets and stroke my ego awhile." He snorted. "Perhaps I was right about the second part."

"And the first. Your point?"

"Because of you," Anselm said in a tight voice circling the edge of real anger, "the city inspector is now under the impression that I'm in the opium trade."

She smiled. "Brietney going under was a good thing for both of us. After how he tried to screw you last spring, no one from our end of the world will feel sorry for him. Besides, that *was* a lot of goods to just walk away from."

"So you did lift the last two thousands' worth."

"Oh, come off it, Ann. It's not as if you haven't pinched something from one of the cases you've informed on before."

"*Before* I've given my estimate of the take, yes," he snapped. "When I said twelve and Gammon found ten, she must have thought I'd lost my edge or my wits. Probably both. And now I'm going to eat her looking the other way on your account."

Rare affected a perfectly beautiful pout. "Do you have a problem sharing your good connections all of a sudden?"

"I have a problem sharing them when they associate me in trades I'm not prepared to work."

"Well." She shrugged. "Maybe you aren't, but I've done my homework." Rare studied the ruby-red candy she'd picked and popped it into her mouth, lips lingering salaciously on her finger. "Go on. Ask. You're dying to, I can tell."

She was right, at that. "And what," Anselm said, sounding the words out coldly, "did your homework yield?"

"Five thousand sovereigns and an offer of future sidelines."

Anselm raised an eyebrow. Her success was an order of magnitude greater than he'd expected. That did more to fan the flames of irritation than to cool them. "No loose ends?"

Rare sniffed. "*Ann*. Really. You're not my mother."

"I've thought otherwise before."

"Are you going to ask me what I know about this Pierce business, or must I beg you to let me be helpful?"

Anselm stalked back into the solar and took Gammon's chair. He spread his hands: *Fine. I'm waiting*.

Rare swung her legs back around to the front of the chair and spoke with the soft, conspiratorial eagerness that always came when she had a good line. Angry as he was, Anselm had trouble not finding that electric intensity engaging.

"Two days ago, I was down at the quayside's Rotten Row, near Misery Bay. I go there once a fortnight, just to keep appraised of who's moving things around on the underside. You know how it is. There was a fagin and his pack of urchins peddling all the usual trash. Ordinarily I'd pay it no mind, but they had a very nice roll of jewelry and oddments, and one of the things laid out was an Ecclesiastical commissionary's signet. The band was engraved. Care to guess?"

"No."

Rare sat back triumphantly. "'NP, ThD, PhD, Order of Physical Sciences.' They claimed it was on a woman's body washed up beside the wharf the night before—black and blue around the neck and not in the drink overlong. Said they threw the body up on the docks after they'd stripped it down, hoping one of the constabulary patrols or perhaps the lanyani pit-poachers would find it before it drew a stink. Someone must have done a little sweeping up. I checked the docks, and there was no sign of a body."

"So you think Nora Pierce is dead."

"How many reverend doctorates of physical sciences with those initials could there possibly be?"

"Usually I wouldn't venture more than one or two in this city, but you forget that Corma has been filling up with the visiting members of the Ecclesiastical Commission. That changes the odds."

Rare snorted. "You can't be serious."

"*If* you're right and the constabulary already got their hands on a body—say a body matching Nora Pierce's description, even—why is Gammon sitting in my solar asking me about a missing person case?"

"She said this is all procedural, yes? She's putting on a show of due diligence to hide what she already knows. Maybe she's trying to cover up Pierce's murder."

Anselm considered the idea. The visit *had* been odd. Gammon smoked a cigarette and took the whisky. For six years, they had exchanged information and favors, looking the other way at all the right times. But as a matter of principle, Gammon had stoically refused all Anselm's hospitality—and, he considered with a frown, other things he had clearly offered, too. He could think of no reason today should have been different. And yet, somehow, it was.

The inspector hadn't quite been herself. That much was plain.

"You are," Anselm said grudgingly, "a very clever kitten for being such a damned reckless fool, you know that?"

"Of course I know it. Now what do *you* know that you weren't giving up?"

He smiled. *Very clever kitten, indeed.*

"Around the time I wrote Pierce's gambling debt as a note, she was looking for a private courier. I recommended Ivor. If there was something between Pierce and Chalmers that could shed some light on this affair, he's probably had his hands on it recently."

"When were you planning on telling Gammon that?"

"Never," he said. "If you're right and Ivor's had some role in foul play, I don't want on record how Pierce met him in the first place." Anselm glanced at a grandfather clock set between two bookcases. He sighed. "It's half to six. I'm going to the club now—shall I expect you?"

"Later. I have a meeting."

Anselm raised an eyebrow.

She smiled her most perfect, petting grin. "Nothing you'll need to clean up after. On my honor."

"Your honor tempts a very particular kind of retort."

Rare aped Anselm's eyebrow raise with needling accuracy.

"Fortunately," he said, pushing himself to his feet, "my nature as a gentleman forbids me to make it."

Rare watched her lover depart, listening for the click of the master bedroom door down the hall. Anselm would dress, would take the back lift down to the carriage garage, and would be late to his casino's nightly opening. He was always late for everything. He would wear his evening jacket with the high, banded collar and matching jacquard vest. That was his habit whenever he made a trip to the Empire Club, crown jewel of Uptown. He would leave a dress lying out for her—almost certainly the red-and-gold corseted affair with the black lace gloves and open-netted stockings. It *was* her most striking gown, and he had both his pride as the club's proprietor and her lover to consider.

Rare waited a full ten minutes before she stirred from the chair. She stole behind his escritoire, opening and closing its drawers, lifting the trays. She knew the catches and latches that led to its better compartments—spaces so well hidden it was only the faintest clue in the wood itself, the slight wear in the lacquer where Anselm's hands had brushed over many years, that reminded her fingers where to stop.

There were two ledgers of private notes, a stiletto like an adder's tooth, a sheaf of documents sealed with sticking gum—even a datebook going back to the summer before she first arrived on Anselm's doorstep, more than thirteen years ago. She leafed through it, curious, and found a few entries that made clear why he had kept it so long.

Even impossible finks, she supposed, were prey to moments of nostalgia.

She found, at last, a folded galvano-gram, sent to Anselm's private line.

It was only a few hours old.

A. Meteron, Regency Square, for immediate delivery
New Vraska Imports, 1st Elevenmonth, 1500

Have unwanted goods—research text collects data. Comes from Pierce and Chalmers. Want clear of it. Have interested EC connections? Spark back today. Ivor.

Gently, Rare set the message down on the blotter and refolded it, following its creases precisely. She returned it to the hatch underneath the file drawer. A smile drew the bow of her lips.

If Ivor had something he wanted to get clear of, the lanyani had given her an idea how to help him be about it.

9.

Ivor Ruenichnov's interest in books had always been limited. He had grown up puddling iron in the smelting houses of Czernobog, six in the morning until seven in the evening, six days a week, and had used very little of his Seventh-days for attending lectures or studying at the EC free schools. His forbearers had been peasants before the Unification, believing in witches and saints and devils. The only difference the marriage of science and theology had made in their lives or those of their children's children had been the names they gave to the many things they did not understand.

Now, Ivor's books were ring punches of shipping manifests, ledgers of transactions, address diaries. The scholarship that passed his office door was always en route from Someone to Someone Else. Such packages usually drew far less notice from him than the letters sent between lovers or conspirators or business partners.

But this book—the book that had been staring at Ivor since he'd snatched it from Rowena Downshire's dirty hands—held him rapt.

It was not attractive or elaborate. It resembled a notebook, unassuming, with a thick paper binding and stitched white spine. The cover was pasteboard, glazed with wax to repel a laboratory's tinctures and acids. It was as thick as his hand, fingertips to wrist. Long stretches of pages sat dull and vacant. Others were crammed with notes written in a rapid hand littered with strike-throughs, arrows, substitutions, corrections. Ivor could make no sense of why some portion of the text would be dense with scrawl and why another would be all but blank.

But that was not the thing he wanted most to understand.

Ivor stared at the page laid out before him, watching its letters and numbers write themselves into existence.

The words were not in any language he knew. Though he lacked schooling, Ivor could work his way through two dialects of Vraskan, bits of Trimeeni, and Corma's particular idiom of Amidonian. The alphabet of these steadily appearing words resembled nothing he knew, its framing geometric and angular. Here and there, he recognized Amidonian words or perhaps . . . initials? Abbreviations? Impossible to say.

Numbly, Ivor reached for his wodke bottle. He was, at present, quite terribly drunk. That knowledge did nothing to dull his amazement at the self-scribing book. He'd noticed a graph taking shape as he riffled the pages long before, when his bottle was still in his desk drawer and still half-full. There had been a field of points being plotted and then some kind of line tracing them, hills and valleys of data without labels on the x and y axes.

The shock of seeing those lines writing themselves had been enough to cut the string of muttered curses he'd been spinning since Rowena returned from Coventry Passage. He'd been happy to see her, at first—glad to say he was done with Pierce and Chalmers and whatever trouble was passing between them. And then he spotted Chalmers' package under her arm. He'd boxed the girl's ears, sending her staggering up to the loft in a daze—and that was before he even knew what the package would *do*.

God, if he'd known, he'd have used his brass fist and made a wreck of that pale, pert little face.

After the first ten minutes of watching the notations take shape, Ivor's amazement gave way to shock, and then concern. That was when he began consulting the wodke bottle.

It simply didn't make sense. There was no such thing as magic—science, yes; God, perhaps; and, to any reasonable folk, no distinction between them. But *magic*? Pierce's letters ended with a plea to destroy their research. Ivor started to wonder if this book—this *thing*—was what she meant. If it was an invention, how did it work? Where was the information coming from, and what made it appear on the page?

He saw the script pause in writing itself. And then a line sliced through the last four words. Ivor shivered. What kind of book *corrected* itself?

If this was the thing Pierce wanted Chalmers to destroy, and if Chalmers was as desperate to be rid of it as Rowena had insisted, was it dangerous? Did destroying it require some kind of specific knowledge, some special equipment? Was it as simple as throwing it into the fire?

Ivor very nearly had, stirred by the bottle's bitter courage. He'd stood before the open stove door, staring at the roaring coals, ready to hurl the book in. And then he'd stopped. If the book could be destroyed, and if it was some mad scientific device, was it full of chemicals or gears, something that might blow up and take the whole warehouse down with it? Ivor considered himself a hard man, but since that moment, he'd been frozen, staring at the text and willing it to tell him what to do.

Ivor resisted the urge to throw open his office door a fourth time to see if Anselm Meteron had sent his response. It was scarcely past eight o' the clock. The scoundrel was probably just starting his rounds of the Empire Club. Ivor supposed he might even still be sleeping with his face buried in some scandalously young thing's tits. In his guts, Ivor knew he could not rely on Anselm to rid him of the book, even if his recommendation to Pierce had, in a fashion, brought the book to Ivor in the first place.

Ivor's guts also knew he'd found his way into something of strange and terrible consequence. What that consequence might be was still a vague effluvium of fear. Ivor only knew that this Bad Thing, this reckoning, was stalking steadily closer.

The writing stopped.

Ivor put the wodke bottle aside. He inched toward the book with his gaff hook and, as if piercing and flipping a venomous snake, quickly turned the page.

Nothing. All blank.

He rubbed his eyes, then reached to close the book. Under the shadow of his flesh hand, sepia-colored lines crawled.

Ivor stared at the growing image, its borders sketched in fine, careful lines. It was as if they followed an unseen straight edge, conforming to careful measurements. Waypoints appeared, one by one. Ivor recognized the slant and cross of the image, the intersections. . . . He saw a grid being drawn, very lightly, over the map itself. He saw street coordinates, the junction of the Blackbottom market square, the immediate environs of his business. In the margin of the page, notations appeared in small, geometric print. Ivor saw something he was suddenly very sure were initials, and two words he *did* recognize beside an arrow.

Subject Six.

The street coordinates were exact. A little carat in the margins pointed at New Vraska Imports.

Ivor felt the galvanizing touch of something more real than he had words for, like the point of a dissecting pin driving through to his heels. It lasted only a moment.

And then he staggered out from behind his desk and through the office door. The clerks had gone for the night—all except Albert, who snored with his face against the blotter, waiting beside the galvano-graph register.

Ivor kicked the stool out from under the boy. He landed in a flailing heap, scarcely pulling himself up onto his rear before the old man crouched over him.

"Get Rowena," Ivor demanded. "Tell her to fetch her bag."

8.

Rowena jogged up Blackbottom End, her breath fogging. Her stomach growled sullenly over her abandoned supper back in the loft—cold salt beef and black bread she'd never get her hands on. By now, Mick was gobbling it up and stacking her straw mattress on top of his own in front of the loft stove. Rowena might once have been able to curl up on Bess's old pallet when she returned, but the fleas had gotten in the first night she forgot to powder it. She'd find no sleep on that pest trap, now.

The old man must have been punishing her for nicking the teaspoon. He'd already given her a drubbing for bringing back the book, and this rage was too fresh to be old business. Ivor'd been slobber-drunk and roaring. Probably the landlady had counted the silver after Rowena left and sent a complaint down. Never mind that it wasn't her *fault*. The spoon was gone, pawned for two sovereigns against Mama's ledger in Oldtemple, and Ivor and his cups now conspired to teach Rowena a lesson about getting light-fingered around the quality.

The lesson wasn't just in the lateness of the job, or the missed dinner, or the lost spot by the stove. It was the job itself—Westgate Bridge, nearly the whole city's width away. It would take far more than an hour on foot, even at a jog, to cross it all.

And that was only the *where* of the job—the what of it was far worse.

She was taking the reverend's book to the Alchemist.

Rowena paused at the intersection of Harper Lane and Buskerton to let a dray cart groan by under alchemical lamplight and fog.

The Alchemist.

She would not have said it aloud—not to anyone, and not for anything—but Rowena knew she was powerless. She would have been satisfied with any kind of power. The power to buy a meal with money she earned. The power to tell Ivor to go hang himself from the courier's loft, for all she cared. She would never have any such power, and knowing that was as bad as the powerlessness itself.

The rumored power of the Alchemist, on the other hand, was something unknown and unknowable. No one believed in magic, not even the mad Kneeler beggars preaching the Old Religion to curious passersby. Not even the lanyani. *Magic* was just what the ignorant called systems they couldn't understand in an organized universe. Rowena had heard a young seminarian lecture some pretty girl outside a tavern with that line once. Probably he'd only wanted to get under her petticoats, but it sounded good. The other alchemists weren't quite respectable enough to be scientists of Ecclesiastical rank, but they weren't fairy stories, either. The Stone Scales was different, its proprietor a figure cloaked in contradictory legends. The idea of approaching him for the first time in the dark, unknown, set Rowena's teeth on edge.

This *had* to be a punishment.

She stopped under a globe lamp and shifted her satchel over her shoulder. Across the way, she spied the phosphor-painted sign for the underground lightning rail. The cold was working through the weave of her gloves and into her bones. She'd have to run at least another three quarters of an hour, and she expected her burning lungs to give it up for a walk long before then. And a girl of her age, her size, walking to the east end of town, past the river wharves and fulleries?

There was nothing else for it. Rowena reached into the breast pocket of her jacket and drew out a quarter-sovereign chit. She'd been saving it since midsummer, a little piece of just-in-case. It was enough for one ride on the underground.

The stairway to the lightning rail pitched down from the cobbled sidewalk, burrowing to the tunnels below. Rowena dropped her quarter clink into a brass turnstile and squinted through the dusky air at the platform beyond. The dense crowds of early evening had already gone their ways. The factories were empty, the pubs and clubs filling up. Only big, young men and a few red-faced women, bleary with drink, shuffled about, waiting.

Rowena claimed a bench underneath a guttering alchemical lamp. She set her bag on her lap and drew her boot knife slowly, hoping no one nearby had failed to see it. She laid the knife down on the satchel and folded her hands over its handle, letting the blade stay in full view.

No one strayed nearer. Rowena stared at the empty tracks, lips pressed tight.

The tunnels were hazy with cigarillo smoke and golden chemical light. Rowena's eyes were watering badly by the time a dim, yellow eye appeared in the distance, the low thunder of wheels on rails running close behind.

The lightning rail always ran on time, say what you might about its eerie electric crackle and shrill, screaming wheels. A conductor stepped off the narrow ledge and put his ratchet in the socket of the door, holding it open. The doors scissored apart with a clatter of toothy gears, and as soon as a knot of passengers pressed its way out, another shouldered in after. Rowena waited for the human clog to pass. She darted in just as the conductor ratcheted the doors shut.

The cars had windows, trimmed with patchy blue curtains that looked like false velvet. Rowena wondered why they were even there. There was nothing to see in the tunnels, anyway—just the stutter of signs passing too quickly to be read, arc lights blurring into white-hot smears. She supposed the under-iron cars of the lightning rail were remainders from the upper-iron fleet, old cross-country cabs retired to the shorter jaunts of the cities.

"If you're going to keep your knife out like that, it would serve you better to watch what's going on *inside* the car."

Rowena turned in her seat, her fingers closing around the knife's handle.

Then she smiled.

"Rare." Rowena slipped the blade back into her boot.

Rare wore leather trousers so supple they moved like her own skin, buttoned tight against her curves. Her black under-corset gathered up beneath the shadow blue of her blouse, and a belt with two buckled pouches circled her hips. She rested a hand on Rowena's seat back, steadying herself against the rail car's clatter. Her piled hair was run through with a long, heavy pin, tucked here and there with clips as useful for working at the tumblers of a lock as holding up her coif.

She was a thief, a charlatan, and an idol to any girl of Rowena's world—the model of the Way Out. One story had her starting off life as a courier, a bird like Rowena and Bess. Others said she'd been a bawdy house Jill. Whatever she had been, she was a free woman now. They said she had a dozen lovers in Corma, each richer and more sinister than the last. Dozens more men, gentry and underside alike, vowed to have her. They weren't the sort to be turned aside easily, but Rare managed all the same.

"Hullo, Rowena." Rare nodded to the space on the padded bench. "May I?"

She didn't wait for a reply. Rare slid into place and offered Rowena a concerned look.

"Have Ivor's hours changed?"

"Just for tonight. Well, just for me."

"You don't usually go east. Where's Bess?"

"Gone. Ivor gave me her routes."

A little line appeared between Rare's eyes. She scowled. "You shouldn't be running new routes this late."

Rowena shrugged gamely. "He's been acting off—all of a sudden, he wants me to move this package along, so—" again, a shrug, "—I'm moving it."

"Be careful. East of the Compass Square, you should keep to the low-streets. I grew up around Westgate Bridge. They aren't bad people, but they're tough, and a stranger won't get much help if she gets turned about."

"Thanks."

Rowena knew better than to ask what Rare was doing on the under-irons. Almost certainly she was on some job. Rare was a professional. She'd know better than to say much. That thought brought the heat to Rowena's cheeks. She shouldn't have said the bit about Ivor wanting to dump the package. *Stupid eejit.*

"You know . . ." Rare reached into a belt pouch. "I have a letter for Ivor. I meant to take it to him today, but I had an appointment that ran late and thought he would have closed up for the night. Do you think—well, it's an extra bit of work, maybe, but when you get back to the warehouse tonight, could you give it to him?" The letter wasn't in her hand; she held a tight roll of sovereign bills discreetly.

Rowena blinked at the roll. She had never had much money of her own, but she'd handled enough to eyeball a sum quickly. It was as much as she might clear in two months of deliveries.

"I wouldn't dream of asking you to do it just as a favor," Rare said gravely. "It's a job. I understand that."

"You've got the letter now?"

And there it was, an envelope with Ivor's name written in a tall, tilting script.

Rowena slipped it into her bag with the paper-wrapped book. She tucked the roll of bills under the leather thong wrapped around her forearm.

"Suppose I can be back at the warehouse by eleven. Urgent message?"

Rare smiled. "I imagine Ivor will think so."

The rail car slowed. Beyond its greasy windows, Rowena saw the dim light of a station platform and a sign, its letters a faded jumble.

"*Thank* you," Rare breathed. "It was going to bother me the whole night if I had to wait on that any longer."

"Anytime."

"Remember," Rare said, stepping out of the car onto the platform's edge. "*Lowstreets* after Compass Square."

"Lowstreets. I've got it."

And Rare was gone.

The Compass Square was an intersection of six streets that left an impression, when viewed on the city map, rather like the points of the compass rose. The square lacked only the northwest and due east arms.

Rowena studied the eastern paths, southeast and northeast—the lowstreets and highstreets—and considered Rare's advice.

The lowstreets ran far south of the Stone Scales, skirting the banks of the tidal River Corma. They were broad, well marked, and well lit. There would be some merchant seamen, perhaps, and some night watchmen, but the streets would be quiet and Rowena could see well by the lamplight, especially with the cold clearing the fog.

The highstreets were old, unnamed routes, lit with alchemical globes that were broken as often as not. One had to climb long sets of stairs to go higher into the borough's old quarter, where the oldest businesses sheltered between row houses of slate and plaster. Those streets were crooked and steep, full of Reason only knew who at this hour.

Rowena shifted her bag on her shoulder and blew on her gloved hands.

She was four steps down the southeastern road, heading low, when she felt her hackles rise.

Seven times in seven years of courier work, Rowena Downshire had been robbed. With each experience she'd learned a little more about how to sense the next coming.

Rowena looked to her right and saw a hulking shape slip free of an alley's shadows, not far from the lowstreet path. There was no mistaking its hunched shoulders or its curious, high-stepping gait.

The aigamuxa raised its left leg and held it aloft. The pink eye on its heel seemed to stare right through Rowena, slicing skin and muscle, bone and sinew.

Rowena closed both hands around the satchel's straps. She tightened them slowly.

And then she turned heel toward the northeast, taking the stairs to the highstreets three at a time, scrabbling with her fingers as her feet slipped.

She was at the first summit and running. From somewhere below, she heard the aigamuxa's furious bellow.

The fear left Rowena almost as quickly as it had come. She had her wind and felt good. The aigamuxa were worse than bad runners, all but blind with both feet on the ground. They were confined to a plodding pace to keep from careening into walls or stamping through some debris that would grind into their eyes.

The alchemical lampposts flashed by Rowena's head, one after another. When she passed the sixth, she realized the flashing movement in the corner of her eye wasn't from her own passage into and out of pools of light.

It was from the aigamuxa swinging in the upper reaches of the street above her.

The highstreets were old, narrow things, full of houses with porches and railings and gutter works, washing lines and window ledges, a perfect jungle for the aigamuxa to swing through. The creature bounded against the face of a laundry house and was suddenly two buildings ahead of Rowena, dropping hand over hand toward her on a route of downspouts and balcony rails. The aigamuxa's legs dangled, angry pink eyes blazing downward.

Rowena ducked a swipe from the creature's swinging arm, lost her footing, and skidded on both knees into a wall. She scrambled to her feet just as the aiga scuttled, spiderlike, within an arm's reach, swaying from a row house shutter.

Its clawed hand grazed the satchel as she bolted again.

That was when panic took her.

Rowena rounded a curve and plowed down a short stair, climbed back up around a bend to her left, and tore through a straightaway, dark except for moonlight pooling between broken cobbles. She ran hard, trusting the straps and buckles of her bag to keep it from flying off. She ran until her chest tightened under a screw and her breath tasted of cotton and copper. Rowena turned another corner she hoped would bear toward the lowstreets and found only a dead-end yard with a tumbledown well and broken ash cart.

There was another flash of movement at her right and then a blow that crushed the wind from her lungs.

The cobblestones were black with lichen. They surged up to meet Rowena's chin, rattling her teeth. Her eyes watered as she bit her tongue. Her mouth filled with blood.

The aigamuxa's hands planted in front of her, long, four-jointed fingers splayed wide, wrists touching. Slowly, Rowena looked up.

Even in its customary crouch, an aigamuxa was the height of most any man. This one seemed a little larger than most, or perhaps it was the darkness and the way its eyeless, hairless face loomed. Its legs were swung up over its back, ankles resting on its shoulders. Its eyes glared at her from either side of its head.

"Give," the creature hissed and lifted one of its huge hands, fingers flexing slowly. "Or I will take."

Rowena blinked the tears from her eyes and spat at the cobblestones. Trembling, she pushed herself up to her grazed knees.

"I don't know what you—"

The hand lashed out with blinding speed. It cuffed Rowena to the ground, and for a moment, the world was filled with explosions of green-and-yellow light and a horrible keening between her ears.

Slowly, the sound died away. She could hear the aiga's voice again.

"*Give*," it rasped, "*or . . . I . . . will . . . take*."

Rowena rolled onto her side and bucked her shoulders, trying to worm free of the bag. It took two tries to get the first shoulder out; the second came away with a jerk as the aigamuxa tore the satchel from her.

The creature's shadow passed over her, its eye heels on the ground, and then she heard scuttling, scraping noises and the roof tiles slipping high overhead.

For a long time, Rowena lay still, waiting for the lights in her eyes to clear and the sick feeling in her belly to sweat itself away. When the nausea passed, leaving a throbbing pain behind her eyes, she sat up.

The yard was empty. Quiet. It seemed strange that it could be so quiet again. There was that thundering sound, though. . . . She clenched her jaw and realized the pounding in her teeth was her heart coming down from full speed.

When she finally stood, Rowena didn't think about her ringing head, or her skinned knees, or the blood coating her tongue.

She thought about Ivor and the Alchemist.

Running from the aigamuxa had been frightening, but she had at least known what she should *try* to do. Get away. Keep her bag. Failing that, keep her hide.

Now she was terrified, wondering what to do next.

Slowly, Rowena retraced her steps, hoping to wend her way back to the Compass Square. She didn't remember running into a rain barrel or kicking over a wire caddy of empty milk bottles, but she found these things, and a scattered crate of old gazettes, and an overturned dustbin. Her route back to the square was clear enough. She'd done a fine job marking its way.

If I tell Ivor I lost the package, she thought, *I'll be lucky to crawl back up into the loft after the beating he'll give me.* Rowena remembered the courier girl from the Brixton workhouse Ivor had beaten unconscious the spring before, and the three days she'd lingered, black and blue and feverish, before finally dying. When Albert and one of the stock loaders carried the body away, three teeth fell from her slack mouth—the only teeth the poor bird hadn't spit out the night Ivor took the hawthorn to her.

If I go to the Alchemist without his package, Rowena thought . . . And then, the thought trailed away because she didn't know what to do with it.

If I go to the Alchemist without his package . . . what then?

Rowena kneeled beside a downspout, tugged off her gloves, and cupped a little water from a puddle beneath it. She threw the water in her face, sipped some from her fingers, then rinsed and spat. The water had been brackish. Now it was pink with her blood.

If her brother Jorrie had been here, rest his soul, he'd tell her to go with the devil she knew. Probably Mick would say the same. They never went in for gambles. But they were strong boys. Rowena was an underfed scrap, not at all likely to come away from Ivor's beating as well as they would. She tried to remember what Bess had told her about the Alchemist. Bess knew him better than anyone, Rowena supposed—had gone to the Stone Scales dozens of times over the years.

Nothing came. It wasn't just that the tables of her mind had been upended by the aigamuxa's blows. There was simply nothing there. Bess had never said anything about the Alchemist at all. But whatever happened to her once she found him, Rowena wagered it wouldn't cost her any teeth. That seemed more hopeful than the devil she knew.

She was standing back in the Compass Square. This time, checking all the shadows before she chose her path, she headed for the lowstreets.

9.

The coroner on duty was William Knox, a man City Inspector Haadiyaa Gammon considered both cautious and incisive—traits Gammon usually desired in her staff. Tonight, they gave her pause. Knox was a bent creature with a look at least half as sepulchral as the subjects he tended. His rheumy eyes goggled under the magnifying lenses cinched tight around his bald, spotted head. Still, Gammon knew they missed very little.

Very little. Gammon breathed deeply to steel herself and immediately regretted it. She'd never gotten used to the smell.

Knox stood over the examination table, its cured slate top glossy with scrubbing, its trough drained. He regarded the woman's naked, fish belly corpse with utter dispassion. The principal examination had been conducted some hours before. Now, she was slit up the middle and held together with surgical clamps and vises, her skin drawn tight like a white pudding's wrappings. The woman had not been beautiful. She had a soft, round body and a square jaw better suited to a man's face. Her black hair was cut with severe, conservative precision—disturbingly familiar, too much like Gammon's own coiffeur to pass unnoticed. Even in death, the woman somehow looked reprimanding.

Knox donned a pair of thin gauze gloves, careful to draw them on slowly. Inspector Gammon had ruined three pairs already, forgetting as she tried to gentle them on how easily they would tear. Now she stood across the table from Knox, the phonocorder whirring along at her left.

Gammon had been a constable almost twenty years. She'd seen her share of corpses yet had not lost the feeling of sick sympathy that always accompanied an inquest. Here was the way of all flesh. Its indignity had not ceased to shake her, and that, she supposed, was a good thing.

Gammon watched the paraffin cylinder of the phonocorder as it revolved steadily on the bobbin. A crooked needle scratched a groove into the creamy yellow cylinder. Waxy curls thin as spiderwebs peeled away, drifting to the morgue's cold floor.

Knox cleared his throat and began the formal record.

"First-day Elevenmonth, year 276. Subject Jane Doe, found 0530 Thirtieth-day Tenmonth, Misery Bay docks. Chief Medical Examiner William Knox presiding, City Inspector Haadiyaa Gammon attending. The subject, female, approximately thirty-five years of age, shows signs of contusions to the ventral region of the neck, just below the windpipe, suggestive of strangulation. . . ."

In the dimness of his study, the alchemical globes illuminating only the surface of his cluttered desk, the Reverend Doctor Phillip Chalmers read over the letters many times, thinking he could tell their intended order and then realizing he had lost the front page with the date, or that in his haste he'd skipped one ahead. It had taken some hours, but finally he'd worked the sequence out. Still, he scratched his head over the whole affair. Nora was gone, yes, and it seemed from these letters it would be for good. But why?

He lifted his gin and tonic to his lips but felt only the stones, long since warmed to room temperature, butting against his lip. Glancing down at the glass, then the gin bottle three fingers emptier than it had been an hour before, he shook his head ruefully.

"Can't make whole sense of it with or without you, girl," he sighed. There was something to gin's character that had always struck him as particularly feminine. He addressed it as such, and often.

He returned to the last letter, poring over its final paragraph.

> I hope these notes have found you well, Phillip, for that would give me some hope for the days to come. Keeping them has been hard. I hope they will be much remembered and that I will, too, someday. That will fall to you, for I am afraid it is all out of my hands now. You've done

a little of the mapping before, and so I trust you will find your way through it—with any luck, a little better than I have done.

The sooner you can destroy our notes, the better, Phillip. They will be following not far behind these letters.

He ran a hand through his thinning hair and muttered several phrases unworthy of his office as a reverend doctor.

"The level of decay suggests the subject has been dead approximately seventy-two hours," Knox continued. "Distally, the digits and hands show abrasions consistent with attempts to fend off an attacker, but coagulation and skin condition suggest these wounds preceded death by as much as forty-eight hours."

Gammon regarded her shoes to avoid seeing Knox lift up a flap of skin cloaking the larynx. The jar of camphor cream was near at hand. She considered dabbing it under her nose to combat the odors rising from the gray-and-purple mass of the body cavity, which the old man had methodically ratcheted open.

"Was it murder, Master Knox?"

"The contusions on the neck are principally ventral and dorsal, with fainter bruising around the lateral regions. Typically this suggests manual strangulation."

"Typically?"

"Typically—but not this time."

"'Much remembered,'" Chalmers drawled, swiping the cut-glass bottle up once more. "Sending me a bloody obituary, isn't she, girl? Biggest ruddy find in all Post-Unification research, and what do I get for it? Pat on the back, a new heap of work, and my colleague's wish for bloody remembrances. The *nerve*."

A knock at the study door jerked him from his bleary rumination.

Chalmers squinted at the clock on the wall and scowled. "Told you already I wasn't going to Regenzi's cursed ball, Mrs. Gilleyen. Breakfast not for hours. Do be a love and sod off, there's a girl, eh?" The laugh began as a drunken snigger, then a splutter. Finally, he was dabbing at his nose and the unseemly snort of phlegm his humor left behind.

The knocking continued, a good deal louder than Gilleyen's usual thumping. Chalmers's temples throbbed with each blow.

"Bloody Rood, Gilleyen, it's not even morning!" he bellowed, slapping the desk. "Have you completely lost . . . your . . . ?"

He peered at the water clock again, just making out the steady motion of the wire-thin second hand passing round the hour mark once more. . . . She *was* early. Far too early.

Chalmers looked down at the letter in his hands. . . . *Much remembered . . . all out of my hands now. . . .*

"Oh dear."

The boozy sickness surged from Chalmers's belly up to his ears, and he reeled to his feet, pawing at the catch under the center desk drawer.

The door wasn't knocking any longer. It was thundering in the jamb, buckling inward. Chalmers heard it splinter just as his fingers fumbled over the switch, and the little hatch beside his right leg popped open to reveal a dainty alley pistol. It had been a gift from a colleague, a rib at his faintheartedness. It had never been out of the drawer. His colleague had had to load it for him before leaving it there with a wink. Chalmers desperately pounded at the safety hammer.

By then the splintering sound was a rending noise, and what was left of the door flew into the room like so much kindling. The aigamuxa crossed the space in three strides, vaulted the desk—

Chalmers raised the pistol. There was a sudden flare of powder and the smell of carbon. Then, his head was full of stars and clanging bells.

"It's not often done, hanging by this means," Knox said, clucking tongue against yellowed teeth with something very much like admiration. "It takes a *will*."

He showed Gammon his meaning with a gloved fingertip. The woman's neck was circled with a black, almost perfectly continuous line. It was less than a finger's width, a black adder of bruising curled about her throat.

"Probably used a bodice- or bootlace. She'd have tied it up in a noose and hooked it behind her. Probably attached to a closet bar or something of the kind. They noose up and stand there, leaning *forward*."

Gammon grimaced. "I can't imagine it works. You'd black out before you were dead, fall over, and probably catch your breath while unconscious. A garrote would make the same wound, and the victim's hands being bound would account for the lack of defensive clawing. It's a more reasonable cause of death, given the evidence."

"But, there are no binding marks around the wrists, and no contusions on the upper or lower arms to suggest she was grappled. As to the hanging?" Knox wagged a finger, a schoolmaster scolding his pupil. "Think *masses* and *vectors*, Inspector. You fall unconscious, but if you've made the lead short enough, you're still pulled taut even after sinking down. Tie your knot well, keep your resolve as the lights are flaring and your lungs are screaming, and you'll buckle with your arse off the floor. Your own weight will finish the job. This girl had weight enough to spare, I should think." He returned his gaze to the woman's heavy body, fishing into her belly. "And she had a will."

It might have been hours later or only minutes. The room was dark and Chalmers's head full of dull noise and dirty cotton. Bile coated the back of his tongue, but it was less horrid than the pungent, animal reek stifling him, or the pounding in his head.

Chalmers opened his eyes, blinking, the room swaying. It was not his study.

It was a long, blurry time before his head made sense of the floor above it, the hooded alchemical lamp thrust impossibly upward from a hook. The swaying . . . He groaned, and when the vomit choked out and ran down his forehead, he knew he'd been strung up by his ankles. Sputtering and spitting, he blinked his vision clear. He reached to wipe at his brow, relieved to find his hands weren't bound, too. He studied the spare, dim room and began mentally inverting its contents. Soon, things made as much sense as they were going to for a head full of gin and a face full of aigamuxa.

Being upside down was, perhaps, the only thing that could have made the beast's body look even more *wrong*.

The creature lurked a few feet away, crouched with its feet perched atop shoulders and calves hugging spine. Eyes the size of Chalmers's fist glared out from the creature's heels, flanking its sloping not-face. Two serpentine slits passed for a nose, and a broad, slack mouth full of teeth as jagged as a shark's worked at some invisible cud. A featureless, oval dome of skull rose above that, sickeningly smooth and empty without a brow or eyes. Its hide was glossy gray, like oiled sealskin, shoulders etched with the white ridges of old scars. It crouched an arm's length away from Chalmers's suspended form, pelvis bent horribly backward, arms thrust down between its legs, the long, four-jointed fingers splayed wide.

"You had something," the creature hissed.

Chalmers swallowed, tasting acid.

"I . . . I did. Maybe. I've had many things."

One of the hands struck his chest, emptying him like a bellows.

"You had the *book*."

Chalmers nodded, gasping.

"We have need of it."

He shook his head but curled an arm protectively around his belly as he did so. "Must . . . be some . . . mistake. . . ." Chalmers gulped air. "It's nothing anyway. Piece of Post-Unity mythology. Apocryphal."

The egg-shaped head tilted to the side, like a dog contemplating some conundrum.

"Your judgment in this is unimportant. We prefer ours."

"I'm afraid I don't know who we—who you, rather—are. And I don't have the book."

The head tilted back to midpoint. Chalmers realized with sickening clarity that the aiga seemed to have two parallel-running spines, each an inch or so off true center. They moved below the skin of the neck where a human's carotid might be found. Perhaps that allowed for its exceptional flexibility, even asymmetrically, the bizarre contortions so perfectly a part of its form.

"But you did have it, once," it said.

"Out of my hands now. And besides," Chalmers said, too quickly, "it's all a bunch of theological speculation. Doctrinaire at best. Most people, actually, think it's all just metaphors, you know. It would be mad to take it literally."

"Humor us." The creature narrowed its gaze. "Tell us what you know."

Chalmers blinked. His vision blurred; his face felt flushed and swollen.

"I know a . . . a lot of things." He winced. *No, no, no, idiot—you don't know* anything. *It needs to let you go.* "Or, rather, some things. Small things."

Seeing the shift of the creature's weight on its arms, Chalmers corrected course hastily. "The doctrine states— My God, it's hot in here. I can't— Look, you're twice my size, and I think my head's half caved in. I couldn't run from you. Could you be bothered to, perhaps—"

With a savage swipe, the creature severed the rope. Chalmers fell like a sack of stones. He heard the aigamuxa's voice over the ringing in his ears, but barely.

"Up, Reverend," it called with rasping gentleness.

Groaning, Chalmers pushed himself to his knees and ran his fingers through his hair. They came out damp and slick. Then he remembered being sick.

"My thanks."

"Thanks are not what we want. Tell us what you know."

Chalmers eased out of the ropes binding his feet. He rotated his ankles and found them in working order, pins and needles notwithstanding. He felt he might be sick again.

Simplify by reducing, he thought. Phillip Chalmers closed his eyes and revised the room, imagining it without the aigamuxa, the cold, the ringing in his ears, the fear. He spoke as if he were back in seminary rehearsing a lecture for exams.

"Since Unification, science and theology have mutually believed that God is literally an engineer and something of a researcher. He creates. He observes the functions of His creations. He records. He draws conclusions, and from those conclusions, He will determine the meaning of the whole Experiment. . . ."

Chalmers opened his eyes. The aigamuxa stared at him. He felt what little courage he'd summoned slipping away and tried to tether it with words.

"Usually, you test a theory by gathering data to support or refute it. That's good science. This time, we—Nora and I—found data and searched around for the theory it fit *into*. We were going to present the data at the conference but hold the book it all came from back. How could we share it? After all, we—" He pursed his lips, then considered. "We just *found* it. Or Nora did. She never said quite where when she called me in to help compile the data for the project." He paused and considered the beast's expressionless face. "Once we ciphered the data, we found its readings corresponded to readings of certain particles in the immediate atmosphere. That's what my work had been about before Nora. Measuring god particle concentrations to see if they corresponded to environmental shifts."

"*God* particles," the aigamuxa repeated.

"It's a . . . a pet term, I suppose. Trace energies, invisible to the naked eye. The Ecclesiastical Commission has noted the particles' presence as a kind of background phenomenon for some time now. Meteorological teams and physical scientists measuring the particles' charges have detected them, but as they seemed to be just some kind of neutron soup of variable concentration, they've been dismissed as atomic detritus. Someone got in the habit of calling them 'god particles' because of their ubiquity. It stuck. A little joke."

The aigamuxa's heel eyes blinked.

"Very little." Chalmers swallowed. "In any case, Nora came to me about the book because she thought it might have something to do with the particles. You see . . . it updates itself. Seems to be independent of any observable, guided hand. The pages just fill up as some kind of data is gathered."

"We know."

Chalmers opened his mouth to carry on and stopped. "You know?"

The creature showed no interest in the reverend's perplexity. "What about the Nine?"

Chalmers felt his heart stop. It was neither an exaggeration nor a figure of speech. For a moment, he felt a horrible nothingness in his chest, the sudden awareness of *not* feeling something once taken for granted.

And then, his vision swimming, he felt it start again.

"I don't know what you mean."

It was a lie, and it earned him another blow, this one from one of the legs, which spun nearly a full circle from its perch over the aigamuxa's shoulders, clouting the reverend under the jaw. He crashed backward, his mouth full of hot metal. Yet Chalmers barely felt the rebound of his head against the bare stone. He was too engrossed in feeling his heart come back, thundering away, sliding back down from its leap up into his throat.

The aigamuxa reached down and hauled him to his knees, lips spread in a horrible pantomime of a smile.

"Do not make me strike you again. You are not very strong, and I have need of you."

"You want the book," Chalmers gasped, "because you think it has to do with the Nine?"

"We *know* it has to do with the Nine. You use another word for them."

"The Vautneks. It's from the old languages—part of a number, meaning 'thirty-six.' It seems . . ." Chalmers paused uncertainly and found himself rattling on, trying to soothe himself with words. "It seems the old estimates of the Vautneks' numbers were a little high. They are supposed to be the subjects God watches, the ones whose actions are used to justify humanity's continued existence to the Divinity. Theoretically, humanity exists only as long as the Vautneks are pleasing to God—or . . . or interesting to Him. Or useful. The EC has been debating for ages what God wants to verify in them, assuming the Vautnek theory is real."

"We know this already. We have come here to collect their names."

Chalmers blinked. "We?"

Again, the jagged smile. "We have different purposes, but we are a 'we,' of a kind. He will tell you his motives, if it pleases him. Or he will not. I wish to have the names because I have been called by God to find them."

As a member of the Unified Ecclesiastical Commission, Phillip Chalmers was a believer in the supremacy of humankind, in Reason, in God the Experimenter, and in the Grand Hypothesis. The Unified church maintained that there was, indeed, an intelligence that had designed the universe. Its choices could be understood only through humankind's scientific explorations. The whole purpose of science was to determine and record the will of God, to demonstrate the objective truth of Reason as the ultimate object of Faith. Other beings—intelligent beings like the lanyani and the aigamuxa—had the capacity to observe God's workings, true, but their disinterest in the scientific process was a priori evidence of their distance from Him and His undoubtedly mutual disinterest in their existence.

The Reverend Doctor Phillip Chalmers, therefore, believed a great deal. None of it prepared him to accept that God had anything to do with these illogically formed, ill-adapted beasts from the jungles of faraway Leonis.

"You want their names," he scoffed. "You're mad."

The smooth, eerie head tilted. "This is an expression I do not know."

Chalmers considered clarifying the idiom but balked when he opened his mouth. One of his bicuspids moved with suspicious looseness.

He opted for a different tack.

"If the Vautneks—the Nine, I mean—are real, if they are the true focus of the Grand Experiment," Chalmers began, "then their actions must be recorded, cataloged, and assessed by God. Nora and I started calling the book the 'Vautnek text' because it seems to show exactly that happening. Nine subjects, different locations, patterns of actions and interactions recorded. Periodically, the group's membership shifts.

Human mortality requires this. No single subject's lifetime could encompass the duration of the Experiment. But you must understand: *no one* knows the Vautneks' names. If you know enough to ask these kinds of questions, you must know that the Experiment only works if the experimental population remains unaware of *being* its focus. They are meant to justify the existence of Man to God—unconsciously. Organically. No one has the names of the Nine because to have them would endanger the Experiment. Endanger all of us."

"Perhaps. But this thing you call science is not our concern." The creature swung up to its feet and snared Chalmers by the collar of his shirt. Its leathery, featureless face pressed close to the reverend's. The many-jointed fingers circled his neck, wrapping nearly twice around. It was like wearing a lobster's tail as a scarf, a segmented horror pressing deep into the flesh.

"I'm sorry?" Chalmers wheezed.

"We do not require apologies. We require you."

"Why me?"

"You traced the particles. Tied them to the text and deciphered it. Now, you will read the names from it."

Chalmers blinked at the aigamuxa in perfect stupidity.

"That . . . was really more Nora's business. My research partner. The—the Reverend Doctor Pierce?"

"She is dead."

Chalmers remembered the galvano-gram from earlier in the day and compared its businesslike tone to the panic of the letters he had only just read, kept secret by long delay. Had she been taken in Lemarcke? Perhaps. But then why had her tone changed so much, in the weeks between her missives? He swallowed back a knot of fear, inching closer to a realization he did not wish to have.

"How did she die?"

"She would not give us the names."

Chalmers was not a man of vivid imagination, but he could easily visualize the aigamuxa's cruel hands cutting into Nora's neck. He knew what he should say. To reveal the most crucial elements of the Experiment, to open not only the Nine but the whole of creation to some terrible and unforeseeable consequence? It was more than irresponsible. It was unthinkable. Chalmers struggled to marshal his strongest invective, but the courage wasn't there. Nora had had courage. Conviction. Even something a little like genius. For her sake, he offered up a protest.

"You don't just . . . *peek* . . . into God's laboratory notes."

The look that played across the aigamuxa's eyeless face was more grotesque than its smile had been, more chilling than its bared, snapping maw. There was a placidity there, a northward shift in the flesh near the crest of the skull—perhaps what passed for a brow? Perhaps a look of bemusement.

"And why not?" it wondered aloud.

"Because . . . Because . . ." And it dawned on Phillip Chalmers that he had no good explanation, not even one that made his own actions—the research, the proposal, the keynote, the eventual publication—defensible. He could feel his convictions yawning like an unknotted purse, dropping in bits and pieces from his mental vault.

"You simply . . . don't."

The aigamuxa's chuckle was a desiccated thing. "That is not the answer of a devoutly curious mind, Reverend Doctor."

The fingers released. Chalmers's legs wobbled beneath him. There was still a faint ringing in his ears.

"I am called Nasrahiel," the aigamuxa said, turning on the balls of its feet, heel-set eyes winking up from the ground as it padded toward a door barely visible in the lamplight. "There is much for you to do, if you expect to live. Come. I will take you to the other half of 'we.'"

Chalmers didn't ask who "we" was. Nasrahiel seemed to have his own sense of how this business ought to be done, and he had little strength and less will to challenge the creature anymore.

The aigamuxa walked. Phillip Chalmers followed. It seemed all he could do.

Inspector Gammon peeled off her gloves and dropped them into the bin beside the morgue's frosted-glass door. She winced at the thick, steady *chunk-chunk-chunk* of Knox's suturing gun punching its way up the body. The reek of viscera steeping in bowls of formaldehyde had soaked into Gammon's skin and hair. She ached to return to her flat and pump up the tap for a good washing.

"I'll need your report on my desk by midday tomorrow," Gammon said. With a handkerchief, she dabbed away the camphor gel under her nose. "File it as a Jane Doe and send up a disposal request. It's getting crowded down here. We need to clear the decks."

"Inspector," Knox called. Gammon turned back. "One last detail. The digitus annularis on the right hand—"

"Plain language, Knox."

"The subject's right ring finger," the old man continued. He was moving the bowls of excised organs onto a little trolley. "It's broken."

"And?"

"Usually that's consistent with the forcible removal of a ring. Lividity and rigor suggest it occurred postmortem."

Gammon made a mental note to check with her confederates come morning. The ring was supposed to be gone, yes, but breaking the finger taking it was sloppy. Sloppy was the same as dangerous. She concealed her consternation under a shrug.

"People will steal anything," she said grimly.

Knox began shuffling the trolley away. "It's a devil of a world we live in, Inspector, I'll tell you that."

The old man butted the cart through the swinging doors opposite the morgue entrance, rolling back to the laboratories. One bowl splashed a carnation of blood on the ground, narrowly missing his feet.

Gammon watched the doors swing in Knox's wake. "Indeed it is," she sighed.

She cut the gases running to the globe lamps, plunging the room back into darkness and silence, leaving the body of the Reverend Doctor Nora Pierce to its empty rest.

10.

Rowena Downshire stood in the shadows outside the Abbey, a single-storied pub sprawled across three storefronts. Inside, she heard a din of voices, the mob monotone interrupted by laughter. Rowena hadn't the schooling to read, but she knew her letters well enough to make out the sign and assure herself the local folk had steered her right.

When Rowena arrived at the Scales a half hour earlier and discovered it locked up for the evening, she'd nearly bloodied her knuckles banging on the door before realizing it had a knocker. Hammering with it had proven equally useless. Rowena pressed her face to the window glass. She'd squinted and could make out the shapes of shelves and tables. A dog started barking within, but that was the only answer her ruckus raised. If the Alchemist was in, he was determined not to answer, and if he wasn't . . .

That was the devil of it. If the Alchemist was expecting his package, why wasn't he there? And where was he?

She'd spied a sooty sweep and a ruddy-faced longshoreman making their separate ways down to the lowstreets and asked where she might find the Alchemist at this hour.

They'd answered her with a look as if she was half a fool to have not already known. *Everyone* in Westgate Bridge watched the comings and goings of the Alchemist.

Rowena put her hand to the Abbey's door, the smell of ale and the warmth of a peat fire hitting her full in the face.

The pub was crawlingly busy, better than a hundred people playing out an old neighborhood's nightly theater. The bar maids carried trays of food to long trestles with built-in benches that broke up the field of snooker tables and six-sided card tables. There was no musician's stage, but a few buskering types sat about, strumming a guitar or sawing a violin.

Rowena knew how to move through a crowd—and, just as important, when not to. She danced to a clear space near the scullery entrance and stood on a chair. Usually, her height was an asset in her trade, in that she didn't have much of it. Nearly fourteen years old, she had only recently crept an inch closer to five feet even. She could dart and duck about with wonderful ease, but if she didn't get the lay of the land before she started, she was as good as trod underfoot.

In less than a minute, she'd found her mark.

There was a booth at about two o' the clock, horseshoe shaped and large enough for five with room for elbows. It afforded a good view of the main room and probably should have belonged to some little knot of chums who came regularly. It was clearly the home of a regular—a solitary one.

It would take an effort to move about the front room of the pub without passing that booth, but all the patrons managed it—or managed, at least, to pass by with the widest possible berth.

If that man was not the Alchemist, Rowena was the bloody governor's mistress.

She stepped off the chair and glanced about, looking for her reflection, and finally caught it in the mirror behind the bar. There was some blood matted about her right temple and a hot-red mark on her cheekbone. It would turn black soon enough. She reached up to scrub the blood away, but the wound stung fiercely. She let it be. Rowena needed courage. She manufactured it by practicing her best look—her tough and savvy look, the one she'd used on Sticks, the lanyani fence, that morning.

Her brow furrowed, darkening her stark, blue-gray eyes. She considered adding a curl to her lip, or perhaps—

Rowena sighed and gave it up. One didn't glower at a man who could half-clear a room just by sitting in it. Perhaps she should try something pathetic, something wounded and fearful? She played at that look for a moment—

No. She'd sooner convince the Alchemist she was a guppy than a damsel in distress.

Disgusted, Rowena stalked from the mirror, spitting curses down at her grazed knees as she picked her way across the room. It was no good. She had lost the Alchemist's package, and now she would interrupt his leisure, and nothing—no face, no words, no perfectly affected pose—would keep him from skinning her down to her marrow with nothing more than the blade of his gaze. If she was lucky, that would kill her faster than Ivor's truncheon, and she could at least be done with running and hiding and scraping up every last unguarded coin to drop into the gaping maw of Oldtemple.

Sorry, Mama, she thought as she neared the border of the Alchemist's kingdom. *Mags tried. Jorrie tried. I tried. Maybe there's no use in trying after all. I'm never going to buy you out, am I?*

And then, she was standing before him, hands balled at her sides. She was sure these words would be her last. There seemed no point in dragging things out any longer, so she spat her story in a breathless rush.

"Sir, I'm sorry to trouble you, but I had a delivery for you and it's gone now."

For a moment, his only response was silence.

His eyes were dark, flecked with some glinting, uncertain color. They might have seen through stone. There was no doubt they saw clear through Rowena. He had a beard, trimmed short and shot through with the same gray salting his close-cropped hair. Broad shoulders. Tall enough, he looked Rowena in the eye from his seat, the crow's-feet set deep in skin as black as saddle leather. Older, but not precisely old. Not to the order of magnitude she'd imagined. There was a beaten frock coat hanging from the peg at the end of the booth, brown like his trousers and boots and bracers. He wore a linen shirt with its sleeves rolled up, and there was tobacco staining his right thumb and forefinger. He looked more like a shopkeeper than a scholar or an EC squint. For a moment, Rowena wondered if she'd approached the wrong man after all.

And then she realized the silence belonged not just to the Alchemist but to the whole room. The neighboring patrons stared, nodding her way, nudging each other.

She had chosen right, Reason save her.

"I'm sorry," the Alchemist said at last. "I'm afraid I don't know what you mean."

Rowena stepped closer, keeping her voice low. "I'm from New Vraska Imports. I had a package for you."

The Alchemist surveyed her critically. "You're injured."

"When the aigamuxa—"

His dark eyes narrowed. "Aigamuxa?" He pushed his pint aside. "Come with me."

The Alchemist slipped out of the booth and into his coat. It was as if she'd thrown a switch and it had simply turned his intentions for the night off. The bar maid headed toward them stopped short of the booth, looking down at the tray held before her—a second pint of ale, a bowl of something hot, a half loaf of bread, and a slice of beef.

The Alchemist dropped a folded bill on her tray as he passed. Rowena snagged the loaf and tucked it inside her jacket before hustling along in the old man's wake.

Rowena almost tumbled into the Alchemist's backside as he stopped to let a velvet-curtained clockwork carriage roll by. She stumbled into a puddle instead.

"Where are we going?"

"You said you had a delivery. Even if it will never make it to the Scales, we can."

And then he was off again. The Compass Square fell away as they wound past the quay and the fullery on its banks, the steady beat of its automatic clubs thumping the woolens keeping time.

The Alchemist took a short staircase that curled off the quayside, away from the sounds of the fullery and the murky waters pooling around its dyeing house. The stairs were narrow, their edges worn and crumbling. Soon the quayside lane joined with a terrazzo level winding between the slated roofs of shops down at the water's edge.

And there they were, back at the Stone Scales, a building crooked as a constable, tucked between a haberdashery and a money changer's offices. The shingled sign showed balances and an odd beast, a bit like a rooster with a lizard's tail. It was drawn over a rough line of script—

The Stone Scales

The Alchemist turned an iron key in the lock and ushered Rowena past the threshold. He reached up to the left and right of the doorframe, where two brass sconces waited, and flicked their tiny switches. The alchemical globes set there burst to life as the gases in their chambers mingled. In a moment, he had a kerosene lamp beside the till going and the alchemical chandelier at the room's center, too.

"Sir?" Rowena ventured.

"Hm?"

"Why is there a rooster on the sign?"

The Alchemist stooped under the front counter. "Rooster?"

"The sign calls this place the Stone Scales. But there's just a rooster and balances on the sign. No stone."

"It's a cockatrice. A creature whose gaze *turns* things to stone," the Alchemist clarified. Some expression must have crossed Rowena's face, for he paused in his search and regarded her flatly. "They're entirely fictional beings, girl."

Rowena nodded. She glanced back outside. Her mind clicked along, summing the situation, dividing it and moving remainders about. The old highstreet was empty. Foreboding. She was indoors, and that meant she might be able to stay the night, and that meant she'd have time to think of what to tell Ivor about the lost package. Perhaps, she might dodge going back to him altogether.

She started sizing up the place. The Alchemist let her wander as he arranged bottles and gauzes on the counter.

To the left, the room was a maze of bookcases, some only as tall as Rowena, others high enough that ladders ran along rails before them. Most of the shelves were too full to justify bookends, but here and there a sable statuette or miniature globe broke up the lines and rows and ranks and columns.

The alchemical lamplight stretched shadows across the walls. To Rowena's right stood display tables and glass cases. Skeletons of tiny, flightless birds. Strange, rune-covered jars and bundled herbs. Stuff Rowena had seen being carried onto ships by sailors: astrolabes and barometers and spyglasses. Along the wall stretched a map of the six continents, looking as if it had been skinned from the surface of a globe and had only to be folded around some ordinary sphere to make the world over again.

"I like this place," Rowena announced.

If the Alchemist regarded that as a compliment, he felt no need to acknowledge it. Instead, he beckoned Rowena to a stool beside the cash counter.

"Let's have a look at that face, girl."

Rowena had nearly forgotten her scrapes and bruises. She'd never seen a physick before. There were never enough of them to look after the prisoners' health during the years she spent at Oldtemple, and Ivor didn't go in for coddling his birds. Still, she did as she was told. The Alchemist knelt before her, paused to polish the spectacles lifted from his collar, and started his work.

In the light of the cash counter, Rowena could see him better. Even crouched before her, the Alchemist looked big.

"I'm sorry about your package," she said.

The Alchemist dabbed at her temple with gauze treated in something brown and pungent. Rowena squeezed her eyes shut at its acrid sting.

"I mean, it en't really my fault, exactly," she continued. "Aigamuxa don't usually bother with the likes of me, and I don't see what I was supposed to do about it. But still, it's been an age since I lost a package, and I know Ivor's got a lot of good business with you and I don't want you to think I wasn't trying, or—"

She stopped talking and opened her eyes. The old man was using his little finger to swab an ointment from a pot. His half-rolled sleeve shifted as he raised his hand to apply another dose. Rowena saw the dim tracery of an old tattoo on the dark skin of his forearm, blurred letters and a seal, the image half-familiar.

"Anyway," Rowena finished lamely, "I'm sorry."

Time enough passed that Rowena began to wonder if he'd heard her words at all. Then he spoke: "What's your name, girl?"

"Rowena."

He grunted. "Family name?"

She focused on holding her head still as he traced his finger along the rise of her cheekbone, spreading the ointment with a pressure just at the edge of what her bruise could bear. "Downshire, if it please you."

"I can't imagine what your name has to do with my pleasure, Rowena Downshire." The Alchemist studied her carefully, taking an inventory of something quite apart from her injuries.

Rowena's heart fluttered. It was like locking eyes with a hawk. She sat frozen as a mouse waiting for its talons. Her mind bolted for a piece of cover.

"What's *your* name?" Rowena blurted. "I mean Ivor, he tells me, 'Bring this to the Alchemist of Westgate Bridge,' and that's all. Everybody knows who the Alchemist is. There's only one."

The old man returned to the ointment, then her face. "Not true."

"Only one who matters in Corma. En't heard anyone call *you* by a name."

"Then in my case—" he set the pot aside and lifted her chin with a finger, squinting, "—a name would be superfluous."

Rowena felt her tongue volunteer itself to be swallowed.

He fetched out his chronometer. "When was your last meal, Rowena Downshire?"

"Midday, I think. What time is it now?"

The Alchemist made a dyspeptic noise. He stood and waved her on behind him, muttering something that sounded cross and involved Ivor's name. They shrugged behind a heavy curtain at the back of the shop, Rowena's hopes—and her stomach—suddenly lively.

A half hour later, she sat cross-legged on a spindly stool in the back storeroom where a potbellied stove warmed a crock of beans and rashers and a pot of black chicory. A ragged, old hound slept in a knot near the coal bin, snoring. Rowena shoveled the food down. She'd singed her mouth on the chicory, leaving her tongue in cinders, but she didn't care. Ivor's grub was cold sandwiches and watered ale. He'd once treated Rowena to a wedge of good cheese and a jack of wine, a reward for running four important jobs in a day. But that was the best it had ever been. Apart from the puddings or chestnuts nicked off carters' traps, she hadn't had a hot meal in six years.

The Alchemist sat in a high-back chair made of driftwood. He watched Rowena demolish her supper, a smile threatening the corner of his sober mouth. There was a table between them built of scrap from a shipping crate where he let his mug of chicory cool. When Rowena hauled the half loaf of bread snatched back at the Abbey from her jacket and dredged her bowl, the old man snorted. He busied himself stuffing his pipe, then struck a lucifer against the table. A bluish smoke, smelling like damp leaves, marjoram, and fennel trailed from the pipe bowl.

Her dish molecularly empty, Rowena wiped her mouth on her sleeve.

The Alchemist set his pipe down to stir another lump of sugar into his chicory. Rowena was fairly sure it was his third. She'd lost track, with her face buried in her meal.

"What do you know about the aigamuxa?" the Alchemist asked.

"The one who took the package? Nothing."

"I meant generally."

"They're ogres of some kind, aren't they?"

"You might as accurately say we are monkeys of some kind."

Rowena frowned. "But we aren't."

He waved dismissively. "A matter of scientific debate. Not important. What do you know about *what* they are?"

"Well . . . nothing special, I suppose." Rowena rolled her mug between her palms, thinking. "I know we used to keep 'em—the business folk and the gentry types, I mean, used to keep 'em—as servants. Or slaves. I guess the difference was if you paid 'em. Then the governors changed the laws to get more human folk back in labor, and they've been sort of shifting about Amidon ever since."

The Alchemist nodded.

Rowena spoke into her mug. "I know I'm afraid of them. Everybody is. They're huge and strong and angry." She looked up. "I know it's because of the way they've had it here in Amidon, but still, they're *so* angry. You can feel it on 'em when they walk by. It's like a cloud. Why are they *that* angry?"

"Imagine having to walk on your eyeballs all day," the Alchemist suggested dryly. "It might put even a saint in a bad mood."

Rowena laughed, then clapped a hand over her mouth. The last answer she'd expected was a joke.

The old man shrugged. "It's only a theory, of course."

"So, what am I *supposed* to know about them?"

"*Supposed* to know? Well—" the Alchemist rose, "—that's another matter."

And he was gone, shrugging past the long curtain separating the front of the shop from its ramshackle back. Soon he returned with a hefty book bound in peeling orange leather. He set the book on the table and opened the dusty front cover, spinning it the right way round to show Rowena, then resumed his seat. The frontispiece boasted a fine etching of a snake coiling around a pillar made of the heads of many creatures—wolf and mist-ox and chimer and eagle and such—and a long title in a gothic typeset, the words far longer than any Rowena had tried to read before.

"Find 'Aigamuxa.'"

"I don't . . . I can't really read."

The old man raised an eyebrow. "You read the sign outside."

"I knew what the shop was called *before* I came."

"Start looking in the A's."

Rowena grimaced at the book. She pawed back and forth through its stubborn pages, the paper a thin onionskin, its dog-eared corners needing to be teased apart. Finally, she spied something powerfully long staring with an "A-I." Rowena turned the book back around and pointed.

"Is this it?"

The Alchemist reached down to his shirt front and donned his spectacles.

Nodding, he read:

"'*Aigamuxa*, singular and plural. See also "*aiga*." The aigamuxa are a tribalist species originally descendant of ogres in the jungle regions of eastern Leonis. Males grow roughly half again the size of human males, with females equal to males in height, but lesser in weight. Their physiognomy is distinct for its structurally stooped posture, their fourth joint on each digit, and the seemingly ill-adapted location of their visual organs on the soles of their feet. While walking, aigamuxa must stop at regular intervals to raise their feet and look around with them, a process made easier by the great range of motion afforded in their extraordinarily limber hip and ankle joints. Xenobiological field reports indicate aigamuxa are capable of approximately two hundred seventy degrees of motion in these areas and can see in the dark through some ill-understood process of heat recognition. The jungle environment and the range of motion in their limbs have combined to make brachiating their most efficient locomotion.'" The Alchemist paused, looking at Rowena over the rims of his spectacles. "Brachiating. That's swinging from tree to tree."

Rowena nodded. She remembered the pink eyes staring down at her from the awnings and window ledges as she ran. The Alchemist searched the page for his lost spot, then continued.

"'Among the few jungle creatures capable of seeing with equal facility, night or day, the aigamuxa tend toward nocturnal habits. The awkward placement of their eyes has also led to species adaptation of the other senses, which are strikingly keen. An aigamuxa hunter can smell its prey on a windless night at a distance of roughly two miles. They are omnivorous and thrive on highly variable diets.

"'Aigamuxa are intelligent, but (apart from those assimilated through forced labor into human civilizations) do not generally exercise this intelligence to use human languages, considering themselves above condescending to lesser beings. Aigamuxa racial lore declares them the "first people" of the world, rationalizing their unusual physiognomy as a sign of their eternal connection with and attentiveness to the earth itself. Many aigamuxa legends describe the first people as the inevitable rulers of the world of *sapiens*. Shortly after Unification, large populations of humans native to Leonis became victims of a rise in aigamuxa tribalism, marked by a campaign to "cleanse" humanity from the continent. This began the

Ecclesiastical Commission's aggressive relocation of Leonine refugees to human settlements in Europa, the Amidonian continents, and across the Indine and Lemarckian territories. The historical record remains unclear as to whether this genocide preceded, or was in response to, humans capturing aigamuxa for use in industrial labor. In recent generations, free tribes of aigamuxa have known considerable success working in human lands as heavy laborers, mercenaries, and bodyguards.'"

The Alchemist closed the book. "I wouldn't call that an objective piece of scholarship, but it's accurate on the most significant matters."

"So, they hate us because they think they're the superior species and they should be in charge of things?" Rowena ventured.

He nodded, removing his spectacles. "Do you know what was in that package?"

It was the question Rowena had been dreading. She'd been under the Alchemist's roof for nearly an hour, and barely anything had been said of the package. She'd hoped that he'd put it out of his mind.

"Not exactly, sir."

"If you know something *inexact*, you know more than I."

Rowena stared at him. "I don't understand."

"I've ordered many things from Ivor over the years. He has always carried out the process in the same way, sending me notice in advance of a delivery so nothing is left to chance. There were no arrangements this time. And I had nothing on order awaiting delivery." The Alchemist picked up his pipe again and stabbed at its burnt-out bowl with a tobacco-stained thumb. "You don't know what was in that package. Neither do I."

"But . . . the aiga know now."

"Very likely they knew what it was when they took it."

"It might've been just bad luck. Lots of people get mugged by aiga these days, since they were turned out of the factories."

"True. But it takes very little study to see you haven't any money."

"The satchel was big. Could've made it look valuable," Rowena noted. "It was a book. Belonged to some EC doc—Reverend Chalmers."

The old man shook his head. "I've never heard of the man."

"Then why would Ivor send you the package? I can't figure it. He en't one to just give things away."

"Ivor," the Alchemist said, "had something he wanted to keep *from* someone. Sending packages to me has been such common business for so long it shouldn't raise suspicion. If whoever wanted the book believed Ivor wanted it, too, and knew anything of his nature they wouldn't suspect he'd part with it. But Ivor didn't contact me. That alone tells me something is quite wrong."

Rowena frowned. "The book you just read said that aiga don't care much for human languages and stuff, right?"

"Right."

"So if *you're* right and they knew what the delivery was, why would they even want it? What good can they get from a human book?"

"None, perhaps. But they're often hired by humans. They might be taking the book to someone else entirely."

It was an answer, but not one that really *answered* anything, Rowena supposed. The water clock on the pantry shelf showed eleven. She bit her lip.

"So, what do I tell Ivor when I go back to the warehouse?"

The Alchemist picked up the bestiary book. He turned it over in his hands. "I think it's a fair assumption Ivor won't be there if you do."

Rowena opened her mouth to ask why, but the set of the Alchemist's jaw gave her the answer. She recalled the wild look in the old smuggler's eyes when he shoved her through the door and felt an icy knot in her stomach.

The Alchemist turned back to the curtain again. "You'll need a place to sleep tonight. It might as well be here."

11.

The look Smallduke Herridge gave Bess was somewhere between gracious and hungry, a leer that made the skin along her shoulders crawl when he kissed her hand. He was as broad as a barrowman's cart, and bald except for a ring of hair above his ears, the rest seemingly migrated into the dense bush of ruddy beard covering his throat. Every movement was accompanied by the music of his medals clinking. None were military. Tokens for philanthropy or civil service, maybe. Bess wasn't entirely sure. She withdrew her hand, grateful that her long lace gloves shielded her from his fleshy fingers.

"She is," Herridge said, speaking with his eyes distinctly appreciating Bess's cleavage, "very lovely, Regenzi. Your godchild, you say?"

Regenzi nodded. "Our families have long connections."

"I'm sure they do."

Bess adjusted her mask of peacock feathers. She hoped that its flourishes hid her surely deepening color. Herridge had to know she was no more Regenzi's godchild than the lanyani servers were. Still, her lover had been telling the lie for two hours. It seemed courtesy demanded the assembled ignore their host parading his courtesan around as an honored guest.

The ball Bess had been anticipating all day turned out more opulent than she had dared dream. It was a midnight masque, though it had truthfully begun at eleven o' the clock. The Regenzi manor comprised a half block of row houses merged together with a bit of architectural ingenuity years before, carving from the crowded splendor of the Upper Districts space enough for yet another self-made noble. Now, it was teeming with wealthy merchants; famous debutantes; dukes and duchesses both great and small; most of the members of the city governor's cabinet; elegant companions and escorts of all descriptions; and exotically skirted lanyani serving girls, whose fibrous flesh had been planed raw, down to bare sapling skin with the perfect feminine curves of bodies utterly devoid of nipples, of hair, of navels. Men and women alike watched them sway among the guests, carrying trays of cordials and cocktails, little canapés, folded serviettes, and every other nicety Bess could imagine. Their long, leafy manes were all autumn fire. Regenzi had been very particular that none of his lanyani spend time out of doors in the days before the masque, lest their colors fail and their fine, smooth-grained skin shed all its ornamentation. Everything had to be perfect.

Everything *was* perfect.

Bess had been afraid of her looks measuring up before entering the grand ballroom. As she came down from the private apartments above, she'd heard the string quartet playing—one of six stationed throughout the sprawling manse. The strings rang high and sweet and every bit as tight as her nerves, each step down the brocade stair a descent into scarce-concealed panic.

Panic left in a rush as she stepped into the room and saw the rest of the women.

Except for the professional courtesans, the ones with papers and licenses, the women of the ball were creatures of money, and it had made them plump, or enervated, or merely dull. Bess had seen a glossy-haired woman with the wide, round face of a Malay, her belly and breasts so vast she might have been mistaken for one of their pre-Unity fertility idols. Another woman, stick straight and bound up in a buttercream-colored wrap only a shade deeper than her sallow skin, drifted between the long halls as if she'd lost something. Bess had begun to wonder if it was her wits. Countless others, their features only half-hidden by understated opera masks, wore faces of powder and stain that had already crazed like old pottery, doubling whatever age the cosmetics had been meant to hide. Bess could barely breathe for the tightness of her corset, but she knew it was *worth it* to show up these crones. Her fine auburn hair was pinned with silver and amethyst clips, her bosom swelling up from a wine-colored bodice slashed with silver satin. Regenzi looked very fine, too, his tawny whiskers trimmed and his jewel-colored coattails pressed.

He wore no mask. It was important, he said, for his guests to be able to find him readily.

There had been applause from the assembled as he swept her into the room. No one could have heard Bess's gasp over that roll of thunder when Regenzi pinched her side, hissing into her ear.

"Smile, my dear. *Always* smile."

Bess offered him the smile again—the painted one, the porcelain one. The one he liked best.

"Of course."

The next two hours were a blur of dances and introductions. Bess shook hands, curtseyed, chatted, and laughed her best nightingale giggle, her skirts swirling as she bustled from one room to another. Remembering faces to go with the names was impossible, so Bess remembered masks. There was the minister of streets in his leopard face; the third Greatduchess Salend and her tamarind's mane; the owner of the six grandest hotels in the city wearing a wolf's snout. Bess had met dragons and demons and eagles and even a hedgehog, though she couldn't remember which guest belonged to that bit of whimsy. Abraham said her mask was the tropical dove, a bird common to Trimeeni cities in the distant southern hemisphere. Bess had never seen one, but its exotic details appealed to her, so she wore it with pride—and relief, when men like Smallduke Herridge let their gaze linger overlong.

There were many members of the Ecclesiastical Commission attending, each one an invited guest of some other guest. Bess saw so many black collars and dresses it seemed the Decadal Conference must have moved its sessions to the manse. The EC guests hunted after Smallduke Regenzi, plying him with requests to fund some experiment or other. He took their calling cards graciously, making certain that each knew Abraham Regenzi was a friend to the Grand Unity.

Bess turned to hail a lanyani girl carrying a tray of *vinas* when she noticed Regenzi turning the other direction. A florid, middle-aged deacon stood beside a short, broad-hipped woman. Both wore the simple domino masks provided at the door to those guests who had come unprepared. This included nearly all the Ecclesiastical commissionaries.

Regenzi gripped Bess's arm and turned her back toward the pair now crossing the room to meet him. "Stay a moment, will you?"

"Do you know them?"

"The man is called Fredericks, I think. . . ."

"Re*genz*i!" the man the smallduke called "Fredericks" cried, arms and smile wide. "I had thought I might go the whole evening without seeing my host. Do you remember me?"

"Leopold Fredericks, Order of Historical Statistics," Regenzi answered with absolute confidence.

Fredericks shook his head admiringly. "You've a mind like a trap, my lord. There must be a hundred black collars here to remember."

"I always remember the *important* ones." Regenzi turned to the woman. Her dress bore the pin of a reverend doctor: balances resting on a set of books, overlaid on a silhouette of the globe. "Might I have your help, Fredericks, in expanding my repertoire?"

"Of course. Reverend Doctor Nora Pierce, I give you Lord Abraham Regenzi. And Doctor Pierce, this is . . ."

"Beatrice," Bess said helpfully. "I'm Lord Regenzi's goddaughter."

Fredericks bowed, touching his brow. He was an awkward-looking man, a little rumpled, but he had a good smile—sincere and content to leave her bosom to its own devices. Bess smiled back.

Bess studied the Reverend Doctor Pierce carefully, trying to figure what was so unusual about her. All evening she'd been watching people sporting the oddest affectations, yet something about this woman in her black dress with nothing more than a domino mask covering her dark-eyed face struck Bess as . . . odd. That was the only word for it. Odd.

"My lord," the woman said, curtseying slightly. "I am honored to have been invited."

"Invited. . . ." The look Regenzi offered her was, for a moment, absolutely blank. "Wait, *Pierce*. My God, you're the keynote speaker for the conference! Some villain told me you'd missed the galleon out of Lemarcke or some nonsense. Your coauthor, Chalmers, is supposed to carry on alone."

"The galleon had a malfunction. Things looked very bad when I sent

Phillip the spark, but enough passengers complained the owners called a new ship up from storage and had us in the air a few hours later. I arrived after supper, and I haven't had the chance to stop by Coventry Passage and sort out the confusion. That can wait till morning."

Regenzi patted Bess's arm and flicked his eyes toward a sideboard of refreshments some yards away. She nodded and untangled herself from him with a murmured apology, hearing his voice behind her: "You must be exhausted from your travels. Let us get you a drink."

Let "us." Bess sighed inwardly. It was only a little thing. Regenzi was handsome, powerful, still quite young. He had a temper and a certain proprietary air, but he'd never raised his hand to her, let alone had her across the back with a hawthorn—or worse.

At the sideboard, a teenaged page dressed in the bright green house livery prepared trays of *vinas* for the lanyani girls. Barely looking up, he passed two flutes to Bess. She opened her mouth to ask for something different—Abraham had told her once that *vinas* gave him a sour stomach—but the page's back was turned. Two lanyani girls were looming nearby, their white, pupil-less eyes staring through her. Bess realized she must be standing in their way and stepped aside, whispering an apology.

She regarded the flutes of *vinas* in her hands grimly. She might ask for a replacement, but still. . . .

Better not make them wait longer.

The room was far longer than it was wide, a sort of gallery with space cleared toward the center for the most determined dancers. Bess paused, scanning the room for her smallduke and the reverend doctor. For a moment, she couldn't find them amid the strolling and dancing forms, or tucked in the knots of chatting gentry. Finally, just as she began to wonder if they had moved on to another room without her, Bess spied them standing near the quartet, half-hidden by a decorated paper screen.

She frowned. If conversation was their aim, it was a strange place to take it up. Standing only ten or twelve feet from the musicians, the smallduke dipped his head down to better hear the Reverend Doctor Pierce.

Bess studied them as she skirted the dancers. She hoped she did not appear to be watching—or stalling.

Jorrie Downshire, rest his soul, had known a few things about reading lips. He'd taught Bess some of the trick one slow afternoon as they lay in the loft above the warehouse. Bess recalled his curly brown hair and his mischievous eyes. The memory of the rest—his hands on her new-budded breasts, her lips against the warmth of his throat—was faded, though it had been barely three years before.

Bess narrowed her eyes, standing almost inside a school of Ecclesiastical fishes. She watched the smallduke's lips.

Doing well. . . . Not much longer, an hour . . .

Fragments, at best. Jorrie would not have been impressed. Bess kept trying. The Reverend Doctor Pierce's back was to Bess, but she glanced over her shoulder. For a flashing moment, Bess could see her mouth.

. . . make sure sees me?

No, this is good . . . too far . . .

And then Abraham Regenzi saw Bess. For a moment, his eyebrows lowered and his nose scrunched, a mime of a snapping comment: *Where have you been all this time?*

Regenzi met Bess halfway. Two other guests came up to stand with Pierce, ushered into the gap by Fredericks. The little crowd was all handshakes and well-wishing for the upcoming keynote.

Bess offered Regenzi both drinks, but he ignored them, instead turning in a fashion that concealed their conference from passersby.

"*Vinas*," he sighed with relief. "Perfect. Good. This will do."

Still, he didn't take the flutes. Instead, a gold-ringed hand slipped with surreptitious grace into a pocket of his dress coat, fishing briefly—

Bess sighed her own relief. "She likes *vinas*? The page gave me them before—"

And then she stopped, staring. Regenzi's hands hovered over one of the flutes, tilting a slender aluminum flask. It held a crystallized rod of something Bess remembered seeing in a liquid form so many hours before. Her heart thundered as the thin, brown blade sagged into the *vinas*, finally dissolving. The music and people and porcelain smiles had all but washed the Alchemist's words down the basin of Bess's mind. But now, she remembered.

"Your lover has need of rather dangerous things. Be mindful what that might mean for you."

"Abraham," Bess whispered. "Abraham, what are you doing?"

Regenzi took the doctored drink, his fingers brushing the back of her hand. When their eyes met, Bess felt her color drain.

He was *smiling*. It was the same smile he offered her in the moment before they made love—the same smile that accompanied a good dinner, a useful introduction, a piece of good news. It was, Bess realized, the only smile Smallduke Abraham Regenzi had, utterly utilitarian, and if hers was made of painted porcelain, his was forged of iron.

He kissed Bess on the lips, pressing painfully hard. His breath burned against her ear.

"I'm tidying up a mess, Beatrice."

Regenzi straightened and raised the glass in salute to a passing member of the governor's cabinet. The minister raised his in reply.

And then he was gone, excusing himself back into the Reverend Doctor Pierce's company. Bess stood frozen, the heels of her ankle boots driven into the ground. When Pierce took the flute of *vinas* from Regenzi's hand, Bess managed to pivot one boot, pull the other up from the polished granite floor, and walk away.

She achieved her retreat quickly in spite of the crowd. Old instincts from the courier's loft took over. They knew how to slide through busy spaces and still look natural, even if Bess herself hardly knew where she was anymore.

At the farthest end of the room, Bess paused and looked down at her *vinas*. No one seemed to be paying her any mind. She drained the flute and clutched the emptied crystal in her nerveless hand.

She stood beside a waterfall clock draped in green sashes. Two o' the clock in the morning—a new day, Second-day Elevenmonth, sixteen days since she'd first walked through the doors of the Regenzi manor.

The room was full of whirling animal faces. She caught her own in the reflection of the clock's glass door, the jewel-bright plumage haloing her face.

Bess felt a sudden, stinging certainty that there was no such bird as the tropical Trimeeni dove. Whatever looked back at her in the glass was splendid and lurid and an absolute fiction. A storybook creature. Something children would believe in because they wanted to. Or needed to.

Over the strains of the string quartet, half a world away, Bess heard a shriek and an avalanche of china. In the glass, she could see a space clearing at the far end of the gallery where a page boy's serving cart lay on its side, toppled by the spastic form of a small woman, a convulsion of black-clothed limbs on the dance floor.

A man's voice called, without irony, for a doctor.

INTERMEZZO

The diary of the Reverend Doctor Nora Pierce
Sixteenth-day Threemonth, year 269:

I have received a reply from Phillip Chalmers; he is willing to discuss the project. He believes the equipment he designed to check atmospheric concentrations of the particles can be modified to suit my present objectives. We'll meet on the morrow. I pray it goes well. I need a partner.

I am afraid.

Now that I write the words, I feel a little better. It is good to be honest for a moment: I, Nora Pierce, scholar and researcher, the Shrew of Semiotics—was that what they called me in seminary? I think that was it. All those man-children, thinking themselves so clever. Damn them. I, Nora Piece, am afraid.

I remember Phillip from my post-seminary in Rimmerston and hope he's grown a little since. He lacked something in the way of discipline; I will need someone with me who can be reasonable and steady. My strength for that is nearly spent, and it's only six months I've had the text.

Usually it unfolds before me slowly. The recorder is very precise. But now, that invisible hand has drawn an "X" through the whole of the last page.

I can't decipher the notes well enough to fathom what the error might have been—not without Chalmers's equipment to test my hypothesis first. Meantime, I am struck by how carefully the recorder's work is done and how much of it is still being undone.

Does God make mistakes? Does He—can He—misperceive?

If anyone finds these notes, they'll think me mad. Let them. I am a reverend doctor, a theosophical scientist. It is my duty to record without passion, and so I will carry on. The observations are all here; I can move on to constructing my claims.

Claim #1: I am looking at the shadow of the hand of God, tracing the silhouette of the universe.

The silhouette has only nine figures comprising it. Only nine. I am a long time from my Apocrypha seminar, but I remember that number and the theories of Ruchell Bennington in 236. She thought she had finally traced a liturgical path to an exact number for the Grand Experiment, and she proposed the term Vautnek, with its Old Religion translation of *thirty-six*, be revised to the Nine.

She was pilloried in the journals for her ideas—called a raconteur. Arrogant. Self-serving. She retired three years later, though she was only forty-eight.

But there *are* nine sections to the book, only nine sets of data.

Such an absurdly small number, nine. And if it truly is an experiment—the Grand Experiment of Creation itself—there must be (Claim #2) a control out there, somewhere. That is another reason I shall need Phillip. His paper on the Many-Worlds Interpretation suggests there could be many other earths the Creator might compare ours against, many sets of nine or ninety-nine or nine billion to compare against these, our Vautneks. It makes the madness of it all at least a trace more . . . Rational.

I wish I had been there with you in 236, Ruchell. I wish I had had this book in my hands when you gave the lecture in the old cathedral of Aerion so I might have stood up from the pews and shouted down that sneering Bishop Meteron and his pedantic objections. I wish I had known that I would sit in his study some thirty years later, that I would agree to make a delivery for him to the grand librarian in Nippon—and that I would agree to take something from the librarian too.

Did he know it was true, all those long years ago? Or did he find out later?

I wish I had been at Aerion, Ruchell, so you could see these pages, too, and tell me I'm not mad—or if I am, save me from it.

It's been two years since I saw Phillip Chalmers last. I should put my vain hopes for some miracle in him aside. He was always a fool. People do not change, even when they must. I will need his equipment, his maths, his ciphering, and he can keep his nervous, narcissistic nonsense and go to the devil with it. I will have to find the answers. I will have to save myself. If the nine shadows on these pages are who I think them to be, I may have to save them, too.

I didn't bring the book back to Rimmerston. And the bishop has not forgotten.

DAY TWO

2nd Elevenmonth

12.

Anselm Meteron stared at the pages spread before him, the spidery ink of some dead scribe's calligraphy swimming in his vision. He stifled a yawn and stretched. The water clock ticking away on his solar's mantelpiece showed eight thirty. *God's balls.* His temples throbbed with the dull, persistent pain of a sleepless night—not such an unusual thing for him, perhaps, but still. He had his limits.

He glanced at the escritoire's right-hand drawer and considered the bottle of ether lurking there.

For as long as Anselm could remember, insomnia had been his bedfellow. He could never stop his mind working. Perhaps he should have been a chronometician or an engineer. He thrived on moving parts, following their intersections and cascades of consequence. Without something to grind his own gears down, sleep was little more to him than a rumor invented by others for his particular torment.

A book that writes itself.

Anselm pressed his hands to his eyes.

It was entirely possible that Ivor had finally lost his wits. Anselm knew his ether bottle a little too well to cast aspersions, but Ivor knew his wodke better and had been its intimate far longer. Still. The Vraskan was many things but never a blind alarmist.

Anselm leaned for the bellpull and gave it a slow, certain draw. A gong rang, far below in the concierge's offices. Moments later, the brass speaking tube set beside the bellpull released an echoing, tinny voice.

"Yes, sir?"

"Coffee," Anselm said, then paused, considering. "With a little rum in it, there's a good girl."

"Very good, sir."

Anselm passed the time before the tray came up sitting beside the empty fireplace. Rare had never come to the Empire Club, and his half hope of finding her in his bed had been dashed. Ivor's strange question and his own books had been the alternative to her arms. A poor substitute. *Damn them both.* He should have turned to the ether hours before. It was too late, now.

The long night's unanswered questions gnawed too fiercely to be ignored. How could he have spent so many hours and have found so little? Found, really, nothing at all? Anselm loathed failure. This particular morning, it galled him like a stone.

Anselm had made a career of knowing a little something about almost anything. His first professional expertise had been more physical than intellectual, but knowing the right people and the right things had kept him out of more than a few scrapes. He prided himself on being every bit as dangerous in his retirement as he had been in the years before. It was just a different *kind* of danger.

He kept a library of surpassing eclecticism, full of volumes of Decadal Conference proceedings, gazettes from each of the major Amidonian cities indexed on lamp film, files of names and business cards, a host of scientific treatises and histories. Yet nothing in the Ecclesiastical Commission's official literature so much as mused about self-writing texts. Nothing in the abstracts of the current conference suggested a new means of transmitting information was being presented—certainly not a *wireless* mode of transmission. Could such a thing even be possible?

Ivor's galvano-gram inspired Anselm to dig about his other sources. He'd hired an informant in the Coventry Passage rectory, the landlady Mrs. Gilleyen, in an effort to keep some track of the much-indebted, often-traveling reverend doctor Pierce. Gilleyen had furnished no new report on Pierce's partner Chalmers since Gammon's inquiry, and rumors moving about the Empire Club the night before, spread by young deacons and reverends visiting that most exclusive venue, said the landlady had been taken in by the constabulary overnight. In the dawn gazette, Anselm read an article about a death at Smallduke Regenzi's masque, but the story supplied no names, no details. Nothing remotely useful. Anselm had had a spree once with the journalist who was now that gazette's editor in chief. It was not in her nature to hold back—not without the proper inducements, of course.

All that work and he'd earned nothing more than the ache of an abortive search and the annoyance of his spark back to Ivor going unanswered.

Damn him. Anselm glanced at the clock on the wall. Quarter to nine. *He was supposed to have been here by now.* He ought to call down to the concierge and tell them to give up the breakfast preparations.

The footman shuffled in with a silver-laden tray. He deposited it on the sideboard, sketched a quick bow, and scurried off.

Anselm poured coffee into a cup with two fingers of rum at its bottom, nearly spilling the cup's contents on a folded note tucked under the saucer. He returned to his desk with coffee and note, its ink still fresh from the spark clerk's pen.

> A. Meteron, Regency Square, immediate delivery
> 2nd Elevenmonth, 0830, Private Address
> Unexpected courier from our old friend last night. Package intercepted by aiga. Reason to believe your girl involved. Need to meet, your terms, spark back. E.

Anselm tossed the note in the rubbish and made a mental note to carry the bin down to the furnace himself later.

"My girl," he mused dryly.

Yes, he supposed, *that is one way of thinking of her.*

Anselm reached for the bellpull again. The speaking tube hummed in reply.

"Yes, sir?" The voice was unfamiliar, male. The new footman, perhaps.

"Bennie—" Anselm began experimentally.

"Benjy, sir."

"Of course. Benjy. Send a spark down to Stillhampton, the addressee under 'R. J.' in my logbook downstairs."

He could hear the sound of paper tearing from a notebook. "Very good. What's the message?"

"'Here in an hour, or I'll feed you to the Bear.'"

A long pause. "I . . . Feed to the bear, sir?"

"Make sure it's a capital 'B,' there's a good lad, hm?"

"Yes, sir."

The connection cut off with a click.

Anselm smiled ruefully.

Rare would not take an hour, of course. She never did. But Anselm had a certain love of drama—there was a time he had written all his contracts out for a term of a year and a day, simply as an aesthetic gesture. But an hour, even as an overstatement, still had its value: it was time enough for Anselm to wash up and change his clothes, to roll two cigarettes, and to smoke them down to the tips of his fingers before calling up his carriage.

And so, he did.

13.

For the first time she could remember, Rowena Downshire awoke to breakfast smells.

It was still early, pink morning light seeping through the high dormer windows of the attic bedroom. Yawning, she sat up and felt a tingling deadness in her legs, something pinning them down.

The dog raised its head and beat the mattress with its tail. Motes of dust swirled everywhere.

"Oh," Rowena said.

The beast wormed forward on its belly a few inches, snuffling her fingers wetly. It was a russet hound with a blocky gray muzzle and one ear ragged-ended from some old wound. The dog from the coal bin. She scratched all up and down its neck, laughing at its eager trills.

"Friendly cuss, en't you?"

It shook, ears to toes, and jumped down, trotting to the door with several backward glances. One back leg seemed a little off, somehow. The dog's rear didn't canter after its front so much as hop along in its wake. It whined insistently.

"All right, all right. Let me put my knickers on already."

Rowena slid to the floor and found a good rust-colored coat and a pair of fine woolen britches draped over the bedstead. She fingered them as if they might have been imagined: lightly at first, and then with eager, grasping hands. The coat's pockets still had a few cedar shavings stuck in the lining. The britches were creased along the seams, as if they had just recently been unfolded from long years of storage. Her old jacket and knickers smelled of the courier loft's moldering hay mattresses. She wriggled into the new clothes and buckled the britch-cuffs about her calves, finding they fell a bit too long.

Still, she'd take an odd fit over rags and holes in the Elevenmonth cold. An oval mirror standing in the corner threw back the image of a lean, canny-looking girl, her rough-cut hair all chocolate waves and snarls. Rowena struck a pose, buttoned the coat's double-breast, then unbuttoned it. She affected a casual air and examined a phantom chronometer drawn from its inner pocket, tapping her foot with theatrical impatience. But—wait.

She looked in the mirror again, gaping. Her face should have been a map of bruises, yet somehow her cheekbone was still only red. Rowena touched the mark gingerly. A film of the Alchemist's ointment, smelling of aspic and something grassy, came off on her fingers. Whatever it was, it had done its job well.

Again, the dog barked, then thundered down the stairs without her.

Rowena turned to follow the shaggy thing as it bumpity-bumped down, but something spied out of the corner of her eye made her pause.

Rowena studied the nightstand beside the sagging old bed. A candle, a washbasin, and jug, just like the night before. She remembered the Alchemist carrying them in after he pulled the tarp from the bed and beat out the rug. But the candle, she was sure, had been new. This one was burnt nearly halfway—and hadn't the cane-back chair been under the window before, not at the bedside?

Something shivered the hairs on the nape of Rowena's neck. She rolled her shoulders, as if to shake it off, and followed the breakfast smells downstairs.

The Alchemist sat at the improvised table, flipping through a morning gazette. There were two crockery bowls laid out, one full of hominy porridge with honey, and the other only traces of the same. He glanced at Rowena, grunted something that might have been a greeting, and nodded to the untouched bowl.

Rowena tucked in so fast she forgot to offer a thank-you until she was nearly half-done. The Alchemist waved absently. He set his empty bowl beside his feet. The hound slavered it clean, full of noisy gratitude, and collapsed on his master's boots with a contented wheeze.

"Your dog," Rowena ventured. "He's—"

"Lame. An idiot, even as beasts go." The old man set his pipe down and folded the gazette.

"*I* like him."

He indicated her dirty dish. "Offer him that and you'll win a friend for life."

Rowena copied the Alchemist's technique and watched the dog come trotting awkwardly around the table, all tail and earnestness, to bury his nose in her dish.

"It's a shame about that leg."

"Always been that way. We call him Rabbit."

She looked up. "We?"

The old man removed his spectacles. "I," he amended. "Old habits."

Rabbit turned three tight circles, half-hopping his way through the last, and settled with his head on the toe of the Alchemist's boot, still licking his chops. Rowena glanced at the old man, wondering if she should ask—if she *could* ask—if he'd been in her room.

"Rabbit," she echoed. "That's a nice—"

"Why didn't you tell me about the woman you met on the lightning rail?"

For a moment, his tone left Rowena frozen. She cursed herself for rattling so easily. "What woman?"

The Alchemist's dark eyes narrowed. Rowena propped up a rickety smile. She had her own habits, her need for secrets, and they'd served her well and long. She sized him up, figuring the next move. He was angry—and, she saw, something more than that. It was the something more that made her shift uncomfortably in her chair. She thought of the candle again but pushed it aside.

"I'm sorry," Rowena said finally. "Rare just wanted a letter delivered to Ivor. We've met a few times before, and she en't ever done me wrong. I didn't mention it because . . ." She shrugged. "It just didn't seem important. I guess the aigamuxa have the letter now, too."

"You guess," he snapped "Did you give it to the aiga?"

"It was in the same bag as the book."

"Then you can spare yourself guessing."

"*I said* I'm sorry."

"And what will you say to Rare if the aigamuxa decide to look for her?"

Rowena's cheeks burned. "But . . . they won't. Why would they?"

"The letter shows she's connected to Ivor. Ivor was afraid the book would bring him trouble. That seems a fair assumption, given what befell you. Why should it stop there?"

"*I said I'm sorry*," Rowena insisted. The room had gone blurry. She swiped a hand across her eyes. It came away damp.

The Alchemist's jaw was tight below his graying beard. "You did." Abruptly, he stood. "Sorry begins the redress. The rest is yet to be done."

"Can it—" Rowena asked then stopped when he turned and leveled those piercing eyes at her again. "Can it wait for a little more breakfast? I'm really very hungry."

The old man opened his mouth, some reply about to come. He closed his teeth on it and sighed. "I need to check for a spark," he said, passing through the curtain to the front desk. "Tell me when you're ready to go."

"Go where?"

The curtain closed. The Alchemist let silence make his reply. Rowena stared at the table, then reached down to the empty bowl on the floor. She carried it to the little copper sink to rinse away the dog's spittle, emptied the last of the porridge into it, blew on it awhile—and found she couldn't bring the spoon to her mouth. Her hunger was still there, but her guts roiled, full of something indigestible.

She put the bowl on the floor, her head on the table, and listened to Rabbit enjoy second helpings.

14.

With Anselm, a message directing someone to meet him "here" might have any one of a dozen meanings. Long practice had taught Rare the trick of telling to which "here" a given message referred. It was all in the context, and the hour of day, and the weather, and the smaller subtleties of his temper. She'd learned to read all these things, sifting them out of the thin phrases of a galvano-gram. This particular day, in this particular circumstance, "here" would mean the Hangman's Market, already in its midday rush. It was a place she had learned to lose herself in years before, a trick mastered under Anselm's watchful instruction.

The Hangman's Market owed its name to the disused gallows casting skeletal shadows across its snarl of tents and carts. Men and women were still hanged in Corma, but now the gallows were shut up in the outbuildings of the Court and Bar, away from the riot of the streets. The Ecclesiastical Commission didn't much involve itself in the business of law and order, but it had lobbied against public executions years before with a compelling study of the crime rates in the days following them. If the goal of such spectacles was to scare the people straight, it was a goal better reached by other means. That had been enough to shift the custom's location, though not to stay its practice. Now only the hotels and public houses ringing the Hangman's Market recalled its past with winking names like the Pine Box Inn and the Bitter End.

Passing the rotted scaffold, Rare recalled that a younger Anselm had been among the last to take the long ride to that infamous stair. He'd given the clumsy gendarme left in charge of him the slip and escaped in spectacular style. Years after, Anselm had purchased a café called the Last Drop. He still owned it, a little snub directed toward the Fates, though no one but his accountant and the maître d' ever recognized him as more than a wealthy patron on his occasional visits.

Rare found Anselm in a perfumer's tent, browsing phials of every shape and hue with practiced disinterest. The space reeked of jasmine, sandalwood, and cherry bark. Rare wondered how the wizened, hood-eyed merchant could bear so much oppressive scent.

She slipped between two matronly women in broad, feathered hats and settled in beside Anselm.

Rare lifted a phial the color of sunset. "Your message was uncommonly direct."

Anselm made a tsking sound. "Not that one. You need something with wood undertones." He offered her an alternative and moved a few paces off.

Curious, Rare sniffed. Beech and amber. It *was* a good fit—a dark scent to balance her fair features. She set the bottle down, following Anselm's path.

"But lavender is most certainly your color," he observed. "Where did you find that gown? It's lovely."

"You only start with nonsense when there's something important going on."

"I had thought my uncommonly direct message should give you some idea of it. You've gotten into something that concerns the Bear. He's asked to see us about it."

She put a hand on Anselm's elbow, directing him out onto the boulevard. The market air was comparatively free, its treacle puddings and cinders and ales mingling with the closeness of humanity.

Rare twined her arm with Anselm's. "I'm listening."

"I had always thought you clever." Anselm's voice dripped acid. "But you seem determined to make me regret that assessment. What have you put your nose in now, kitten?"

She shrugged. They turned a corner and walked past a lanyani busker pulling sovereigns from the ears of idiot children, the shining coins secreted between its willow-whip fingers.

"Nothing that involves me with the Bear."

"I hear different."

"And what *do* you hear?"

"Ivor sent him a package last night. He ended up with an empty-handed courier instead. Now he thinks you're connected. I was hoping you might clarify what led him to that conclusion."

"I *may* have met one of Ivor's birds on the lightning rail last night."

Anselm pulled them up beside a stall half-buried in an avalanche of shoes. A cobbler knocked away at the heel of a lady's boot, the hammer punctuating Anselm's words.

"You *may have*. And if, peradventure, you did?"

Rare rolled her eyes, untangling her arm from his. "I *may* have given her a letter to pass on to Ivor, encouraging him to consider me a candidate for a mutually beneficial partnership." Rare smiled at Anselm's narrowing gaze. "You really should lock your desk drawers. Not all the help can be trusted."

"Nor all the houseguests."

Rare spread her hands innocently.

"You planned to lever Ivor with your knowledge of Gammon hunting for foul play between Chalmers and Pierce," Anselm said. "The letter was an offer to take their goods off his hands, perhaps find a buyer for them?"

"I had a buyer for them."

Anselm raised an eyebrow. Rare bristled at that, hoping the claim was not so plainly an exaggeration. The lanyani's aigamuxa housekeeper had said the clan might be interested in Ecclesiastical goods, in light of the conference being in town. But that was enough. It was a lead, and she intended to make it useful.

Rare added, in a honeyed tone, "I learned from the best."

Anselm scoffed. He stalked toward the Last Drop.

"Kitten, I daresay you've forgotten half of what I taught you. Do you even know what those goods were?"

She tossed her hair dismissively. "Some kind of research text. There was something in the message about it containing data. Lots of EC collars have records full of data. It's all worth something to someone. With so many of them mucking about the city, nosing into one another's interests, what better time to move it along?"

"You didn't pay attention to the grammar of Ivor's message."

Rare laughed. "Did you just use the words 'grammar' and 'Ivor' in the same statement?"

"The book," Anselm said in a cool, poisonous tone of correction, "*collects data*. It was the subject of the sentence, in the active voice. It *collects* data *by itself*."

"A ridiculous conclusion. If Ivor wanted to tell you something so incredible, he'd put it plainly."

Anselm shook his head. "No, kitten. Ivor is cheap. You pay for galvano-graph transmissions by the character. And the constabulary has a whole department listening in on the shorts and longs. They can't catch everything, but they get enough to keep savvy people nervous. Helps keep Ivor running a brisk trade in letter delivery. He'd know better than to make matters plain."

Rare cursed inwardly, keeping her face neutral. If the delivery hadn't been stolen, she might have made something of the debacle—brokered a deal for the package with the Old Bear. Things were not so bad between them, she supposed, that she couldn't at least make a show of mending fences. But it *had* been stolen, and Ivor—

"Ivor's already had his trouble," Rare said, taking Anselm's arm again. She patted it consolingly. "When he didn't respond to my letter by the morning deadline I gave, I strolled by Blackbottom End on my own. New Vraska Imports is a wreck. There's a lot of blood in the offices above the loft." She considered mentioning what she'd taken from Ivor's office before leaving, the half-rifled sack of correspondence squirreled away from customers. She'd had to leave it unexamined in her apartments to make this meeting. But . . . no. That was her business, at least for now.

Anselm pinched the bridge of his nose. He and Ivor had their history. Rare knew that very well—and she knew equally well the look of a man expecting the other shoe to drop.

"So you left a letter with a courier implying that you wanted to work with Ivor and obtain this self-writing book for your own purposes. The delivery and the letter were stolen, and now the old bastard appears to be dead. Does that roughly embody your recent escapades?"

"I do try to keep busy."

The blow was not the hardest Anselm could offer, but it was cruel—the back of his hand, knuckles grazing her mouth. Curt. Punitive. Rare's eyes misted before she could push the pain back down. Nearby, a governess holding a little girl's hand tugged her charge away from the row.

Rare gentled her lip with the lace of her sleeve. "You bastard."

"I'm not the one who contacted an old ally contemplating usury and extortion," Anselm snapped. And then, the sigh. It was the one he'd used when she was still a girl, learning her way around the dark places at his heels. His sighs were a language unto themselves, complete with tones and grammars. Once, they'd had the power to pare Rare down a size. Now, they slid into her, silent as a sharpened knife, and turned.

"You've rattled the Bear's cage," he continued. "Probably the girl confessed the whole business to him."

"Who has the delivery now?"

Anselm stared at her for a long time. He pulled her forward, a hand about her waist, another cupping her chin, and kissed her. She felt the familiar rasp of his tongue and shivered. Then he held her at arm's length, a gesture of mock admiration, the teacher sizing up the pupil and finding her wanting.

"Some aigamuxa, silly kitten. And because of your clever little note, now it has your name, too."

Rare pushed him away. "What of it?"

"Nothing. Everything. If there are aigamuxa willing to steal this delivery, and someone willing to kill for what Ivor used to have, why should you fare better? Even if there were no monsters to contend with, there's still the Bear to shake off. You've put a deal of effort into avoiding him."

"I'm not afraid of him. Or them."

Anselm sniffed, shaking his head. He resumed his walk down the cluttered lanes of the Hangman's Market, hands folded behind his back, the stump of his shortened finger tap-tap-tapping. Rare set her jaw and followed, shrugging her shawl close.

It needled her to see him so knowing, so contemptuous of her work. He had always taken pride in her skills, her charm and aptitude as his apprentice. She'd been fifteen when she came to his doorstep, looking for someone to console her for the family she'd lost. He'd been the best choice. Their loss, after all, had been shared. And he was hardly a stranger to her. For years, he'd been a kind of uncle, wicked and wily, and she'd pined for him with a schoolgirl's fancy. He was charming, rakish, canny. She had *needed* that kind of man, back then. He might even have needed her, too.

The thirst for consolation had brought the younger Rare into the bed of a man twice her age. It had seemed better than a dream. She was *his*. His ward, his apprentice, his lover. It was a pleasure beyond any she'd known to belong to someone so completely.

But Rare *had* been a child. To be reminded, thirteen years on, that he still saw her as an amateur was an indignity she'd earned an end of long ago.

She walked beside Anselm. She did not take his arm.

I am not a child, Rare thought fiercely. *I've been on my own five years and made more than enough clink to show my worth. He should know that by now.*

Very likely, he *did* know that. *Perhaps*, she considered, *he even resents it.* Anselm had his wealth and his success, true. He was retired, though he rarely used the term. And didn't that prove he hadn't accepted it? A surge of triumph filled Rare's breast. Anselm's reputation was considerable. Cutpurses and cat burglars swapped stories of his exploits across smoky card tables. They regarded his legend as a yardstick against which to measure themselves. But Anselm was nearly all legend now—an object of admiration, yes, but so was a fossil or the shroud of some long-dead king.

As they passed through the thinning edges of the bazaar and entered the Last Drop's portico, Rare tried to recall the last time Anselm himself actually ran a job. It had been . . . Her brow furrowed as she fumbled through memory. *Six years?* That long, at least. They nodded their way past the maître d' and took up a padded corner booth. Rare had trouble suppressing her smile.

"You look a deal too pleased with yourself," Anselm said, "for a woman who might need to run for her life before supper."

The smile unfolded in earnest.

"You," she purred, "are a *relic*, Ann. Do you know that?"

He pushed his menu aside. A waiter sidled up to their table. Anselm dismissed him with a flick of four and a half fingers. The man disappeared.

Rare slid closer, coming round the curve of the bench to press herself against Anselm. Beneath the table, she traced a hand up the outer hem of his trousers and began to play her way to the inner thigh, imagining her smile laced with poison.

"You think because you taught me this trade, you'll always be my master. You think because we've shared a bed, I'll always be your lover. Or that reputation will carry you through this lovely *retirement*." Rare felt the heat in her cheek where Anselm's knuckles had clouted her. He didn't blink as she leaned very close, kissing him just below the earlobe, along the angle of his jaw, pausing just shy of his lips—and pulling away.

Curious, Rare's hand explored. The dance of two fingers along his trouser laces confirmed her power over him—and those, too, she pulled away.

"You've certainly retired. Into the storybooks. I'd bet all the sovereigns in my purse you're not fit enough to scale a building anymore, nor well enough connected to the prowlers to *really* loosen a body's lips. You had your big take, wrote your great legend, and you settled for them. Now the dust has settled on you."

Anselm's face might have been etched in stone. "Are you quite done?"

Rare smirked. "I'm sorry. Hit a nerve?"

"Better to say I hit one of yours. You dealt yourself into a game not even knowing what was being played, and now it's gone bust you'd rather get picked clean than have the good sense to be dealt out."

"Marvelous. I tell you you're an irrelevant bastard using facts, and you tell me I'm an ungrateful child in an atrocious extended metaphor."

"More or less."

Rare slipped back to her place an arm's length away. "So is that what you called me here to do? *Deal me out?* How chivalrous."

Anselm rolled a cigarette, not looking down at his nine and a half fingers. It came together fast and tight. Rare had to credit him that much—whatever else might have rusted over, his hands were as fine a device as ever.

"To be frank, kitten, I don't know that I can do that, even if I were still standing at the razor's edge of relevance. But there *are* things I can do, assuming I cared enough."

"Oh, my. You're pouting."

He shrugged and lit his cigarette with a lucifer. "No more than you. We make a lovely pair—your bruised face, my bruised ego. The Old Bear will find us an absolute hilarity."

The waiter peeped around the frame of the swinging kitchen door. He scuttled forth at a gesture from Anselm, scrawled down their orders—two cocktails, a basket of figs and lean bread, a plate of herbed oil, and roasted aubergine—and was gone again after much bowing and muttering.

Rare spread her napkin on her lap and smoothed it with exaggerated care. "So he'll meet us here. When?"

Anselm consulted his chronometer. "Half past the hour. He's a man of principles, which means he's punctual as well as damned irritating."

"His principles haven't prevented him from dealing with Ivor's kind."

The plates arrived, and they split up the meal amid the electric tension of two people putting up a show of mutual indifference.

"He won't be coming alone," Anselm said at last. "He'll bring the girl, of course."

"The delivery girl?"

"Naturally."

"Whatever for?"

"A certain nostalgia for lost, broken things, I imagine." Anselm's mouth was an ironic curve. "I had thought you'd remember it."

Rare flashed him a cold look. Anselm continued with an air of careless musing. "Or perhaps just those dusty principles. Given what's probably become of Ivor, the Old Bear wouldn't have sent the girl back where she'd come from—whatever's left of it."

"Foolish choice. The aigamuxa have seen her already. They've followed her once. If you're right and it turns out they wanted the delivery *and* to shut up people who know anything about it, they'll find her again."

"They would probably come his way, in any case. The package was meant to be delivered to him. That links him to whatever business they care so much about. In the final analysis, there's little risk added to his account by that charity."

Rare dabbed her fingers with her napkin. "I've no use for charity."

"I know. It's one of your most seductive attributes."

She frowned.

Anselm smiled over the rim of his drink. "There's an immeasurable sweetness added to the pleasure of a woman putting your cock in her mouth, kitten, when you know she only ever does things for her *own* pleasure."

A long moment passed, the two staring at one another.

Gradually, Rare returned the smile. "You are a magnificent bastard, Anselm Meteron."

"A magnificent, *irrelevant* bastard," he corrected. "Curious that the odor of disuse never kept you from my sheets."

His hand was on her knee, warm and insistent, traveling upward, slipping under a drape of fabric. She felt his touch below and shuddered.

"The Bear," she whispered, "he hasn't started rambling in his old age? Won't expect a lot of our time?"

Anselm was close now. She could see the fine lines at the corners of his mouth, the white hairs at his temples blending with the blond. His other hand cupped her face.

"Still not the loquacious type, no," he murmured against her lips.

"Good. I'm afraid we've a very busy calendar today."

"Do we?"

They kissed. She tasted gin and lime and felt for the laces of his trousers. "Oh, yes."

Anselm slipped from the booth, pulling her after. They were nose to nose, trading a galvano-graph line of kisses, shorts and longs and longer still. If they had opened their eyes, they would have seen the sidelong glances of the other patrons, the winks and jabbing elbows between men out for dinner who now found themselves taking in a show.

"Why wait?" Anselm asked. "There's a room upstairs. The maître d' will keep his peace."

"You old dog." Rare opened her eyes and ran her fingers along his whitening temple. "I thought you said the Bear will be punctual."

"Because he's scrupulous," Anselm replied. He walked backward, ushering her to a stairway half-curtained by long strings of beads. "We are not."

They were gone in an instant, leaving behind the chuckles of the rest of the room and an uncommonly large tip.

15.

"I've told you and told you: *he* gave her the drink."

Bess sat in the stony gray confines of a constabulary interrogation room, head in hands and hair unpinned. The phonocorder was spinning off its second cylinder. It wouldn't tell the coppers much more than the first had.

They'd been going through the story for ages. Sometimes, the city inspector asked her to start at a different place—an hour before all the guests arrived, say, or the day before. She was probably trying to check her for inconsistencies, but there was nothing to be inconsistent *about*.

I didn't do anything wrong. Why can't they see that?

"Miss Earnshaw," Inspector Gammon said, tapping her quill against a little pad of paper tattooed with notes and curlicues. "There's no evidence corroborating your story."

Bess wasn't sure if she wanted to cry or to scream. She shook her head hard enough to drop the last pin still threaded in her hair.

"But it's *true*. Abraham took me shopping for the ball, and we made a stop after at the Stone Scales. He talked to the Alchemist about buying something, but they wouldn't do it where I could hear. And then the Alchemist told me that Abraham seemed to have a need for *dangerous things*."

"Lord Regenzi has already told us of the trip to the Scales. He said the Alchemist spoke to you candidly—twice. The second time Lord Regenzi was out of the shop."

Bess bit her lip. "That's true."

"And that he made an order for you, apparently free of charge."

"That's true, too, but—"

"Did you already know the man?"

The question froze her. If she said yes, she'd have to say how. That would bring Ivor up. If she dragged his name into this mess, the old man would see her pay hell for it. And if she admitted to having been one of Ivor's birds, Gammon would have to know her employment wasn't actually legal. Then she'd be collared for another charge altogether.

"No," Bess said at last. "I didn't know him."

"Why would he give you anything in gratuity, then?"

For that, at least, she had an honest answer. "I don't know."

Gammon shook her head. "Regenzi's admitted you're not his goddaughter. You've only known him a fortnight."

Bess looked down at her hands twisting the fabric of her skirts. *God.* It all seemed so foolish now.

"He also tells me," the copper went on, "that you came to him by Smallduchess Avergnon's recommendation."

Bess looked up brightly. "That's right. Ask her—she'll vouch for me."

"We sent a constable with a notary and a sketch of you to take a deposition in her home. She says she's never seen you before in her life."

Bess felt her breath leave in a rush, as sudden and sharp as when her maid cinched up her corset. "That's a lie."

Gammon leaned forward. "Miss Earnshaw, you're asking me to believe you, a woman with no legal identity, over two members of the governor's peerage. You entered Lord Regenzi's life by apparent duplicity at the perfect time to gain access to many people of stature and renown, including a reverend doctor whose research might have changed the face of the EC's public doctrine. There *are* people who would like that sort of thing stopped."

Bess closed her eyes. She fought for an even tone. "I don't *know* those kinds of people."

"You insinuated yourself into proximity of Reverend Doctor Nora Pierce, and you poisoned her."

"*No.*"

"The only thing I don't yet know is who paid you to do it."

"*Nobody.*" Bess's eyes snapped open even as her voice caved in. "I wasn't hired, and I don't know anyone, and I—"

Gammon stood, speaking over her papers in a flat voice as she swept them together. "If I called upon the Stone Scales with a warrant for the Alchemist's financials, I might find some record of who paid in advance for whatever drug he passed to you. It was nothing subtle, in any case. Whoever hired you must not have cared much if you were caught murdering a woman who was about to become the most famous scholar in a generation."

Bess shot to her feet. Her chair skittered back and toppled, the crash jarring the phonocorder's needle out of place. "I didn't poison her! I saw Abraham put the phial he bought at the Scales in the drink. He took the drink from me, and he passed it to Pierce. That's how it happened!"

Gammon shrugged. "No one else seems to have seen things that way, Miss Earnshaw. If there's anyone you should like to have sparked, or have sent a runner, let the sergeant on duty know."

She rapped at the heavy steel door.

Bess's legs buckled.

The door opened, a chorus of chattering galvano-graph scribes tumbling in through the gap. Outside, a man only a few years older than Bess snapped to attention. He wore the uniform of a junior officer, all blue and buttons without a single band or stripe. Gammon exchanged a meaningful look with him, a curt nod. And that was all.

Bess realized she was backing toward a corner, hands up as if to fend off the approaching officer. The door closed between her and Gammon, cutting short her sobs and the sound of the cuffs clinking free of the gendarme's belt.

Haadiyaa Gammon entered her office in distraction, flipping through a folder full of freshly pressed reports and notes. None of them were the note she wished most to answer. Jane's spark from three nights before still rested in her inner breast pocket, promising Sabberday luncheon and gently teasing about what she meant to do with Haadi after. The very thought made her ache. Haadiyaa had not seen Jane in nearly four weeks. Her present docket promised little hope of that changing anytime soon. Indeed, it promised little hope of even knowing the time of day for certain as she raced from duty to duty. It was past midday, she was fairly sure, but alchemical lamps still glowed, for her office was deep in the guts of the constabulary's meandering second floor, far from windows and the promise of daylight.

"*There* you are. Blessed Reason, I thought you'd never get free of her."

Gammon looked up at the voice's owner.

Abraham Regenzi occupied her office chair, his feet on the desk and his hands behind his head. He still wore his ballroom finery, brocade tunic and vest and hose, looking damnably uncreased. He'd spent the long morning in a conference room with coffee and breakfast and whatever comforts he pleased. Beatrice Earnshaw had been moved from an iron-sided prison wagon to a holding cell to the interrogation room, all without a sip of water or a trip to the loo.

"These things take time," Gammon answered, "if you expect them to look genuine."

"Do they?"

Gammon closed the door. "I'll thank your lordship to get out of my bloody chair."

Smallduke Regenzi traded places with Gammon, who sat and began moving papers with perfect disinterest.

"You didn't answer my question, Inspector," Regenzi noted. He stood with arms crossed, whiskers impertinent as a ferret's.

Gammon looked up at him. She had long since decided Abraham Regenzi was one of the most presumptuous, insinuating bastards she'd ever met—and given her work on behalf of justice and the Court, she'd known more than her share. Gammon wasn't rich. The bribes she'd accepted to rise in station were infusions of information and allegiance, not coin. She had as little respect for the smalldukes and smallduchesses of Amidon as other folk of modest means. Less, really, as the daughter of Indine immigrants, converted Hindoo pantheists eager to work any job that might carve out an honest place under the Unity. Since she was a girl, Gammon had known the smalldukes were little more than wealthy merchants or well-connected raconteurs. Their chief merit was possessing principal enough to buy a place in the governor's peerage. Their titles were manufactured, hereditary only if the family could afford the yearly retainer. Abraham Regenzi's accounts could pay that astronomical fee several times over before he'd feel the strain.

But there were worse things in Corma than men like Regenzi—things that had made it worth Gammon auctioning a piece of her integrity to the likes of Anselm Meteron. There had been city inspectors before her who had helped make Corma a metropolis of orphans and vagrants, rapists and smugglers, and God only knew what else. Gammon believed her citizens ought to be safer. And she believed all good things had a price.

"So far," she said at last, "it seems your story accounting for last night's events will take root."

Regenzi smiled. "Excellent. Good." He pulled a chair under himself. "That will do." And then he glanced at a little wet bar in a dim corner of the office, clearing his throat.

Gammon regarded the smallduke narrowly. If Regenzi expected she should act as his waitress, he had best think again.

"When you first asked me to . . ." Gammon paused. The verb Regenzi had used was telling, and it tried now to elude her.

"Consult," his lordship suggested. He looked again at the bar and sighed, finally pouring himself a short glass of something brown.

"When you asked me to *consult* in this business, I had a different idea of what you wanted than what's been happening, my lord." She ticked a manifest of complaints off on her fingers. "I've helped conceal Pierce's kidnapping. I've made a dumb show inquiry into her disappearance, suppressed details of Chalmers's abduction in the gazettes, let you set up some wide-eyed child courtesan as the murderer of a *new* Pierce . . ." Gammon paused. "Who is this fresh corpse in my morgue really, Regenzi?"

The smallduke resumed his chair and shrugged. "An actress. She actually did come from Lemarcke. She was led to believe she was participating in an avant-garde audition for a part in a new form of immersive, audience-involved theater."

Gammon raised an eyebrow.

"I chose her," Regenzi continued, his pride in the plot growing more obvious, "because she had a certain resemblance to Nora Pierce—the right height and age, more or less the build. The hair was wrong, but women change their hair so often it hardly mattered. I probably needn't have been so careful. The Ecclesiastical Commission is such a large fraternity, when you toss the lot of them together, you find that everyone knows a lot of names but not many faces. When your global conference takes place just once a decade?" Again, the shrug. "Well, you can imagine the difficulties."

Gammon nodded. Now the Ecclesiastical Commission had good reason both to stop the search for Nora Pierce that Chalmers's panic had engendered and to cancel her keynote address. A public murder, enough witnesses of appropriate station and credibility. It was a tidy piece of work. No one would ever look for Nora Pierce again. The body from Knox's inquest—the true reverend doctor—could be safely recorded as a Jane Doe and incinerated. Procedure could take over from here. Gammon realized she'd already opened a drawer and reached for the necessary paperwork.

"There will still be an inquest," she murmured over the forms.

"I want one. The case needs to be complete."

"Then there's the matter of the Alchemist. I'll need to question him about the purchases you and Beatrice Earnshaw made yesterday morning."

Regenzi frowned, his whiskers prickling. "That's really necessary?"

"At some point, you'll need the girl to go before the Bar and be convicted. The judge will expect either your story or hers to be corroborated by the Alchemist's testimony. I doubt we'll find him very cooperative. He would need to admit to selling a virulent poison. We used to give the rope for that. It's prison time in the hulks now, but some men would rather just swing."

"I can buy him," Smallduke Regenzi insisted. The way his knee jogged suggested he was less than sure of that. "I can do it if you promise to look the other way on the poison sale."

Haadiyaa Gammon laughed—a humorless bark. "How many crimes do you expect me to *commit* or *forget* in this cause, Regenzi? I have my limits."

"*Haadi*," the other man soothed. Gammon could already feel the ache in her jaw as she fought the urge to grind her teeth. There was something about her familiar name, something in its two syllables that the most devious men seemed unable to pronounce without a petting tone. "Haadi—remember why I came to you in the first place."

Haadiyaa Gammon did remember. She was a God-fearing woman. An earnest and a Rational woman. She believed in God the Creator, God the Experimenter. She believed in Him because her mother's grandfather had abandoned a thousand years of culture and history to put his children's children on the side of Reason. She even had an aunt who had become a deaconess. Whether Regenzi had known of Gammon's background or had simply wagered on the chief officer of the constabulary's investment in the common good being authentic, she didn't know. Still, the wager had been a good one.

"If this theory is correct," the smallduke said gravely, "then the whole human race is held hostage by the actions of just *nine people*. Nine! It's madness, Haadi. A bad gamble, if there's any truth to it."

"But you don't really believe there is."

Regenzi smiled. "I'm not sure a theosophical debate is essential to the present discussion."

"I prefer to know when I'm being fed a line."

"Whether I *believe* there really are nine people whose actions will determine if God throws the plans for this world into the furnace or lets it click along awhile longer isn't important. There are tangible benefits to our present course."

"Tangible benefits," Gammon repeated, skeptical.

Regenzi shrugged. "I have certain needs my benefactor is seeing to, in compensation for my pains. One can only go so far on one's own with a purchased peerage, but making an ally in high places can clear the most *bothersome* hurdles." He reached inside his dress jacket and removed, with the air of a street-corner magician, a carefully sealed envelope. The smallduke passed it to Gammon with a smile.

She felt a stack of bills tucked within.

"The bishop sends us both his regards," Regenzi explained.

Gammon put the envelope aside, though not without wondering just how much it might contain. She chased the thought away with a shake of her head. "But if this Vautnek text is what Chalmers and Pierce claim, it's already happening. God's already collecting the data and making His judgments."

"That's why we've got to *find* the Nine. Gather them in. Keep them from making some damn fool mistakes that will make the lot of us look even worse than we truly are. Why should the rest of us lose what we have, our whole lives and fortunes and legacies, because some idiot we've never met makes a poor showing, and then God decides to snuff the whole species and start from scratch?"

"We don't even know what behaviors God's looking for."

"The Old Religion had some ideas."

Gammon raised an eyebrow. "A social doctrine held together by dogma and superstition. Tablets of stone from a mountaintop. Mythology. That's the best you and your bishop have to go on?"

Regenzi spread his hands. "After the Unity, the Ecclesiastical Commission threw away the social conscience of religion and turned it into the worship of Rational design. We don't say little prayers for moral guidance or beg for absolution because the sin of ignorance is all that matters. Go to a Sabberday lecture, then, and be freed. We took down the blocks and unified the mental resources of the best human minds. Now we've got Savery motors and algebraic engines and particle physics. They're even starting to use petrolatum to make something for building that won't rust or chip. I heard about that from a guest at the ball. Plastics, I think he called it. Bloody awful stuff. I'll take brass, polished or patinaed. But isn't that the problem? We don't have the plastics yet, but it's where we're going." Regenzi tapped his breastbone meaningfully. "It's where we already *are*. If we were honest with ourselves, looked at our little inner cranks and cogs, we might finally clean house and straighten up a bit. But we won't. We'd rather be *Rational*. If the problem of the soul is that it corrodes, we'd rather build it all over again out of something durable and new than remember the art of tending it."

Gammon stared at the smallduke. "Tidily done. Did you have to practice that lecture long to get it down?"

Regenzi shifted uncomfortably, his brass a little tarnished. "It's an . . . approximation of an anti-Rationalist argument I saw in a tract once. But does it matter if it's not really in my heart? If we're wrong, and the book is a hoax, and the bishop and all his collared cronies mad as hatters, then there's no God and nothing to punish us for what we've done. But there will still be men in high places willing to pay out rewards. And if we're right?" He shook his head. "It's not impossible. Listen, Haadi. Deciding a little moral stricture was inefficient and subjective doesn't prove it was actually the *wrong* practice. And just because we stopped demonstrating a behavior doesn't mean God ever stopped looking for it. I'm certainly not convinced that when the bishop of Rimmerston promises me a seat in the governor's cabinet that he'd do it on the strength of a fairy story alone."

Haadiyaa Gammon looked down at her desk, its surface awash with a week of case files. She was desperately behind. Her lieutenants and sergeants had begun orbiting her office days before, wanting clearance to close this murder, to pick up that warrant, to transfer that prisoner. On the chalkboard of active cases, there were six reports of larceny, two rapes, a murder, eight assaults, two missing persons—

And that was only the last five days. She would most assuredly not find her way to Jane's luncheon, or her arms, with the board in such repair.

Regenzi was right about one thing, at least. The EC had brought an end to religion's stymie on science, had made science adopt religion as a valid narrative—and had, in its description of a dispassionate and watchful God, replaced a being of divine guidance and judgment with a figure not unlike itself. Who knew what such a Creator wished to see from its labors? They had only assured the world that it *had* been looking.

If Pierce and Chalmers were right, that gaze was far more considered than Gammon had ever suspected.

Abraham Regenzi leaned forward, smiling consolingly. "I know you don't like me, Haadi. But I also know you've dealt with men you don't like before, when it makes the right things happen."

Gammon knuckled her eyes. It was past the dinner hour—early afternoon. She had not slept since . . . she couldn't remember. She had no appetite yet, but her last meal was far off, too, sometime long before she'd stood in the gallery of the Regenzi manor over a bug-eyed, buckled woman in a black reverend's dress. Regenzi was making sense—maybe more sense than he deserved credit for, but enough that Gammon couldn't find a way to buck his argument. It was true, at least in its constituent parts. She had done ugly things to become the constabulary's chief officer because she believed she was, at bottom, a better and truer soul than the other likely candidates. In the end, she would do whatever was necessary to make her city safer.

"I'm going to issue a warrant for the Alchemist," Gammon said. "We'll take him in for questioning. I can offer him a deal, some kind of immunity. The kind of man who sells poisons will sell anything."

Regenzi nodded and blew air—he looked relieved. "Good. Fine. There was another matter, though."

"Go on."

"When Nasrahiel's aigamuxa got the Vautnek text, there was something else in the bag—a letter to Ivor Ruenichnov. Seemed some kind of blackmail or extortion about the book. I've never heard of the woman it came from. The name sounded like an alias. 'Rare Juells'?"

Gammon cursed and knuckled her eyes again. "She works the underside. Cat burglar. Spy. Seductress. We haven't been able to pin much on her definitively. She's Anselm Meteron's lover."

That name, of course, could not be lost on a man of Regenzi's means. People of his station wallowed in Meteron's empire—his casino, his hotels, his cathouses and burlesques. And his present business, Gammon supposed, had acquainted him with the surname for entirely different reasons.

"We don't know how much she knows," Regenzi said.

"You could say the same about the courier girl. Or the Alchemist."

Regenzi nodded thoughtfully. "We've been trying to clean up as we go. We've only just gotten Chalmers in hand and tidied up the question of Pierce's fate. We can't afford another mess." He strolled back to the bar and set his emptied glass down. "Am I free to go?"

"You were never charged with anything."

"Good. Chalmers should be settled nicely with Nasrahiel by now. I really should pay him a visit." The smallduke wrestled into his overcoat. "I'm going to send him to you later tonight. Nasrahiel, I mean."

Gammon had been about to usher his lordship out the door. Instead, she frowned and held her place. "Why?"

"It seems there are a lot of people who *might* know a lot of things. The Alchemist, the courier girl, this cat burglaress, Meteron." Regenzi dusted off the shoulders of his coat and perused himself in the little mirror hanging on the back of the door, approving the state of his moustache. "Perhaps you'll need a little help."

"I can manage well enough."

Regenzi arched an eyebrow. "Is that pique I'm detecting, Inspector?"

"I will make arrests with *constables*, if that seems prudent. That's all. I don't need aigamuxa thugs."

"Perhaps. Still, they're quite useful. Absolutely devoted to the cause."

They were. That bothered Gammon. The fact that it seemed only an unexpected boon to Smallduke Regenzi did little to put her mind at ease.

As Regenzi reached for the doorknob, a page boy stuck his head in the room. Seeing the smallduke, he flushed and looked at Gammon.

"Ma'am, I'm sorry, I can—"

"He was just leaving, Matthew. Message?"

"Sergeant Ren says the landlady from the Coventry Passage rectory is getting mighty sore, sir. She's talking about wanting a barrister."

Gammon glanced at Regenzi. To keep Chalmers's kidnapping quiet, there had of course been the landlady to consider. She could only keep her so long on the excuse of needing a statement about her honorable tenant's disappearance.

Cleaning up messes, indeed.

"You seem to have your hands full, Inspector," Regenzi said with a half bow. "I'll see myself out."

"Of course." Gammon turned to Matthew. "I'll see Ren in a few minutes. Stay here. I've a warrant request you can run to the Bar for me."

16.

It was past the dinner hour, and the Alchemist was restless. Rowena watched him peer out the arched windows of the café, squinting through a cloud of pipe smoke. Rowena didn't mind waiting. She was on her second plate of roasted chicken and potatoes and had nearly finished a pint of weak ale. Between this, a full night's sleep in a real bed, and the new jacket she was sporting, Rowena Downshire felt her fortunes running jake. She'd almost put from her mind their row in the kitchen hours before.

They'd departed the Stone Scales after breakfast, silence like a curtain between them. A young man coming up the highstreet to call on the shop had stopped, watching the Alchemist turn the shingle to the "Out of Doors—Call Again" side. He stared at them as if he was not sure what was queerer—the proprietor's departure at the dawn of the business day or the scrap of a girl following in his shadow.

The Alchemist was in the habit of using his legs rather than the rails. That suited Rowena fine. The free air and wary distance the locals afforded gave her a chance to order her thoughts over the long walk to the Hangman's Market. Now that they were settled in the Last Drop, she was ready to try them out on her companion.

"Do you mind if I ask you a question?"

The Alchemist blinked, looking almost as if he had forgotten her. "If you like," he said.

"Why are people so afraid of you?"

"Are they?"

Rowena suppressed an incredulous snort. "You must have noticed."

"I suppose."

"It doesn't make sense."

"Doesn't it?" He weighed his pipe in his hands.

"Well, no," the girl insisted. "You're just a . . . I don't know . . . a scientist, basically. Right? That's what a *good* alchemist is. His craft's all Rational stuff."

"It should be."

"So, people should know better than thinking you're some kind of silly magician." Rowena watched the old man's face change very slightly, a smile playing at the edges of his features.

"And I suppose you have never been prey to such superstitions," he said.

Rowena opened her mouth, then let it snap shut. "Well, I know better now. You en't so bad."

"Why, thank you."

She rolled her eyes. "You know what I mean. So you're a little, I dunno, *stern*. What's that got to do with anything?"

"For one thing, I'm not a reverend doctor."

Rowena shrugged dismissively.

The old man tapped the table with a finger, as if pinning down an axiom. "Any fraternity that seems to have a grasp of knowledge others lack will inevitably appear powerful. Any outsider to that fraternity with similar knowledge will inevitably appear to be a heretic."

"So why didn't you just join the EC, go to seminary? Then you wouldn't have to worry about people getting queer ideas about you."

"Fraternity of that kind isn't exactly in my nature."

"Maybe you just need a little practice," Rowena said. She tried to fox him with a smile, testing if his morning's temper had run its course.

Perhaps it had. He made no reply. The Alchemist was back Somewhere Else, that place high above ground, his raptor eyes trained out the window once more, studying the middle distance.

Rowena watched him, an inspection to which he seemed utterly indifferent. He looked . . . not angry. Not like he had before, when he asked about Rare. There was a Something Else in this look, too, but a different Something Else altogether, something new.

"You're nervous," she said.

The old man glanced at her. With exaggerated care, he tapped his pipe out into the ashtray. "I suppose I am."

"Because these people are late?"

"What do you think?" There was no drip of sarcasm in his voice. "You seem to like puzzling things out," he clarified. "Try this."

"These people we're meeting, Anselm Meteron and Rare," Rowena began, "they're sort of . . . crooked folk, right?"

"You could say that."

Rowena warmed to the task. "I know plenty like that. Sometimes, they're late just to push you around, show you who's boss. Or sometimes it's because they're hanging back, being careful. They know you, but not me, and so maybe they're trying to get a read of what I'm doing here. If they don't like what they see, maybe they'll never show at all."

"God's balls, Bear. It seems the urchin does have a brain rattling about up there."

Rowena turned and saw a man standing behind her, arms crossed. He wore a black vest and leather trousers as tight and tailored as his smile. His hair was a pale blond tipped with white, his chin sharp and imperious. She'd never met him before—had never even seen the kind of money it took to meet him—but he had the look she'd expected. He had to be Anselm Meteron.

"*Bear?*" Rowena asked.

She recognized the woman standing beside him with four cups of mulled wine on a tray. Rare was a different creature by daylight. The leathers and belts had disappeared in favor of a lavender day dress pinned into a high bustle about her hips, gathered to show her tall, heeled boots and a few inches of crocheted stockings. She set the tray down between the Alchemist and Rowena, winking conspiratorially.

"Men have their pet names for each other," Rare purred. "They're like schoolgirls, all pigtail pulling. Before he turned into a fossil selling antiques and hokum potions, 'the Alchemist' was a rather formidable sellsword. Men like that always earn names in the trade."

Rare took her place on the old man's side of the booth and pecked him on his bearded cheek with perfect chastity. "Hello, Father," she said, in the same tone she might have said, "Sod off, bastard."

"Hello, Rare."

Father? Rowena searched back and forth between them. She found nothing but her puzzled face reflected in the Alchemist's eyes. Looking for a resemblance between Rare's golden mane and blue eyes and his ebonwood features was more than hopeless. It was absurd.

"On the matter of your theory, Rowena," he said, "I had begun to regret bringing you here and exposing you to their general depravity."

"Very noble of you to think so much of a jaded young courier's innocence," Meteron answered dryly. He smiled an apology at Rowena. "We called him Bear for his manners, among other things. Now, will you introduce us properly, or am I simply to talk around your young companion all afternoon?"

The Alchemist was stuffing his pipe again. He nodded toward each in turn, without raising his eyes. "Rowena Downshire, I give you Anselm Meteron and Rare Juells, for what they may be worth."

"Master Meteron." Rowena shook his hand. Something about his grip felt strange; when they released, she glanced down to see why, but his hands were beneath the table as he slid in beside her. "I've met Rare before, but I didn't know your family name." Rowena stared at her. "*Jewels?*"

"Spelled a little differently than you'd think."

"But *still.*"

"My mother had an insipid sense of humor. Now—" Rare spread a napkin on her lap and rested her hand on the Alchemist's, "—we've already had our dinner, but I could do for something sweet. You're buying, Father."

He raised an eyebrow at her.

She nodded toward Anselm. "You know *he* never would. And I've heard a rumor that you're lately quite a gentleman to women in need."

With something between a sigh and a growl, the Alchemist hailed a passing waiter and put in another order for the table.

What unfolded afterward seemed to Rowena like watching auctioneers running the quayside blocks. Rowena was certain she knew all the words her companions used, and yet the talk moved so fast, and was strung so oddly together, that whatever the rules of this cant might have been flew by her completely. They seemed to be confirming whereabouts, comparing pieces of insight, going through a list of possibilities and striking them off. Over a plate of cheese and grapes that arrived before Rare's sweets, they came to the package, and that turned their eyes and questions onto Rowena. She explained the delivery to Chalmers, his panic, and the book he'd been so eager to lose.

Master Meteron looked up from rolling a cigarette. "Do you know why he had to be rid of it?"

Rowena frowned. "He seemed to think he was in danger. He's a twitchy cove. Didn't seem like it would take much to set him off. But when Ivor went dead white looking at the book in his own turn, I knew there was something to it."

"He sent me a spark about the book, hoping to find someone to pass it on to," Meteron said.

"Before he sent me out, Ivor was in his office looking through the book. He got panicky after. That was when he sent me to the Alchemist with the package, and I met you on the under-irons." Rowena looked to Rare. "An aiga jumped me for the bag later. The book's gone. So's your note—but it *really* en't my fault. I had planned on the lowstreets, like you said, and then it started after me—"

Rare's only answer was a sharp, silencing look. The waiter had returned. There was a general shuffling of crockery to make space for an architecture of pastry. Rowena was too full to even look at it overlong. Apparently the Alchemist had been too absorbed in getting the meeting going to count her out of the order. No one paid the food much mind.

When the waiter had bowed his way off again, the Alchemist spoke: "What was your letter about?"

Rare seemed about to lash him with a bitter comment, but Meteron's eyes narrowed. She stared back with her lips tight. Rowena bounced a look between the three, utterly perplexed. She might as well have been watching hurlers at play.

At last, Rare shrugged. "It said that I had some knowledge of what Ivor was trying to be rid of, and I knew others who would want to know about his involvement with Pierce and Chalmers—City Inspector Gammon, for one. I didn't know Rowena was delivering the book at that moment, or I would have put the matter differently. Still, with what I knew, and what I pretended to know, I could have had him for quite a sum."

The Alchemist's face was a portrait of disgust.

"Oh, I'm *sorry*," Rare sighed, favoring him with a long-suffering smile. "You're probably prepared to moralize at me awhile, Father. I wouldn't deny you your little pleasures. Go ahead."

"Ivor was a criminal, but he was my friend once. He was your mother's friend, too." His tone was flat, edgeless. It bludgeoned where another man might have cut.

Meteron spread his hands. "I told you, kitten: principles."

"They're an ironic affectation for a man who sells as much out of the back of his shop as the front," she snapped.

The Alchemist's voice turned cold. "Affectations are so fashionable in this company. I hate to be left out."

Meteron cleared his throat. "What happened after the robbery, Miss Downshire?"

"I wasn't sure what to do. I en't been robbed by an aiga before, and I'd always been told . . . you know . . . *things* about the Alchemist. Stuff about him being powerful and whatnot." Rowena felt the old man's gaze purpling her ears. "Anyway, I thought if I told him what had happened, he might talk Ivor out of whipping me, or firing me, or whatever else. I think we've all got the rest from there."

And then, thinking of that rumor of power—any one of the dozens that were supposed to make her fear the man who had given her a bed and a meal and a clean set of clothes—Rowena felt a question pluck her sleeve. It took a moment for her to construct it. But as the others watched, she could see in their eyes it had been written on her face.

"What I don't understand, though," Rowena wondered, "is how you knew I'd talked to Rare at all. I didn't tell you. I *never* told you. It's like—" and she laughed at herself, a dismissive little hiccup, "—I dunno, you read my mind or something."

Rare's ice-blue eyes flashed victoriously. "'Principles,' indeed."

The Alchemist watched Rowena over steepled fingers, his mouth hard and drawn. She stared at him. The raptor eyes weren't looking down from their impossible distance. They were almost begging her to keep her peace. All the fables about the Alchemist she used to believe gathered around him, rising from the dust of memory as if they'd never been discarded.

Suddenly, they became very real.

It couldn't have been possible. And yet the candle had been burned, and the chair had been moved, and *someone* must have sat there, looming close in the night.

"You— You *did* go into my mind," Rowena murmured.

It wasn't a question. The Alchemist sat back and closed his eyes. Rowena's stomach knotted.

"You bastard. *How* did you—? No. You know, I don't care."

All at once, Rowena realized she was caged in, surrounded by strangers, staring at a man who somehow heard inside her things she'd never said. The thought of what else he might know, and how, pulled on her oldest instincts.

Run.

Rowena scrambled in her seat, butting against Master Meteron. She dropped under the table and darted between its posts and his shins. She clambered from under the booth, banging her shoulder on the table, upsetting the dishes. Meteron recoiled in time to miss catching his wine in his lap.

Rowena saw the Alchemist on his feet, reaching for her. She bolted for the street, Meteron's string of curses unspooling behind her.

17.

After a third set of calipers died a groaning, twisted death in the padlock's tumblers, the Reverend Doctor Phillip Chalmers began at last to consider the possibility that he was well and truly buggered.

The holding cell clearly wasn't meant to serve as such. At first, that had given him some hope of jiggering his way out. It mattered very little that he'd only seen a few kinotrope shows of dashing actors picking their way free of unlikely prisons. He was, after all, a *scientist*, and acquiring knowledge through systematic observation was his stock and trade, and *therefore*—

Therefore, it seemed things should have been going a bloody lot better than they had been.

Throwing the ruined instrument down with a curse more befitting his father's trade in costermongery than his rank in the commission, Chalmers returned to the practice that had occupied most of his confinement—a vocation in which he seemed more naturally gifted.

He paced the room, gnawing his cuticles, and took stock. His inventory of the situation had become quite thorough.

First, there was the room itself, clearly an old wine cellar, and—judging by the pearly condensate on the mortared walls—far below both ground level and the frost line of whatever building it occupied, perhaps some manor on the outskirts of Corma. That last idea was an impression gathered over the long, circuitous route Nasrahiel had traced, Chalmers thrown over his shoulder with a sack on his head.

The room boasted a wide, grated door with a heavy padlock. Empty wine casks held long boards up to make trestle tables and improvised walls of shelving. These bore an impressive and largely irrelevant array of scientific equipment, a shrine to his captors' ignorance. Every time Chalmers completed a circuit of the room, he spotted something new among the treadle-powered centrifuges, distillation kits, aiga bar-cranked dynatron coils, microscopes, and miniaturized sum boxes imported straight from Nippon, every bead and lever and counterweight within their open bodies stamped with the Lemarckian protectorate's seal.

And there was the Vautnek text itself, resting in the midst of an almost quaint improvised desk, flanked by pen and ink, blotter and notepad.

Chalmers wasn't certain if he found the reckless array of supplies amusingly eclectic or quietly terrifying.

A low, snarling sound prickled the hair of Chalmers's neck. He whirled. An aigamuxa padded by, stopping to lift a foot and thrust its heel eye against the grating.

A few blinks later, it carried on into the dimness beyond the cellar.

Terrifying, Phillip Chalmers decided. *Most definitely terrifying.*

At the washstand beside his blanket and cot, Chalmers took off his soiled shirt and began washing up, splashing water through his hair and working out the worst of the sick still crusted in it. The face staring back in the glass was a pale, wild-eyed phantom of the one he knew. On the streets of Corma, he would have passed such a man by, thinking him a lunatic—but only after crossing to the other side of the street.

Chalmers frowned at that face. He practiced a few expressions that were meant to convince him of its strength, its resilience.

None of them proved credible.

He turned his back to the washstand, approached the Vautnek text, and stood over it, one hand hovering above its cover. He wondered just what had become of the courier girl he'd given it to yesterday. The dull aches and pains of his body suggested her fate. He wasn't a strong man. Certainly not a courageous one. How much battering could such a slip of a girl take before an aigamuxa caved in her skull?

Chalmers leafed pages, scanning, looking for signs of change since he'd last reviewed the book's contents.

His breath caught somewhere about the last third of the pages.

"Well," Chalmers said to the open air, "you've been busy, haven't you?"

In a moment, he had the desk shrouded with leaves of paper. Nine pages. Soon, nine piles of pages. He labeled the top of each sheet and returned to the Vautnek text, thumbing forth and back. The top of each page in his notation piles was labeled in the blocky, half-completed geometric shapes of the old script, a language he'd learned very quickly when his and Nora's theory suddenly fell into place. Necessity was a wonderful teacher, and Phillip Chalmers was her most eager, if not always her most gifted, pupil.

He sequenced his recordings as he'd always done, beginning with the subject whose location was closest to his own—Six—and working to those progressively more distant. Subject Six, Subject Three, Subject One, Subject Seven . . . The remaining five were ordered thus simply because he liked the euphony of the numerical sequence he'd assigned to them—Nine, Four, Five, Eight, Two. He hadn't the faintest idea of their actual locations relative to Corma because he hadn't gotten that far. The assigned subject numbers corresponded to the amount of data the text had accumulated in the section of the book apparently set aside for them. The earliest subject numbers—One, Two, Three—had long, rich histories but comparatively little new activity. The later numbers, presumably more recent additions to the experimental population, had much slimmer records and seemed to be accumulating data with a speed relative to their ranking. Very orderly.

But not today.

Today, Subject Six—the subject that had been in Corma as long as Phillip Chalmers had worked with Nora Pierce—was running away with the show.

Soon, Chalmers gave up trying to make separate file copies of the other eight subjects and focused on transcribing only Subject Six.

There were coordinates, equations, data points . . . Chalmers all but flew across the cramped room, weaving between a lamp-film reader and a silver specimen table, to tear into the shelving. He had been supplied a whole rack of atlases, unbound and threaded on long bamboo staves as in a library. The aigamuxa knew very little of what equipment might actually be needed to cipher the book's notations, but they had been practical to that extent, at least.

By the time the aigamuxa guard came loping along again, Chalmers was absorbed in applying the fast-changing sets of coordinates to various atlases of Corma and its surrounding areas, narrowing down, drilling deeper. Now that he'd started into it—found his rhythm and found in Subject Six a blur of activity he might spend a week tracking backward to make full sense of—he had to keep narrowing his gaze, lest he lose all sense of the narrative the data strained to tell.

And finally, there it was.

He crossed a straight edge and a drawing triangle over a map detailing the public square once used for hangings, and could see from the steady changes of the last three coordinates that the figure was moving hurriedly to the southwest, one tiny point pushing toward the sea.

Subject Six.

For an absurd moment, Chalmers wanted to say hello. *I see you. I know we've never met, but really, in a sense, I know you. You wouldn't believe the day I've been having.*

In the corner of his eye, he could see new numbers taking shape, and he moved his improvised crosshairs accordingly. To cover that ground so quickly, Six would have to be running—running hard.

It was impossible, looking down through the glow of low-hanging lamps, to judge if he was running toward something or away from it.

Chalmers did the only thing he could do.

He kept taking notes. And, very quietly, he said an old and thoroughly irrational prayer. He could not have said with certainty if it was for himself or for Six, wherever he was going.

18.

The Alchemist had been chasing her. Of that, Rowena was certain. She'd had a good head start, though, and knew from her footraces with constables that she could make a fair distance on jangled nerves alone. She'd ducked under the traces of parked hackney carriages and side-shouldered through clusters of pedestrians. Somewhere along the way she'd lost him, and herself, in the long avenues of Midtown. From there, it had been back to the alleys between hostels and tenements, threading her way to Blackbottom End.

The sun hung low over the horizon, haloing the spires of church laboratories and the blocky faces of tenement towers. The buildings of Blackbottom End cast grim shadows, the phosphorescent street lamps winking on, one after another.

Three quick turns, then down a narrow alley.

Rowena stood, her breath steaming, and gazed at the hollow of New Vraska Imports. A murky gas lamp showed a door swinging on a bent hinge. She glanced up and down the street, then scurried through the splintered entrance.

The main floor was completely turned over. Broken crates, scattered cargo, and banker's boxes of paperwork were strewn around as if a hurricane had cut a path through the building. Rowena picked her way through the rubble, reaching out in the darkness, hands scraping over brambles of broken furniture and crates. Her boots crunched glass. She winced at the sound, afraid someone would hear.

The last rays of daylight seeped down from the courier loft's high windows. Rowena peered around, her eyes adjusting to the darkness.

No one would hear her. Not anymore.

She spotted the ladder to the loft perched in its usual place, as if nothing were amiss.

Rowena's eyes stung. When she realized she was crying—crying in relief that her ladder was still there, that she might climb back up to her little straw pallet and pretend all was well—when she realized how much she *wanted* to, and how safe it would make her feel, she hated herself.

Stupid girl. You weren't ever safe here. This en't your home.

She was still thinking that, even as she scaled the ladder. She chided herself for being a soft-bellied fool, wishy-eyed and sentimental, as she stepped onto the loft floor. Then she hooked her arms under the ladder's rungs, hauling for all she was worth.

The ladder was all wood, and nearly twenty feet tall, but Rowena had only to think of the Alchemist putting his fingers—or whatever he used—in her head, fishing around, and she found the strength to wrestle it up. She angled it back, and back, fighting for balance. Finally, Rowena dropped it across Mick's dusty mattress by the coal stove. She fell on the boards beside it, gasping.

Why did I trust him?

Rowena stared up at the soot-blackened rafters, their edges silvered in the fading light. She *had* trusted him. That was the strangest part. She knew better than to trust anybody. Even Bess had skimmed off Rowena's deliveries when she was first learning the trade, claiming it was "guild practice." It had been a fortnight before she'd learned there *was* no guild and that "practice" among courier birds only meant the "thing we're doing this week to get by." She had trusted the Alchemist because he offered her a bowl of something hot and a place by the fire for a night.

That's how you tame an animal, Rowena thought. *You're as easy a mark as a terrier. He looked at you like a cold piece of meat, and he wouldn't tell you his name, and still, you trusted him.*

Worse, she had found herself *liking* the Alchemist. Under all that silence and brooding, there seemed to be more than a bag of myths and witchy tales. She thought she'd caught a glimpse of a real person. But she'd been wrong—and being wrong, in her world, wasn't far from ending up dead.

Well, whatever the Alchemist was, Rowena wanted nothing more to do with him. She found that in her distraction, she'd begun searching the loft's flotsam and jetsam for something, picking about the chaos. *A light*, she realized. She needed a candle or a lamp.

She found a cracked hurricane glass with a taper still in it, long enough she could reach its wick with even a broken stub of a lucifer. Pawing about the wreckage, she found one, and soon had it glowing well enough to see properly.

Rowena surveyed the loft. Hay mattresses torn open. Coal bin overturned. The lid of Bess's trunk had been smashed, a fistful of clothes pulled up through its shattered ribs. The hatch to Ivor's private storage room, built into a copse of the rafters above, swung from one hinge, leaning drunk against the ladder falling from its mouth. Elevenmonth wind whistled through the warehouse walls, wafting a sharp, coppery smell down from Ivor's room. Rowena turned away, stomach churning. She didn't wonder anymore what had become of him.

Rowena set the lamp on a window ledge. The street was empty. Quiet. Strangely quiet—but then, any cove could see something dark had gone down in Blackbottom End. The usual lot would keep their distance awhile longer, she supposed. Maybe long enough for her to pick over the wreckage and pawn a few unbroken things against the Oldtemple ledger. She might save a bit of clink to line her pockets—to keep her while she looked for a new situation.

She might.

Or the pickers might be here by morning, and then she'd be scrapping just to keep the new coat on her back.

Remembering the coat, Rowena remembered the Alchemist. She felt the garment's charity burning her, mocking her. She wrestled free of it, spitting curses, and tossed it into the rag pile beside the coal bin. She hugged her knees, certain her anger would keep her warmer than any woolen hand-me-down. Even if she was wrong in that, she was sure of one thing.

If the Alchemist knows what's good for him, he'll leave me be.

The sound of crunching glass made Rowena start. The crick in her neck told her she'd fallen asleep against the railing, and the candle's guttering nub showed the hours that had passed. A haze of sooty moonlight filtered through the window.

Rowena's ears pricked at the shuffle of feet below. *Pickers?* She reached for her boot knife, trying to scoot silently into shadows.

Her heel nudged something. She winced at the scraping sound it made.

"Rowena?"

Rowena plunged a hand back into her boot, fumbling for the knife, then stopped. The ladder lay beside her, out of his reach.

Don't be stupid. He can't get you up here.

She shuffled to the loft's railing, peering down. The Alchemist was a shadow moving amid tumbled crates and twisted shelving.

"Go. Away," Rowena called.

He squinted up against the glare of moonlight. "Are you all right?"

"You were right 'bout one thing." Rowena put her candle beside the railing. "I think Ivor must be dead."

The Alchemist closed his eyes and sighed. "Where is the body?"

"Upstairs, maybe. Haven't gone up yet. You can smell the blood, though, up in the attic. His apartment."

He frowned. "It's not safe here. You should come down."

"I feel perfectly safe," Rowena spat. "I'm home now. *I love it* up here."

The old man cast about, looking for the ladder. Then he spied the open rectangle in the loft overhead. He squinted at the ladder's feet, pulled far out of reach.

Rowena smiled smugly. "I'm not coming down."

"Rowena, please. I am sorry."

"That doesn't help! I don't know how you did it, but the more I think of it, I'm sure it's true—you went into my mind. If I think hard, I can tell. There are . . . there's something in there," Rowena said, her voice rising. The words piled up in her throat, threatening to choke her. "Some kind of footprint or fingerprint or I don't know what. You left *tracks*. I wouldn't have noticed them if I en't thought to look."

"People typically don't."

She'd had another volley ready, the fires lit and the launchers cranked, but the Alchemist's honesty snipped the wicks. But only for a moment.

"Who *are you*? *What* are you? What kind of a person can go knocking around other folks' heads like it's nothing at all?"

"None of that is important now," he murmured, looking about as if he expected something to emerge from the shadows.

"The hell it en't! What if I ran off right now and found myself some squints down at the pubs around the Commons, taking a pint after the day's lectures? I could tell 'em all about you and your . . . your . . ." Rowena pawed through the jumble in her head, sifting for the right word. "Your *irrational* powers. Some of 'em might even be down the pisser enough to believe me. I bet it would seem pretty damned important to you then."

The Alchemist looked up at her, his dark face gone ashen. Suddenly, Rowena knew she had him.

"They'd be giddy to get their hands on something like you and explain it, huh?" Her heart pounded with anger. And fear. She wanted him to feel that pain, too. "Probably send you straight to Lemarcke, to the Logicians. You hear all kinds of stories about how far their work'll go in the name of Reason. Savvy?"

"You aren't safe here," the Alchemist insisted.

"*What do you care, anyhow?*"

Silence filled the space between them. The old man looked down at his boots for a moment, his jaw working, chewing his response. He spoke at last, words tight as garrote wire.

"If the aigamuxa came here to look for other parcels from your reverend doctor, and if they killed Ivor, they're looking to tie up loose ends. You're one of them, girl."

"Seems like you know a lot about folk who take care of loose ends," Rowena answered. "Where's our lovely dinner company now? Out knifing people for chronometers?"

"Looking for you," he snapped. "Because I asked them to. You can't afford to be alone."

She snorted. "And what, I'm safer with you? Sleeping in your spare room, waiting for you to come tiptoeing into my head? I was wrong. You're not some scientific bloke with a shop and a shingle. You're a creature out of fairy stories. How many girls have you pulled up into that room before and played your games with, huh? Bet Rare could tell a pretty tale if she was of a mind."

The Alchemist's eyes narrowed. Even at that distance, she could see the fury clenching his jaw. "That's none of your affair."

Rowena glared down at the wrecked warehouse, her eyes suddenly blurry. "And this en't yours! So shove off to your stupid shop and your stupid dog and your stupid—"

The rafters creaked, a weight shifting among them.

Rowena's words tumbled back down her throat. Slowly, she looked up.

It must have come down from the apartment above. She stared at the aigamuxa spidering its way through the skeleton beams, saw-teeth bared in a growl.

"Oh, *balls*," she breathed.

"Rowena!"

Her head snapped toward the Alchemist's voice. He'd leapt atop a tumbled pile of grain sacks, gesturing to her.

"Jump down!"

Rowena gaped at the drop. Already, her stomach was plunging, but still—she looked back at the aigamuxa, almost near enough to swipe with its clawed hand—

She grabbed the railing, vaulted to the top bar, and leapt.

The Alchemist's landing place felt about as hard as the floor itself. The sacks split, pouring out barleycorn and something else: the tiny, whistle-nosed bullets sifted secretly into the freight. Rowena gagged on a cloud of dust. She swam free of the spilling grain and ordnance, her left side screaming with pain.

Big hands pulled her roughly to her feet.

The Alchemist shoved Rowena behind him. He reached into the lining of his frock coat for something, eyes searching the ceiling.

"Why hasn't it come down yet?" Rowena whispered. The aiga prowled along a roof beam, rumbling, its gaze stabbing at the floor.

The Alchemist pulled Rowena into the center of the room, away from the cover of the tumbled sacks and crates. She struggled, trying to twist free and turn for the door, but he hauled her close, dragging her heels through broken glass. *Is he barking mad? Shouldn't we be running away? At least running for cover?*

A twisted piece of metal jabbed between Rowena's laces. Suddenly, she understood.

Its eyes.

Rowena looked down. She stood in the center of a shattered sea, full of reefs of nasty, jagged debris. The aigamuxa bellowed and flung itself onto the loft. But it stayed there, perched on the rail. It couldn't come straight down on them without getting its eye heels full of metal and glass. Rowena gave the Alchemist a knowing smile, but he paid her no mind. He'd found what he was looking for in his coat—something small, the size of a lump of coal. He turned it in his hand, searching for the right grip.

The aigamuxa's shoulders tensed. It folded in, readying to spring.

"Stay behind me," the old man murmured.

Rowena glanced back at the exit. There was another hunched form bending its way through the splintered doors.

Rowena fished her boot knife out. "Okay, but . . . behind you en't actually a lot *better*."

The Alchemist followed her gaze. That was when the aigamuxa in the loft hurled itself down, arms spread wide.

The Alchemist grabbed Rowena's shoulder with his left hand, pulling her around and under him as he hurled the tiny parcel in his right. It sizzled through the air, cutting a bright arc and then smashing with a burst of searing yellow light against the creature's chest. The old man's coat half-covered Rowena's face. Through a buttonhole, she could see the aiga hit the ground, writhing and howling. It swatted at the burning chemical splatter on its chest but only coated its hands and arms in the smoldering stew. Its back arched up from the glass-covered ground, feet stamping in agony, eyes pouring blood.

Rowena *wanted* to look away, and yet—

The Alchemist turned on his heels, his coat sweeping over her face. Then he yanked it away, like a conjuror tugging a tablecloth free. Rowena pushed herself up, wincing at the shards of glass stabbing her palms. The old man had gotten his feet just in time to take the crashing weight of the aigamuxa from the doorway square in the chest. It barreled them both backward, tumbling over Rowena's back like a sawhorse.

Rowena fell, gasping, in the dust. She blinked stinging, gritty eyes, following the fight as best she could through the light of the chemical fire still licking at the dead aiga's chest.

Somehow, the Alchemist had rolled free of the aigamuxa. He had some kind of a short weapon in his right hand—a stiletto or dirk the length of his forearm. With a flick of his wrist, the weapon more than doubled its length, telescoping out and ending in a glinting, strangely forked blade. He danced away from the aiga, which bounded over the most treacherous ground to perch on slouched desks and overturned chairs. They swiped, and ducked, and stabbed, winding in close and parting again, and twice the aigamuxa nearly raked the weapon from the old man's hand, forcing him back, coming nearer and nearer to hemming the Alchemist in.

Rowena looked to the door again. Beyond, Blackbottom End promised open space for running, and empty stoops for sleeping, and the comfort of an alchemical lamp's glow. She crept closer to it, fingers tight on her knife. Then she glanced back at the fray.

The old man spotted her hiding in the shadow of the doorframe. He seemed about to say something when the aigamuxa snared one of the columns holding up the loft and swung around it, slamming its legs like a club against the Alchemist's head.

He fell in a heap, rolling to the side only a moment before the aiga's fists crashed down where his head had once been. The creature crouched over him, hands at his throat, teeth bearing down. Too close for the Alchemist to raise his blade.

Rowena knew she should leave. Leaving would be easier. She had every *right* to go.

She kept telling herself that, even as she dashed toward the aigamuxa's unguarded rear. Rowena drove her tiny knife into its bent knee. It howled in pain and whirled, snatching her up by her wrists and straight into the air, all teeth and slaver and blind, twisted features.

Over the creature's shoulder, Rowena saw the Alchemist's hand close on his sword's hilt. There was that wrist flick, and then the blade collapsed down, short enough to slip into the space between himself and the aiga.

The blade streaked toward its throat.

Rowena closed her eyes. There was a meaty, stabbing sound, a sizzle. Something made the hairs on Rowena's arms lift, her skin prickling. And then, all at once, the aigamuxa's crushing weight slumped over her.

A moment later, there was moonlight again, and air. The Alchemist rolled the dead aigamuxa away with a grunt. A stench like charred offal wafted from the seared wound in the creature's neck. The old man's face was pouring sweat, his grayed temple matted with blood. The strange weaponette coughed blue sparks where it lay at his side. They stared at each other, panting and powdered with grain.

"You might have been right," Rowena said. "About it not being safe here, I mean." She stood, knees trembling more than she wanted to show, and dusted herself with bloodied, stinging palms.

She offered the Alchemist her hand and levered him up.

"You'll need a place to stay again, I think," he observed.

Rowena surveyed the room. "Might be, yeah."

The Alchemist sheathed his weapon and let his coat fall back, covering it. Without a backward glance, he walked toward the broken warehouse doors. "Come along, girl. Anselm is expecting us."

19.

Rare Juells had watched them arguing under the Last Drop's portico arch for nearly a quarter hour, amused at first at how well she could read them—their little snipes and jabs and negotiations, the Old Bear and Anselm reflecting one another like a pair of beveled mirrors. But the amusement wore thin as she considered how they both expected her *to wait*. To stand aside and to be a good girl, or whatever paternal nonsense ran through their heads.

She knew these men better than they knew themselves. When Anselm clasped the Old Bear's shoulder, casting a glance back toward her in the doorway, she saw already what would, inevitably, follow. He'd passed the old man a look of assurance, but it became a warning when it fell upon her.

Don't be difficult.

And Rare had smiled in return. *I'll do as I like.*

Then the Alchemist teased his way through the knots of the Hangman's Market, moving westward. Rare had watched his retreating form, a fire rising in her belly.

"You're taking the north."

She blinked at Anselm. He was slipping into his greatcoat, adjusting its cuffs.

"I beg your pardon?"

"You know the markets and squares in the upper quarters better than most," he continued. Rare bristled at that qualification—better *than most*, was it?

Anselm's pale eyes flicked up from his buttons, looking irritated that she hadn't already flown like an arrow. "The idiot girl is liable to get herself into trouble. The sooner she's roped back with the Bear, the better for all of us. Especially you."

Rare stared at him, incredulous. "You volunteer me to hunt for the Old Bear's pet urchin, and now you want to sell me the notion it's for my own *good*? How kind of you."

He'd taken her arm, then, as if to turn her toward the lane. She snaked free with a venomous glare.

"And what will *you* be doing while I run about looking for the girl? Asking after her welfare among the locals? Setting up a cozy bed back at the Regency?"

He turned to walk away. And she knew she had guessed exactly right.

"For thirteen years," Rare said, her tone simmering, "you've taken his part. Over and over and over again."

Anselm flipped an impatient glance. "And for thirteen years, you've expected that to change."

"Shouldn't I?"

"No," he said. "You shouldn't."

They were too far apart to have traded blows, but the words had hit her like a slap, all the same. Rare had felt her jaw tighten, clamping down on a little cry of pain she wouldn't permit Anselm to hear. Not now. Not ever.

"Be sure to offer the girl my old room," Rare answered. She swept past him, chin high. "The north, you said. Coventry and the Cathedral?"

Anselm nodded.

"I'll see what I can do. Meantime, do yourself a favor. Don't wait up for me."

That had been hours before, the midafternoon. She returned to her apartments in Stillhampton and traded her lavender dress and shawl for working clothes. She packed a little belt of tools and gathered it up under the short, slitted skirt worn over her long boots and leather trousers. By nightfall, Rare had sorted out a route for herself, and a plan, though they had nothing to do with Coventry Passage or the Cathedral Commons.

They had to do with the Stone Scales.

She approached the skeletal building from the shed yard at its rear. A musty, old hound lay roped to the doorjamb, his lead coiled up beside a box of bones and rags put out for his comfort. Rare's heels barely rang against the cobbles, but it was enough to make the dog start from slumber. His hackles lifted, his rumbling throat making noises between a whine and a snarl.

"*Rab-bit*," Rare chided sweetly. "You useless old rug. It's *me*."

The gray-muzzled hound sniffed Rare's hands, wrists, boots, and finally her face, the half snarl's back broken by the force of his wagging tail.

"How's mummy's good boy, eh? Old Bear left you hanging, did he? Wretched Old Bear! Here." She opened the clasp of the lead and unwound it from Rabbit's neck. The dog's good back leg thumped the ground as she scratched *that* place behind his scarred ear. "Come along, poppet. Show mummy where Daddy keeps his lovelies."

Barking like a puppy, the dog bounded up the back steps and through the swinging flap of his cutout door. From within, he nudged the drop latch with his nose, and the outer door swung open obligingly.

"That's my boy," Rare purred.

Smiling, she entered. Rare felt like herself again, wearing her leathers and silks, her boots with steel-toed innards, an alley pistol halter strapped to her thigh. Rabbit danced in the doorway eagerly.

Still a useless watchdog, she mused, thinking back on the wiggly, lame fuzzball that had once been her puppy.

There were many things Rabbit would never be—but he *was* utterly loyal to whoever did him a kindness.

The first lesson Anselm Meteron had taught Rare Juells was to begin a job knowing what you're looking for.

"Never," he'd said as they crouched on the roof of Regency Square, scanning the skyline of Corma and its brocade of galvano-graph cables. *"Never go into a place looking for something to make the trip worth it. Know where you're going. Know why."*

Rare Juells had come to the Stone Scales looking to take the things that would hurt the Alchemist the most.

She ignored the till. She walked past the padlocked side room where the rarest and most valuable goods were kept. Rare climbed the elderly stairs, remembering at each rise precisely where the wood would groan.

She stood at the door of her old attic bedroom, sweeping her magnesium torch's unsteady beam over the room. She had left the Stone Scales and her adoptive father thirteen years earlier. Her bed looked as ready to receive her as Rabbit had.

Know where you're going. Know why.

Rare continued down the hall to a smaller room, perhaps half the size of the last. She almost raised a hand to knock at its closed door. Then she stopped.

Mother wouldn't be there, of course. She hadn't been for thirteen years. And yet . . .

Rare turned the knob.

The bedroom was not quite as she remembered. Its tall standing mirror was gone. The curtains badly needed laundering, but the bed was made and the chest of drawers' surface clear of all but a little catchall holding a watch chain and cufflinks. An ivory comb rested in that little dish, the sort used to pin up a woman's hair. Rare touched it, memory shivering through her. She lifted her fingers, and it faded, leaving only a familiar, creeping anger in its wake.

Know where you're going.

Rare shook her head, as if to sweep it of debris. Then she rifled the chest of drawers with a purpose.

Tonight would be her last in Corma. She had already bought a ticket for the lightning rail out east and would have it punched at first light. There were two valises under her bed, packed with everything she needed—everything, at least, that might fit in a bag.

The business with the book and the aigamuxa had made things a bit hot, true, but Rare had had those bags in mind long before Rowena Downshire got herself cornered on the highstreets. If she was honest with herself, her life had been ending by degrees ever since the woman she called her mother died in the hull of an air galleon somewhere over the Western Sea. The Alchemist had disembarked that ship half the man he'd been when he'd boarded it. The half that remained hadn't been strong enough to hold up an angry girl desperate for consolation.

Though the Alchemist had opened the door of the Stone Scales and given Rare money enough to see her way through most anything—though he'd said there was nothing left for her in the place she'd called home, that she might be happier putting him behind her—it was Rare who crossed the threshold. Some nights, she imagined that if she'd only planted her feet, he might have relented. He might have forgiven her anger after Mother's death, her outbursts and tantrums, and she might have forgiven him for giving up so easily. He might have held her in his arms and allowed himself, at last, to cry.

But she hadn't. And he hadn't. And so Rare was put out, or put herself out, and turned to Anselm, with his new fortune and his stunned silence, too raw and wounded to turn her away.

That was thirteen years before. Things had been that way ever since.

Rare found the tight leather roll of the surgeon's field kit, earned at the end of an apprenticeship almost forty years gone. She unfolded it, examining its gleaming residents, fingering each in turn. There'd be a half dozen others like it in the shop's stock, but *this* was the one she wanted, because it was *his*.

Rare would leave Corma at dawn carrying a bag stuffed with everything that meant anything to her father. She would pith him, scrape out what remained of his core, and carry it off with her, proving beyond question that however much his abandonment had hurt her, she could do him far worse. Taking the surgeon's kit first seemed poetically right.

Now, she could cut deep.

In ten minutes, she found a chronometer inscribed with unfamiliar initials, its yellowed faceplate frozen on a date passed weeks before. She found the Alchemist's wedding band, a wide, plain ring of silver large enough to sit loosely at the base of her thumb. In a trunk at the foot of the bed, there was a little wooden box with her mother's matching ring, a necklace and two pendants, and an iron skeleton key.

At the bottom of the keepsake box was a stack of notes, folded neatly and tied off with twine. Rare slipped the string away and opened one.

Letters from Mother, written in her familiar, left-leaning hand. Rare pondered them a long time. Not love letters. Not all of them, anyway. Notes. Little arguments and harangues. Lists. Reminders. And some tendernesses, too. The creased edges were well-worn hinges now, yawning apart and quartering the pages.

Rare wrapped them up and reached to stuff them in her bag, only to find she lacked the space.

The letters from the warehouse.

She might have told Anselm that she'd done more on her trip to New Vraska Imports that morning than confirm Ivor's death through blood and bedlam. She might have told him about the packet of correspondence from the office she'd lifted before leaving for the Hangman's Market. But it had seemed wise to give herself the chance to review that little haul first. Now that she knew she'd be leaving Corma on the next lightning rail bell, it was time to toss the excess, find what could be sold to the lanyani quickly. A little spending money for a little effort. It was worth the time.

Rare sauntered to her old bedroom, riffling papers with a thumb. Rabbit lay on the foot of the bed now. She flopped onto her belly beside him, ruffled his ears, and rolled onto her back.

The packet was all letters and little parcels in overstuffed envelopes, the stamps showing they'd arrived in Corma as mail freight from a galleon out of Lemarcke. Some might have been from clients of Ivor's, but many, she supposed, had simply been lifted wholesale from the anchor yards of Quayside Down during unloading. Ivor would have sent that fink of a boy, Mick, to pose as a porter and sift the best of the baggage. The boy had probably snagged the correspondence on a guess: a galleon full of EC squints, all penning letters to pass the time, would *have* to turn up some missives worth the effort of a bit of blackmail. The date of entry into Corma flashed by again and again—*26th Tenmonth*, *26th Tenmonth*, *26th . . .*

Rare's fingers brushed away an envelope, reached for another, and froze over its delivery address.

Phillip Chalmers, PhD, ThD, 16 Lamplighter Circle, Coventry Passage

The envelope was tiny, like the ones a lady might use for a courting note, but the writing was meticulous and unromantic. A professional hand. A *reverend doctor's* hand.

Rare tore open the flap. Inside was a piece of galleon stationary hardly larger than her hand, its center watermarked with the seal of the good ship *Hipparchus*. At the bottom, below Nora Pierce's hasty signature, lay a blob of postal wax—just enough to bind a tiny key to the paper.

She read, and on the third sentence, her breath caught. Rare pulled her hand from Rabbit's shaggy head. She sat up, scanning the letter, then started over again. *It couldn't have said*— Rare's eyes burned into the page.

And yet, it did.

"Bloody Reason," she breathed.

Rabbit lifted his head and stood on the wobbling mattress. Then the air split with his barking, huge belting yelps that nearly covered the sound of the front door being hammered by something very large. Not a fist but a shoulder. A whole *body*. The dog charged downstairs, baying alarum.

Rare was on her feet before the sound of shattering glass ended the thunder below. She stuffed the package of the Alchemist's things in her satchel, cramming Pierce's letter in among them. Then she stepped up on the nightstand beside the bed and jumped for the exposed rafters. She swung her legs up over a beam and lay with her belly hugging its cobwebs, staring at the darkened room below. She dialed down her magnesium torch, let it cool a moment, and thrust it into her bag.

Voices. Three. All male, one with that particular grating quality, that sound of sandpaper over skin.

Rare mouthed her curses. The aigamuxa would smell her all over the upper floor, and soon.

The stairs groaned. She counted their protests, could tell the intruders had ten steps to go before they came to the landing outside this room. Rabbit's barking ended with a heavy, thudding noise, a sharp yelp, and the sound of the dog scrabbling through the back door's hatch.

Rare fished Nora Pierce's letter out of her bag. She snapped the seal over the key and pressed that tiny thumbnail of brass into a crack in the rafter beneath her. The oval of the key handle showed a stamp and a number: *49*. It would serve her well as a hiding place—but only if she got away.

Reaching forward with her arms and pulling, hugging with her knees and releasing, Rare inched along the beam toward the dormer and nudged open one of its panels. She kept her breath steady. *"Almost everything a good thief does starts with the breath,"* Anselm had said a thousand times over. *"Lose that, and you lose control. Lose control, and you're done for."*

Slowly, her fingers plied the window catch. She pulled herself out into the night, belly pressed to the gabled roof, peering past the casement edge, reversing the upside-down room in her mind's eye.

"Hullo! This is the gendarme! We saw your torch. We know you're up here somewhere."

Rare closed her eyes and sighed. It would just be her luck that some bloody gendarmes of the constabulary made their patrol as she was sweeping the place. At this hour, a light moving furtively around the upper stories of the Scales would draw attention—might compel them to knock after the welfare of the proprietor and justify forcing the door.

But it didn't explain the hunchbacked shadow looming in the bedroom now, casting its crookedness along the moonlit floor. One of the two junior constables had already bypassed the old attic room. A beam from his magnesium light grazed the walls and floors and moved on. The aigamuxa was one step into the room, one foot raised, ankle pivoting, pink eye blinking and peering.

The aiga's flat face twitched, *snf, snf, snf*. Rare's pulse bucked. She fought to keep her breath.

The creature set down its foot.

"Nobody here," the gendarme called back. "Not even the Alchemist."

Slowly, the creature nodded its blind head. "He will keep. The girl was here." And it pointed toward the bed.

The gendarme was a young man, younger than Rare, and he looked green as grass, trying to avoid looking at the aigamuxa's face.

"Then we can leave. Inspector Gammon said to get the Alchemist to open up the records and come down to the station if he was here, and he en't. She didn't say boo about any girl."

"A courier girl. She is becoming important."

The gendarme shook his head. "What's important is what *I* got told. Nothing about a girl."

The other voice called, from the storeroom below: "Nothing here, Mills!"

The first one, Mills, nodded and hung his torch on his belt. "That scratches it. We're done."

"No." The aigamuxa prowled forward, paused, lifted his other foot. His back was a quilt of bright, white scars. "There is the other one. The woman. The letter-scent is everywhere. New."

Rare's haunches tightened. She looked for the downspout, shimmying close enough to curl down onto it and start her descent to the moonlit yard below.

If they're looking for the Bear, and for Rowena, and if the aigamuxa knows my scent—

She didn't quite know how to finish that thought. But it coalesced into a very firm conviction of Things Being Wrong and cleaved to the vision of the officer and the aigamuxa speaking in confidence. To Bishop Meteron's name in Nora Pierce's letter. If the aigamuxa who took the book and the constabulary itself were searching for people connected to that botched delivery—if Bishop Allister Meteron were part of that—Anselm would need to know. She could tell him, and leave after, go farther than she'd first intended, and never return. Regency Square was a long way off, but she knew Westgate Bridge well and could cut a path through it like a hot knife, make it to Uptown within the hour, even taking the time to be careful.

Rare's feet touched the cobblestone yard. Something about that solid ground cleared her mind and pricked her ears.

From the shadows around the stoop came a piteous whine.

Rabbit cowered, the hairs of his spine a rusty set of quills. His eyes fixed on the old machine shed behind Rare.

There was a sound like a pot at the edge of the boil.

A second aigamuxa waxed into view from the shadows of the alley, his arms reaching for the ground, ready to launch toward her. Rare knew it could clear the space. Aigamuxa were hideous leapers, muscle springs always tight and twitching.

Rare sprang up, snaring the downspout again. Her feet dug against the building's backside. Behind, she heard the aiga's bellow and pounding, bounding stride, and the sudden silence that was its eye heels leaving the earth to wheel in the air, a shadow growing over the frame wall before her, faster and wider and closer and suddenly upon her.

INTERMEZZO

The diary of the Reverend Doctor Phillip Chalmers
Second-day Elevenmonth, year 276:

They've left me alone long enough I suspect they've done with me for the night—or, perhaps, the morning. There is no telling time down in this beastly hold. All the instrumentation I could dream of, and no clocks. I shall have to ask for one, of all simple, stupid things. I could laugh, but . . . no. I don't have the will for irony now. Not after our meeting.

I have decided to start a diary. It once seemed to me a rather womanish habit, something too indulgent to suit the character of a reverend doctor. I own hundreds of old lab books filled with scrawls, and drafts and galleys of papers I've published. But no diaries. Thinking on that, it seems I've had no life to speak of—no personal thoughts and reflections. Just a lot of papers.

I've seen four different human guards, all of them uncharitable in their long stares. There are at least six aigamuxa. I am learning a few tricks for telling them apart, mostly by their scars and limps and such. Certainly there is no mistaking Nasrahiel for any of the others.

He came an hour ago, with the other half of "we."

Some EC are devoted to knowing the peerage of their district. I left that business to Nora, so much better at small talk and digging gently in pockets for pious donations. If I'd followed her example, I should have known Smallduke Regenzi without the introduction. Were I not presently sleeping on a cot and making my water in a bucket, I might have called him a gracious host.

He came in as I was calibrating the phosphor display, Nasrahiel loping behind him. The aigamuxa's sacking trousers had blood on them, a handprint on the outside of the thigh, long trails marking where fingers lost their hold and fell away.

Regenzi gave me his name—his card, even.

"Fascinating little array you've put together here. Could you show me, perhaps . . . ?" And he let the question trail, gesturing coaxingly.

I eyed Nasrahiel. Regenzi tsked. "I am sorry for that roughness back at the rectory. Nasrahiel is an enthusiast for our cause. That has its detriments, I'm afraid."

"The display is rather technical," I said, at last. "I'll try to keep things simple."

And I began adjusting the apertures. I had done it so often before I had the display ready in moments.

"And what *is* your 'cause,' exactly, my lord?" I wondered aloud, wheeling the particulate scanner around on its dolly cart to face a little band of blank space between my captors.

The smallduke shrugged. "More easily explained, perhaps, once you've shown us the tricks of your trade."

I checked the connections, then waved to the aigamuxa, pointing and signing at the creature to ensure its comprehension. "This is, ah, a *generator. A treadle-powered dy-na-mo.* It collects, um, demons of energy that are enslaved by these conduits to provide—"

Nasrahiel's shark teeth bared. He slammed his foot down on the treadle board, hard enough to send the flywheel spinning in a mad, clattersome rush. The screen sparked in response.

"I . . . see you already know how it works," I said sheepishly.

He folded himself into his customary crouch, pink eyes glaring from his heels.

Regenzi laughed. "The aigamuxa don't practice science, Doctor, but they *are* really quite a bit more clever than we've given them credit for. Did you know they also believe in God? Granted, there are some philosophical differences separating us, but that was also true of human societies three hundred years ago. We've enjoyed quite a profitable partnership: I'm looking for scientists who can tell me how to find the Vautneks. Nasrahiel believes God has asked him to do the same. Perhaps we're both right."

I was about to ask what either of them could want the Vautneks for, but Regenzi looked suddenly quite eager, and so I took my place at the treadle board and began pulsing it along, bringing the phosphor array up to a warm, steady glow.

"Turn down the lamps, please," I said.

The screen was thick glass, its color dilute amber. It lent that sepia tone to everything seen through its face, the movements of particles and waves curling and sparkling. The particles pulled right and left, trying to gather around the reflections of man and aigamuxa in turn, and then, as if losing interest, drifted back to the middle. Nasrahiel reached a leg out and held it at the height of my head, ankle turned toward the screen, the pose an impossibility of anatomical angles.

My stomach knotted, threatening rebellion. I held it in place. I am getting rather too experienced in that business, I think.

I gestured to the drifting matter. Regenzi leaned close. A particle, tiny as a needle prick, dashed off screen in an arc, following his movement.

The smallduke gave a low whistle. "So these are they. The god particles."

I nodded.

"We called them god particles because they exhibit patterns one might call behavior. That's unusual because they lack any kind of charge—a sort of neutron waste, the particle physicists used to think. They should experience neither attraction to, nor repulsion from, any other kind of matter. They should behave more or less like dust. When I was studying volatile weather patterns, I had a theory of the particles being connected to pressure systems, perhaps as a form of atmospheric fallout. Instead, once I compiled the data from the various arrays, I found different patterns entirely. There were nine zones of concentration, and they were mobile."

"The particles follow the Nine," Nasrahiel said with certainty.

It was a strange thing, having part of what might qualify as his face hovering by my left shoulder, and the voice of the creature itself in front of me.

"That's . . . what we ended up theorizing, when Nora's Vautnek text and my readings showed the same coordinates. The movement in particle fields corresponds quite precisely to the changes in the book's data set."

Regenzi leaned back and stroked his side whiskers. "But how do you know that?" he wondered aloud.

I nodded toward the nine piles of papers stacked up on my ersatz drawing table. "My own notes. Some algorithms. About a year ago, I used a coordinate set from the text to identify a survey area. Here. In Corma."

"And?"

"Subject Six," I said. "I set up a little station for myself in the Cathedral belfry, connected the array to a telescope, and was able to follow a path Six had moved through a few hours before, according to the textual record. The particles linger for quite a long time in the wake of the Nine, you know. Hours, at minimum. Perhaps days."

Nasrahiel swung back up to his feet. "You could hunt by such a trail."

I should have said nothing. I should have tried to turn the idea aside, but something about *talking* the work over made me feel safe again. I felt cradled in the presence of knowledge and reason, in a world that knew my purpose.

I forgot I was looking at a monster.

"It would be cumbersome, but once you narrowed the plat of survey with a little mathematical modeling, it could be done very . . ."

Regenzi looked at Nasrahiel, and though the creature's eyes were planted on the floor, I think he was looking back at the smallduke, as well.

I considered the aigamuxa uncertainly. "Nasrahiel . . . why are you called by God to find the Nine?"

"*I* called him to serve me," Regenzi snapped. And he smiled reasonably. "For all practical purposes, that's what it comes down to. Doctor Chalmers, may I ask you a question?"

He carried on before I could have given a reply. "Are you quite comfortable with the idea of mankind's worth being measured by the actions of just *nine* individuals?"

I started shuffling the papers on my drafting table, stacking and secreting them.

"I'm a reverend doctor of the Ecclesiastical Commission," I answered. "Our first belief is that God is the creator of a Rational and organized universe, and that He uses His infinite observation and wisdom to render judgments about that universe. His nature is the model of science itself, and our pursuit of its processes a meditation on His being."

"Lovely speech. It's not an answer to the question, though."

"Our *second* belief," I continued tightly, "is that God must carefully observe His creation in order to judge its value—its efficacy, worthiness, substance. He does so without interference in our actions. God preserves the conditions of the Experiment."

"Until such time as the Experiment has demonstrated conclusively its significance." Smallduke Regenzi was still smiling.

"Yes. Exactly."

"It hardly qualifies as a *proper* experiment, though. Where are the control subjects?"

"If God is truly ubiquitous and omnipotent, there is no Rational cause to doubt He created other worlds with other conditions and populations, against which we might be measured." The smallduke stared at me. I shrugged at his bafflement, a little pleased with myself. "I wrote a paper on the Many-Worlds Hypothesis using string theory."

He frowned. "And so you're at peace with the idea of our being watched at all times by God."

"Observation is the second tenet of our doctrine. A cornerstone of the scientific method itself."

"Are you equally at peace with *only nine of us* being watched?"

My hands were on my transcription of Subject Six's information. I evened the papers' corners and set them in the stack, perpendicular to the next subject down, building my way up to Nine. He had me ready to say what I had been stewing over for years, for the first time really *wanting* to say it aloud.

"No, my lord. It's a frankly atrocious sample size, even given the likelihood of many worlds. If God is all-powerful and all-knowing, He shouldn't require such a narrow view. He should be able to see everything, judge from everything, all at once."

Regenzi nodded sympathetically. "There are others who feel quite the same way."

Others. Of course there were more than two to this conspiracy—a hand pushing Regenzi, just like the hand of God Nasrahiel claimed pushing him. I should have pressed on that, but then he was prowling the room with curious confidence. He gestured to the phosphor screen, then laid hands on the cart and wheeled it toward the Vautnek text. The amber screen was suddenly afire. It magnified a hail of golden motes, raining and darting and swarming down into the text, seemingly absorbed by its bindings.

"There used to be a theory that eyes *cast out* light, wasn't there, Doctor?" he asked.

"Emission theory. It's been discredited. The ocular apparatus reflects light. It can't produce it."

Regenzi shrugged. "Perhaps that's true of humanity. Why should the same rules apply to God?"

"I fail to see your point."

"Perhaps I'm just a wealthy businessman," Regenzi answered, letting go of the cart and straightening up, pausing, dusting off the banded arms of his very fine green coat. "A purchased title. But my father worked hard to become such a thing so that I might become such a thing, and he was quite a decent man—paid the workers in his mills well and kept the aigamuxa fed and unfettered. The first man of business in this city to do away with their chains—did you know that? When my benefactor shared the little apocryphal tidbits the EC had been keeping from common knowledge—these things that are, given the work you and Reverend Doctor Pierce produced, more than just apocryphal—I felt the ground shift under my feet. The thought that God might shrug His mighty shoulders and wipe the slate once He's learned all He wishes to about mankind? Or He might clear the board if He found us displeasing, or simply got bored and wished to make the world over again? Well. That means my destiny and everything I've worked for belongs to someone else, doesn't it? And for all we know, they're sinners. Or saints. Or backward aboriginals. I don't *like* that powerlessness, Doctor. And I do not accept it as the necessary condition of my world."

I sat on the edge of the shabby little cot. "There's something to be said for not disrupting the conditions of an Experiment we can't fully understand."

Regenzi snorted. "We don't bother to make claims about what God wants of us anymore, morally or ethically. So what harm could it do to take nine souls under aegis and protect them from the depravities of the world?"

"You can't expect people to live under quarantine, forced to live out someone's guess of what may or may not be good for all of us."

"We do it in laboratories with mice."

I was about to protest that, too—claim that these men and women were not lab mice, but that was patently untrue. They were. God's lab mice, no less.

"According to the Old Religion," Regenzi went on, "there's quite a storied tradition of sacrificing the one to secure the salvation of all. We're merely expanding on tradition."

I looked up at Nasrahiel, still standing, looming. He has no other way of being. The aigamuxa are built to loom.

"You, ah, never answered my question," I recalled. His head tilted, as if he knew I must have been addressing him.

The teeth parted, smiling. But it was Regenzi who answered.

"I felt I owed Nasrahiel and his clan a certain employment after the labor acts were passed, something to keep his people out of the streets. When I was . . . recruited into this endeavor, I knew I would need help of his kind. Besides, his wanting to keep the world turning should hardly be a surprise."

They left not long after, but I swear the creature's smile is still hanging in the air, two rows of saw-teeth bared against the dark.

DAY THREE

3RD ELEVENMONTH

20.

It was morning, well past first light. Rowena Downshire had awoken in a cloud of pillows and satin sheets perfumed with chamomile and rosewater—alone.

The last she remembered, she had been with the Alchemist in Master Meteron's apartments. There had been supper, and a bath, and a change into a nightgown laid out in a guest room. The Alchemist had called down to the concierge for a lady's nail kit, some iodide, and a roll of gauze. He waited for Rowena to emerge from the water closet, then gestured for her to sit on the edge of the bed.

She had watched him suspiciously as he donned his spectacles and examined her red, raw palms. The bath had soaked the glass splinters to the surface of the skin, prickling them out like tiny quills. She'd had a notion what the old man meant to be about with those tweezers and tiny scissors. It made her creep backward on the coverlet.

"The quality can just call down to a desk and get what they like easy, huh?" she piped nervously.

The Alchemist had said nothing. The little silver instruments glinted, waiting.

"I think I'll be fine," Rowena had insisted. "I mean, it hurts some, but—"

"Sometimes you have to open a wound up for it to heal properly. Now stop squirming."

The Alchemist dabbed something retrieved from his coat all over Rowena's skin. It was clear and smelled of wool factories and dye shops. It tingled a moment, and then he settled into the task, working steadily, drawing forth the needles of glass in perfect silence. Somehow, it didn't hurt, though she could still feel a dull probing and pulling. They'd said nothing more. Rowena's head was so full she could barely think how to pry words from it, let alone what they ought to be. The silence grew strangely comfortable. Finally, the Alchemist had finished, painting her palms with the iodide, bundling her hands into two gauzy mittens.

As the old man gathered up his things, Rowena was still deciding if she was cross enough to withhold her thanks.

He'd gone altogether before she made up her mind.

Now, hours later—awake, alone—she climbed into the morning clothes the help had laid out: an oak-colored woolen skirt and a white tunic that tied behind her back. A breakfast trolley waited in the hall. Her stomach rumbled, but she suppressed the urge to wheel it into the room and tuck in.

The place was deadly quiet, so it seemed a good time to give it the once-over. She unwound her bandages and found her hands only a little stiff, if very orange from the iodide. Then Rowena tiptoed down the bright, broad corridors of Anselm Meteron's penthouse.

There was a dining room, narrow and long with a table fit for twelve, all cherrywood and marble and crystal chandeliers. She considered the china cabinet, opening one of its drawers. The other guest room's door was open, but she paused to knock anyway, expecting to find the Alchemist with his gazette and a coffee. But there was no breakfast trolley, and the bed was made, though in a loose fashion that suggested it had been occupied not long before. Rowena paused by the room's vanity, fingering an ivory comb with a golden palm leaf handle.

Across the hall was a room that could have held all three of the others, the biggest bed she'd ever seen at its center. It was all white and fine and very neat, except for the sheets, knotted up and spilling to the floor.

Last, Rowena approached the solar, two voices echoing within. She crept to the doorframe and peered around.

Anselm Meteron paced between divan and pianoforte, his back to the door. A secretary sat at the escritoire, taking dictation:

"On the matter of Twentieth-day Fourmonth, I see no cause to delay appropriation of the assets from the Brietney sale, and give you leave to execute the remaining terms of the contract." Meteron paused and pinched the bridge of his nose. "You can craft some kind of conclusion from there, I assume, Miss Ennis? The usual pleasantries."

The secretary scribbled on, nodding. She wore a tiny pair of spectacles on the tip of her punctilious nose. "How far shall I go, sir?"

Master Meteron smiled. "Make it none *too* pleasant."

"Of course. Will there be anything—"

And then a footman came through the front door and bumped another breakfast trolley against Rowena's unsuspecting backside. A clatter of china and the boy's apology turned all eyes toward her hiding place.

Rowena glared at the boy.

"No, Miss Ennis," Master Meteron said. "I think we're quite done for now."

Rowena's host had the footman, Benjy, lay both their meals out in the solar: coffee, toast, a soft-boiled egg, and a sectioned orange—even slices of black pudding, the sort Rowena had only seen in the windows of expensive butcheries. Her head was a tangle of hope and suspicion. There she was, eating like the governor's peerage, wearing a clean set of clothes, fresh from a good bed and a sparkling washstand—

And she still wasn't sure if it was good luck or bad that put her there.

Master Meteron poured coffee. Rowena filled her cup with as much cream and sugar as it could hold. He kept his black, though there was something already in the bottom of his cup waiting to mingle with the pour.

"Thanks," said Rowena, blowing at her coffee. "Where's . . . ?" She paused, searching for the name Meteron had used. "Where's the Old Bear?"

"Visiting the Council Bishopric. Apparently he believes the EC graybeards will answer his questions about Pierce and Chalmers's work."

Rowena frowned. "And you don't think they will?"

"I don't think they have the damnedest notion of what's *really* going on. And if they did, I very much doubt they'd let it out to the likes of him."

Rowena sawed at the pudding. "Thanks for all of this. It's really jake of you to put me up the night."

Master Meteron hadn't touched his plate. He sat far back in a roll-armed chair, holding his coffee, one hand lifting the cup and turning it a few degrees, setting it down in the saucer again, lifting it, turning it. Corma's skyline, ringed with gray clouds, filled the window at his back. Rowena ate until the chinking rhythm of his game with the cup worked under her skin.

"Are you, um . . . ?" She looked at her plate of food, then at her host. "Are you just going to watch me eat, or what?"

"We talked awhile after you were abed, the Bear and I. It seems you came into some trouble last night."

Rowena studied him, chewing slowly. The corner of his mouth had turned a little, crooked and knowing.

She lifted her chin. "We managed it all right."

"We?"

"There were two aiga," Rowena said briskly. "I done for one of 'em."

"Did you."

Meteron's tone raked down the back of Rowena's neck. She shifted in her seat.

"You don't believe me?"

His head tilted, as if to take her in by another angle. "Should I?"

"I'm being straight with you. Least you could do is stop staring at me like some constable query man."

"Perhaps," he allowed. "But you're in *my* home. And I've been thinking. Perhaps you haven't been as straight with us as you've pretended."

Rowena sat back, arms crossed. "So ask me something instead of sitting there playing games."

Meteron raised an eyebrow. "We can make this a game, if you like. It would even be fair."

Something in the cold calm of Anselm Meteron's voice told Rowena there were very few games he played that were at all fair to his opponents.

"What . . . would we be gaming for?"

"Pieces of things. Truths. There must be things you've been wanting to know."

Rowena looked all around the bright, white room, taking in its gilded edges and deep cushions. It was nothing like the Scales with its aching old stairs, and even less like Ivor's squat over the courier's loft. Somehow, those men had something to do with each other, and that something had to do with the book, and the delivery, and her sitting there with a plate of eggs and black pudding and blacker worries pushed to the back of her mind.

"Some things," she admitted. "I suppose. But there's nothing left for me to tell you. You know everything about me already."

"I doubt that very much, cricket."

Rowena opened her mouth to snap at him, then faltered. "Cricket?"

Meteron nodded toward Rowena's feet, tucked up and peeking out sidesaddle from her skirt. Her cheeks burned.

Rowena's bare feet rubbed against one another, sawing together in little anxious strokes.

Meteron chuckled. "At our rendezvous yesterday, I could fairly hear the leather of your boots rubbing away. You're a nervous thing, aren't you, cricket?"

Rowena shifted, hiding her feet, and stared daggers. "What are your game's stupid rules, anyway?"

"Every truth you give me, I'll give you one back." Meteron leaned closer, his eyes hard. "But feed me some clever street lark lie and all you'll get is birdseed."

"What makes you think you'll be able to tell the difference between when I lie or tell the truth?"

"I've met your kind before."

Rowena snorted. "I've met *your* kind, too."

"Have you?" Meteron sipped his coffee. "What's my kind?"

"You," she said, "are a rich, pompous, lazy sonovabitch who en't got the least idea of what it's like to scrap every day just to get by. That's why you don't think a thing of making me play games like this when I en't done you any wrong. It's as much nothing to you as that girl writing your letters because you can't stand getting the ink on your pretty hands."

Rowena folded her arms tight to her chest. She hoped her eyes looked as hot as her face felt.

"Passion," he observed mildly, "makes you strikingly eloquent."

"Privilege makes *you* an arse."

Meteron set down his cup, reaching for a cigarette and a lucifer from the smoking box on the table. "You're right on some counts. I think nothing of testing you, and that requires arrogance. But you also missed the mark. Twice. First, it requires an extraordinary amount of work to achieve and maintain the rich, pompous life I enjoy. I'm afraid you can lay all manner of veniality at my feet *except* sloth."

Rowena ate with sharp stuffing motions. "And the second miss?" she asked through a mouth crammed with toast.

Meteron held up his right hand, unlit cigarette between his middle and ring fingers. Rowena stopped eating, staring in spite of herself at what she had felt the afternoon before—the oddness lurking in his grip. He wagged the stump of his index finger, its scarred tip sickly white.

"Miss Ennis takes my dictation because my penmanship is simply beastly."

Rowena wiped her mouth to cover a grimace. Meteron lowered his hand. She was happy to have its ugliness out of sight. She felt his gaze and weighed her options. There were things she wanted to know. If this was the way to be about learning them—

"So you'll match me?" she asked. "Truth for truth?"

"Birdseed for birdshit."

Rowena nodded.

"But remember: you're in my house," Meteron added. He struck the lucifer and lit his cigarette. "So I'll ask the first question, if you don't mind." He didn't wait for her response. "Have you really told us everything you know about this delivery and the aigamuxa?"

"Yes."

He breathed smoke through his nostrils. "Very well. Your turn."

"Wait. That's it? You don't think I lied?"

"No, cricket. You're a terribly easy read."

"Stuff 'cricket,'" Rowena snapped. Anselm Meteron might put a roof over her head for a while, but that word went a bridge too far and crossed it too often. She knew very well why men like him used such names. "I'm not your pet."

"Do you have a question?" He sounded bored.

"Rare called the Alchemist 'Father.' But she can't properly be his daughter . . . can she?"

"Many things are proper where adoption's concerned."

"So if *he's* her lawful father, why do you both have girls' clothes about that suit me?"

He sighed. "Keeping a wardrobe of Rare's old things might make me a rather too tolerant custodian of her clutter, but that's between us. The Bear and Leyah adopted Rare when she was a little younger than you are. After Leyah died, she came to live with me."

"Leyah?" Rowena paused. "Is that . . . ? He was married?" Rowena studied Meteron, her brow furrowed. "But what's Rare doing with you if you en't family, and you en't—" And then, the tumblers in her mind rattled into place, and she knew the answer. "Oh. I see. Sorry."

"That was two questions in a row, Rowena Downshire."

"So even us up. Try me a hard one."

He raised an eyebrow. "How much have you stolen from me since you came here last night?"

Rowena's jaw slackened. She scrambled to shape the look into a glare, something suitably offended. "I en't taken anything. God's honor. It's my turn now. How'd you lose the finger?"

"Tragically deep paper cut opening the morning post."

Silence, sudden and absolute. Meteron's eyes scraped the pieces of her up on a set of balances, massing them out. To Rowena, all those jagged bits seemed suddenly, impossibly small. She stabbed at her food a sullen while.

"You'd be surprised what you can stuff up a good set of bloomers," she said at last. "I've got an ivory comb. A little clasp mirror, like for a lady's handbag. And three of those tiny silver forks—what do you call 'ems?"

"Crab forks."

Meteron set his cigarette in the ash stand, finally cutting into his cold breakfast. For a time, only the scrape and clink of silver and plate filled the room.

"How'd you know?" Rowena asked.

He tossed his serviette onto the tray. "You work for Ivor," he said. "You must be desperate."

She didn't nod. She didn't need to.

"He's quite taken with you," Meteron suggested in a consoling tone. There must have been panic in Rowena's eyes, for he added, "The Old Bear, I mean. You've slid right under his thick skin."

Rowena bit her lip. "Can't think why."

Her host shrugged, a movement of one shoulder. "I had been hoping this little interview might help me figure that."

"So, have you?"

"Life doesn't afford many second chances," Meteron said, examining his cigarette's ember end. "Things didn't go well between him and Rare, after Leyah passed. Perhaps a new orphan will assuage his conscience."

"I'm not an orphan," Rowena said, then winced. "My mum's alive. She's just . . . she's in Oldtemple."

Meteron nodded. Even a man of his means, Rowena supposed, would have to know the only thing Oldtemple was famous for—a debtors' prison four thousand inmates strong, all but overflowing.

"Silver and ivory fetch a good price if you hawk 'em at market," she explained. "Helps me keep ahead of her fees a bit, make a dent in the debt. I'm getting close. Just five hundred left. That's . . . that's not too bad."

Now that she was saying it aloud, it came rushing out, like a pumped tap running dry. "I think I can get it paid off, if I find a good job with some other courier or something. I can do my sums a little, and I work hard. I'm used to it. The accountant clerk tells me I should have it all settled in about four years."

He nodded again. Rowena could tell his agreement was as much a lie as her claim had been. The accountant clerk had told her no such thing. And no job she could get would keep ahead of the keeping fees or wear down the debt in so short a time. Certainly not if she expected to feed herself in the meanwhile. But Rowena had decided on the lie long ago and told it to herself over and over again, until it seemed true.

"It's a worthy plan," Meteron answered, toneless.

Rowena scrubbed at her nose. There was a little tingle in it, and she had to drive it out before it brought along a company of tears. "I have another question."

He spread his hands.

"En't you afraid of the Alchemist?" She saw the crease between her host's brows deepen. "You're a liar. I mean, begging your pardon, but that's about the size of it, right?"

"So I've been told."

"Seems to me the last person in the world you'd want to be hanging about is some witchy mind reader."

"We've had a long time to reach an understanding."

Rowena pulled a face. "About irrational magical hoodoo?"

"It's not quite so prosaic as that."

"But are you *afraid of him*?" Rowena pressed. "That's the question. Birdseed for birdshit, remember?"

He smiled darkly. "Of course I am. But I'd be much more frightened to call him my enemy than my friend, after all we've done together."

Rowena pursed her lips. Meteron was following the rules. She almost wished he wasn't. *After all we've done together. . . .*

"How'd she die?" Rowena asked.

"Sorry?"

"The Alchemist's wife. Leyah."

"Ah." Meteron's brow furrowed. He stabbed his cigarette into the ash stand. "Badly, and a long time ago."

"How's an alchemist's wife die badly?"

He studied her face. "You missed a room," he said at last. "Follow me."

Meteron touched a wall plate, opening the gas chambers in the dining room's alchemical chandelier. The long, draped table shimmered under the crystal lights. He walked to the china cabinet, and Rowena followed.

"No, I've been here before. The crab forks, remember?"

"You've been here," he allowed, pulling the second silver drawer out and reaching deep into its back, his four-and-a-half-fingered hand groping for something. The wall shuddered, the whole cabinet rattling porcelain music. "But you haven't been *here*."

Master Meteron shifted the china cabinet aside, moving it as easily as the ladders on rollers at the Stone Scales. He gestured through the open passage. Slowly, Rowena approached.

It was an office or study, though not the paneled and rustic sort like in Chalmers's rectory. Like the rest of the suite, it was white and cream and gold and silver, startlingly clean, with polished fixtures and shining wood. It *was* like Chalmers's study in that it had shelves full of books, but that was as far as it went. All similarity ended with the display case, glass-fronted and running the length of a wall, filled with equal parts stringed instruments and weapons.

Rowena stood by, gaping. She had never seen such an arsenal before. It was arranged like a museum, old wheel locks and trumpet-mouthed muskets mounted beside lean flintlock rifles and snub-nosed alley pistols. There were punching daggers, and blade breakers, and stilettos half the length of Rowena's arm. The case even boasted a few of the heavy carbines the gendarmes of the constabulary carried in the rougher districts. Here and there, the wall of weapons was broken up with a violin, or a guitar, or other things with necks and strings and bows.

"This," Meteron explained, "is a little remnant of what you might call the family business."

Rowena pulled her gaze from a fierce, broad-barreled contraption that seemed practically a hand cannon. "What exactly did you *do*?"

"You must know why men like Ivor make a brisk business smuggling."

She shrugged. "You need things, and there's no way of getting 'em lawful, or maybe there's something you want moved around that needs the wrong hands kept off."

"Our business was like that, but with people. We did things the constabulary doesn't do, or won't. Some things even criminals can't do for themselves. Or won't."

"Like . . . what?"

"Kidnapping—sometimes, rescues. Theft or retrieval. Keeping secrets or exposing them. Different sorts of jobs, different sorts of clients." Meteron sank with a yawn into a wingback chair. "This is a world of plutocrats, Rowena Downshire. Get your hands on enough money and you earn with it problems requiring creative solutions."

"How's a body go from that to running a nightclub?" Rowena was still looking around at the cases as she took up the chair opposite her host's. "Or an alchemist's shop?"

Meteron's face shifted into an expression Rowena didn't recognize. Slowly, she realized it was the nearest thing to uncertainty she'd yet seen in his flinty eyes.

"You retire. And then, for a while, you unretire," he answered, scanning the weapons cases as if they were points on the horizon, impossibly distant. "And then, things go very wrong. As they do."

"So, this is how you knew Ivor and the Alchemist."

"This is how."

"Why are you letting me see all this?"

Meteron smiled faintly. "You really have to ask?"

Rowena bit her lip. *No. Not really.* The room was a warning. Meteron was leveling with her, all right—leveling his watchful gaze, the sights of a gun, and a promise that whatever she took out of this room or any other, it would be only and exactly what he chose. He was telling her the absolute truth in little parcels of half-truth.

And then he stood, dusting absently at his silk trousers. "I hope you'll pardon me, but there are a few matters to which I must attend. There's still breakfast in the solar, of course. Finish, if you like. Benjy will clear up if you ring for him."

Rowena stood, then felt awkward in her skirt and tunic, not knowing what to do. Follow her host out, so he could close up his little nook and the secrets it held? Shake his hand? Curtsey? Meteron was no gentryman, but he was *something*.

It turned out not to matter. He sketched his shadow of a bow, and a moment later was in the passage beside the china cabinet, stopped short by Benjy.

The boy carried a note on a silver charger—a hastily scrawled clerk's rendering of a spark.

Meteron plucked the note up and scanned it. Rowena noticed his jaw tighten, chewing something his scowl suggested was a curse.

"Something wrong?"

"There should be a coat with an ermine collar in your room's chiffarobe," he said irritably. Meteron balled the note and flung it into a wastebasket. Rowena watched him reach into the china hutch, searching for its switch. She scrambled up, nearly tangling her ankles in her skirt in her haste to avoid being entombed behind the sliding cabinet.

Meteron rolled the cabinet into place, his face dark. A teacup toppled and ran free on the shelf.

"Get that coat and a pair of shoes," he instructed. "Meet me in the hall in five minutes. We're wanted at the constabulary."

Rowena blinked. "But why?"

"So we can bail the Old Bear's fool arse out of trouble."

21.

Though anyone attending the Decadal Conference's laity lectures that cold, bright Elevenmonth morning would have had a cache of rumor and superstition ready to describe "the Alchemist," most had no clear sense of what kind of man belonged to the name. The two young gendarmes Haadiyaa Gammon dispatched to find him, though, left the constabulary armed with a good description and a sense of urgency. Their city inspector's orders had come on the heels of a message brought by a runner in the Ecclesiastical Commission's own livery. It complained of an unexpected request for a meeting with the Council Bishopric, and was signed by the Decadal Conference planning committee—Xuahtili, Chatham, Bonaventur, Tran, Grigori, and Meteron. Only the last name of that list mattered. It was the name that had made Gammon pull the bell rope for the gendarme's bull pen and summon the two lads to her office, with orders to double-time down to the Cathedral campus.

The boys were back in an hour, bearing a full report and a foul-tempered old man they'd left sitting in an interrogation room down the hall.

"Went well enough, ma'am," Cortes said with a crisp salute. "No fuss. Some reverend doc was raising a ruckus with a page about missing equipment as we were calling the old man in. She wanted us to stay on and start an investigation, but we had our orders, so we told her to send a page down to central."

Gammon glanced up from the reports and warrants littering her desk. "Missing equipment?"

"Stuff gone from her lab overnight, a good crate's worth of galvanic testers and such. En't so odd given all the folk coming in and out of the lectures, I suppose."

Missing equipment. Gammon made a mental note to discuss the matter with Regenzi. If his lordship's agents were getting sloppy, then the bishop would have to intercede before long, and His Grace had already been moved to do more than Gammon would have wished for one day.

"He did ask for his right of contact, ma'am," Cortes said hastily, following Gammon to the holding room. "Regency Square. We had a boy see to it."

"The boy sent the spark already?"

The young officer flinched at Gammon's tone. "Yes, ma'am. Quarter hour ago, I think. He wasn't under arrest, exactly, so we couldn't just put the clamps down."

Gammon nodded, sighing. She'd known she would have to deal with Anselm Meteron sooner or later—but did it have to come so *much* sooner? "It's fine, Cortes. You did well."

Cortes looked relieved. "And . . . that'll be all, ma'am?"

"Here." Gammon passed the lad a folded sovereign note. "Be sure to tell Madigan I'm pleased with you both. Buy yourselves a round tonight."

Cortes lacked the grace to resist unfolding the bill then and there. It was enough to stand their pints for a whole night.

"Much obliged, ma'am."

Another quick salute and he was gone, trotting down the hall to find his partner and report their spoils.

Let them be happy, Gammon thought. *They had to collect the bloody Alchemist and keep from soiling their trousers doing it. It's the sort of thing they'd be proud of.*

Gammon turned the knob of the holding room's door. She wondered what she'd have to be proud of come day's end.

The Alchemist stood by the narrow window cut into the room's outer wall, his shoulders squared and arms crossed. Whatever he saw out in the dusty alley below commanded his full attention.

Gammon cleared her throat. "Thank you for com—"

"You're welcome," the Alchemist said coldly. "I've been nearly half an hour in this room, so I assume whatever brings me here isn't urgent."

"I'm sorry for your wait. The Decadal Conference has us busier than usual. Petty thefts and larceny always rise when the city is full."

The Alchemist grunted something that might have been agreement—or indigestion.

"If you'd like to sit, I can explain the situation more fully," Gammon offered, gesturing to the room's single teetering stool.

"There's no reason my standing would prevent you from doing that, Inspector?"

"None, sir."

"Then I'll keep my feet, and you'll keep matters brief."

Cortes and Madigan earned every clink of that bill. "Last night, two of my men went to the Scales to execute a search warrant. They found the premises had been robbed and someone murdered there."

The Alchemist's dark eyes narrowed. "Home breaking, robbery, and murder. I'm surprised that doesn't take precedence over petty larceny."

"We recovered the stolen goods on the thief. They're in case storage down below. I had hoped you might be able to identify the body."

"I can try. Why was there a warrant in the first place?"

"There's a lift down the hall. We can speak candidly as we go down."

They walked the building's central corridor, stopping in a vestibule where a brass-gated lift waited for Gammon and her ring of keys. She turned one in its lock and scrolled the grating aside, letting the Alchemist enter before her. Inside, Gammon hauled down the lift's segmented inner door, latching it at the floor, and put a hand over its ivory-handled lever.

"The Reverend Doctor Nora Pierce was murdered at Smallduke Regenzi's manor yesterday. Toxicology shows some kind of a conium concentrate in her bloodstream, probably administered through a spiked drink." Gammon looked at the Alchemist meaningfully. "Regenzi tells us he was in your shop earlier that day."

"A lot of people were in my shop that day."

"He claims his mistress made a purchase—or that you donated her something."

"Did he tell you of his own purchase?"

"He may have. The case is complicated, and we're very busy. I find it hard to recall details at a drop."

"Conium. Thirty percent of a solution, suspended in glucose."

Gammon lifted her eyebrows, incredulous. "You're confessing to acting as an accessory in Reverend Pierce's murder?"

"I'm confessing to the preparation and sale of a substance used in the treatment of arthritis."

Gammon snorted. "At thirty percent concentration?"

"Conium is toxic in any concentration. Regenzi purchased a fortnight's supply. If it were taken *at once*, it would be fatal." The Alchemist shook his head. "I can't assume liability for customers who don't heed my usage instructions."

"I see." Gammon pulled the lever for the lowest level. The carriage lurched down its chain. "Smallduke Regenzi and his mistress remember things differently."

"Is there a version of the truth you would prefer to hear, Inspector?"

Gammon considered the Alchemist.

"No," she said at last. "That's a question you'd be better served to ask yourself."

The carriage staggered to a halt, and Gammon set about opening it once again.

The lift opened onto a dim, alchemically lighted corridor with just two doorways, one labeled "MORGUE AND LABORATORY" in vivid block letters, the other "CASE STORAGE." There was a tall desk beside the second door, manned by a bleary-eyed clerk who looked as if he saw the light of day about as often as the contents of the room he managed.

The clerk scurried back into storage and emerged with a large canvas envelope, a claim tag dangling from it. He checked the tag against a ledger and handed it over for Gammon and the Alchemist's signatures. As Gammon turned toward the morgue doors, the Alchemist paused to rifle the envelope's contents.

Gammon stopped. "Something wrong, sir?"

She waited in the morgue's threshold, its door propped against her polished heels. The Alchemist looked up at her.

"You said there was a body."

"This way, sir."

The constabulary morgue was a vast room, lined with thick vault doors and half-frosted tiles. The cold dampened the sweet smell of the dead, pushing it down to hug the ground with lingering, malevolent vapor.

Gammon stopped at the medical examiner's table, painting camphor under her nose. She offered the pot to the Alchemist. The old man waved it off.

He was already looking at one particular vault, weeping water where its ice bevels met the tiled wall. Its surface beaded with perspiration. The other doors were dry.

Number eleven. That was where the body would be.

Gammon cracked the vault's lever and pulled the slate tray out.

Even in death, Rare Juells had a kind of pale splendor. It was a stark and distant beauty, a cool radiance faintly blue beneath the curve of her cheek and the bow of her lips. That, more than the ruin of the rest, forced Gammon's eyes away. She did her best to cover it by studying the Alchemist's face for some reaction, some sign of recognition. Of surprise. Distaste.

The old man's blank face was almost as terrible as Rare's bloodied body.

A gash ran just under her armpit, showing winks of bone and rags of muscle. Her blood filled the slate table's long grooves. The left side of her face was a shattered mirror of the still-lovely right. The orbital bone was caved in, piercing her eye with shards of skull, the nasal cavity left gaping. Through the mats of blood and bone in her hair, Gammon could see the pulp of gray matter.

She cleared her throat.

"The evidence suggests that after she robbed the Scales, she was murdered by an accomplice. The goods we found on her were of negligible value, and likely that started a row. Perhaps the accomplice wanted to go back in for more. The neighbors awoke to the sounds of a fray. One of them came round the backyard and found her there. No weapon, but I imagine the devil ran off with his cudgel. Happens all the time."

The Alchemist nodded distantly. Gammon felt a lurch in her stomach—bile at the lie she had told, or unease at that blank, stony face beside her. Both, perhaps. She frowned.

"Do you know her, sir?"

"I do."

"Take your time."

The old man surveyed the woman's face. He seemed to be searching for something, a line etched deep between his brows. He spoke more to himself than Gammon.

"If you check the family records division of the Court and Bar, you'll find papers on the adoption of Rare Juells. Her adoptive mother's name was Leyah." He paused, seeing Gammon remove a notebook from her jacket, and repeated the names, spelling each in turn. "You'll find my name in that record, as well."

Gammon's pencil stopped scratching. She stared at her hand, then cleared her throat.

"I'm sorry, sir. Do you mean to say she's your daughter?"

"It's all in the records, Inspector." The Alchemist drew in a slow breath. "Would you mind, perhaps, giving me a few minutes?"

Mechanically, Gammon reached into a drawer beside Rare's vault and produced a white sheet, drawing it up over her nakedness.

"I'll send someone down later to take your deposition."

"Thank you."

"And, sir?"

The Alchemist's gaze locked on Haadiyaa Gammon. For a moment, Gammon said nothing, chewing her words, trying to work them into something whose taste she could stomach. *I could have prevented this*, she almost said. Instead, as if it belonged to someone else, Gammon watched her hand drift up to touch the Alchemist's sleeve.

"I am sorry."

That, at least, was the truth.

There was another truth in the Alchemist's hard, dark look. He turned his gaze back on his daughter's corpse, the line between his brows deepening again. As Gammon left the morgue, she could not shake the feeling that there was something the old man was looking for in her shattered face—and that he was close to finding it.

22.

"There's nowhere to park," Anselm's driver grumbled.

The streets of the Upper Districts were a snarl of clockwork buses, hackney cabs, costermonger carts, and darting pedestrians. The line of iron posts for hitching drive teams that ran half a block outside the constabulary's central offices had been cordoned off, probably to keep a path clear for the officers' own coaches and carts. Anselm's driver had boxed in another secretariat coach in the scrap to get as close as possible to that broad building, toothy with windows and colonnades.

Anselm donned his grandee hat. "Drive around the block awhile, then. We should only be a few minutes." He stepped off the platform beneath the coach door and reached a hand up to Rowena.

The girl looked something between charmed and frightened under the ruff of Rare's old overcoat. He supposed she'd never ridden in a coach before. The thought of her finding anything novel in something so mundane amused him. Then again, a good deal about the girl and her provincial penury amused him.

"My lady?" he said, smiling at the flare in her cheeks. It was wonderfully satisfying to see her disarmed. He considered it compensation for his temporary services as governess. Still, those services seemed in danger of becoming less temporary with every passing hour.

Certainly the Old Bear's message gave the impression that this might be a concern, if a congenial party able to offer alibi or bail failed to make a timely appearance at the constabulary offices.

They started up the long stairs, Anselm in a fine gray doublet with a long, woolen coat buttoned halfway to his ruffled cravat. It took only a moment for Rowena to forget herself entirely and bound three steps ahead. He plucked her sleeve, holding her back until they were side by side again.

"On my arm." He threaded her right through his left. "We'll be in and out a good deal faster if you look a lady."

Rowena's mouth twisted. "Instead of a what?"

Anselm started up the stairs again. She was obliged to keep his pace.

"Instead of a street urchin in borrowed clothes. This is the wrong place to raise suspicions. The people here are *paid* to have suspicions."

The sergeant at the front desk had the good sense, at least, to pretend that he didn't know Anselm Meteron on sight. Anselm and the girl had discussed this moment in the coach. Rowena noticed his hand squeezing her forearm and reached into her clutch for his card.

Anselm let the other man review the token. "I'm here to see Inspector Gammon on the matter of the Alchemist. There is no appointment."

The clerk began jotting down a note, then paused. "Master Anselm Meteron and . . . who else, may I ask, is calling?"

"This is my daughter."

When the clerk returned to the appointment diary, Rowena cast Anselm an exasperated look. He smiled, winked, and enjoyed himself thoroughly.

"I'll ring down to her office, sir. You can take a seat down the hall."

Anselm took Rowena with him, still steering her by the arm. Her eyes darted as they moved through the central waiting area, crowded with benches of sour-smelling ruffians and half-fed whores with gendarmes looming over them, working out papers on their writing slates for this crime or that. A pair of rough-looking lanyani sat strapped in separate metal chairs on a concrete dais—far enough from each other and high enough off the scuffed wooden floor to keep them from easily rooting into the boards or vining together before the officers could see to them.

Anselm opened the door to a private waiting room and held it for the girl. Then he threw his hat on the seat of an easy chair. Rowena rounded on him.

"What the hell was *that* about?"

Anselm quirked an eyebrow. "I could have said you were my courtesan, but you're a bit young, even for me. Besides, Miss Downshire, I have a certain aesthetic standard to consider, in which regard you are rather wanting."

She swatted his hat off the chair it had claimed and flounced down in its place, her arms crossed over the less than ample bosom of her dress.

"A lady," Anselm suggested as he bent to recover the upended grandee, "takes her coat *off* before she takes her seat."

"Stuff it."

"You're in a mood, aren't you?"

"I don't like this place."

"Been here before?"

"Is that some way of asking if I've been arrested?" Rowena shook her head. "Well, I en't. Known lots of coves who have, though."

"You're on the right side of the law this time," Anselm said, draping his coat over his arm. "At least insofar as anyone here is aware. Relax."

"I'll relax when we're well and gone, thanks. Do you really think you can just walk off with the Old Bear?"

There was a note of actual distress in the girl's voice, quite a different quaver than her little rage moments before. "What would it matter to you? I thought you were furious with him for the liberties he took. Frightened of his unnaturalness."

Rowena lifted her chin stubbornly. "He saved my hide, so I suppose I owe him a lookout."

"Ah. Now, I thought *you* were the one who 'did for' the aigamuxa last night." Rowena gave Anselm a searing look. "Where would I have gotten such a notion, I wonder?"

"Can you get him out of this hole or not?"

"As there hasn't yet been a formal arrest, absolutely. The inspector and I have an understanding."

There was a rap on the doorframe. Anselm winked at Rowena. *I'll do the talking.* She wriggled free of her coat, folding it demurely over her clasped hands just as the door opened.

Sometimes, they can be taught.

Inspector Gammon always had a pinched, stiff cast to her hawkish features. Anselm expected that sail-in-a-gale tightness, the propriety the inspector couldn't, for all her pragmatism, shed. Now, though, there was something else at play.

"I left him in the morgue," she said from the doorway, without preamble. "Perhaps—" Gammon looked tentatively at Rowena. "Perhaps the young lady should wait for us here."

Anselm frowned at the girl. She'd gone stock-still at the word "morgue."

"No," he replied. "Let's all go."

Gammon fastened the latches on the lift's scrolling doors and cranked the lever. Anselm looked up at the ceiling as the carriage jerked downward.

"Where did you find his body? The warehouse?"

The inspector regarded him uncertainly. "The Alchemist isn't—"

"I know *he* isn't dead," Anselm snapped. "You do have him down there identifying a body, yes? Ivor Ruenichnov?"

Anselm returned Gammon's gaze, saw its passing blankness, and felt his own prickle of misgiving. Rowena fidgeted, her petticoats whispering. Gammon shook her head.

"I'm sorry, Anselm."

The lift felt oddly cold, the walls closer than they'd been. Anselm's hackles rose.

"Haadi," he said, drawing out the name, dismembering it with lingering care. "What precisely is going on?"

The lift stopped. Gammon attended to the doors. Anselm swept past her as soon as they released, his hat and coat under one arm. He clipped Rowena's shoulder, stalking through the morgue doors.

Rare lay on the slate table. The Alchemist slumped on the floor beside it.

Neither of them moved.

Rowena bolted in, her skirts whipping her ankles, and rushed for the Alchemist. The old man's back rested on the body-vault wall. His legs spread out before him as if they'd given way, his whole frame sinking to starboard. The girl pushed and tugged at him, trying to shift him upright.

"I'll call down a physick," the inspector said, turning to the bellpull and tube beside the doors.

Anselm grabbed her shoulder. "No. He'll be fine."

"He's in catalepsy or had a palpitation. God only knows what."

"*He'll be fine*, Haadi. Stay here."

They locked eyes. Gammon nodded, stepping aside.

Anselm walked to the slate table and instantly wished he hadn't. From across the room, he couldn't see what had become of Rare's face. He had seen worse deaths before. Sometimes, he had even been their cause. But to see Rare wearing its grisly colors silenced him. He was aware of that sudden stillness—the echoing halls of his whole system, so full of clamor and incidence, ground to a sudden halt. Usually, that peace was a good thing, the most longed for of all uncommon things.

Peace, Anselm thought distantly, *was Rare.*

He focused on the right side of her face, the angle of her cheek, the blueness of death bleeding through like ink. Rare had been chaos itself. He would pet, and she would purr, or scratch, one nearly as often as the other. He loved that willfulness, though the part of him that was something other than a lover watched her exploits with a fist of anxiety tightening in his belly. Some nights, it took all Anselm's energy to match her impulses, her wits, her audacity. Rare exhausted him. He *needed* that. No other woman was brazen enough to insult him, sink in her claws, and then sink into his bed a moment later. She had been utterly, unchangeably herself, the whole of his joy and his grief.

There was a voice nearby, insistent and shrill. Anselm turned. A wide-eyed girl crouched beside him, flailing in a dress cut for a woman's curves. She seemed familiar. The clockworks slipped back into motion, anger turning the winding spring. At last, he could put a name to her face.

"What's *wrong* with him?" Rowena cried.

Anselm stooped and felt for the Alchemist's pulse. It was there—dogged and strong, perhaps even too fast. Out of the corner of his eye, he spied Gammon lingering by the doors, arms folded, bottom lip white between her teeth.

"You should have known better, you old fool," Anselm murmured. He looked at Rowena. "He must have been looking for answers. He's been . . ." He tapped a finger to his temple meaningfully. "Traveling abroad."

Slowly, the girl seemed to understand. "He went . . ." She stared at Rare's body. "He went *in there?*"

In there. To a place. A thing. Anselm's stomach turned.

"Will he be all right?"

"Damned if I know, but he can't stay here. Gammon!"

The city inspector looked up.

Anselm stood, reaching into his folded coat. He drew out a gold clip of sovereign notes and tossed it on the sheet covering Rare. It thumped into the valley between her breasts. For an instant, he watched her, waiting for her to start up at the indignity, hoping a hand would swat the bundle away.

Nothing.

"We're leaving," Anselm announced. "We're taking this man with us. Send anything of his you have in holding to my apartments. I'll expect the delivery within the hour."

Gammon looked at the bundle of bills—thousands of sovereigns discarded. Her face twisted. "I can't take your money, Anselm."

"The hell you can't," Anselm spat. And then his lip curled. He shrugged. "Leave it here, if that pleases you. Let some lucky ghoul in your staff turn up rich and quit his post on the morrow. It would be a laugh. The Trimeeni bury the dead with all their riches, you know. We should be so generous with our own."

Anselm knelt beside the Alchemist and slapped him once, hard. The older man groaned, stirring. Anselm began packing up the little altar of items arranged by Rare's corpse, stuffing them unceremoniously into the canvas envelope lying at her feet. Chronometer, wedding rings, surgeon's kit . . .

"Help the man get his feet, Haadi, if you're so determined to be a gentlewoman."

Haadiyaa Gammon said nothing. If she had, Anselm knew he'd have done something unwise, something his right hand and its missing finger ached to do to someone. Instead, Gammon strode over, slipping an arm around the Alchemist, and levered him to his feet. Rowena kept prodding and chirruping until, dazed, the old man accepted the help silently, making a slow, uncertain path to the door.

Gammon was holding the door open for them when Anselm called.

"Haadi?"

Gammon looked over her shoulder. "Yes?"

Anselm stared down at Rare. *Get up, kitten.* He stared at the right side of her face, willing warmth into the flesh, willing open eyes and smiling lips. *Get up. You never sleep this late.*

"Anselm?"

Anselm flinched. For an instant, his gaze strayed to the other side of Rare's face. Its bare meat and bone flashed bright as lightning before his eyes. He winced, shutting them. "She's been through quite enough," he said. "No inquest."

"Given the circumstances, it would be difficult to justify denying one."

"Ask me if I care."

"There's the possibility you might never know what happened without it."

"I have a rather good idea of what's happened." Anselm looked at the Alchemist darkly. "We can determine the finer details on our own."

Gammon sighed. "I'll have the chief medical examiner transfer her to the mortuary of your choice. You can leave their information with our courier when you receive the Alchemist's effects."

"Just burn her." Anselm shook his head. "There's no decent place to bury the dead in this city."

Wordless, Gammon guided the Alchemist and Rowena away. The door shut.

Anselm lingered, studying the right side of Rare's face. It was almost as he'd always known it, cool and dark in the night, waiting to turn into gold and fire with the dawn. Yet there was no flush of life coloring her throat, no steady rise and fall of breath. It was *too still.* The stillness stretched over Rare's restless loveliness like a winding-sheet. Then, he considered her left side, crushed by a strength greater than any a man could bring to bear. It was bitter and brutal, as vicious as the lacerations running down her body.

Anselm slipped on his coat. He tucked the Old Bear's belongings under one arm. He almost donned his grandee.

And then he paused. Anselm laid the package and his hat atop the bundle of bills. He leaned close to Rare's face—

The right side.

His nose brushed her eyelashes. There was a smell skulking in her fine, long hair like old meat and an open privy. His lips drifted over her cheek, close.

Very close. And yet—

"Sorry, kitten," Anselm murmured. He straightened, taking up the parcel and his hat.

Anselm Meteron walked to the morgue door and doused the light behind him.

23.

Rowena knocked once, firm and loud. For a long time she stood in the dim hallway, trying to choose the right interval to knock again. She counted slowly—*one-will-you-won't-you, two-will-you-won't-you, three—*

She came to ten, prayed against Reason for an answer, and figured the Alchemist wouldn't. Best just to head back to the solar and tell Meteron that he was still . . . what? Sleeping? Was that what they left him doing there in the guest bed, all those hours before?

Master Meteron asked you to check on him and bring him to supper, so . . .

Rowena turned the knob as she might tear off a hangnail and stepped hastily within.

The curtains were drawn, filtering in the harrowed light of a sunset struggling through coal dust and saltpeter. The Alchemist lay tangled in the bedsheets. A bare leg, pocked with the scar of an old wound, balanced on the mattress's edge. *A bullet wound?* Master Meteron's words came back to her: *"After all we've done together."*

The Alchemist twitched fitfully. She could tell he'd been left to sort himself out naked under the covers. Rowena froze, fighting the urge to fetch Benjy in her place.

She imagined herself retreating to the solar to ring down for the footman. And she imagined Master Meteron's cold, burning stare, his quiet contempt at her for being a yellowbelly under all her streetful sneers. Her fingers tightened on the candlestick she carried.

You en't afraid of some old cove shut up in a room having nightmares.

She put the candle down on the nightstand. Half the sheets had slid from the bed, lying in a satiny puddle still smelling of laundry perfume.

It wasn't fear of waking the Alchemist that left Rowena knotting her hands in her skirt. Whoever he was—whatever he was—she doubted he could turn her into a toad or some other silly fairy-book nonsense for interrupting a rest that was clearly not restful in the least. No. The thought assembled itself awkwardly, with all the wrong words and pieces jabbing at strange angles, but when Rowena pushed it around, setting all her worry and wonder in order, it came together clearly.

She wasn't afraid *of* the Alchemist. Not anymore. She was afraid *for* him—afraid of what he might need. Afraid of not knowing what to say, and what that failure would cost when he finally fumbled his way back into a world where his daughter was dead. What would she say about that? Surely the moment *required* something.

Sorry your daughter's dead, Master What's Your Name. That's some sore luck.

As if he'd heard that thought, the old man writhed again. His graying beard rasped the pillowcase. Perspiration beaded his hairline. He seemed to be pushing away from something, straining for distance. And then he whimpered.

A big, growly man folk called the Bear, and something in his head was making him *whimper*.

That tore it. Rowena took the Alchemist's bare shoulder and shook it, hard. He twisted, waving a hand to shoo her off. She tapped his chest, knocking on his breastbone at first gently, then harder and harder.

"Hey," Rowena called, "Alchemist . . . Bear . . . what's your name . . ."

Her knuckles stung as if she were laying into the door again, and then, suddenly, a door *did* open.

Rowena felt herself stagger forward, a wobbly momentum pitching in her guts, though somehow she knew her feet hadn't really moved at all. She felt a lurch, and then her eyes flooded with a sunlight that glowed through the sky and her skin and the blades of grass in the field all around. A summer wind brushed her cheek. It carried none of the city's damp, doggish smells. The wind mounted into a gale that whipped her hair across her eyes, curtaining a vision of a distant hill—a man lying under a tree, a small, feral, naked thing digging into his chest, his back arching and scream rising—

The Alchemist awoke with a strangled cry, the sound jerking Rowena back into herself like a hook in her spine. She found his hands closed on hers, clamped so hard her fingers had gone numb. He scrambled back from the thing he might still have been dreaming, half-throwing her onto the mattress. Then his head struck the board with a sharp crack.

The Alchemist cringed. Blinking, he looked down at his tight-knuckled hands smothering Rowena's, as if puzzled how they got there. He saw her sprawled before him—and finally himself, bare-chested and tangled in the sheets. Flushing so deeply Rowena could see the color despite his dark skin, he let her go and gathered the covers up around his hips.

"How did you do that?"

Rowena stared at him. "Do what? What happened?" She looked down at her hands and wondered if it was just the feeling coming back into her fingers that made the rumpled bedspread feel like grass, or only the blood thundering in her head that felt like wind.

The Alchemist rubbed his face. In the dim light, Rowena could almost make out the tattoo on his forearm again. It reminded her of the insignia on constables' coats. Some kind of rank—something military? But then it was gone, out of sight. The Alchemist's hand drifted down to his breastbone, lingering where Rowena had been rapping. She remembered the twisted, naked thing tearing at the man under the tree.

"You sounded . . . um. Are you all right?"

"What day is it?" The Alchemist's voice was dusty. He handled it cautiously, like a curio taken from a stranger's shelf.

"Same day. You've been down for hours. Master Meteron's ordered up supper, and I was thinking you might . . . well . . ."

Eejit. Ask him something. "Are you hungry?" "Would you like me to send down for some clean clothes?" "Your things from that parcel are in the solar."

Even in her head, she wasn't doing it right. "*Are* you all right?" she asked.

The Alchemist closed his eyes. "How is Anselm?"

"He's . . ." She thought better of it. "Maybe you should just come to supper."

The old man squinted about the room. His eyes followed Rowena as she stood again, leaving the candle on the nightstand where his clothes waited in a bundle.

"I'll let him know you're coming."

Good. Done now. And yet, Rowena couldn't make herself go. Absurdly, she looked down at her feet peeking out from the hem of her skirt. *Move, damn you.*

"You can ask," she heard the Alchemist say.

Rowena turned. He was making a too-careful study of his shirt buttons as he worked them, as if they held some mysterious interest. *You can ask.* But trying to pick just one question was like fishing the bottom of the quay—the hook would always snag, and when you tried to pull it up, you'd discover the whole muck of creation dangling on the other end.

She swallowed. "You were really in Rare's head, weren't you?"

"What remained of it."

"What did you—"

"Tell Ann I'll be down in a few minutes, girl." The old man's gaze was too plaintive for her to hold long. "I cannot tell it more than once."

Rowena nodded, backing away another step.

And then, suddenly, she felt absurd—full of small, stupid fears she had to outgrow. Her feet stopped moving, and so did her heart, wedged like a cork in her throat. She struggled to work it free.

"I'm sorry," Rowena said. "I don't know what else to say, because I don't even really know you. But I'm sorry about Rare all the same. For what it's worth."

The Alchemist's hands stilled over the buttons. He nodded. "Thank you."

Rowena stared at him a long time, trying to puzzle out what to say next. Then she was back at the threshold, and leaving seemed the only thing that could come next. Slowly, she shut the door behind her, wondering why the carpet felt so much like grass.

In the hours since the morgue, Rowena Downshire and Anselm Meteron had developed a system. Wordlessly, they divided the solar, occupying its opposite poles with the wary tension of enemy states. Rowena kept to the armchair beside the empty fireplace, hugging her knees to her chest and following Anselm's movements as he unpacked papers from his escritoire in large sheaves. Rowena's business was waiting and listening. Master Meteron's was industry.

He sent a spark to the Empire Club, ordering a detail of three men to stand watch over the Regency's foyer, the penthouse roof, and the back lift to the carriage garage. He rang down for Miss Ennis and canceled all his appointments for the next day. He searched for something in the escritoire's bowels. When he found it, he stared at its many pages, leafing through the dense, hand-printed lines with a look entirely too calm for Rowena's comfort.

After waking the Alchemist, Rowena returned to her post and found Master Meteron still manning his, comparing two documents spread on the blotter. She looked to the pianoforte bench, where the Alchemist's frock coat and the canvas parcel lay in a heap, as forgotten as the supper tray on the coffee table.

"I hope you got my pipe back," Rowena heard from the doorway.

The Alchemist studied his partner's frozen face. The younger man smiled grimly, staring at the papers as his friend entered and began a search of his coat's pockets.

"You couldn't pay a man to steal that damned dirty lump of beech," Meteron snorted.

The Alchemist retrieved the pipe and began stuffing it. Silence. Rowena stared at them, wondering if that would be all. Could they possibly act as if there was nothing more to say? Or could it be that two grown men were as afraid of what to say as she had been? The thought left Rowena's stomach in a knot. If none of them knew what to do with the death poisoning the air around them, what would they do about the rest of it? The aigamuxa, and the constables, and the book that still felt as though it hung from a satchel around Rowena's neck?

"I am sorry, Ann," the Alchemist said at last, mostly to his pipe.

"Of course you are." Meteron's voice dripped acid. "Ready to do something about it?" He looked up with eyes keen as daggers.

Rowena didn't need to be a mind reader to know what that look meant: *Tell me who to kill, Bear.*

The old man took the chair beside Rowena. He struck a lucifer from the cigarette box and touched it to his pipe. Meteron stuffed the documents before him into a barrister's envelope.

"What are you doing?" The Alchemist frowned.

"Rare is the principal heir of my estate. I had a secondary version of the will drawn up a few years ago, though, after she made a rather large gamble with both our hides. After that, it seemed a little less certain she would survive me than I'd once imagined." He threw the envelope into an "out" basket flanking the blotter. "I had hoped to be wrong about that. I'll have it sent down to my solicitor in the morning. We can settle the finer details in a few days and refile at the Court and Bar. Too busy before then to possibly keep an appointment."

Rowena looked between the two men. "Busy doing what?"

Meteron swept into the settee opposite her. He plucked a few olives from the dinner tray. "Killing people," he said. "Lots of them."

"*Ann.*"

He smirked innocently, but the anger still glittered in his eyes. "Sorry, Bear. Afraid I'm going to scar the little gamin again?"

"I'm afraid you're going to get yourself killed."

"Of course. You're right," Meteron answered coldly. "I should wait until the first business day of the week to take action, settle up with the solicitor first. Probate is a bloody mess."

"Ann, you don't even know who killed her."

"Then *tell me*!" Meteron struck the coffee table with the heel of his hand. The platters jumped and rattled. They took a long time to stop ringing.

The Alchemist muttered a curse. He set the pipe in the ash stand, letting it smolder.

"Light the fire," he murmured. "Have something to eat, both of you. It will take some time to pull it all back together."

24.

Rowena couldn't muster herself even to think of food. She let the supper tray sit by, ignored, and watched the Alchemist sitting fireside with his head in his hands, staring a hole into the cherrywood floor. Perhaps Master Meteron ate. She had little sense of what went on around her as she watched the old man, the struggle to sort out Rare's fragments written on his face. When her ankles started to burn and ache, she realized she'd been rubbing her feet together, for how long she could only guess. Meteron said nothing of it, this time.

The solar's long windows showed only the distant glow of alchemical lamps and the prow lights of merchant ships threading in and out of port, like constellations reflected on the murky waters. It was full dark when the Alchemist sat back in the chair, pressing his hands to his eyes. He reached for his pipe and tapped out its cold ashes.

Questions had been eating at Rowena. They were still hungry.

"What's it like?" she blurted.

The Alchemist was using the end of a burnt lucifer to scrape out his pipe bowl. He seemed to understand the question's context.

"Every mind is different. A platitude, perhaps, but true, despite."

Rowena waited. She thought she'd finally gotten a feel for the old man. He would tell her what she wanted to know, if she kept at it long enough.

"Minds are abstract things, girl," he continued. "A bit of memory, some personality. A trace of the organic elements of the brain itself. You can't walk into an abstraction, and so you enter the metaphor of it."

Rowena pulled a face. "What's a . . . metaphor?"

"A description of one thing in terms of something else. The mind is full of memories, and so you might say it's a library. Or a museum. Those are common images. Some minds are sprawling manors or rambling estates. Some places in the mind are forests, with memories hanging from trees like fruit or covering the ground like moss."

"And so, with Rare—you went into her metaphor?" Rowena chewed a nail, puzzling the notion out. "You can really just go into minds anytime? Even dead ones?"

The Alchemist turned his pipe in his hands. He looked up, gazing past Rowena. She checked over her shoulder. Master Meteron stood at the foot of the pianoforte, his back to them, a whisky bottle and tumbler at his side. He looked down on the city with a back so stiff he might have been a corpse himself.

"It's not something I've done before," the Alchemist answered. Something in his voice pricked Rowena's ear. *That's a lie. Or near enough.*

The old man shook his head. "It's almost impossible to guard an abstraction or build a shield around a metaphor. So, yes. I can go into minds more or less as I will. But unless the mind in question is distracted, or disabled, somehow—confused or drugged or frightened—"

"Or sleeping?" Rowena suggested. The Alchemist's expression showed he'd noticed the edge in her question.

"Or sleeping. Without those distractions, it's all too easy for a person to realize I'm there. And as a rule, I don't *want* anyone to know I'm there."

Rowena had warmed to the topic, almost forgetting the grim business that had brought them to it. "So, what's my metaphor, anyway?"

"Are we ready, Bear?" Meteron called. He threw a look at Rowena that made her wilt back into her chair.

"Ready."

Meteron sat down on the settee, leaving the whisky behind. Rowena glanced between the two men and realized they were preparing for something. Then it dawned on her.

This isn't the sort of story you can just tell.

Rowena looked at the Alchemist, hoping she had it wrong. He sat back in his chair, nodded once, and emptied his hands. Out of the corner of her eye, she saw Meteron had done the same.

In for the quarter, in for the clink.

Rowena Downshire closed her eyes and nodded—and sat on her hands to keep them from shaking.

It began like a lamp-film ring with the slides all unseated and sliding around pell-mell. Each moment a frozen frame, the Alchemist had lifted them up, peered at them, studied their details to put the sequence together. Now, with each section finally in order, the vision clipped along, the chop-chop-chop of passing images blurring into smooth motion, shapes and shadows and light wheeling into players on a stage.

The story began with the letter in Rare's hands and the sound of glass shattering.

Dear Phillip,

If my recent luck holds, this letter will find you after we've already met, and after you've read my other warnings; that would be best. I did not wish to risk this letter and its contents in a personal meeting. Bishop Meteron's snares are considerable, and I might yet suffer some accident of his design and lose this message with it. He set me on this path from the first, Phillip. I'll be damned to let him lay hands on what lies at its end. That honor falls to you.

Please settle our account with the courier. I've borrowed a little money and laid it by for you in the rectory finances; it should more than cover. Use what remains to pay Gilleyen for her confidence and buy your passage.

The bank is the First Principles Unity in Lemarcke, box 49. Ask for Miss Aneyru. She knows your name and some quite personal details by which to verify you, and will accept the key from no other hand.

Once you've been to the box, you'll know where next to meet me—or how to carry on, if I'm absent.

Yours, etc.

Nora

Rare sees the beast, then starts up the side of the building, in spite of the pistol holstered on her thigh. Its safety knot is still tied, and the aiga is closing fast.

Rare has good hands, strong arms, sure feet. She doesn't look back, because that's the first thing that happens before a fall—even when there isn't a monster on your bootheels. "You never need to look down," *Anselm always said,* "because everything your feet will touch, your hands touched a moment before. You already know where you're going. Down is down—it's gravity; it's a broken neck. Keep your damn eyes up, kitten."

And so she does.

One stretch shy of the gutter framing the tiled roof, a sudden pain shrieks down her right side. The freezing air stings her torn flesh. The aigamuxa has reached up with its wicked hand and pulled down, hoping to drag her off the wall, but its reach is badly aimed. Its eyes show only the ground, not its prey. It loses hold of her leathers and slices them open, instead, claws flensing the flesh below.

Rare screams at the pain, throws her left arm up, pushes with her right foot, feels the scrabbling grasp of the long fingers on her heel.

And then she hauls herself up on the roof. She scrambles back and wrestles her pistol free in a two-handed grip.

When the aiga lifts its head over the roof's edge, it can't see the barrel ten feet away, can't see the muzzle flash. The smell of gunpowder and ozone splits the air, and the heavy shot drills into the center of its eyeless face. Its body plunges into the night, black limbs flailing.

One of the gendarmes in the yard blows his whistle. Rare finds her feet and reels for a moment, the sky full of whirling stars. She puts a hand to her side. It comes away gloved in blood, slick and blue in the moonlight. Her breath saws in her throat.

She is aware of the other aigamuxa only when she turns and its hands close around her throat. Blackness crowds her vision, but she hasn't forgotten the gun.

She raises it.

The aiga has not forgotten the gun, either. It punts her, driving an eye heel into her breastbone. She tumbles end over end, and then there is the free air, her hands flailing for the gutters. The iron ducts cut into her palms as she snares them, her fall broken. She almost loses her grip. Below, the gun clatters on cobblestones.

Above, a shadow spreads over her bloody fingers.

The aiga prowls to the roof's edge. It drags her into its embrace.

A moment later, Rare lies on her back in the yard, heaving for breath. She sees a sky full of stars hovering above and the moon-white faces of the young gendarmes. The aiga's flat, fierce face rises between them like an eclipse. Its body shifts, and then the eye heels flank its head, blinking red rage.

"The one you killed," the creature rasps, "was a bond brother to me, Rare Juells. It will not go well by you now."

"We had . . . a misunder . . . misunderstanding."

The shoulders shift again. She can see they are a map of scars—long, white snakes crawling on gray skin. She shuts her eyes, expecting a blow. One of the junior constables speaks.

"Hold up. She's collared now. Inspector Gammon will want to talk—"

Rare opens her eyes at that name.

The aiga's face turns toward the green policeman, but its eyes stay fixed on Rare.

"She is a murderer."

"En't any criminal statute for a human killing an aiga," the other gendarme snaps.

The creature bares its ragged shark teeth, growling. The sound is something between a rattlesnake's tail and a gorilla's bellow. The men shrink back a step. They share a look. Then they go rigid, distant, back to being coppers.

"What do you know about a delivery girl who came by here yesternight?"

Rare blinks. She realizes the copper must be talking to her. She considers sitting up, but the aiga is nearly squatting over her, and the thought of moving closer to its teeth and its horrible, corded arms— No.

Rare shakes her head. "Nothing. She's just a delivery girl."

They've used her name already, which means they must have been the ones to get the book and the note meant for Ivor. No way to undo what they know already, but still—

"Where is she now?" The aiga speaks this time.

Rare smiles thinly. It is the first time she's ever answered two questions truthfully in an interrogation. She almost laughs. Almost. The aiga is so very close. She remembers the letter in her bag, the name it contains, and that looms every bit as dangerous.

"No idea. Might have gone back to her warehouse."

The constables exchange another look. The one who tried to cut off the aiga starts in again.

"Who else knows of her and the delivery?"

Rare is surprised by how long she hesitates. The satchel with her father's life stuffed in it lies in a heap just a few yards off. She wanted *to pith him. She could send these thugs after him, end him for good and all.*

And she can't do it.

"I'm not sure."

An aigamuxa's bones are heavy—far heavier than their rangy movements would suggest, but they must be to hold up all that muscle and anger and hate. The fist comes down like a hammer. Rare's face explodes in a bloom of pain. She feels her nose break, sees a spray of red in the air.

She gags on the blood. Things are moving in her face that had no hinges before. The voices all clamor together now, half-drowned under her bubbling breaths.

"Dammit, Nasrahiel, she can't tell us anything if you kill her!"

"There's a signal station down the way—I'm going to hail the inspector."

"Bloody hell . . . we're good as dead if this gets out to the rest of the force. They say Regenzi kills folk who let things slip."

"Let the inspector take care of the goddamned lordship."

"Tell her we need some kind of backup to keep this blasted monkey—"

There is another sound, a thud like a fuller's club pounding a hundredweight of cloth. Then the night goes quiet.

Rare smears the blood from her eyes. The second gendarme lies in a heap, doubled over by the blow to his belly, silently heaving up his guts.

The first gendarme has drawn his pistol, but he points it at no one as he backs away. His eyes dart all around. His partner reaches up, beckoning to him from his knees and his pool of bile.

The other man runs.

The aiga curls its feet back down and draws Rare's face up to its featureless brow. Slowly, it rises to its full height. Rare's feet dangle. For a moment she kicks, but it pumps the blood away faster; she loses the will to struggle as quickly as she found it.

"I am expected," the creature called Nasrahiel says, "to make a report. It should be a full one. Help make it so, and it will end quickly."

So Rare gambles. She learned that from Anselm.

"You can find the girl and the Alchemist," Rare gasps, "if you look for Anselm Meteron."

"All three know what the book is?"

"It . . . writes itself?"

The face creases in something too terrible to be a smile. "The reverends thought God writes it." The head tilts left, right, center, considering. "Perhaps you will carry a question, on behalf of Doctor Chalmers? He has been very busy."

"What . . . what question?"

"Ask God if the reverends are right."

The head rears back, then surges forward, heavy brow ridge bearing for her pulped face.

After the pain, everything is stars and stars and stars and stars.

Rowena heard a quailing sound so near it seemed right on top of her. She flinched and realized when she looked at the Alchemist and Master Meteron that the sound had come from her. She found her arms wound round her knees, hugging them close.

Master Meteron reached for his cigarette. There was nothing left in the ash stand but curled paper and cinders. The anger was still on his face, a hard sheen of ice. The Alchemist massaged his temples.

"Neither of you can leave here now," Meteron said after a time. "Not with things as they are. I've called down three of my better security men from the club and put them about the Regency. It will do, until the conference ends."

The Alchemist shook his head. "This won't end when the conference ends. Not with the bishop involved."

Rowena put her chin on her knees. The fire was still going, crackling as bright as if it had just been fed its logs. She stared at the water clock on the mantelpiece, wondering if its gears were somehow done in. Then the second hand flickered once, and again, and again, and she realized the whole vision dug from Rare's mind had passed between them in no time at all.

The fire didn't matter. Rowena still shivered.

The Alchemist rose and walked unsteadily to Meteron's escritoire, taking the lounge coat draped over its back and draping it over Rowena's shoulders. Her hand reached for his, clutching on reflex, as if it could keep her from falling back into the black, starry end that swallowed Rare. Then Rowena remembered to whom the hand belonged and made herself stop short. She bit her lip and wrapped the garment close.

"I don't understand. Who's Bishop Meteron?" Rowena looked back and forth between the men, trying to pry open their closed faces. "Family of yours?"

"My father," Meteron said.

Rowena frowned. "When Rare read the name in Pierce's letter . . . it felt like she was scared of him."

"He has a certain reputation for . . ." He considered the contents of the ash stand and smiled ruefully. "*Implacability.*"

"But he's your *da*. He wouldn't hurt you—would he?"

Meteron's eyes trained on the Alchemist, hard and cold. "No. I don't believe he would. But he's been looking for a chance to kill the Old Bear for better than twenty years." He seemed at last to notice Rowena's puzzled face. "Old business between them. His Grace despises leaving an account unsettled. We have that in common. And you heard the ape, Bear. 'Carry a question for the doctor.' They've kidnapped Chalmers."

Rowena frowned. "But why would 'they' want him?"

"Now that the conspirators have the book they wanted, they need someone to decipher it," Meteron answered irritably. "Do you really think God writes His notebook as plain as a housemaid's shopping list?"

"But that assumes we *believe* God's got a book or something He's writing in for some reason or other. And that we believe these coves have got it," Rowena protested.

"Believe it," the Alchemist said flatly. "If Bishop Meteron asked Nora Pierce to pursue the book and has employed agents in Corma to retrieve it, it's very real. He is not a man who entertains simple curiosities."

Rowena looked to Master Meteron, scanning for his approval. The hard line of his mouth was all the confirmation she needed of the Alchemist's claim.

The Alchemist returned to his chair and lit his pipe. "This morning I made it as far as requesting an appointment with the Council Bishopric and sitting in waiting before the constabulary came to collect me. Bishop Meteron must be the one who tipped the constabulary after my request for an audience. I should have suspected it earlier. I saw the title of the keynote in the conference program. 'God Is with Us.' Chalmers and Pierce seem to think their research revealed objective proof of God as observer. Probably these aigamuxa and their allies captured Pierce some time before the conference and tried to force her to reveal her findings in greater detail. She didn't have the book or the information they wanted. Then they killed her."

Meteron shook his head. "His Grace wouldn't go to the trouble of getting her just to kill her for lack of a few resources. He'd have his men get the book, if that's all that was needed to make her useful."

"How do you account for the body Rare heard about by Misery Bay?"

"There were marks around the neck. She might have made her own way out. A suicide—a hanging."

The Alchemist nodded. "So they needed another scientist. They got Chalmers, but not until after he'd sent the book away. We know how they got it back."

"But who are 'they'?" Rowena repeated.

"Apart from my father? Smallduke Regenzi, apparently," Meteron answered. "Inspector Gammon. The little mysteries make more sense now—the lack of press about Chalmers's kidnapping, the vagueness in the gazette about the death at Regenzi's ball. He would need someone like Gammon to have kept his mayhem quiet."

"Gammon told me the victim from the ball was Nora Pierce," the Alchemist added. "But that would have been some cover agent Regenzi employed. She was killed with a compound he purchased from me two days ago. I've been wrapped up in this business longer than I knew."

His partner clucked his tongue. "*Bear*. You've been holding out details."

"Until recently, that detail was irrelevant. And for most of today, I've been less holding out than catatonic."

"I suppose that's a valid distinction." Meteron looked at Rowena. His mouth twisted into a smile devoid of humor. "Well. They got the EC docs responsible for the work they wanted. They finished the smuggler who ran their correspondence, and the thief who offered to market their research to the highest bidder. If it's loose ends these conspirators hope to tie off, you and the Old Bear would have to be next on the list. Especially given my father's grudges."

Rowena opened her mouth, then let it snap shut.

Meteron raised an eyebrow. "Go on."

"Rare gave up your name, too."

"Well," he murmured, "we all have our bad days. As it stands, I'm more interested in my father's head than he would be in mine."

And then Meteron was on his feet and across the room, opening the glass doors of a bookcase. One section was shaped like a honeycomb, its cells full of long rolls of heavy paper bound with twine. He scanned the shelf and drew two rolls out. The Alchemist lowered the pianoforte's hood to make a flat surface. Together, they rolled out the papers, and Rowena knelt on the bench to get a better view.

One was a map of Corma drawn in black and blue and red, detailed down to its narrow alleys and side streets. The other was a nervous system of jagged lines and cross hashes: a schematic of the under-irons, with the names of the tubes and lines coded by color and distance and the year they were opened.

"What are you looking for?" Rowena looked between the men flanking the maps.

"Our angle," Meteron murmured.

"A way out of this mess," the Alchemist corrected.

Rowena studied the Alchemist, watching him don his spectacles to consider the map. "You're going to look for Chalmers," she said. "Try to kidnap him back."

He grimaced. "Usually 'kidnapping back' is called a 'rescue.'"

"If he's important enough for his work to create a heap of bodies," Meteron added, "I'd like to meet the man—particularly since this cabal seems to think we should join that heap simply because we came into contact with his work." He frowned. "And there's also the small matter of his being the houseguest of some people who owe me restitution."

The Alchemist pointed at the constabulary's central offices. "There are lockups in the lower levels, between the morgue and the main offices. It could be here, if Gammon's in control."

"But she isn't. She's hushing up kidnappings and tracking down loose ends. She's a gopher, not a principal. Pragmatic, but not ruthless. Certainly not devious, and too cautious to keep a serious liability that close at hand." Meteron waved dismissively over the Upper Districts. "Forget Regenzi's manor, for the same reason."

"Here's what I don't understand." Rowena scowled at the maps over her folded arms. "Say Gammon isn't in charge. Say she's taking somebody's orders. Why did she let us all go? There we were, right in the belly of the bloody constabulary. Rare had been dead for hours already. She had to have heard from her officers and maybe even that aiga that we're all wrapped up in this thing with the book. And she lets us *go*? It en't sensible."

"She might have been letting us out into a trap," the Alchemist suggested. "Or hoping Rare's death would scare us into keeping our peace."

Rowena pulled a face. "You couldn't catch a pigeon in a trap that clumsy—and any trap she'd let us out of is no trap at all." But there was something else, too. She chewed her lip. "When you were . . . you know . . . *out* . . . she was acting funny about things. All apologetic and concerned. That's not a copper who's looking to scare anybody straight."

The Alchemist grunted, eyes still on the map. "Perhaps, though I wouldn't leave our fortunes after tonight to the mercy of her conscience."

"Count out all the markets," Meteron decided. "Too mobile and exposed."

Rowena craned closer. "The shipping district? There are lots of old warehouses."

Meteron offered a disparaging noise. The Alchemist shook his head. "Too obvious," the old man said. "Hard to keep secured against thieves or squatters."

They eliminated the Regenzi family's textile mills on the eastern outskirts of Corma; their fulleries on the Westgate Bridge quayside; the five blocks of tenements surrounding Oldtemple Down; the debtors' prison itself; the aeries of abandoned construction sites and rope ladders and fire escapes of Southwater, where the dispossessed aigamuxa tribes squatted; and each of the three prison hulks, ruins of slag floating derelict in Misery Bay. They ruled out locations with more than three angles of entrance. The whole of the Ecclesiastical Commission's campus and the Decadal Conference facilities were scratched off. They were too busy now for some laboratory or even a humble storage room to remain conveniently unused.

Rowena stared at the map, her eyes aching, the colored lines and cross-hatched districts blurring together. *Something* had to fit. Something close by, still in the city. Something you could guard. Something . . .

She felt the prickle of inspiration along the nape of her neck and blinked at the map as if seeing it for the first time. Rowena realized the Alchemist was watching her. She wondered if he'd felt—if he'd heard—the thought ringing through her head.

"What kind of stuff d'you suppose he'd need?" she asked.

Meteron was studying the lightning rail schematic. "Who?"

"Doc Chalmers. To use the book and tell them what they want to know from it."

"Damned if I know."

Rowena felt a smile tugging at her lips. "Well, so—they wouldn't either. But they'd need to get him stuff to work with. All kinds of stuff."

She jumped off the piano bench and looked around the room, scanning its shelves of books and maps and lamp-film cases. "You know, it's funny. I'm not all that different from the aigamuxa. The book about them you read to me—it said they don't care much for human languages and science, right?"

"Not generally," the Alchemist agreed.

"Well, *I* en't sure what *half* this stuff is here, Master Meteron," Rowena announced. She felt oddly proud to make some use of her ignorance. "Most of the stuff back at the Scales is way past me, too. I couldn't name more of it than I could count on my fingers."

"Your point?" Meteron sighed.

"If Regenzi's got a bunch of aigamuxa doing for him, they probably were told to kidnap Chalmers *and* set up a shop for him, but they wouldn't know what to get. They'd do what I'd do—grab a little of everything and hope it would suit."

Meteron nodded. "But they'd need to get it all from somewhere."

"They'd *steal* it." Rowena shrugged. "I would, if I needed it right away. Costs a bloody mint to get all that technical stuff, I bet, and there'd be receipts and deliveries and all sorts of things you could trace."

The Alchemist looked up from the map again, as if something had just jolted into place in front of him. "When I was waiting for my appointment with the Council Bishopric, there was a reverend doctor giving a page hell over equipment gone missing from her demonstration lab. She wanted the gendarmes who were taking me for questioning to record her complaint."

Rowena crossed her arms and grinned in triumph. "Best place to steal science stuff in all Corma's *got* to be the EC's Cathedral campus, especially with the conference in town. And if I was stealing that much stuff, I wouldn't take it far and risk getting caught or busting things. I'd hole up close to where I could get more if I needed it."

"So close by, in fact," Master Meteron murmured, pushing the lightning rail map aside to expose the outline of the Cathedral campus, "that it would be mad to keep him there. Mad enough nobody would think to look there." He tapped the sketch of the Old Cathedral itself. "The foundations could go a hundred feet deep. Who knows how much of that space is stuffed full of old reliquaries and sacramentals the EC has no use for anymore? The old girl's bloomers are practically apocryphal."

"So they kidnap the keynote speaker, and they hide him in the very Cathedral where he's scheduled to speak," the Alchemist said. "It *is* mad."

"And brilliant," Meteron concluded. "Ballsy. Hell, Bear, we might have done the same in their position." He shook his head at Rowena. "You are a passing clever cricket, I'll give you that."

A little part of Rowena glowed at the compliment. She returned to the piano bench. "Doesn't count for much if we can't get in."

The Alchemist's expression darkened. He snapped off his spectacles. "*We?*"

"What do you expect me to do? Sit around here and hope it all goes okay when I could be helping?"

"Point of fact, yes."

Rowena opened her mouth to snap back but stopped short. Meteron was peeling the onionskin backing away from the lightning rail schematic, separating its two pieces—the mounting paper and the overlay, a hazy film with the network of rails threading its surface like lines of frost.

He laid the schematic film over the city map, squared the corners, and there it was.

The foundations of the Old Cathedral were skirted on all sides by the single and double lines of passing rail tunnels. One of the double-lined routes boasted a little purple X drawn just below the bones of the Cathedral's eastern transept.

"Maintenance tunnel entrance," said Meteron. "There's one every half mile."

The Alchemist donned his spectacles again. "I'll be damned. . . . Based on that position, it would almost have to intersect with the Cathedral's drainage system."

Rowena smiled. "Now *that's* jake." She looked between the two men eagerly. "So—what's next?"

Master Meteron and the Alchemist exchanged a glance.

"We've a little more research to do before we could move on this," the old man said. "The kind that takes a trip out in daylight."

"So," Rowena pressed, "what can *I* do?"

"You can go to sleep, Miss Downshire," Anselm Meteron answered, his voice flat and cold. "It's past your bedtime."

INTERMEZZO

In my mind, I've written all this down. I held a quill in my hand, and I made it look easy, guiding that scratching thing all up and down the page. Maybe that's foolish. There must be half a hundred things folks would sooner write about. But I can't help thinking they must choose all the wrong things. Little moments will tell you everything, sometimes. So I've written it all down—in my head, at least. I have a feeling I won't want to forget.

That night, I was passing tired, curled up under one of Master Meteron's housecoats, but I watched everything from under my eyelashes. The sound of the gun parts clacking startled me properly awake, my head still tucked under the coat as I shammed sleep. It was strange, listening to them talk between themselves. You can tell a lot by how they say things—and by what they en't saying, too. I don't know if there's a way to write down what people don't say, but I'm trying, here in my mind. I'm trying to get it all right.

There was a mess all about the solar—long guns and short guns and spring guns and other gizmos, too. Bags of equipment and things that must have come from the room hidden behind the china hutch.

"Don't bother with the carbine."

(That was the Alchemist. I've seen carbines before—gendarmes carry them around Blackbottom End. Meteron had one across his knees, a gun about as long as my arm. Like a rifle but shorter and nasty.)

Meteron showed him something like a pepper box, stacked full of studded rings. "It takes the same caliber as the caplock pistols. I'd rather carry one kind of ammunition."

"If that's a thirty-eight, you'll wish you had more stopping power."

"That's what this is for."

And Meteron showed him something else. Bear glanced up from checking a revolver's cylinder and looked about poleaxed by the pistol in Master Meteron's hand. He took it, weighed it, one hand at a time, real careful. The gun looked like a cannon and a pistol got mixed up together in some armorer's shop. A long, narrow nose, with a flaring trumpet at the end. Shiny. Blunt. Brutal.

"What the devil is this?"

"Enthusiasts are calling them 'semi-automatic grenadiers.' New thing I bought from a dealer in Vraska a year ago. They're common enough there, but the Vraskans won't export them or sell the design, so you don't see them beyond their borders. It'll shoot three times faster than anything else we could carry at five times the power."

"Weighs a bloody ton. You'll never hold it steady long enough to pull a decent shot."

"I don't have to." Master Meteron winked. "It's for you."

Bear tried to pass the blunderbuss thing back, but Meteron wouldn't take it.

"Humility isn't my forte, Bear, but you *are* stronger than I am, senescence notwithstanding."

"Go to hell, Ann."

"You first."

Bear sighed and set the weapon aside. "Given the circumstances, I might oblige you."

"Tsk. It's not like you to have cold feet."

"Cold feet, hell. Cold facts. I'm seven and fifty."

Meteron snorted and did something with his hands that hinged open the stock of some kind of arquebus. He squinted down its barrels. "You're an alchemist," he said at last. "Everything you're good for is age irrelevant. It's all brains—" he tapped his temple, looking serious, "—and this business. You seem to have kept those faculties in working order."

"And what about you?"

Meteron didn't say anything. He looked angry again—angry like he had in the hours before the Old Bear finally came to, the stewing anger that made it hard to be near him.

"After thirty, second-story men age in dog years," Bear pressed. "That makes you around ninety-eight, assuming one only counts the dog years."

"Our assets are *different* than they were, but we still have them.

And I still have a rapacious interest in living out my threescore and ten."

The Old Bear grunted.

"You don't believe me."

"Of course I don't. You've caught the bishop's scent on this business. The chance to foul up whatever game he's playing is enough to send you to the Cathedral on principle. Never mind that you're also furious and vindictive and starving for someone to kill. If you caught Rare being this reckless, you'd have taken her to the woodshed twice over."

Then nobody said anything. The guns clicked as Meteron snapped things into place. Bear kept himself busy with a notebook, making a list—or pretending to. It didn't look like he'd written anything new in a while.

"That was coarse of me," he said quietly.

Meteron snorted. "You might be right. So, are we in the woodshed now? Is that what this conversation is?"

"I'm coming with you, remember?"

"To keep me from getting myself killed."

"Partly that. Partly for Rare. She was my daughter, in spite of everything. She died finding that letter and the key. I saw in her mind where she hid it. Pierce arranged that only Chalmers can use it. We need him, if their deaths are to come to anything. If we're going to get our lives back."

"You don't *have* a life, Bear."

It was a dirty shot, but the Old Bear let it go. He seemed to know what Meteron meant—even nodded a little. When he looked up, he studied his friend's face.

"When was the last time you slept?"

"Last night."

"And?"

"It was fine."

"How long?"

"Maybe four hours. I don't keep track."

Bear frowned at his chronometer. "It's nearly three. If you expect to have those assets you're so sure of come daylight, you should turn in now."

I couldn't really see Meteron's face clearly. He stood up and started rearranging things on the edge of the writing desk—boxes of cartridges and bullets and firing caps. The Old Bear was talking again. The words were tough, but his voice was gentle.

"You're still addicted to the ether?"

"Naturally."

"I can help you use it."

Meteron barked a bitter laugh. "I'd have predicted a temperance lecture from you. Enablement is rather novel."

"Another time. You need the rest. I know how to dose you."

"I've managed well enough myself."

"Fall asleep with the gauze still in place and you won't wake up. Now, are you going to yield to my professional wisdom or shall I threaten you with this new present?"

"You make a compelling argument." Meteron stretched out on the settee and waved back across the room. "Right-hand desk drawer."

"You don't want your own bed?"

"I want to sleep by myself. Not with ghosts."

"There are two other rooms."

"*Here*, Bear. Just here."

I heard some rummaging around in the drawer, the sound of glass being handled. "What dilution have you been taking?"

"Dilution?"

"For God's sake, Anselm—"

He had rolled so his back was to me, no chance of seeing my eyes half-peering from under the coat. "Scold me later, Mother Bear," Meteron sighed. "Just put baby to bed."

I heard more sounds—the Old Bear working with the bottle. The air was full of his tobacco, all marjoram and fennel and damp autumn leaves, but the ether had another smell. Sweet, almost sickly. It tickled my nose, then stung so hard it was all I could do not to scrub at my face.

Meteron talked in a faraway voice—the one people use when they don't mind if what's inside their heads wanders to the outside.

"I think I loved her. Did I ever tell you I asked her to marry me?"

The sounds stopped. "You're joking."

"Six years ago. I was drunk at the time. But I meant it. She said no, of course."

"Usually that ends things between people."

"Usually. But she had good reasons," Meteron conceded. "I could hardly blame her. If I had asked her when I was sober, she said she might have considered it. It was the other thing she said that kept me from asking again."

Bear came and sat on the arm of the settee, his body shadowing Master Meteron's. I couldn't see anything of him but his legs.

"She said it was all in our heads, anyway," he continued. "We could call it anything we wanted. It would be the same."

"I'm sorry, Ann. Truly."

"Do me a favor, Bear. It's very bright and busy up here tonight." I had a feeling Meteron was pointing at something, and I had a fair notion of what it must be. "Make it dark for me. . . . There are dreams I'd rather not have."

"Eventually, you're going to have to face whatever's waiting for you up there," Bear said. His voice had that weary patience people use when they talk to children. I expected Meteron to snap at that, but he didn't. He took it straight—sounded, for a moment, very small.

"I know. Not tonight."

There was something in the Old Bear's right hand, a little wire thing shaped like half of a shell or a sliced egg, a piece of linen lining it. It was sized to cover a man's nose and mouth.

"Not tonight," he agreed and reached out with the mask.

At first, I saw Meteron's legs move, one knee bending up. Even after the dilution, the smell was all honey and acid, strong enough to make my eyes sting. Then I saw his legs relax, his body falling still.

The Old Bear knelt down and put his fingers on his friend's neck, like he was feeling for the life beat. He stayed there a long time. I watched him. The corners of his eyes creased. He studied the air in front of him, or the space inside of Anselm Meteron, or I don't know what, and after a long, slow while, he slipped his hand away and seemed satisfied. He went back to the desk to put away the ether mask.

I squeezed my eyes shut and felt tears leak through my lashes. *It's the ether smell*, I told myself, but it was a lie. There was a hot coal burning right in my throat. I was angry at myself for ever hating the Alchemist. For threatening him. For being afraid. It seemed a cheap thing to do—an easy, cowardly way to make things simple.

Nothing was simple. Not now. Maybe not ever.

A moment later, I felt him gather me up in his arms like I weighed nothing at all.

I don't know why I pretended to be asleep. He must have known I was shamming and just let me have my way. I think— Really, I just wanted him to hold me awhile and take care of me, too. He's good at that, taking care of people. Better than he knows.

Bear carried me to the bed I'd slept in the night before. He left my clothes alone, except for my shoes. He set them by the radiator, then came back to tuck me in. By then I was finally really tired, sinking down into sleep.

Things were pretty dark in there for me, too, that night. A good dark. I don't know if it was all my own doing or if he worked a little something to rest me.

I didn't mind, either way. The pillow smelled of chamomile and rosewater. I could smell the Old Bear's pipe smoke, too, where my hair had rubbed his shoulder. I could write about that scent pressing into my cheek a thousand times over and still not find the words to say how much it mattered.

DAY FOUR

4TH ELEVENMONTH

25.

Rowena Downshire lingered just outside Regency Square's mahogany and granite vestibule. She was back in the trousers and coat borrowed from Rare's trunk at the Scales, happy to have shed layers of skirts and ruffled tunics. She felt fast and ready. For the first time in days, she was completely herself, and that made it easy to watch Anselm Meteron's back with an intensity usually reserved for unwary carters and greengrocers.

Meteron scratched out a message on the concierge's galvano-graph pad. His maimed hand gripped the pen awkwardly between middle finger, ring, and thumb. If his penmanship was as bad as that grip, it was a wonder he didn't just keep Miss Ennis on a lead.

Satisfied that she was in the clear, Rowena walked briskly through the lobby. She did her best to look purposeful, as if she absolutely belonged there and was just on her way out, thank you kindly. She had one hand on the front doors' brass bar when she heard Meteron call her name.

Rowena froze, cursed, and looked back over her shoulder.

He hadn't lifted his eyes from the paper. "Have an appointment somewhere, cricket?"

Rowena let her hand fall from the bar. Several reasonable-sounding responses occurred to her; she chopped each down, wondering *how* he'd even spotted her. Then she noticed the mirror running halfway up the wall of postboxes behind the front desk. Inwardly, she groaned, realizing how easy it had been.

Meteron handed the pad back to the concierge and joined her at the doors.

"Well," he said, "let's be off."

Rowena blinked. "You don't have your hat. Or your greatcoat."

"I wasn't expecting to leave when I came down. Plans change."

"I . . . sort of hoped to go alone," Rowena admitted.

"Hence the sneaking off. I'd gathered as much."

"I'd *rather* be alo—"

"Do you really think," he said, eyes narrowed, "that my father's people will call a moratorium on the hunt so you can run a private errand?" He nodded toward a broad-shouldered man with a folded gazette and a cigarillo standing under the Regency's awning. "Do you think that once you leave this place where I can put a man on every floor and another on the roof you'll be *perfectly safe*? I could have every potted tree in this vestibule replaced with a lanyani bowman and it still wouldn't help you out there."

Rowena said nothing. She glared in his face and crossed her arms.

Meteron shook his head, disgusted. "No wonder the Old Bear likes you. You're cut from the same stubborn cloth." He pushed one of the gilded doors open, raised an eyebrow at Rowena, and waited.

"It's a long walk to Oldtemple," Rowena said. "And it's cold."

They'd been walking ten minutes already. If the cold bothered Meteron, he was of no mind to let it show. He kept his hands in his trouser pockets and stalked beside Rowena as they wended their way out of the Upper Districts to the rough-cobbled streets of Old Town.

There was a feeling to his tension like the air just before a thunderstorm. It gathered around him and drove him forward, like the crackling power suffusing the lightning rail. She kept his pace and kept her peace. It seemed about all she could do.

"It's twelve blocks from Uptown," Meteron said after a time. "We're practically there already. Shouldn't you be making a stop at some pawnmonger's shop to hawk that ivory and silver?"

"I put it all back. I've got some money—what Rare paid me, for carrying the letter she meant for Ivor. Thirty sovereigns."

"She paid you well."

His voice was toneless. Rowena felt she should say something more, but it seemed foolish. She tried another topic.

"Where's the Alchemist gone?" She didn't bother asking why he was allowed out alone in spite of the aigamuxa searching for loose lips to seal. She remembered the telescoping saber, the packets of things drawn from his coat. He'd probably been pursued many times before, and probably had more things to protect himself literally up his sleeve than Rowena could even imagine.

"City records," Meteron answered. "If there have been any major renovations or repairs to the Old Cathedral, there would have to be formal surveys and permits on file."

"Why does that matter?"

"They would have dimensions and schematics of the interior. There were a few things we needed from the Scales, too—that key in the rafters, for one. And I suppose he needed to cave awhile."

Rowena frowned. "Cave?"

"One of the reasons we called him Bear," he explained, "was that after a long stretch of using his mind tricks, it gets to be too much for him. He has to hole himself up awhile, keep his distance from people. It's a little like . . ." He puzzled over the middle distance for a moment, then asked, "Have you ever seen an ambrotype being exposed?"

"Those are the pictures they use for kinotropy, right?"

"And some police records."

She shook her head.

"The longer you expose the image, the clearer it becomes. But only up to a point. If you overexpose, then the image loses clarity. Sometimes the outline warps, or everything gets washed out. You end up seeing something that is, and isn't, what was actually there." Meteron shrugged. "It's like that, the more he uses the power, except he sees overexposures of minds. That's how Leyah used to explain it. Eventually, he starts picking up thoughts and feelings he isn't trying to find. When that happens, he stays away from people until the worst of it passes."

"Caving," Rowena murmured. "Poor Bear."

Meteron laughed. "Time was, we were the finest campaigning group you could hope to contract, and Bear was our best secret. Of course, we all played our parts—Leyah was a brilliant machinist and a crack shot with a rifle. Ivor was ferocious, true idiot-fearless. There was no better second-story man in the business than me, and I might have been a better marksman than Leyah, come down to a firefight. But those mind tricks of the Bear's?" Anselm shook his head admiringly. "You'd be amazed what he could do—the information he could find out, the communications he could relay, the complexities he could coordinate. You'd face the wrath of the Creator if you tried to get the drop on us. There are people in this world who would *literally* kill to do what he can." He fixed Rowena with a warning look. "Save your pity in case any of *them* should ever find out about him."

"You seem to have a lot of those sort in your life. Folks who'd kill to have this thing or that." Rowena looked at Meteron pointedly, hustling to match his strides.

"We've lived eventfully."

"What about your da—"

"His Grace," Meteron interrupted coldly, "is rarely so heavy-handed. There's something else in play. Something bigger than we know." Rowena could see from the line between Meteron's brows how it dug at him, the uncertainty a burr rubbing him raw. "It's the book they have, and Chalmers—and it's whatever's in that box in Lemarcke, as well."

"I never really imagined that EC types could be *dangerous*."

"You'd do well to exercise your faculties more often, cricket."

She glared at him. "It's not like I'm stupid, y'know."

"Stupid, no. Naïve, clearly."

Rowena bristled. She didn't have an impressive host of words at her disposal, but she knew that one. "How do you mean?"

Anselm Meteron stopped walking. He stared down at Rowena, his gray eyes sharp as a knife's edge. "You believe it all, don't you? The idea of the Grand Unity, the gathering together of science and religion. All the peoples of the earth Rational and objective and wise." He shook his head, looking up and down the street. "You can't take a world with half a hundred faiths and convince them all that whatever they *think* they believe it's really just *science*. Not by pinning a treatise to a church door. Not by calling symposium, or giving lectures, or sending emissaries. Not by trade or marriage or open war. We've done all that for nigh on three hundred years, and there are still people in the world waiting for the Unity to collapse."

"Kneelers," Rowena said.

Meteron snorted. "Call them that. Call them Hindoos and Ishmaelites, Gautamans and Protestants. Call them what you will. There are more of us than them, now, and they waltz in time with the reverend doctors because the commission is too vast and powerful to be ignored. But don't think for a moment that they *believe*. I would ask my father what *his* father had in mind when he shaved his forelocks and gave up his shawl, but I suspect His Grace would take that amiss. He likes to imagine the Meterons have always been scions of the Unity. Never mind that any deacon with a little Hebrew under his hat can tell the name for what it is."

Rowena blinked. "*Your* family are converts?"

"Go back far enough and everyone's was. Mine . . . came round a little later than His Grace would like to admit."

"And the Unity is actually divided."

"In scores of unequal pieces. Factions within factions, each with a different notion of how to bring the rest of creation to heel, and none of them able to prove what course is objectively superior for the Grand Experiment. Now, imagine you got wind of a book that shows you *exactly* what God is seeing, right now—all His little notes and marginalia. Mightn't that motivate some *unprecedented* fervor?"

Rowena gazed down the street, past the ever-shabbier storefronts and slack-faced tenements. She scanned the open jaws of alleys. Her mouth had gone dry.

"We're in a lot of trouble, aren't we?"

"Yes, cricket. Yes, we are."

They began their walk again, silence hanging heavy between them. A huge square yawned at the foot of the steep street, opening around a building shaped precisely like a giant red brick and decorated with equal imagination. The name "Oldtemple" was a relic of the city's earliest days, when this had been a comfortable, middle-class neighborhood popular among the Ishmaelite tribes of Hasids and Tzadikim, whose mythologies were the Old Religion's cornerstone.

Oldtemple had been gradually worn down by disregard and desertion until most of its properties were bought up by the governor and his peerage as a haven for the city's lower classes. Inexpensive housing, ready access to the rails, free Ecclesiastical schools and seminars for those who could demonstrate sufficient penury. Oldtemple became Oldtemple Down, and finally its namesake house of worship was demolished to provide the foundation of the debtors' prison and its adjacent alms house.

Anselm and Rowena walked into the heart of Oldtemple Down. At the bottom of the street, the detritus of the neighborhood gathered like a gutter head around the prison walls, smelling of ash hoppers and fish bones and sour wine.

Rowena stood before the prison's slab doors, feeling her shoulders stiffen with a familiar, focused hatred. She'd spent the first six years of her life in that tomb, choking on its airlessness. She'd bloodied her fingers picking oakum for Corma's naval fleet and merchant air galleons. Her first year sleeping in the louse-infested hay of the courier loft had seemed luxurious by comparison.

Rowena realized her companion was watching her, his breath steaming. She felt herself being moved about on the balances of his mind. It made her squirm to wonder what measure she made.

"There's a waiting room," she volunteered, "before you get to the accountant's desk. You'll probably like it better there."

Meteron shook his head. "I didn't leave my home without a coat or hat to let you out of my sight now, least of all here."

Rowena grabbed the rusted iron handle, pulling hard. It was a beastly heavy door—as much to keep folk out as keep them in. She struggled against it, her heels digging into the cobblestones, and still hadn't split the door's seam.

Suddenly, it moved all at once, and Rowena staggered back. Meteron's four and a half fingers held the handle above her hand, tilting the balance and seeing them through.

26.

Anselm Meteron stood outside Clara Downshire's cell, painfully aware of the woman's eyes searching him. Rowena argued at the accountant-turnkey's desk some yards off. She was a foot shorter than him and not half his weight, but she snapped like a rabid terrier, hands punctuating her protests.

Anselm regarded his shoes with a practiced, fictitious interest. He pretended to ignore the ragged woman and her little hellspawn and pretended he wasn't a good enough lip-reader to have made out the crux of the argument—bedsores and mildewed food and an uptick in the keeping fees since Rowena's last visit, just three days prior.

Anselm cracked his knuckles. He rolled his shoulders. He took an impatient mental inventory of his body and felt alert. Strong. Ready. All of this nonsense was preamble, something to pass the time while the Old Bear readied his part of the affair. Anselm had learned patience through a long effort of will. The hours before a job tested it intolerably.

"I hadn't expected you'd still be here."

The voice made him flinch from the lattice at his back.

Clara Downshire was taller than Anselm would have expected, given Rowena's size. She stood with her face uncomfortably near the grating. It irked Anselm to see she had him by a half hand, and barefoot, too. He was not a tall man, nor particularly large, though he had a compact, tenacious strength only a shade less than the barrel-bodied sorts he'd often met on campaign. Experience had taught him he was a match for most of those inelegant hulks. And besides, a tight, unassuming build was an asset to his particular trade.

But it was still galling to look *up* into the eyes of creatures he saw as little more than bedfellows.

If Clara Downshire had been a month nearer her last bath and better fed, she might have met Anselm's standards for a night of company. She had fine, high cheekbones and a full, expressive mouth. But her long, black hair was a dusty nest of snarls, the dress covering her pale, bony body the murky brown gray of the common washtub. She smelled of sweat and her last month's blood.

And she had a beautiful, terrible smile.

It was the angelic expression of a person with no notion what was going on around them, who suffered the world with infinite, eerie patience.

"I beg your pardon?" Anselm asked. She'd said something to draw his attention, only a moment before.

"Said I thought you'd be gone by now," Mrs. Downshire repeated. Again, she smiled. This time, her teeth showed. They needed very badly to be cleaned—or pulled. Likely both.

Anselm wasn't certain he wanted a clarification. He was even less certain what she offered qualified as one.

"It's good you en't. She needs you here awhile, before she needs you there."

Suddenly, Clara Downshire stretched her arms through the lattice, but Anselm was just beyond reach. She pulled back reluctantly.

"That was forward of me. Begging your pardon, sir. I wanted to say thank you, is all."

Anselm stared at the woman, searching her face. It took a will not to turn away from so much deluded sincerity.

"Have we met before?"

"No, sir. But we will. Can't be helped." And then she laughed, the sound discomfitingly childlike. A hand flew up to her mouth. "Or I suppose we just have, and there it is, en't it? Anyway—I'm glad you're still here. Means it's not as late as I thought, and that's a comfort. I get turned around. Time gets bad down in dark places. I'm sure you can imagine."

I am sure I have no god-fucking-damned notion what you mean.

"Of course," Anselm said. He offered a thin, charitable smile.

Rowena stalked up to the cell. "Idiot scribbler bastard. Does he really think—" she rounded on Anselm, as if he were in a position to verify the accountant's frame of mind, "—that raising the keeping fees ten per quarter is going to go over easy? People in the upper floors will riot."

Rowena stopped cold, noticing Anselm's proximity to her mother. "Oh, God." She bit her lip and looked green. "She's been bothering you. I'm sorry—she just . . . She gets these *ideas*, and . . . Look, Mama, I'm coming in awhile, see? There's something I want to talk to you about."

Clara Downshire smiled indulgently and stepped away from the cell door. There was no lock on it. Anselm doubted very much the woman had ever tried to roam. If she had, he supposed the worst danger she posed was filling some other man's ear with nonsense.

The two women retreated to the bench in the corner by Mrs. Downshire's pallet, well away from the privy bucket. Rowena took her mother's hands, speaking with quiet urgency.

Anselm watched for a moment, though he had no need. He'd determined what fool idea had set Rowena out the door of his suite when he spied her in the mirror below the postboxes. They had the whole walk back to Uptown for him to dissuade her of it.

He went to the trestle table where the accountant clerk scratched out his sullen duties. The man didn't look up as Anselm's shadow fell over the ledger.

"Gave you an earful, did she?"

The man grunted. He was fish belly pale, as bad as Mrs. Downshire, but jowly and soft, the way men who spend their lives hunched over figures seemed inevitably to go.

"Little bitch, that one. Didn't used to give lip, but you send them off to pay the red down and all of a sudden, they're popping off."

Anselm glanced back toward the Downshire women. "They were in together, before the Vraskan bought the girl up?"

"The whole lot of 'em—father and mother and three kids, that one smallest. Father was a carter with some bad loans. The wife, she tried to run the business awhile with what he'd left behind. Got kicked by a horse some 'prentice was trying to shoe." The clerk tapped his temple meaningfully. "Lost her wits after that. The Court and Bar put 'em all in here to keep the kids from turning vagrant."

"What happened to the others?"

"Father died of the bloody flux. Older sister, she was let out to start earning. Went whoring but came down with a belly right fast and died by a stillborn. Middle child was a boy. He and that little shit went away with the Vraskan. En't seen him in a deal of years. Suppose he up and died, too."

Anselm looked at the ledger spread before the clerk. "The girl seems to think she can have the debt settled in four or five years."

The accountant snorted.

"If she's got hold of a money-press, maybe. There's five hundred and a fourth bit left on the account." He tapped the page with judicial firmness. "Then there's three sovereigns a month in keeping, and two in taxes. She puts down about twenty a year, usually, after the taxes and keeping. I give her long odds on making black in fifteen years. 'Course, by then the ague or consumption will probably have the old lady, so it'll be a wash."

Anselm said nothing. He was not surprised by the enormity of Rowena's overestimation. He knew more than most men about Oldtemple. Anselm had lent a great deal of money at interest over the years, and on a few occasions, his debtors had had the bad luck or bad sense to fall short on the note. He had deferred his right to prosecute such cases because of the stunning waste it would represent. A little dumb show of clemency—the promise of something other than Oldtemple's darkness and disease—would turn a man's debt of sovereigns into a debt of service, and that was as hard to pay off as the prison's red ledger. But far more useful to the creditor.

Anselm Meteron had no illusions that the system of Oldtemple was fair or even logical. He had no illusions, either, about why it existed.

It was because of men like him.

Rowena got up on tiptoe to kiss her mother's filthy cheek, said something in her ear, and left the cell, letting the grate fall shut behind her. The alchemical lamps cast her wiry shadow far down the corridor as she walked toward Anselm, fists jammed deep in her pockets.

Anselm gave the clerk his little shadow of a bow. It drew a poisonous glance from Rowena, but she stuffed the look away quickly. They stamped down the corridors and past the close, animal smells, through the heavy front doors, and up the hill toward Uptown.

It was a long time before Rowena spoke. She began as Anselm knew she would.

"I said good-bye to Mama, in case things don't go well. So I'm ready for the plan."

"Whatever plan you're imagining we have doesn't involve you."

"The hell it doesn't." Rowena held her chin high. "I en't just going to stay back with your ham-headed guards and let you two get yourselves killed, you know."

"I hadn't realized *that* was the plan."

"Maybe I can help you, huh? Ever thought of that?"

"Not even once."

Rowena glared at the road ahead, plowing up the hill with red cheeks and damp eyes. "I'm fast, and I'm smart, and I'm actually pretty strong, too."

"I kept thinking that as I watched you work that door back at Oldtemple. Intimidating."

"*I'm going with you.*"

"There's not much good you can do for your mother if you're lying dead in the bowels of the Cathedral, cricket."

"There's not much good I can do for her now," Rowena spat back. "Maggie's dead, and Jorrie's dead, and now it's just me, and I've got no job and nowhere to go. So say I *don't* go with you. The Old Bear ends up dead, you end up dead, and I'm back out picking pockets in the Shipman's Bazaar. Then one of Gammon's shields collars me. Some kind of 'accident' happens and I get a matching bunk alongside Rare down in *her* basement."

"If seeing what happened to your mother can teach you *anything* about what your life's worth—"

"The only thing I learned from what happened to my mother," snapped Rowena, "is that there's some people who get kicked by horses and some who don't. That's all. That's what life's worth."

They were obliged to stop at a crossing to let a knot of aiga bar-cranked omnibuses and frilly secretariats clatter by. Anselm shivered against an icy gust that tore down the lane, marveling at how utterly unprepared he'd been for this journey.

He had needed a great deal more than a coat.

"There's a very real possibility that in trying to help, you could put us all in more danger."

Rowena's face was a mask of conviction. "I'll do whatever you say. I know I'm useful. I've met Chalmers. I'm the only one who actually knows who we're looking for, and he might recognize me, too. It could help if he gets nervy."

The idea struck Anselm as the girl stepped off the curb and looked furtively about, checking for gaps in the press of traffic. He knew suddenly how they would get inside, no matter what the blueprints the Alchemist retrieved would say.

He knew *exactly* what his revenge would require.

"You're right."

Rowena's brow furrowed. "I'm . . . what?"

"You're right," repeated Anselm. "Chalmers knows you. You're exactly what we need to get to him."

The girl beamed. She grabbed Anselm's hand—the right hand, not flinching from its maimed touch—and towed him toward the crossway.

"Well *come on*, then! The Alchemist might be back by now! What are you waiting for?"

She was too excited to linger. She let loose his hand and turned, almost running, stopping on the other side of the street to look back expectantly.

Anselm crossed, offering Rowena his arm and a smile when he reached her side again.

He offered her an apology, too, but kept it in his own mind. There were some things she was just too young to understand.

27.

The lightning rail lines beneath Corma ran between thirty and fifty feet underground, always at least two city blocks from the waters of the tidal river or the Western Sea, in case of flooding after the long spring rains. The tunnels had a bone-aching chill that crawled on the ground, a mildewed odor that worked its way into your skin. Rowena had never walked the tunnels before. The experience thus far was putting her off plans to visit again.

The journey had begun back at Regency Square. Rowena and Master Meteron returned a little before the dinner hour to find the Alchemist checking off a list in the secret office, surveying an array of equipment. His spectacles perched on the bridge of his broad nose, but there was also a pair of goggles hanging down around his neck, all brass and dark, thick lenses. A postman's bag rested against his hip, the telescoping saber sheathed on his thigh. The beastly pistol Meteron gave him sat in a holster under his left arm.

Rowena had taken one look at him frowning down at a notebook through his spectacles and half-choked on a laugh.

The Alchemist glanced at her reprovingly. Meteron swept the old man's coat off the back of a chair, throwing it open to reveal a lining checkered with padded pockets of every size and shape, a patchwork quilt of compartments, stocked and ready. He rifled them, then turned to his partner, a little phial tucked in the palm of his four-and-a-half-fingered hand. The old man took it, raised an eyebrow, and cast Anselm a skeptical look.

Rowena watched Meteron in baffled silence as he hummed his way through gathering up his own kit. He craned his neck to check the Alchemist's list, then exchanged a few comments about the building plans drawn from the Ministry with the older man. He seemed . . . cheerful.

"Be a love, Miss Downshire," he called at last. "Ring down to Benjy for something to eat."

Rowena frowned. "Like . . . ?"

"Anything quick. We'll need a little time after to pull some of Rare's things out for you."

The Alchemist looked up from a sheaf of notes. "The hell we will."

Meteron offered Rowena an indulgent smile. "And be sure to dawdle in the solar after the call so your pet Bear and I can have a little row."

Rowena was about to insist on making her own case when he shooed her with an insistent raise of his eyebrows.

Just go, it said. *I'll take care of it.*

She could hear the range of tones in the argument, though not the words, for they closed themselves up in the office behind the china hutch. She found it hard to resist listening by the dining room door, but a sudden fear that the Alchemist might overhear her thoughts pushed her back down the hall. At the solar door, something nudged Rowena in the back of the knee.

Rabbit sat behind her, sporting a wagging tail and a lolling canine grin. He must have been asleep over by the fire, unnoticed. She lost herself in rubbing his belly, only remembering to ring for food when her own started to rumble.

The two men emerged just as the dinner cart came up. Rabbit thundered over to Meteron, throwing his paws on his host's chest and licking his face. He shoved the dog off and scowled at the Alchemist.

The old man shrugged. "Couldn't countenance leaving him at the Scales again after all that's happened."

"I hope he uses papers."

They ate over notes the Alchemist had scrawled on lithograph duplicates of the Cathedral's various levels, from the clerestory and lower transept down to the cellar. They learned only a little more about what to expect once they entered the drainage system tunnels, but the cellar itself was worth investigating closely.

Rowena returned to her guest room and dressed in the best-fitted combination of leather, wool, and corduroy Rare's childhood castoffs could supply. She slipped her knife into a tall black boot and raked her hair back with two heavy combs. Studying herself in the washstand's glass, she fancied she looked an adventuress—smart and ready and fearless.

Then she spied Master Meteron standing in the doorway behind her.

Seeing the Alchemist outfitted for action had been odd. Seeing Anselm Meteron this way was like meeting him for the first time.

He wore black gauntlets tailored for his index finger's stump, and a charcoal shirt under a black leather waistcoat scored where a blade once sliced it. He carried two caplock pistols and a knife strapped at his thighs. A chest rig held the carbine, broken down in pieces. If Rowena had seen the Alchemist's clothes and Meteron's hanging side by side, she would have been hard-pressed to mark any real difference between them. Both kits were dark and durable, studded with extra pockets and compartments. Both announced a certain efficiency and precision.

But the Alchemist, Rowena realized, could not have worn clothes like Meteron's, even if they had been tailored to his size. His dress was plain and purposeful. Meteron looked like a man who had turned evening formalwear into something deadly.

He offered his bow that was only a nod and swept his coat—cut more like a dinner jacket than a long coat—over one shoulder. For a moment, he looked like a stranger. Then Rowena realized he'd shaved his moustache. Its absence left his wry mouth wickedly untamed.

The Alchemist came up behind the thief. He shifted the bag on his shoulder and shrugged into his frock coat, and without a word spoken, all three left together.

They began in the lightning rail station of Ippining, just on the border of Midtown and the north end of Oldtemple Down. After the first train passed and the platform conductors began a circuit of the station, waving off vagrants and buskers, the Alchemist slipped off the platform to the rail floor below. Meteron handed Rowena down to him, then stepped off the platform, landing in a crouch. A hundred yards farther on was a side passage that they followed to the Ravenswood line. The Ravenswood had been closed by the governor's offices for better than three years, shuttered by a string of derailments.

Since then, they had walked so many long, winding paths lit only by the Alchemist's magnesium torches that Rowena doubted they would ever reach the Old Cathedral. The electric charge of action that had lifted her steps before had fizzled out. There was strikingly little to *do* other than keep her place between her companions as they walked the disused tracks, giving the third rail a wide berth. There were a hundred questions Rowena longed to ask: Had they been in the under-irons this way before? Or the sewers? If Ivor and Leyah were here, what would they be doing right now? Had the Alchemist fired a gun that big before? Just how good a shot was Master Meteron, anyway? She wanted to fill the time with tales of glory and intrigue, but there had been rules set down over dinner. They hadn't been complicated. She meant to show she was up to the challenges of the day by obeying them.

"First," the Alchemist had said, pinning the rule down on the coffee table with the tip of his finger, "no chatter. We'll be in a deal of trouble if we're heard coming. Second, if a fight starts, stay *behind me*. Not Anselm."

Rowena had frowned. "Why not him?"

"Because chances are good that if a fight starts, I'll be the one in the middle of it," Meteron answered. "Assuming precedent holds."

"And if it doesn't?"

The thief chuckled. "Then get behind me and wish you had bigger cover."

"So no chatter. Stick with whoever's under cover. Is that all?"

"No," the Alchemist said. He'd been looking at the map of the clerestory level, examining a staircase curving up toward the bell tower. He removed his spectacles, as if they might put some barrier between his words and her ears, and held Rowena's gaze a long, uncomfortable time. "Rule three is if we tell you to run, run. No stubbornness. No looking back. Get as far off as you can, as fast as you can."

"And then?"

He smiled. It was the weakest of lies trying to hide in the honesty of his face. "I'll find you later."

Rowena nodded down at her watered ale. And then her lips twisted impishly. "Do I get a gun?"

The answer had been no. In a panic, with no aim or experience, Rowena was as likely to shoot one of them as anything threatening. And so, she endured the long walk with her knife scraping inside her boot, somewhere between bored and frightened. The walk supplied no conversation and nothing more interesting than the long, rust-colored trails left in the stone by rainwater seeping down. She had seen twenty-three rats and countless miles of cobweb stitched by long-dead spiders. They passed a tilted, twisted forecarriage and spark engine that had once headed a derailed train. Most of the windows were knocked out. The beam of Rowena's torch flashed across an interior eaten up by mildew and nesting things, some of the old wrought-iron benches pried up and carried off by some squatter king's muddy princelings, hunting salvage.

Rowena stopped wondering how this venture could turn exciting when Meteron gestured with his torch toward a short iron ladder punched into the tunnel wall. The ladder seemed to start much higher off the ground than it should have—eight feet at least, perhaps ten. Rowena blinked at it in puzzlement before she realized he had stopped just short of a place where the tracks twisted sharply down, the rocky floor sinking into a pit of rubble and wreckage. The avalanche of debris had bent the lower ladder rungs, tearing most of them away, leaving the ones farther up the wall just beyond the Alchemist's reach.

"Well," Meteron said, "I think we've investigated the derailment." He waved his torch back toward the wrecked car and engine some hundred feet before.

The Alchemist nodded. "Sinkhole. The train must have been going fast enough to jump tracks over the gap." He considered the rung ladder poised five feet beyond the lip of the sinkhole. The ground that would have put it just barely in reach had long since fallen away.

Meteron dialed down his torch and handed it to the Alchemist. He walked to the sinkhole's edge, checking the distance. "I can reach it if you give me a boost."

"No."

Meteron shot the Alchemist a bemused grin. "*No?*"

"I want to see if the assets we need are still there. Jump it."

"You want me to clear nearly ten feet of height in a leap over a bone-breaking hazard?"

The Alchemist crossed his arms. "If clearing this gap is the worst thing you have to do tonight, you'll be lucky."

"Bastard," Meteron sighed.

He fussed with his gloves. The Alchemist made an impatient noise. His partner ignored it, glancing between the rung ladder, the jagged gap below, and the space between himself and its edge. Ten feet, perhaps.

He walked it back to twenty.

The Alchemist stepped across the path that was to be Meteron's runway. Rowena followed on his heels. They took stations along the tunnel's opposite wall, watching.

At thirty feet back, the thief at last seemed satisfied. He considered the path, rolled his head over his shoulders, leaned forward, and tore into a full run.

He jumped about three feet before the gap, coming off his right leg toward the ladder wall, still several feet short. He pushed off the wall with his left leg for another surge of height.

The distance closed, almost sailing by. Meteron snatched the ladder's lowest rungs, legs swinging past, then whipping back in a pendulum motion. He planted his boots into the wall, grinding to a halt.

Meteron had bounded off the wall like a cat, all power and perfect timing. Rowena clapped a hand over her mouth to stifle a whoop. He winked at her. The Alchemist rolled his eyes.

"Good enough?" Meteron called.

Rowena doubted he could see the Alchemist's smile through the glare of their torches. "The wall jump was a cheat."

"I wanted to be sure. You first, cricket."

"Me first, what?"

"Over by the edge. Grab the sleeve and hold tight."

Master Meteron climbed up a few rungs. He hooked his knees in the ladder and bent back until he hung upside down, within five feet of Rowena's hand, if she got on tiptoe and leaned out over the crumbling lip of ground as far as she dared. He slipped free of his coat, wrapping one sleeve around his hand and wrist, and swung it toward her.

Between the length of his extended arm and the span of the conscripted coat, there was plenty of sleeve left to grab. Meteron hauled her to the lowest rung. She grabbed it, let go of the coat, and edged around him, climbing the ladder to the access hatch above.

Below, Rowena heard a rustle, a grunt, a tearing sound, and two curses. She stopped short of the hatch and looked down. The Old Bear was pulling himself onto the bottom two rungs, Meteron righting himself with a slow, groaning sit-up. One of the jacket's back seams yawned open. Meteron sighed and dropped the garment into the sinkhole with a salute.

"That was one of my better field coats," he sulked. "You've put on a bit, Bear."

"I'm carrying most of the equipment."

"Of course. That *must* be the trouble."

On the other side of the access door was a room so small even Rowena found it cramped—probably a disused storage closet for rail maintenance crews. Beyond it stretched a corridor that eventually found its way into the Cathedral's drainage system, as the Alchemist had predicted.

Rowena wasn't sure what the difference between a drainage system and a sewer was. She had imagined it would be filth, but the smell inside suggested otherwise. The ground was submerged in two inches of black water, drifts of half-frozen mold floating in archipelagoes along its oily surface. Her breath steamed. It hurt to hold the dank room's air in her lungs overlong. There was another iron ladder, rusty and damp. The Alchemist stayed at the rear to catch Rowena's feet when they slipped on the frosted metal.

Finally, Meteron pushed a hatch open. He climbed through, crouched beside the hole, and pulled Rowena up after. She fished out her torch and swept the beam slowly around. Meteron drew a pistol and smirked.

"God's rummage sale."

There were crates stacked up along one wall, the top ones unsealed, protruding thatches of moldering straw and the glossy edges of statuary. Paintings slouched against one another, like books on a shelf missing its bookend. Mice had been at some of the canvases, but Rowena could still make out many of the images—oils of men in robes and sandals, one of them usually taller and more beautiful than the rest, his hand raised in a vague gesture over the other people. Glowing figures hovered aboveground, huge, feathery wings stretching out behind them. It took a moment for Rowena to see the wings weren't decorations *behind* them but *part of* them.

She felt a hand on her shoulder. The Alchemist looked down at her. "Be ready to move along."

Meteron pushed crates and dollies draped in canvas away, revealing a door. "Time?" he called.

The Alchemist flashed his torch over his chronometer. "Three o' the clock. Sunset is at five forty-eight today."

"Good," Meteron answered. "I think we'll manage this yet."

The Alchemist joined him in clearing the largest of the obstructions away. The door was hinged to open outward, into whatever hall lay beyond.

"We'll avoid most of the aigamuxa if we keep ourselves under an hour," the old man grunted to Meteron as they worked, "given their nocturnal habits. But we don't know how many humans to expect."

"The keynote was supposed to have been yesterday. That's got to have caused a stir. Whatever EC confederates Regenzi has are probably off with the other huggins and muggins spreading gossip to keep eyes away from here."

The Alchemist reached under his coat, drew the hand blunderbuss, and checked the pepperbox-sized cartridge jutting down in front of its trigger. "That story requires more luck than I remember us having. Take the right, Ann."

Then the Alchemist put a shoulder into the door. He used its cover against whatever might be up the hall, training his heavy pistol past its edge.

Meteron stared up the right side of the passage, right hand holding the torch at his shoulder height and left holding the gun at arm's length. He gave only the side of his body as a target, Rowena saw, shoulders pointing in a line back toward the Alchemist.

"All clear."

"Lights down this way," the Alchemist said. "Globe lamps, fifty-foot spacing." He flashed a quick look back into the storage room. "Stay close, girl."

Rowena padded into the hall. Meteron took the lead again, but the Alchemist stood between him and Rowena, blocking her view of much of the hall—and, she realized, anyone else's view of her.

"Um . . . excuse me?"

"No chatter, remember?"

"I know, but . . . why're we going *toward* the lights? En't that where people will be?"

"It is," the Alchemist allowed, his voice a murmur. "Human beings need light. The captors will use them as they stand watch, and Chalmers will need them to do whatever work they expect of him. The lights will lead us to him."

"And if they lead someone to *us*?"

"Just stay close and remember the rules."

They put away the magnesium torches. Eventually there were doors to rooms dotting the hall and beyond them a little stairwell. Meteron kept watch over the passage, his flint eyes flicking this way and that, while the Alchemist listened at the doors. It seemed to take longer than it should, until Rowena considered that the old man was probably listening with more than *just* his ears.

She heard the footsteps coming down a moment too late. When Rowena opened her mouth to cry out, the two men wearing the black-and-gold livery of EC security drew their pistols on her.

Meteron had been facing the opposite way, but he heard the guns as they were drawn and whirled.

For a moment, no one moved.

Meteron aimed for the guard standing nearest Rowena. The other man trained his weapon on her, pacing closer, his eyes on the thief.

The Alchemist crouched by the door, the blunderbuss pointing down. He could never raise it and take aim before the guards fired.

"God's balls," Meteron sighed. "Bear?"

The man watching him put the barrel of his gun between Rowena's shoulders. For the first time, she noticed her heart racing. The room swam. She felt too hot, as if she might be sick.

"Drop it, Ann," the Alchemist said.

His partner spat a curse and opened his hand. The gun dangled from its trigger loop before clattering to the floor. The Alchemist set the blunderbuss down, put both hands in view, and stared at the man with his barrel in Rowena's back.

"Take the gun off the girl and we'll come quietly."

Over the blood pounding in her ears, Rowena heard a metallic noise, something coming from the gun pressing into her spine. The caplock hammer being thumbed back.

The guard aiming for Meteron frowned at the blunderbuss and its flaring snout. "Kick that thing over."

The Alchemist rose slowly, hands by his shoulders. He kicked the gun. It spun away. The guard watching Meteron bent to pick it up. His eyes widened as he weighed the huge pistol in his hand.

Then he pointed the blunderbuss at the Alchemist. The barrel in Rowena's back dug deeper.

"Now, how about you come quietly anyway?"

28.

The man who had to be Smallduke Regenzi sat at a long trestle table in the center of a room full of cabinets, shelves, and spiral indices. It reeked of the sweet, archival decay only very old libraries can perfect, full of things priests and parsons used to catalog when the Old Religion held sway—birth and death and marriage records for people hundreds of years gone. Regenzi wore a fine jacquard-trimmed doublet with knee-length britches, all jade green and dark, opalescent blue. He looked pleased by whatever was spread out on that table, a smug, hungry expression sitting between his side-whiskers.

Maps. They lolled off the table's edges, their surfaces scrawled with hasty notes in crimson ink.

The florid man standing beside Regenzi was dressed like a deacon. He looked near as pleased as his lordship. Both watched the guards herd Rowena through the doorway, gun still grinding between her shoulders. The Alchemist and Master Meteron followed after, the second guard covering both men. The hand blunderbuss was tucked into his belt.

Regenzi stood, his eyebrows rising. "The Alchemist. I was unaware you made house calls."

Meteron rolled his eyes. "Oh, for God's sake."

In a blur of motion, he drew his knife and kicked the knees of the guard covering his back. The guard cried out, buckling, and dropped the weapons to clutch at his leg.

The guard threatening Rowena whirled but stopped short of shooting when he saw what was happening.

Anselm Meteron pressed his knife to the Alchemist's throat.

The room fell still.

"I can cope with being marched to your inner sanctum, Regenzi," Meteron said, eyes locked on the Alchemist's shocked face. "I can endure the requisite gloating. But really, *puns* are the lowest conceivable behavior. You might hold yourself to a higher standard."

Regenzi's face was at least as puzzled as the Alchemist's. "I . . . see. And you plan to intimidate me out of the habit by threatening to murder your ally? Ingenious."

"Ann, what the devil are you doing?" the Alchemist growled.

Meteron's eyes flicked to the far corner of the room. Rowena followed his gaze into the shadows and felt her knees tremble.

The aigamuxa who robbed her had been big. This one stood a head taller, even in its crouch. She could see the white trails of old scars snaking down its shoulders, reaching up its back. As it balanced, its long, taloned fingers flexed, drumming the floor. Impatient. Its gaze touched Rowena. The drumming stopped. Slowly, the aigamuxa's head tilted to the side. Its teeth bared, and Rowena realized the aiga was *smiling*.

And that she knew its name.

The Alchemist groaned. "Ann, you stupid bastard—"

"My lord," Meteron called, "I am offering you a trade."

Regenzi frowned skeptically. From Nasrahiel's dark corner came a rattling growl.

"Before you make the offer, it might help if I knew who you are."

"Anselm Meteron."

"*Really?*" Regenzi clucked his tongue. "*Tch*. My condolences. I've heard you suffered a loss. I had hoped it might dispirit your interest in this whole affair, for reasons of your own health."

"My friends always told me I'm rather cavalier about my health. Do you still have Chalmers?"

Regenzi's face was unreadable. The deacon beside him looked damp and nervous.

Meteron watched the Alchemist carefully as he spoke. "If you're going to kidnap a man and litter Corma with bodies, Regenzi, you'll need to learn to stand by your work. If you're keeping Chalmers, it's because you want something from him. I imagine you'd like it quickly."

"Ideally," Regenzi admitted. "But if you expect good work, it can only be done so fast."

Meteron shrugged. The movement turned the knife against the Alchemist's skin. A trickle of blood ran down its edge. The Alchemist hissed, tilting his chin to evade a deeper cut.

"Pain can be a great motivator," Meteron observed mildly. "Even someone else's."

His eyes found Rowena. She felt their bite like the heads of two arrows.

She was the way to get to Chalmers. That had been Meteron's plan—why he'd fought to have her along.

"You bastard," Rowena whispered. "You *can't*."

"For all practical purposes, cricket, I already *have*." Meteron addressed Regenzi again. "This is the girl who delivered the book to Chalmers. He knows her—even let her have a spot of tea in his study. Very cozy. I imagine he would be motivated to operate efficiently and transparently if he were given reason to believe her welfare was at stake."

Regenzi looked doubtful. "Possible. But he has been cooperative."

"It won't last. I've done the captive experience before, from both sides. There's a rather brief shelf life on what passes for cooperation."

"So you're trading the girl . . . for what, exactly?"

"Satisfaction of my curiosity about your motives, and of a grudge."

"Two things in exchange for one?"

Meteron gestured to Nasrahiel, almost inviting. "Two for three. I'm trading the girl *and* consequently tying off two loose ends. All that in exchange for ten minutes alone with your overfed monkey."

Nasrahiel made a sound—the sandpaper slither of a desiccated laugh.

"I take it," mused Regenzi, "you weren't hoping to have a thoughtful conversation?"

"I imagine it will involve a lot of screaming. His."

"Your friends are right about your being cavalier, Master Meteron."

"Perhaps. But those people are dead now. If my outliving them is any measure of their judgment, I like my odds. Besides, if it's a bad bet for me, what loss will you suffer? You keep your killer monkey bastard, and your street urchin hostage, and I've tied up yet another loose end for you."

"Ann," the Alchemist said, "the aigamuxa will take you apart."

Then the old man looked to Regenzi. The guard Meteron had disabled limped to the smallduke's side, showing him the blunderbuss and murmuring something. Regenzi noted the Alchemist's stare. He lifted an eyebrow indulgently.

"Something you wish to say?"

"Let the girl go. She's harmless."

"Before you brought her here, arguably so. Now she's seen things that worry me. And your friend has a point about leverage." The smallduke weighed the blunderbuss in his hands and shrugged. "As for you? Well. You understand I will need him to demonstrate the sincerity of his convictions."

Meteron pressed the point of the blade to the Alchemist's flesh again. He reached a hand toward Rowena's guard, fingers riffling the air in request.

The man looked at the dumbstruck deacon. Slowly, he nodded. The guard turned the gun and offered it to Anselm.

Rowena sprang forward, shrieking. Then the guard had her by her collar, wrapping his arms under hers, hands knitted behind her head. Her neck screamed in pain as she thrashed and spat. With a grunt, the guard tried hauling her away.

"Rowena!"

She stopped shouting because the voice belonged to the Alchemist. Rowena's heels bucked above the slate floor. His gaze held her fast, its grip stronger than the guard's hands.

"Close your eyes," he said.

Rowena's throat tightened. She shook her head.

If I close my eyes, it'll happen. Master Meteron can't do it if I'm watching him. If I close my eyes, the Old Bear will die and I could have stopped it. I won't close my eyes.

"Rowena, please."

"I'd listen to him, cricket." Meteron thumbed the caplock's hammer. Its black nose hovered over the Alchemist's coat.

The girl mouthed the curses she couldn't choke free, her eyes stinging.

"Or you can have it your own way," Meteron sighed. He turned to the Alchemist. The old man looked sick. "Ready, Bear?"

The Alchemist nodded.

"Give Leyah my love, then."

The revolver was small, but it filled the room with a thunder that rattled Rowena's teeth. For a moment, there was only its roar and the pale, trembling silence after. She was aware of her own screaming through the pain in her throat, the feeling of something tearing free of her heart.

The bullet punched a hole between the Alchemist's lapels. There was a thin, red mist, then an arc of blood bursting forth. He lay on his back in a red pool, the grooves between the stones drinking deep.

Sound seeped back into the room. The rest was a blur.

Smallduke Regenzi stooped by the Alchemist's corpse and put his fingers to his neck, waiting. The first guard was gone, and then he was back, an aigamuxa lumbering on his heels.

There were gestures. Words. Some searching around the Alchemist's body. The aigamuxa hauled the big man over its shoulders. Meteron had passed the gun back to Regenzi, or perhaps the guard with the aiga had taken it from him, or perhaps the deacon, or perhaps— Rowena just didn't know. Her head hurt. She was crying, airless and gasping. She stopped bucking in the guard's grasp, her vision smearing about the edges.

Rowena thought she saw Meteron speaking to the smallduke, but her eyes swam, and her ears were so full of her own pounding heartbeat she barely noticed the guard dragging her down the hall.

They followed the shadow of the aigamuxa bearing the Alchemist. A wet, red trail marked its passage.

29.

The Reverend Doctor Phillip Chalmers was making remarkable progress deciphering marginalia on the exploits of Subject Three when his cell door banged open.

The guard shoved a snuffling form with a ragged mop of brown tangles into the room before checking the lock and stalking away. Chalmers sat on his stool, blinking in owlish confusion. The girl's clothes were sodden and foul-smelling, shirtsleeves torn in a struggle. She knelt where the guard had dumped her, staring at her hands. Chalmers chewed his pencil. Twice, he rose to offer some assistance. Twice, he thought better of it and sank back down again. Then he noticed her pale, dirty hands, the knuckles white with scars.

He'd seen them before, holding a teacup and lemon cakes.

"Downshire," he announced suddenly.

The girl looked up. Her face was a soggy, red blur.

"It is Downshire," Chalmers repeated. He dug about his waistcoat for a handkerchief and began folding what he found in search of an unsoiled square. "*Rowena* Downshire, isn't it? I'm rather good with names."

She nodded. He approached with the same furtive care he might use around a strange cat, crouching beside her and offering the handkerchief. Chalmers winced as she wiped her dripping nose then smeared the sodden cloth all about her eyes.

"When the brutes gave me back the book, I had thought they must have—well." He had meant to say something about being sure she was dead, and finding relief in her being all right, but it was evident the girl *wasn't* all right.

"Bless the Proof, you're a mess," he tsked instead. "What on earth are you doing here?"

Rowena blinked at the handkerchief, wringing and balling it

by turns. She gulped air, seemed about to marshal a response, and yet nothing came. And nothing came. And, still, nothing came. Chalmers fidgeted, wondering if there was some way to nudge her along.

"We were going to save you," she said finally. "But now he's dead."

Chalmers blinked. "I'm . . . sorry?"

"It isn't *fair*," Rowena shouted. He recoiled from her snapping face. "I *followed* the rules, and I did what he said, and it shouldn't have happened because I didn't . . . I didn't . . ." Her lower lip trembled. "I didn't close my eyes."

The girl hugged her knees and sobbed as if she might split down her seams. Chalmers watched. He felt he ought to do something. People *did* things at such moments, buoyed each other, offered solutions or comforts.

Inspiration struck. He reached out, patting the girl's shoulder. "There, there," he said. It produced no effect, but, he supposed, he might have used the wrong tone. "There," he added, sweetly.

For a long while, Phillip Chalmers sat dutifully by, offering up adverbs at cautious intervals. Or would "there" be a noun—or an adjective—in this situation? Perhaps merely an interjection? His gifts were not in letters, much less gentling, and so he fetched bits of gauze or muslin for the girl once the handkerchief was utterly exhausted and experimented with the parts of speech until, at last, she peered over her kneecaps, taking in the room. Her bright eyes lingered at turns on the shelves of laboratory glass, the centrifuges, the drafting table, the treadle-powered dynamo trembling beside the particle detector's darkened face.

"It's just like we'd thought it would be," she said, sniffling.

"Beg pardon?"

"Is any of this stuff actually good for anything?"

Chalmers felt a flutter of relief. Perhaps the worst was over. If the girl was of a mind to tour the room, that could prove a fine distraction.

"Well," Chalmers said, standing. He gestured about with a proprietary air. "It's all good for something. I don't have need for very much of it under the present conditions, but— Oh, dear me." He remembered himself, offering the girl a hand up a moment too late to actually perform the courtesy.

She was stepping hesitantly toward his table and notes, touching things with curious, light fingers. "This writing looks . . . funny. Is it Amidonian?"

"Um, no. No, I'm—I'm really not sure *what* to call it. Doctor Pierce liked the term 'Enochian,' but that struck me as melodramatic. Very *Old Religion*, you know."

Rowena scanned the writings, her face blank.

Chalmers frowned. "You . . . don't read?"

"Can't."

"That's dreadful."

She gave him a sour look. "Well, *sorry*."

"No, no, I didn't mean that you . . . or that . . ." He bit his lip and began hurriedly straightening his cot, feeling a sudden impulse to improve upon his missteps through better housekeeping. "That's not what I meant."

Chalmers stole a glance over his shoulder. The courier girl walked the room in a slow circuit, always touching, sometimes lingering. Beside the dynamo and the particle detector, she paused. The apparatus growled as she circled it, throwing up a handful of white sparks.

"Does it do this a lot?"

Chalmers dropped the sheets and scrambled over. He knelt beside the machine, turning its dials haphazardly, trying to calm its protests. *How the deuce was it even active?* Chalmers had left the display itself off. He was quite certain of that. It was one thing to keep the crank battery connected to the apparatus charged, but he worried constantly of damaging its lenses, perhaps burning the phosphor screen. He'd let the detector run overlong the night before, and after that carelessness, he was *certain* he'd turned the display *off*.

"Blast it! It's overheating. I had a notion of asking to take it up to the bell tower with a telescope, so I could compare the diagrammatic path of—" When Chalmers looked up, he found himself and the girl on opposite sides of the glass.

Now the screen was afire with motes of light. They poured in all around Rowena Downshire. He could see her face clearly, a topography of pointillism, its finest movements perfectly animated. Heat poured off the display glass, the air around it trembling.

Phillip Chalmers opened his mouth. No sound came.

On the other side of the screen, two golden eyebrows lifted.

"Is it a short or something? I've heard electric stuff gets those—shorts. Whatever they are. Did you find one?"

Chalmers stared. When he found his voice, it cracked. "Found . . . something."

Anselm Meteron and Abraham Regenzi stood in the open doorway of the sacramental locker, the room dark and still except for a shallow, ragged breathing deep within. They had been standing there a long while—long enough for Regenzi to tell Meteron most of his justifications, refined to a near-theatrical performance.

Anselm could tell it frustrated Regenzi to find his new ally so hard to impress, and that made the worst part of him very happy indeed. The young lord had sense enough to pretend indifference to Meteron's calm. Anselm supposed he might have been a good cardplayer, especially with that hard, knowing smile.

"So, to sum up—" Anselm let himself sound as bored as he felt, "—you're working for agents who are afraid God will give up on the world if these test subjects don't perform as He intends, and for lack of clear information as to what desirable performance looks like, you're hoping imprisonment and total social control will prevent a fatal misstep."

Regenzi offered him that cardplayer's smile. "To sum up, I'm saving the world."

"At most, you're saving your own arse. It's only a happy coincidence that it occupies this world."

"You don't believe my motives are at all altruistic?"

"Call it what you like, but you're no more an altruist than I."

Regenzi raised an eyebrow. "Perhaps so. You're also not the first Meteron with whom I've discussed this matter."

Anselm felt the young lord's eyes picking him over, hunting for a reaction. "I've heard." He gave Regenzi a pointed look. "I'm sure your exploits will make a lingering impression on His Grace."

Regenzi bristled. "I was more hoping for a *profitable* one." He nodded into the dark. "Now, aren't you curious why we've come here?"

"Not particularly. You're clearly not keeping the doctor in this room, and so it's of little interest to me."

"What leads you to that conclusion?"

"You need Chalmers to track, record, and translate data. Not my field of expertise, but I'll wager it requires basic illumination and space enough to turn about once or twice."

"You know your way around rather dark trades, Master Meteron. I'd always thought you were a businessman."

"My present business is wicked enough I had to pass a few other careers in my youth to train up."

Regenzi chuckled. "I could have used you around from the beginning."

The smallduke retrieved the Alchemist's telescoping saber and a leather roll almost the length of his forearm from the inner pocket of his coat. He handed them to Anselm.

"There is a chance," Regenzi allowed, "that you could win your little honor duel against Nasrahiel. If that's the case, I'll need a new right-hand agent. Someone who can do very uncomfortable things without hesitation."

"Technically, I'm retired."

The smallduke shrugged. "It's a notion I'd like you to consider for the future—assuming, of course, that you have one. Now there's someone here I'd like you to meet."

They stepped into the darkness. Regenzi lit a hurricane lamp waiting by the door with a lucifer from his cigarette case. The room filled with a light the color of sepia and shadows like faded ink.

The figure lying in chains stirred. He tugged at his bindings with a hand muffled in soiled gray wrappings.

"Nasrahiel's people have extracted everything they know how to," Regenzi explained as he paced the room's perimeter, well outside the chained man's reach. "The aigamuxa have moved on to keeping him as . . . well, a plaything, I suppose. They're like sporting hounds that way. If they don't have something to chase or harry, they get willful. Still, there's real work I need done with him and they've exhausted their creativity." He stopped. "I have to be sure he knows nothing more."

"So kill him," Anselm said. "Then it won't matter what he knows."

"If he told anyone else, though, before we came for him . . ."

Anselm nodded. "Of course." He removed his gloves and flexed his fingers, waiting for the phantom pop in his missing finger. "I could use the practice before I move on to the girl." And then he looked the younger man up and down. "Stay awhile, my lord. You might learn something."

Regenzi's face wrinkled. He adjusted the cuffs of his jacket with a fabricated nonchalance. "If it's all the same to you, I need to speak with my confederates. I imagine they're concerned about recent developments. They will want assurances."

"Go forth with a glib tongue, then."

Regenzi was walking out the door as Anselm called to him.

"I'll need time with this one. Say two hours."

"That's . . . quite a long time."

"I'm much more creative than an aigamuxa."

The door closed, leaving Anselm and Ivor Ruenichnov alone. Anselm regarded the sunken heap of a man with wonder and pity. He searched his memory, dusting off his Vraskan. Speaking to Ivor in his native tongue seemed a worthy courtesy, under the circumstances.

"God's balls." Anselm chuckled. He knelt by the Alchemist's surgeon's kit, unfolding it slowly. "I'd heard you were having trouble keeping birds to fly your routes. I didn't know it was because you were eating them. You look like a trussed sow."

Ivor's face was a fungus of bruises. He flashed his old companion a snarl with teeth like bloodied tombstones, slurring an idiom Anselm recalled having something to do with birth mothers and the mating habits of livestock. What remained of Ivor's tunic clung to the blood crusting his chest and belly. On the third try, he managed something more conversational. His body rolled feebly, revealing his brass hand twisted into a useless fist of scrap.

"Too much a . . . coward . . . to come alone. Where is the Bear?"

Anselm studied the sparkling tip of a scalpel, turning it in his maimed hand.

"Dead," he said at last. "I killed him."

"*Snake.*"

Anselm snorted. "You never pretended to like him."

"Hypocrite—and a witch. Brave, though . . . Smart. *Loyal.*" Ivor ground the last word in his teeth, powdering it.

"Do you recall Trimeeni back in fifty-six?"

Anselm could see Ivor sifting pain in search of the memory. Finally, the Vraskan scoffed, shaking his head. "That was Iberon. You were always such fools. The Bear should never . . . never have trusted you to—" His face purpled under the strain of words. Ivor gagged, hawking a gobbet on the stones.

Anselm frowned. "Ivor—"

He stared back through an eye not yet swollen shut. Its pupil flared with pain and fury. God, he was pathetic—would have been even if he hadn't been broken. Gouty and gray and gone to waste, a wreckage of the beast he had been, the shadow his shadow might once have cast. Anselm heard a clatter in the old man's throat and saw his chest jump with a wet cough, throwing a jagged landscape of shattered ribs into relief.

Anselm moved closer. Regenzi had had nothing to fear from Ivor. It was amazing, really, that the man was alive at all. Perhaps something of the beast he'd been was in him, still, too stupid and stubborn to die.

Anselm pressed the edge of a scabrous belly wound. Something yellow seeped from its cracks. There was a sweet smell. Foul.

"Ivor," he asked quietly, "did you tell anyone about the book, or Chalmers, or Pierce?"

"Just you," Ivor sneered through bloody teeth. "But you won't believe me. . . . Too . . . *smart* . . . to believe me."

"No, old friend. I do believe you."

Ivor spat, then groaned. He closed his good eye. "You left me with that damned book. . . . You are no *friend.*"

"On the contrary." Anselm returned the scalpel to its sleeve and took the hypodermic injector instead, loaded with the only ampule it had ever carried—the one the Alchemist had scarcely ever used. "I think I am the truest friend you ever had."

Anselm Meteron was no medic, but he knew where to find a man's jugular. There in the half dark, he pressed the needle into Ivor's flesh. Before the pinprick of pain parted his old partner's lips, Anselm pushed down the plunger, and the bodkin mingled with the Vraskan's blood. Ivor sagged, one shoulder twitching spasmodically, a foot kicking. And then he was still. Moments later, there was a damp, earthy smell—the undignified end.

Anselm rocked back on his heels, staring at Ivor's corpse. His right hand ached. He saw he'd been running circles over the stump of his finger with his thumb again, rubbing both raw. He massaged the tightness out of his wrist and hand, shook them, hard, and felt the turn from pain to pins and needles that would eventually fade altogether. It hadn't always taken so long.

Sullen, Anselm seriously considered the possibility that he was too old for this sort of thing. His shoulders still ached from that business with the ladder in the tunnels. He had barely moved fast enough to kick out the young guard's knee and get his knife into the Bear before the rest of the room could act. The odds were against something like that working again. That boded ill for his dance with Nasrahiel. And the more he talked to Regenzi, the less he liked the thought of partnering with him—and not just because he knew better than to tangle himself up with the bishop's business.

Worse and worse, all the time.

Anselm folded the surgeon's kit, noting it had contained only one ampule of bodkin. The Old Bear was more of an optimist than he had thought. There was always a chance someone else would need that mercy—or want it—soon.

He had a few ideas of whom and slipped from the room and its sweet smell of corruption in search of them.

30.

For more than an hour, the Reverend Doctor Phillip Chalmers sat huddled in the farthest possible corner from Rowena Downshire, staring at her like a rabbit cornered by a dog. Something about the big glass screen and the rattletrap machine connected to it seemed to have done in his wits. Perhaps he was sore about its breaking. Moments after he started tending it, there came a sound like the ice on the river giving way, and the glass splintered into a dark spiderweb.

Then Chalmers threw himself back on his rumpled cot, all but crawling the wall to get as far from Rowena as the cell would allow.

Rowena had tried to console *him*, then, though for what, she couldn't say. She offered him back his handkerchief, and he whispered that she should *keep it, please, God, just* keep *it*. She asked after his health, asked if she'd done something to break the machine, asked if she could get him anything, even stupidly asked after his opinion of the weather—anything to stop his shaking.

Finally, Rowena gave up. She slumped with her back to the grated door, hugged her knees, and wondered what she could do. How to get out. If there *was* a way out. How to pull the doctor back together again, to make him useful somehow. When she'd come to the Cathedral, there'd been three of them and a plan, and now she was . . . She considered Chalmers with mounting dread. Now she really *was* alone. She took a composing breath.

It was the breath that undid her.

Rowena lacked the strength to weep loudly anymore, but it *sounded* very loud over the faint hum of gadgets littering the room.

You're an eejit, Rowena Downshire. A stupid, moon-born fool.

The sight of the Alchemist lying in a pool of blood had driven Rowena's last bout of tears. This one was more rage than misery. It was all so *obvious* now. The memory of her joy at being told she should come along, and of setting out from Regency Square with eager pride just hours before, mortified her. Of course Master Meteron wanted her to come along, once he saw she could be used for leverage. If he could get his revenge for Rare's death without fighting all Regenzi's lackeys, why wouldn't he? If there was a way of bargaining an end to the bloody business—well, wasn't that the nature of *his* business? Bets and bargaining and goods and services?

The more Rowena dwelled on it, the more she knew his friendship with the Alchemist was just a bit of scrapbook. Nostalgic. It was a bond between two men who didn't exist anymore, men who had known each other before she was born. Perhaps they'd been more like each other, once, the partnership one of kindred souls. She couldn't imagine any kinship in it now. The Old Bear was—*had* been—a stern, steady, solemn sort of man, hardly the kind to keep company with someone as rakish and elegant as Anselm Meteron. And there were the stories about Meteron, too. If vengeance were better served by a treacherous path, there was no question he'd take it. The Alchemist and Rowena had been perfect assets—trusting, motivated, determined.

Disposable.

Rowena remembered the Alchemist's smile, almost a secret; the touch of his hand on her bruised cheek, and the near magic of his healing; his sharp, fatherly looks over the rims of his spectacles. The books and maps of the Stone Scales. The strength in his arms as he tucked her in bed. Even Rabbit's thundering tail. She wished the smell of marjoram and fennel was still in her hair.

She hadn't even known his name. She wondered if *anyone* had.

There was no use crying any longer. All of that was done and gone. The doctor was useless. If they were going to get anywhere now, she'd have to be the one to make it so.

Rowena Downshire scrubbed her face on her sleeve and turned to the locked door. She rattled bars, climbed tall, teetering stools, and tried to shimmy past a gap in the grating near the rough-cut ceiling. She snatched some pithing wires from a dissection tray, reached a spindly arm through the lattice, and started jimmying at the lock.

All the while, Chalmers watched. At some point, he worked up the will to creep by the long trestle table and snatch up a notebook and charcoal. He glanced between her and the page, writing fast, feverish notes. Rowena stopped to glower at him as she bent a wire into the lock's tangled guts.

"You *could* help, y'know."

"I . . . I think I'll stay here, thank you." His gaze darted toward the trestle table again. Rowena saw he was looking at a thick book—one she remembered disappearing days before under a flurry of brown wrapping and twine.

"*Here.*" Rowena rolled her eyes, stomped over to the worktable, and lobbed the book at the reverend doctor. "Take the stupid thing. I en't gonna bite if you move around."

Chalmers threw himself on the book and scuttled back to his corner.

"Silly twat," Rowena muttered.

An hour later, she was on her belly under a rack of shelves, trying to find some crack in the floor, some chink she could pry open and wriggle her way through. At the sound of a key touching the heavy lock, she scrambled back to her feet, almost banging her head on a rack of balances.

Beside the door, an aigamuxa loomed over Anselm Meteron, its eyeless face seeming to watch him work the key. The creatures all looked mostly the same to Rowena, but this one had mottled black markings in places on its flesh, and its trousers looked new and clean compared to Nasrahiel's. The Alchemist's bag hung from Anselm's shoulder, the flap turned back to reveal the hilted weaponette and the surgeon's kit. There was blood staining the kit leather—dry now, more brown than red.

Rowena stared at him, anger boiling in her belly.

The aigamuxa padded into the cell on Meteron's heels. It paused by the edge of the dissecting table to lift a foot and turn its ankle, like a marble rolling in the palm of a hand, loose and smooth and sick-looking. Meteron still wore his chest holster and the carbine broken down in its slots. He still had both pistols and his knife.

Regenzi must trust him to let him keep all that truck.

Rowena hoped the smallduke got what he deserved for trusting a snake. She hoped Meteron turned on him, bit him and broke him, and that Nasrahiel made good on the Alchemist's prediction, too. She studied the aigamuxa and had no trouble imagining it could tear a man's arms off. And it was a runt compared to its chieftain.

Meteron dropped the bag onto the table. He began unrolling the surgeon's kit with ominous deliberation.

"I'll keep the keys for now."

The aigamuxa tilted its head. "That does not seem wise."

"Fine," Meteron snapped. He wrapped the kit up again. "I understand. We'll find Nasrahiel and Regenzi and tell them I can't begin because the plan doesn't suit you. We can wait. Would tomorrow be better? Will you be in a mood to follow your commanders' orders then?"

"I did not hear of such an order."

"How thoughtless of them not to tell you. I'm sure it's their usual habit to consult you in all things."

The aigamuxa's lip rippled. Meteron glared up at the creature. Even hunchbacked, it was two feet taller than him. He gave it his sharpest, flintiest stare.

"I will need *time* to convince the good doctor how important his cooperation will be to this girl. I need to be able to leave and let them dwell on what I've done. I will need to share details with Regenzi as I make progress. I need the freedom to come and go without your falling all over me, ape. I am keeping the keys. Unless you're of a mind to take them back."

His left hand drifted over the grip of his pistol.

The aiga's flat nose flared, bull angry. It turned, slouching out the door and slamming it shut. Its steady footfalls grew distant as its shadow stretched out of sight.

Rowena bent her knees.

Meteron turned toward her just in time to take her full weight straight to the chest. She flew at him, shrieking and slapping and clawing. For a moment, he was staggered—but that was all.

He tore Rowena's hands from his face with a snarl. And then the whole room *moved* around her as he spun and hurled her down. The floor surged into her back, driving the breath from her body like a bellows. He straddled her and pushed a forearm up under Rowena's neck. Stars exploded at the edges of her vision.

"Listen carefully, cricket—"

Rowena bucked her hips, hard. That moved him enough for her to turn a hip and drive a knee between his legs. She heard a grunt, then a gasp. Meteron rolled away, reflex jerking his arm from her throat. Rowena scuttled back, rattling into a shelf of glassware.

She reached behind herself, felt her hand close around a long, slender neck—

A chemical flask.

She smashed it on the ground and sprang at Meteron just as he curled up from a wounded crouch. Her weight drove them back together, clipping the dissection table's legs. A rain of sponges and steel and trepans pounded them.

Rowena pressed the jagged glass under his chin.

They stared at each other, breathing hard. Faintly, Rowena heard Chalmers scratching away at his notebook.

Meteron smiled. "Gently now, cricket."

Gentleness was the last thing on her mind.

"You *killed* him. He wasn't so bad," she shouted. The words surprised her, but she knew they were true, and they dragged all the other truths along after. "He listened to me, and he cared about me, and you *ruined* it, you bastard." Rowena wept, her voice so thick she could barely make out her own words. "I'm going to kill you. Don't think I won't. I've killed people before—big people. Bigger than you."

"And I've raised the dead before."

Rowena's hand trembled. She felt a trickle of blood between her fingers. "We're not playing your game now, you sonovabitch."

"*You* were lying. I wasn't. I imagine the Old Bear will be sore if you should kill me before he returns."

Rowena moved the glass a hair's breadth from Anselm's throat. "He's *dead*. You only want to catch me off so you can get clear of me. It en't going to work."

"Rowena." Meteron's voice was perfectly level. "*Think*. Do you really believe I'm enough of a monster to kill the only man who will suffer being my friend?"

She didn't want to think that. She didn't know *what* to think.

Rowena squeezed the shattered flask harder. There was a thin, cracking sound. Her palm throbbed as a splinter of glass burrowed into its flesh.

Slowly, Meteron reached up. He closed four and a half fingers around her wrist and pulled gently. Her arm trembled on the descent.

"He's alive?"

"He's alive."

"How?"

He touched his neck, saw the blood lacing his fingers, and sighed. "Why is it young women have such a passion for cutting into my face?"

"*How?*"

"Curare. It's a paralytic. Bear always kept a little in reserve when we were on a job, in case he needed something silent and sure. We were lucky he'd brought some with him when the idea came to me."

Rowena sat back on her haunches, blinking numbly. "What idea?"

"To get caught so we could get out."

He rose and reached a hand down to her. Rowena considered it with weary eyes, unmoving. Meteron took her by the elbows and hauled her to her feet.

"How does getting caught *help* us?"

He looked back toward the hall, scanning its shadows. "The only thing we could be sure of was that we knew little enough of the environs capture was almost a certainty. So we used our last asset."

Rowena scowled. "Me."

"Hardly. *You* are a liability, cricket. Our last asset—" he smiled, "—is the fact that experience and treachery trump youth and enthusiasm every time. Regenzi has distinguished himself by his willingness to take lives, but a more experienced enemy would have a plan that didn't require so much mopping up. We gambled on him making amateur errors."

"Like what?"

"It takes a very particular kind of arrogance to drag your enemy before you when they still have most of their teeth. He should have disarmed, separated, and interrogated us. There's not much angle in it for me to turn on you, but he wanted to believe it. The scene fed his fantasy of being a ruthless, charismatic leader, the sort who can make an ally of a man like me."

Rowena shook her head. "You really figured him out."

"Credit the figuring to our Alchemist. He saw enough of him in his shop a few days ago to make some valuable inferences about Regenzi's character."

"But Regenzi took his *pulse*. He can't be such an eejit he didn't notice the Alchemist was still alive."

"I doubt most physicks would have had a better chance of recognizing our trick." Meteron perched a hip on the trestle table. "The knife was tipped with the curare. Used the usual way, it causes total muscular and respiratory paralysis. It's a quiet death, but horrible. You suffocate and know it's happening the whole time—no struggles or crying out. On the other hand, if you know your way around human anatomy and prepare the poison to a precise body weight and concentration, well—" he shrugged, "—then you can stretch the onset, reduce the mortality risk. The pulse and respiration drop to just a few beats and breaths a minute. It looks damned convincing. And, if you've got a strong heart and a good constitution, there's even a chance you'll wake up none the worse for wear."

Rowena felt herself go cold. "But the Alchemist is . . . he's . . . Well—"

"Not a very young bear? I suppose. He managed it once before, about twenty years back. His odds weren't as good this time, but there wasn't a better candidate."

"What about you?"

"Come along, cricket. If I'm to be the corpse, the Bear has to play the traitor. Could you have believed that of him for even a moment?"

Rowena bit her lip. *No. Send the bastard to do a bastard's job.*

And then, she understood. "You needed *me* to believe it was real, too."

"Lead plate over the target zone, a few packets of drawn blood."

Meteron nodded. "We had the props down, but there's nothing that seals a performance quite like a shrieking extra." A passing sobriety took the edge off his features. "We couldn't be sure if you were a good enough actress to pull your part off. And I knew already you're a terrible liar."

"I am?"

"You blink twice every time. Don't take up cards."

Rowena looked down at her feet, arms crossed. "It scared me to pieces."

"We told you to close your eyes," he answered quietly. It was as near as he'd come to an apology, Rowena supposed.

She scrubbed her nose to chase off the teary feeling that was coming on again. "How does the Alchemist being 'dead' help us get out of here with the doc and the book, anyway?"

Meteron smiled deviously. "No one keeps very close watch on a corpse. My job while the curare ran its course was to learn as much about Regenzi's operation as possible. He's been quite generous in showing me the way around, which let me take stock of the occupied rooms and a rough head count of his men. Meanwhile, wherever Bear was dumped, he'll be able to move about freely, start dispatching guards, and clearing the way for our exit. Between what I've learned and what he'll have determined, we'll have as close to complete intelligence as we could have hoped from a week's stakeout."

Rowena shook her head in wonder. "I can't believe it. He's *alive*."

There was a voice from the corner of the room—hesitant, corrective: "Medically speaking, suppressed vitals carry significant risks of long-term consequences."

The Reverend Doctor Phillip Chalmers watched Anselm and Rowena from his cot, his dishwater eyes darting between them. He flashed a weak smile.

"Arrhythmia. Memory loss. Nerve damage. It's, ah . . . it's really quite dodgy."

"I think," Rowena said coldly, "he's going to be fine."

Meteron made a cautionary sound. She turned.

"Isn't he?"

"The good doctor has a point," he allowed. "But I'm more concerned about the Bear's disposal than his recovery. If the aigamuxa dumped him into an incinerator, or hauled him down to the river, *that* might put a kink into his resurrection."

Rowena and Chalmers cried out in dismay, nearly on-key.

"Still, we're far enough north of the river an aiga would have to be passing industrious to haul him to the nearest quay. If there's an incinerator on the Cathedral campus, it would be in one of the laboratory buildings where the conference has been meeting, and it probably wouldn't burn hot enough to cremate a whole body. And the industrial quarter's too far east to make the journey worth it."

"So . . ." Chalmers began—and stopped when Rowena's gaze fell on him. He looked down at his notes, shuffling papers into superfluous piles. "So, ah, where *is he*?"

"Right now?" Master Meteron considered a water clock on a nearby shelf. "No idea. But he's running late."

31.

Each large building in Corma boasts a refuse catch, a pit dug into the lowest levels of the foundations and fed by drop chutes. The chutes resemble dumbwaiters, with gear-locked doors opening to a compartment about three feet square into which refuse can be loaded. Once the doors close, the user can reverse the crank, releasing the compartment's suspension chain and sending the stinking flotilla hurtling down to the chute's bottom, where it drops its contents on the refuse catch's ever-growing heap. The pits have access bays to the sewers through which the laborers city folk call "mole men" enter to dig the lot out onto skiffs, following a schedule kept as tidy as their smocks are befouled.

Moling is profitable work, if you can stand its stink. There are always things being discarded that have no business going down the drops.

The aigamuxa who loaded the Alchemist into the refuse chute was not overly careful. But then, care hadn't been its first concern. Had it been, it might have considered the regularity with which the refuse catches were emptied, the correspondingly inevitable discovery of a body, and the displeasure of Lord Regenzi at a reeking corpse turning his conspiracy's hiding place into a public travesty. No. The aiga's first concern was that the old human cut a very heavy corpse and that the letter of Regenzi's wishes only required its disposal.

A three-foot square compartment is a tight fit for a man a hand over six feet and a shade over sixteen stone. Stuffing said man into said compartment when one's eyes are obliged to stay planted on the ground meant the aiga's most inventive inflictions of contortionism were met several times with a shoulder blocking the doors' closing, or a foot and ankle wedged between them. Finally, on the brink of a resolution to simply break the corpse's back and stuff it in, the aiga folded it into the happy accident of the fetal position.

And so the doors were closed, the crank engaged, and the platform and its cargo dropped down into the dark on a route that terminated quickly. The aigamuxa had used the drop just two levels above the refuse catch itself.

Under any other circumstances, finding oneself in an overfull refuse heap would be simply and utterly vile. In the Alchemist's case, it was still vile: vile but merciful, its high, damp hillocks breaking a fall that marked the day's second opportunity of breaking his back.

He lay there a long time, adrift in the fog of half death, before a sudden, sharp pain in his wrist woke him. Though the rest of his body lagged far behind, his arm knew what to do.

It jerked back against his chest. The rat that had sunk its teeth near the vein scurried away, bounding over drifts of gazette paper and food scrap and the reeking mountains from the Cathedral's ancient earth closets.

Piece by piece, the world came back to the Alchemist, and he signed off on each of its deliveries with reluctance. All around was darkness. A miasma of rot and its steaming warmth crawled over the waste heaps. The air above that swamp was coffin cold. His right side flared in pain from shoulders to toes. It took on a throbbing enthusiasm as his pulse quickened.

A body sustained at the threshold of life, with only a marginal pulse and the slowest, most shallow breathing, returns to normalcy with a feeling more like dying than lying at death's door itself had been. Sixty beats a minute feels like running a footrace. The lungs' steady bellows scream with the effort of full motion. The blood surges, and the body warms, and with that flush of heat comes a wave of nausea and dizziness.

When the Alchemist sat up, it was only to keep from vomiting on his bloodied clothes.

Once he had nothing left to add to the refuse pile, he was past the smell of the place, past the bruises of his fall. It was the pain in his chest that worried him, until he remembered the shot.

The Alchemist fished under his shirt for the lead plate guarding his heart and withdrew it gingerly. He explored the plate with his fingers, finding it caved in nearly half the depth of his thumb, pinching the bullet tight. He felt a greedy, bone-deep contusion sinking deep into his chest. The bite wound had begun to seep, too, as had the damp line on his throat where Anselm's knife had done its work.

The Alchemist kept a working voice in his head—a version of his own sharper than even his most irascible bark. It ordered him about with callous efficiency.

Take stock.

He started with the coat and found his supplies—secreted in a double-quilted lining—had survived the fall. His bag was gone and with it the torches, some munitions, the grappling fork, the rappelling rigs, and sink pins. The scabbard on his thigh felt light and loose. He vaguely remembered the hand blunderbuss being taken before the shot. The Alchemist reached up to his throat, felt the goggles hanging there, and sighed relief.

Now get moving.

Leyah had been a brilliant engineer, capable of crafting or adapting virtually any device. Good campaigning groups needed such skills, and she'd been a savant. Given a week of preparations and the proper funds, she could construct things her husband had never seen before, things that proved to him that calling God an engineer was higher praise than calling Him an experimenter.

The goggles were one of Leyah's little gifts. The Alchemist donned them and clicked through several lenses, at last finding the glazed optics.

The refuse catch offered dim light from the drop chutes' apertures. The sewer access door was framed in a murky halo by the alchemical globe positioned just outside. The parabolic lenses and their refractive coating amplified that light, letting the Alchemist perceive the outlines of the refuse heap's contents, the mouths of the chutes above. The one directly overhead beckoned, its open hatch revealing the platform from which he'd fallen and the chain suspending it.

Out you go, old man.

Telling his pains he would give them their due sometime further on, the Alchemist gathered the sturdier pieces of the refuse—crates and broken furniture and scrap. He built a platform just tall and steady enough to put the hatch in reach. He snatched its edge, hauling up until he could place a hip on the platform. Resting there, he gave the chains a hard tug, testing their load.

The Alchemist climbed back up the way he'd come down, resting twice with feet and back pressed to either side of the chute. It would have been slow work even if he hadn't felt half dead. The chain was strong, but his hands ached, callused fingers slick with sweat. Finally, he reached the first dumbwaiter doors. Light leaked through their center seam. The Alchemist braced himself again, legs quaking with the effort, and drew a flat iron tool from the sleeve of his coat, tapered to a bit driver tip on one end, flared into an adjustable spanner on the other. He drove the bit driver tip between the doors and levered them open.

For an instant, the hall's globe light blinded him. He pulled down the goggles and made his cramped way out.

The corridor was rough stone and slate, identical to those he had traveled with Rowena and Anselm. And that was the trouble. He had no notion where he was.

Fortunately, he had ways of remedying that.

The Alchemist kept close to the wall, following the lamps to a stairway. He lingered there, back to the corner where the corridor narrowed at the foot of the stairs. He reached into his coat, working with one hand, watching the stairwell. The Alchemist knew the feel of the chemical parcel he sought, its familiar heft, and the stinging smell that already seeped through its heavy linen. He waited. It did not take long for a shadow to stretch down the steps.

The Alchemist squeezed the packet in his right hand. Its crystallized contents ground together, leaving his palm wet. The guard came down the stairs at the Alchemist's right side. With his left hand, cross-body, he snared the man's shoulder and spun into the wall, stepping behind him as he did it. He hugged the guard's back to his chest, stuffing the chloroform packet over mouth and nose.

The guard bucked and thrashed. That only made him breathe harder. When he slackened, the Alchemist let his body slide to the floor.

After tossing the chloroform aside, the Alchemist wiped his hand on the man's uniform and checked his neck for a pulse. Steady and strong. He would live, though he'd have a screaming headache, and not all for the chloroform's sake.

The Alchemist left his hand on the man's neck and closed his eyes. He didn't have to go slowly or pick carefully. He knew what he sought. He shouldered his way through the walls of unconsciousness, tossing the rooms that lay beyond.

In less than a minute, he knew where to find them—Chalmers and Rowena and Anselm. A moment later, he knew the safest way out, and it made him curse.

It was a job, of course. They were hardly ever easy. It was the aigamuxa that would make this exit particularly hard.

32.

Smallduke Regenzi stood beside Deacon Fredericks in the low belfry tower, looking up into a sky full of eyes, winking and glaring against the dark.

"We shouldn't waste time here," Fredericks whispered. Regenzi looked at the deacon coldly, the flushed, fleshy man tugging his sleeve like some mewling child with wet britches. "Things have gone far out of our control. The bishop—"

Regenzi shrugged off Fredericks's hand, dusting himself back into order. "The bishop," he corrected, "proposed that I manage this affair on his behalf. He gave me leave to proceed as I saw fit."

"And he asked *me* to mind his interests as you did so. I don't imagine he had quite this situation in mind, my lord."

"It is my situation now," Regenzi snapped. "Stay or go as you like. When I've seen this matter through and given the bishop professor the book and the names, I'll remember who helped me—and who held me back."

Fredericks's flushed face seemed to pale. He looked back up at the rafters above.

Idiot. Regenzi wondered if he was truly the only one of his company who understood how to use an enemy strategically. *Things would have been a deal easier if His Grace hadn't saddled me with a milquetoast bookkeeper of a second.*

He sighed. Done was done, and there was still much yet to *be* done. Regenzi lifted his face and spoke into the darkness. "I've come to you because I want you to understand this is all a *ruse*, Nasrahiel. Meteron is insane to think he could face you in single combat, but he's useful up to that point. Surely that's plain to you."

One pair of eyes, larger and fiercer than the rest, swung through the rafters, traveling the twenty feet down to the floor where its hulking body landed in that strangely perfect pose. Regenzi stared into the eyeless face and the eye heels flanking it.

"It is plain that I am a tool," the aigamuxa chieftain replied. "You offer me up to this serpent's satisfaction because it serves you, despite the risk to me."

The slithery sounds of aigamuxa speaking in their own tongue whispered through the air. Regenzi knew not a word of it, though he had heard their speech since childhood. But he recognized the tone. Men at the edge of civility murmured their displeasure in just that way—up until the moment of things breaking.

Fredericks cleared his throat. "The risk is infinitesimally small. Even well armed, a single man can't expect—"

"There are such things," Nasrahiel answered, his voice slow and dangerous, "as principles, Deacon. They guide how one honors an allegiance."

"Principles have guided this entire venture, Nasrahiel. You've known that from the beginning."

The aigamuxa tilted his head at Regenzi.

"Fear has guided this venture. This, I have known from the beginning. I am the only one among us with principles."

The air rumbled with the aigamuxa's bellows, so loud the old bronze bell teetering overhead hummed in response. There were many more of them nesting in the belfry, its spare shafts of moonlight the only illumination their blood-milk eyes required.

Regenzi glared at Nasrahiel. "There are certain comments I won't endure from my subordinates. Keep a rein on your tongue, Nasrahiel, or I may find myself with small cause to care what Meteron tries to do to you."

"It is touching to think you ever did."

"I didn't know your kind could pout. It's quite human of you."

The aigamuxa's feet whirled back to the ground. He towered over Regenzi, the white scars along his shoulders purpling.

"Despise me if you like, but do not mock me. There are also comments *we* will endure no longer."

The belfry erupted in a chorus of hoots and jeers, like a pack of wolves set loose in a primate house. Hackles Regenzi had not known he had rose in prickly response.

Another aigamuxa arrived, then, hurling itself up the ladder from the clerestory level below. It spoke to Nasrahiel first, growling several phrases before the chieftain's shoulders relaxed, the rage giving way to a tremble and then a quake.

The chieftain's laughter sawed Regenzi's ears.

"What's so funny?" Fredericks demanded.

The new arrival answered in surprisingly deft Amidonian. "He Who Dared is with the translator and the girl. He demanded to keep the keys. I was told this would be your will."

Regenzi scowled. "He gave you reasons?"

"Poor ones."

"Return with one of your brothers, then, and—"

"Do not," Nasrahiel snapped. "It is already too late."

Regenzi turned on his lieutenant. "We have an understanding: I give the orders."

"That understanding has been outlived."

Fredericks's hand plucked Regenzi's sleeve, pulling him toward the ladder. "Abraham, there's still time to mobilize the guard. Forget the aigamuxa."

Snarling, Regenzi tore his arm from Fredericks's grasp. He fought to keep his voice level.

"There's time enough to get the aiga in place. All of you!" Regenzi shouted over the dissent rumbling through the rafters. "You've been well paid by my family, employed for two generations, made secure by my largesse. Your chieftain joined me in common cause and gave me his word you would follow where I lead. Preserve his honor, if he cannot be trusted to do it. Go!"

Regenzi had been prepared for howls of derision—for more slithery laughter, for contempt, for rage.

The silence that followed was far louder and more terrifying.

Deacon Fredericks stood an arm's length from the ladder, his ruddy, round face gone ashen.

Moonlight slipped through the windows of the lower belfry tower, bleeding into shadows. They crawled down the stone walls, running over the pitched wooden floor, pooling around the heels of his boots as the aigamuxa descended.

Nasrahiel stood beside the messenger. He tilted his eyeless head, thoughtful, almost puzzled.

"Our common cause was finding the Nine," the chieftain allowed. His voice had turned chillingly reasonable. "We needed the book and the reverend doctor. We needed you only to come this close."

The aigamuxa fell into place around Regenzi like withered fruit dropping from a skeleton tree. His shirt collar seemed unaccountably tight. He reached up to loosen it and found his fingers unable to work the button.

Slowly, Abraham Regenzi remembered a question Revered Chalmers had asked.

"Why are your people seeking the Nine, Nasrahiel?"

The head tilted again, as if drawn by the same force pulling the aiga's thin, black lips into a smile.

"God made three intelligent races, equal in gifts, and scattered them in this world. Only Man has strived so hard to strike the other two down. He took the forests from the lanyani to make the cities of iron and lay the rails between them. He turned them into vagrants where once their roots drove deep. He took the aigamuxa, we who walk with our eyes on the earth of creation, and cast us in chains to do labor, because we are twisted brutes in his eyes. Man made us fit for the meanest tasks because *he* wishes to follow the Creator and live by knowledge and Reason, not the sweat of his brow. And then, when the world grew too large for every man to be a scholar, they had to give up their pride and return to the labors of old. So they turned us into the streets to act as the brutes we were taught to be."

Abraham Regenzi looked around the circle of blinking feet, their dagger gazes sharpened by servitude.

"God created the Nine to prove the worth of Man," Nasrahiel continued. "But my people have always known your worth, and we spit upon it. If the Nine are the witnesses, the test subjects, the pillars . . . Well.

We will end the trial by killing those who would testify. God did not see fit to test our people—did not see fit to test the lanyani. If Man is too weak to defend the Experiment that gives him purpose, he is judged and found wanting."

"I won't deny your people have been ill-used by some," Regenzi insisted. "But my father *paid you*. Paid your sire before you and all his tribe. You were never truly slaves to my house. And even for those others . . . For every man who whipped an aigamuxa in chains, there were ten ordinary men laboring beside them. You can't paint us all with a slaver's brush."

"Perhaps," Nasrahiel allowed. "But even if *some* men never forged or latched a chain, even if the Nine themselves are guiltless, this world was still built upon my people's backs. Is it so wrong that I should wish to rebuild it on humanity's?"

"Don't waste your time with me, then," Regenzi said. "You'll need Chalmers to find the Nine. If this one is right—" he nodded toward the messenger, "—Meteron may already have freed him."

"Let them run. They are rats in a maze. There is only one sure way out. When they find it, they will be weary, and we will be ready."

"I *gave you* a path to finding Chalmers: you owe me something."

Nasrahiel nodded solemnly. "It is true. I owe you a debt for paving the path to my people's satisfaction. I owe you, at least, your life."

Regenzi looked around at the crouching aigamuxa and swallowed. Deacon Fredericks's gaze crossed his for a moment, and then he was gone, faster than a rabbit into the warren hole, scrabbling down the ladder to the clerestory below. Regenzi reached into his coat, his hand on the beastly gun taken from the Alchemist. His mind was racing to decide where to shoot first when Nasrahiel's voice startled him back into focus.

"I cannot raise a hand to you, in the name of this debt." The chieftain stalked backward, shaking his head. "But my brothers owe the tribe the defense of its chieftain's honor. I am sure you understand."

Nasrahiel disappeared into the shadows. Regenzi yanked at the gun, but it hooked in the sash adorning his coat. One of the aiga darted forward and struck him down with a forearm heavy as corded wood. His vision exploded in red light, and his mouth filled with hot, liquid copper. Regenzi heard the gun clatter to the ground, then spin away, kicked by the beast's horny heel.

The other aigamuxa lunged, closing the circle, stabbing inward. Regenzi had time only to see their shadows leaping about the belfry walls. And then his own voice, shrieking higher and longer and louder than anything he'd heard before, joined the sound of his arms tearing free of their sockets.

33.

"We need to take all of this," Phillip Chalmers said. He stood before the trestle table of notes and papers, hugging a thick lab book. His eyes darted between Anselm and Rowena, as if he wasn't sure from which quarter to expect resistance.

Rowena snorted at the riot of materials. "How? The Alchemist's bag is already full—with stuff we'd actually *need*."

She looked at Anselm for confirmation, her tear-stained face once more tough and canny. He wondered when she'd developed a notion of being his sidekick. *Master Meteron and the Wonder Waif. Preposterous child.*

"The girl's right," Anselm agreed. "Carrying the book will be hard enough without taking the whole ruddy lab."

Chalmers wrung his hands. His eyes flicked toward the girl, the most overt of covert glances.

Anselm pinched the bridge of his nose. "Rowena, keep by the door while we get this sorted."

She opened her mouth to protest.

"I'm half deaf from all my years at gunplay," Anselm said apologetically. "I need your ears on alert."

And that was all it took. The girl was humming with energy, past ready to be useful. Tell Rowena her pet Bear was still alive and she was ready to stand off in front of Nasrahiel barehanded. It was foolish energy, wasted confidence. It could very well get her killed—but for now, it had a use. She crouched by the locked gate, still as a pointing hound, and listened.

Anselm felt Chalmers take him by the elbow. The reverend doctor spoke in a stage whisper, loud and painfully articulated.

"*The—notes—are—what—*"

Meteron fixed Chalmers with a withering look. "You're a bloody idiot. Just keep your voice down, savvy?"

The younger man blinked like a confused bird, and then, slowly, understanding crept over his features. He dropped Anselm's arm.

"*Ohhh.* Yes, I see. Terribly sorry." Chalmers edged closer, conspiratorial. "You must know what the book is. That's what brought you here."

"A powerful desire to do lots of killing brought me here, actually."

The doctor's eyes widened.

"But I suppose the book has its charm," Anselm allowed. "Writes itself, hand of God, the Vautneks, all that."

Chalmers seemed disappointed. Then, gradually, the nervousness written in his features sloughed away. Underneath it rested a badly tailored solemnity, two sizes too large for his reedy frame.

"Here." He set the lab book down and opened it, turning pages until he reached its middle. "Seeing for yourself might help you appreciate the situation."

The page Chalmers selected was half-filled with lines of numbers, some in sets, some long, unbroken strings. An inky-black script crawled along on its own, then paused. The third line from the top was lanced by a strike-through, two notations made in the margin beside it in a blocky, serif-heavy hand. The bottom of the page began filling again, very slowly.

Anselm felt something in him stir, old and better than half-forgotten. He had no words for the feeling trailing in its wake. It dwelled somewhere behind his breastbone and traveled down his arm to tingle in the tip of his phantom finger.

He blinked at the page and leaned closer. "Those are coordinates."

Chalmers turned back several pages. "It's His habit to step away from recording events and environmental details to confirm precise positioning—happens once a week, sometimes more. The coordinates are tied to other numbers that seem to identify persons relevant to the subject at hand, but I haven't had the opportunity to test that theory. This section of the text refers to Subject Six."

Anselm put a hand on the page Chalmers was about to turn. The stump of his finger hovered over a sketch of streets and alleys, a grid.

"That's the Regency," he murmured.

"I don't know what that—"

"I live there."

Chalmers looked between the page and Anselm. He took a slow breath. "I've transcribed most of the last several days for each of the subjects. Subject Six has been the most active. Translating from the cryptograms is slow work. I do it in scratch through the notes. They show where she's been, who she's been with, what's unfolding right now."

"She," Anselm observed.

"She."

Anselm nodded. He turned the pages, considered their notations. He found very little recognizable—but there were a few things. A sketch of the cellblock in Oldtemple. The lightning rail station at Ippining. Not much . . . but enough. He closed his eyes, suddenly very tired.

There was a thump—Chalmers closing the book.

"I need the notes," the reverend said, voice low and resolute. "Leaving them behind would be like losing half the key for a cipher. Without the notes, working the text isn't much more than educated guesswork."

"If we left the notes behind, would they reveal enough for Regenzi to follow her?"

"Perhaps," Chalmers whispered. "But it's not a matter of Regenzi following her. It's a matter of Nasrahiel killing her." He looked furtively at Rowena's backside. "He has plans of his own—something Regenzi's blind to. I'm sure of it. He's seen my maps and my notes of where the nearest subject has been these last few days. He knows where *you* have been. If he's already seen she's here . . ."

Anselm stared at Rowena. The girl was hunkered down with her fingers twined in the grate's lattice. She looked impossibly small—a dirty, desperate thing with her heart pinned to her sleeve. And she was as fierce and loyal as any wounded creature half-healed by an act of charity, yearning to be made whole. Born to a diet of fish broth and day-old bread, she'd called fleas her bedfellows, stolen flatware to pay a prison penury, and carried on her slim shoulders one-ninth weight of the human future.

Anselm unpacked the Alchemist's bag. He left behind the grappling fork and the four crank work grenades. For an uncertain moment, he held the surgeon's kit in his hands, then put that aside, too.

"Won't somebody need that—perhaps?" Chalmers asked nervously.

"Ever seen a battlefield surgery?"

The younger man blinked. "Ah . . . no. Not my sort of thing, really."

"They happen after the dust settles. If we're still here then, it's because we're already dead. Give me your damned papers. And, Chalmers?"

"Yes?"

Anselm's eyes were hard. "I can keep my peace about the girl, if you can keep your nerve."

The reverend doctor nodded vigorously. "We can't say a word to her. Not now. Not ever."

"Good." He thrust the bag into the reverend doctor's arms, staggering him. "It's your rutting library. You carry it."

Rowena turned, her voice playfully cajoling. "Come on, Master Meteron. You gonna take all day?"

Chalmers had been adjusting the bag across his chest. He abandoned the buckled strap and gaped at Anselm. "Wait . . . you're Anselm *Meteron*? *That* Meteron? Your father—"

"I know who my father is." Anselm snatched the keys off a shelf and tossed them to Rowena. "You've got skinny arms, cricket. Get us out of here."

Rowena caught the keys one-handed and turned back toward the grating. She passed her arm through just in time to find herself looking three EC guards right in the brass buttons of their coats.

"Bugger me," she groaned.

The guard standing nearest the grating snared her wrist. He shoved her back, then jerked forward, driving her face into the door. Rowena cried out and fell in a heap, hands covering her eyes.

The second guard turned the key and opened the door for the third. He entered, gun drawn, three sets of leather strapping cuffs in his other hand.

"Deacon Fredericks was right," the guard with the straps announced.

The other men entered. He passed each a pair of cuffs, the barrel of his gun tracking between Chalmers and Anselm.

Chalmers scurried behind Anselm. He shot the doctor a dark look and earned a shrug in response. "I'm a pacifist, really."

Anselm looked back at the advancing guards, working the odds. One drew close enough to reach for his wrists.

He had nearly decided in what body part he was willing to take a bullet graze, had figured how to turn the guard with the cuffs into a human shield, and was adjusting his weight to put the process in motion when a thought—not his own—came sharply to mind.

Smoking the room in three. Get low.

And he smiled.

The guard had just taken Anselm's hands and slipped a cuff around one wrist when everyone heard something roll under the grating.

It was ticking.

The key-crank grenade was a sphere as large as a fist. It wobbled to a stop right between the feet of the guard holding the gun.

He looked down.

The crank work's capped ends blasted off, spinning it round as it hurled up a cloud of smoke.

Anselm threw an elbow into the cuff man's temple, dropped to a knee, and hauled Chalmers down by his waistcoat. Through the gathering smoke, he could see Rowena crumpled against the wall, her wrists strapped tight.

The Alchemist kicked open the door. It swung hard left, clipping the guard beside Rowena on the back of the head, stunning him. The guard with the gun whirled, eyes streaming. He aimed his pistol in time to take his dazed partner's bulk hurled across his chest, sending both to the ground in a tangle of limbs. The gun clattered free.

Anselm swept the weapon up and shoved it against the nose of the man who had moments before been its owner.

The Alchemist stood over the three reeling guards with a heavy pistol lifted from one of their compatriots. He levered back the hammer. Chalmers's coughing fit broke long enough for him to quail in alarm.

The Alchemist was a big man, gifted with a stare that could curdle milk. In that respect, the goggles were a mercy, though their bright golden lenses looked alien above the double-valve filter mask. It covered his nose and mouth in a fearsome triangle of metal and tubes like the flaring muzzle of a wild beast.

The crank work's spin slowed to a wobble. Its smoke grew thin and watery. Then, finally, the gases cleared.

"You," Anselm observed, "look like shit, Bear." He stood, offering his leather-looped wrist to Chalmers. The doctor frowned at it before realizing the implicit request.

Chalmers fumbled with the strap. "This is your partner?"

The Alchemist lifted his goggles and pulled down his mask. Under the gear and his dark complexion, his face was ashen. The ragged, bloody mess of his shirt suggested something more like an evisceration than a bullet wound. He could have passed for dead again had he just lain down and closed his eyes.

"'Give Leyah my love'?" he growled. The Alchemist stowed the mask. He fished for something in his endless pockets. "That was going a bit far."

Anselm smiled. "It made for excellent theater."

The Alchemist eyed the man standing between them. "Doctor Chalmers?"

"*Reverend* Doctor Phillip Chalmers, at your serv—"

He tossed the doctor what appeared to be a tin of dentifrice. "Put this on their hands, then place them over their mouths. Keep it off of your own, whatever you do. Use the cuffs on their ankles."

Chalmers glanced at Anselm, frowning. "And, um, what will Master Meteron be doing while I'm about that?"

"Making sure they don't try to kill you." Anselm weighed the gun in his hand suggestively.

"Ah. Very good."

The doctor set about his business, muttering apologies as he glued the guards' hands to their faces.

The Alchemist knelt beside Rowena. One of the joints in the iron grating had split the skin above her left eyebrow. The eye would swell shut soon, if the red scoring of lattice around the orbital bone was any indication. He found a styptic in his breast pocket and a square of clean gauze. Rowena moaned. She winced at his touch, jerking away. Her eyes fluttered, then shot open, wild with panic.

And then, she truly saw him.

"Bear?"

Something about her using that name—that small piece of personal property—shook him. The Alchemist worked at Rowena's cuffs. If he held her eyes a moment longer, something would happen, and the fear of what it might be made his heart hurt.

It's only the bruise from the bullet, you old fool.

He released the pinch latch on the cuffs, put the gauze in Rowena's hand, and guided her to press it against the wound. "Keep still. I need to—"

Rowena flung her arms around the Alchemist's neck, burying her face in his collar. Something between laughter and sobs heaved up from her shoulders. Slowly, he put an arm around her.

From the corner of an eye, he saw Chalmers hesitate while cinching one of the straps around the second guard's ankles. The reverend watched the crying girl hang from the old man's neck. His brow furrowed. Anselm prodded him back to work with a boot.

Rowena shoved the Alchemist back on his heels.

"I can't believe you let me think you were dead, you rotten bastard!" The indignant flare in her eyes changed to worry. "You look awful. Doc said coming back wouldn't be easy, but I didn't think you'd look so—"

"First rule, girl: no chatter. Now tilt your head back. We won't get far with you bleeding down into your eye."

Rowena obeyed. The Alchemist cleaned the wound, staunched it with a line of styptic, and began to seal it with a milder form of the adhesive presently silencing and immobilizing the guards.

"Why is it," Rowena mused up at the ceiling, "big, nasty brutes always want to hit me in the *face*?"

Anselm chuckled.

The Alchemist sighed. "I've missed something, or you've both lost your minds."

"A little of both," Anselm answered. "What's the path out, Bear?"

The Alchemist stood and offered Rowena a hand. The girl fairly bounded to her feet, a puppy spoiling for a fray with mastiffs.

"Same as always. Up."

Anselm smirked. He offered the gun to the Alchemist. "Good. I love up."

"That makes one of us. Are you ready, Doctor?"

Phillip Chalmers looked at the other three—the sneering rogue and the bedraggled Alchemist and the skinny, dirty girl. His expression was well beyond skeptical.

"When you say 'up,' could you, perchance, specify?"

"The fastest way out to the roof is from the clerestory level," the Alchemist said. He spotted his weaponette on the dissection table and strapped it back in place. "There are two belfry towers there. We're taking the higher of them up and out."

"Climbing?" Doctor Chalmers chirruped. "I, ah . . . Climbing really isn't my forte, you see."

Rowena peered down the hall, jockeyed to go. She started across the threshold. Anselm snatched her shoulder, trotting her backward.

"Rule two, cricket."

"Why the higher tower?" she asked the Alchemist. She brushed off Anselm's hand with a scowl.

"Because the aigamuxa are living in the lower one."

Chalmers had been about to walk out. He stopped. "*Living* there?"

"Come along, Doctor." Anselm swatted the younger man's back. "Stay close. The girl will teach you the rules."

Anselm peeled out of the room, facing right, his gun raised. The Alchemist moved left, mirroring him. A moment later, he beckoned for the others.

Rowena tugged Chalmers's hand, smiling. "Don't worry, Doc. They en't much to remember—just three rules."

He nodded numbly. Once in the hall, she let go of his hand and followed after the others, running to keep up.

From somewhere far behind the Alchemist came Phillip Chalmers's curse. Running, he supposed, was not the doctor's forte, either.

34.

Haadiyaa Gammon stepped out of the secretariat coach at the foot of the hill rising up to the Old Cathedral. She paid the driver, donned her officer's tricorn, and walked up the hedgerow-lined path, hands in her pockets against the night chill, hiding from the burdens she was bound to carry. Tomorrow would be Sabberday; Jane's spark still rested in her inner breast pocket, unanswered. Her shoulders ached as they always did when she wore her constabulary-issued pistol. She had no plan of using it tonight, but then a lot of things had gone astray where plans and working with Abraham Regenzi had been concerned.

Gammon had avoided the constabulary offices all that day, accounting for her absence by the manufacture of a nasty head cold. A more accurate accounting of what ailed her would have been much too difficult to capture in a hastily crafted spark. The ledger started with mortgaging her position's integrity and carried on through a record of profits and losses ranging from the ineffable to the decidedly bloody. The last entry had no precise figure: it was the half ruin of Rare Juells's face, her father standing glass-eyed over her slab, the gratuity Anselm Meteron had hurled atop of her corpse. She supposed by now it really did line some morgue technician's pockets.

And the girl, Gammon thought bitterly. Beatrice Earnshaw's case had passed quickly through the Court and Bar, sailing on the authority of a few official seals and affidavits. She'd be sitting on a prison skiff bound for one of the hulks by now, reeling at how swift the hand of justice could strike, given the proper scapegoat. Gammon had a plan, and a few favors, set aside to help the girl, now that she had made up her mind of what must be done. Still, it would have been better had Haadiyaa Gammon never made choices that required so much undoing.

With neither a head cold nor her integrity, Gammon walked the paths that fanned out toward the many laboratories, auditoriums, and libraries of the EC's Cathedral campus. It was past the supper hour. The buildings were dark except for the odd lighted window—a reverend doctor tidying up a lab or readying one for the conference's final morning. Only a group of lanyani treelings scavenged the grounds, searching for odds and ends worth pawning out of the rubbish bins. They froze, peering with their white, inscrutable eyes as Gammon passed. Behind her, she heard whispers moving among their branches, whether words or wind, she couldn't say.

Gammon squinted up at the Cathedral, half-expecting to see the shadows of aigamuxa moving between its buttresses and crenellations. She'd marked it a week before and had words with Regenzi about the creatures' keeping. There were places the aigamuxa were expected—their skyline shanty kingdoms strung up between the alleys of the south docks, or the markets, sometimes, standing strong-arm outside a merchant's stall. Folk had learned to tolerate the aiga moving about Amidon without a master's guidance. Seeing them crawl over the surface of a treasured landmark was quite another matter—one likely to draw unwanted attention.

Tonight, she spied through the glaze of moonlight two forms, then three, then four moving down the side of the high belfry tower. Their movements looked too right, and that rightness was as alarming as the aigamuxa's crooked swinging forms had ever been.

Humans.

"Damn it all," Gammon murmured. She checked her weapon in its holster and put a hand to her hat, running up the path and through the Old Cathedral's peaked Gothic doors.

One custom of the Old Religion, at least, had endured through the Unity. A church's doors were never locked—though, times being what they were, they were often under guard.

The Cathedral vestibule held six guards in black-and-gold EC livery, milling about with the uncertain dignity of men with orders they didn't understand. One whirled, pistol raised, as Gammon entered. He froze when he recognized her, not quite lowering his gun.

"What's going on?" Gammon demanded.

"Some coves come for the reverend doc," a man with a poorly trimmed beard answered. He nodded toward the nervous one with the gun. "Sturges says Deacon Fredericks wants the ground floor secured—"

"And the lower floors, and the triforium, and the whole rutting grounds," the one called Sturges snapped. "There's twenty of us—least there should be. Only twelve came 'round to report, and there en't much sign where the rest gone. En't seen Fredericks or the other collars, neither."

Gammon stepped past the man, scowling. The gun was still in Sturges's hands, muzzle pointing to the ground. He watched her cross the vestibule into the cavernous Cathedral. Inside, Gammon heard the distant sounds of aigamuxa bellowing, grunts and howls raining down on the Cathedral floor. Alchemical globes, their gases nearly spent, wavered beside the niches where the preserved bones of Neanderthal and Cro-Magnon mingled with golden imprints of the Logarithmic Equation and the Fourier Transformation, taking the place of the Stations.

The stairs up to the clerestory level, Gammon saw, were littered with bodies. More guards.

"I've found some of your twenty," she called.

Sturges came up and looked over her shoulder. "We know about those, ma'am."

"What's *happened*?"

"The aigamuxa've gone wild," the bearded guard answered, shifting about on his flat feet. "Leastways that's what folk are saying."

Sturges nodded. "Fredericks wants Chalmers back so we can move him somewhere else, start over. The ones who came for him broke in from below, and that's been sealed off. We en't heard a peep from the men keeping the levels between the cellar and ground. We figured the invaders would run clear out the front, then. And now Mathers just spotted 'em up on the roof."

"Half of Coventry Passage will spot them on the damned roof," Gammon snapped. She reached into a little case fastened at her hip and drew out a silk chute, a gas tube, and an alchemical bulb. She assembled the three pieces into a tiny signal balloon and passed it in a bundle to

Sturges. "Find the clearest patch of land you can, shake the bulb, and toss the rig up over your head. The gas tube will lift the chute up where the constabulary's spotters can see the signal bulb—my signal, a call for all available units." She scanned the other men's nervous faces. "The rest of you, go home."

"Ma'am?"

"*Go home*. You don't want to be here when the gendarmes show up expecting answers about who you're trying to guard against or why, do you?"

Gammon had thought many times that Fredericks's choice to increase security using his own Ecclesiastical escort was unwise. True, most of Fredericks's immediate circle was part of the scheme, but that didn't make the EC regulars any more qualified. If you wanted trouble, you joined the constabulary or the army; if you wanted a uniform and a lot of talk, you joined EC security.

This sort of talk, the guards were happy to hear. They left the vestibule in a rush. Sturges even dropped his gun.

Gammon drew her weapon and started up the stairs, passing the fallen men with their broken necks and blank eyes. There were two hatches to the belfries, each fitted with a folding ladder, the first leading to the high tower. It was the second that drew Gammon's notice. She stepped beneath the opening and its unfolded stairs. Silhouetted by the moonlight, something hung there, limp and dripping.

Haadiyaa Gammon had seen many corpses, but most still resembled men. The arm that hung down from the belfry hatch was not attached to the body lying nearby, but it was still in its sleeve. Gammon recognized the jewel-toned brocade and silver buttons.

It was easier to resign a position when one's employer had already resigned his life, she supposed. She turned her back on Lord Regenzi's remains. Her shoes struck something hard and heavy at her feet. It spun away, falling between two shafts of moonlight slicing the clerestory colonnade.

Gammon crouched and examined the weapon.

The pistol boasted a long barrel with a crosshair mounted toward the grip end, its under barrel fitted with a blunt magazine. It was damnably heavy. There was a slide catch on the left side of the barrel. Gammon worked it with a curt snap, and its magazine dropped free. She fitted it back into place and pushed the slide. Something inside the gun's body shifted ominously, accepting the rounds.

This, she thought, *is going to see some use.*

In three minutes, the central offices would signal the units stationed around the Cathedral district and Coventry Passage. They would arrive perhaps five minutes later. With a little luck, another complement would come up from central inside of ten.

Haadiyaa Gammon didn't believe in luck. She believed she had a good sense of who had come after Chalmers, though. That suspicion pushed her up the lower belfry ladder, the heavy gun shaped like a cannon tucked into her harness's strap.

35.

From the pitched copper roof of the Old Cathedral, Corma resembled a distant galaxy of stars the color of umber, glowing under a blanket of cold, yellow night fog. Rowena stared down between two blocky gaps in the raised roof's edge, the panorama marred by the sharp, luminous towers of Regency Square and the wilted rooftop garden of the Court and Bar. A gust of wind filled her coat like a sail. She staggered, hugging her arms against its hems, struggling to keep her feet. The wind had pushed her farther from the edge, but just the same, her heels had left the hammered metal roof for an instant. Reluctantly, her stomach slithered back down her throat.

Far below, the hedgerows of Coventry Passage sketched a maze, junctures of walkways and parkland framing the seminary and university like tiny monuments in a museum diorama. Rowena's head reeled at the distance and how quickly it would fly past if the wind bucked her from the roof.

A big hand closed on her shoulder. She looked up at the Alchemist. "En't ever been up so high before."

"Nor again," he said. The moonlight flared against the roof's green patina, casting an eerie glow. "The doctor's made it down. We need to cross to the lower roof. Take my hand."

She did. The memory of the wind filling up her coat made her grip a vise.

Master Meteron and Doctor Chalmers had descended the belfry tower together, with Meteron obliged to pick an easy route for the young scholar. Chalmers looked white as a pudding as he hugged the tower's foot, inching with painful care until Meteron snared his collar and ushered him into position. The Alchemist took the front, Rowena pacing him. Meteron kept the reverend in the middle and took up the rear.

The four moved in a half crouch, keeping as low a profile in the wind as could be managed. Their hurried steps echoed, mice scurrying over upturned kettles.

"Is there a reason we didn't go back down through the tunnels?" Rowena asked the Alchemist.

"We came that way, and they know it. They'll have covered that exit already."

"But, why the roof—" Rowena's question was suddenly cut in half.

"It's going well so far," Chalmers declared.

Rowena winced. "*Rule one*, Doc."

"*You* were talking, too," he protested. "But, really—" he glanced back at Meteron, "—we haven't had any trouble since leaving the cellar. Dodge a few guards, head straight up to the main floors, and then—"

"And then this," the Alchemist murmured.

He had dropped to one knee, peering over the edge of the belfry level roof. Rowena could see the flat expanse of the clerestory below and the line of pitched gargoyles and rust-stained, soot-blackened relief work where it ended. For a moment, her sense of direction turned on its head. From the ground, she'd stared up at the Old Cathedral many times, but its steep rises and graceful slopes had seemed a single, continuous shape from that vantage point. Now she could see how many levels and pieces comprised the structure, how complex it really was. Rowena searched her memory for the terms the Alchemist had applied hours earlier as they reviewed the schematics.

The Cathedral's interior had three levels. She couldn't remember the names, except for "clerestory." That was the one that mattered—the highest interior level. The clerestory had a roof spanning the whole building, from the front porch to the back of the chancel, where the EC collars gave their lectures on this thing or that. Rising up from the clerestory was the belfry level, joined by gutter works and spans of buttresses to the building's tall sides and the clerestory roof that made up its floor. There were two towers, high and low, on the belfry level, the lip of that middle roof extending over the main. That was where Rowena crouched now. And if she peered up to her left, there was the central tower, the

Cathedral's highest structure. It bridged out from the upper belfry tower, seated just behind it and squarely over the chancel.

It's a bit like one of those wedding cakes in bakers' windows, she thought, *with all the tiers stacked on one end, crowding up together.*

The clerestory roof was perhaps sixty feet down, linked to the belfry level by several short buttresses set at terrible angles.

You could get down there, Rowena supposed, *if you knew what you were about.*

She looked to her three companions, certain there were only two among them with any notion what they were about. She studied the Alchemist's grim expression and considered revising that figure downward.

"Well, we've got the rappelling lines," Rowena observed.

The Alchemist and the thief were already at work setting one up.

"The way down isn't the problem," the old man replied. He set down a spool of line and sank a bracing pin into the mortar just behind the last line of crenellation.

Chalmers frowned. "What, then?"

Meteron threaded something through the heavy eyelet of the rappelling harness, wrapped it twice, then handed it to the Alchemist. Hands freed, Meteron reached for the stock and barrel of his carbine and had it assembled in time to gesture with its snub nose.

It touched six points of the clock—three, one, twelve, eleven, nine, and eight. For a moment, Rowena saw nothing. Then, sheltering in the puddles of shadow gathered below statuary and scrollwork, she saw glinting eyes, pale as bloodied milk.

"*They* are the problem," Meteron said. He handed the Alchemist the carbine.

The old man was already strapped into the harness. He threaded the weapon through the leather saddle pressing against his back. Below, the aigamuxa shifted positions, speaking to one another in slithery sounds the wind sliced apart and carried away.

"Listen carefully," the Alchemist said to Rowena and Chalmers. "I am going down first—with you, girl. When we're down, stay behind those ornaments near the buttress arms. Ann will reel the line back and send you down after, Doctor. Then he'll take up the line and come down on his own."

Chalmers blinked. "I don't understand."

"I'll provide cover while you come down." The Alchemist patted the carbine. "Ann has to be last because he can manage the descent without a rig, and we need it brought down to this level to complete the escape."

"Can't he come down with *me*, like you with the girl? And then he could, you know?" Chalmers gestured breezily, made a little *ffwhpp!* noise, demonstrating the utter simplicity of his plan. "Head back up, disassemble the rig, shimmy down?"

Meteron snorted. "Waste of bloody time. Eventually the apes will tire of being held off. Then they'll close with us."

The Alchemist loosened a strap and gestured to Rowena. She leaned against him, felt a strap pass between her knees, then a pressure under her rear as it cinched tight. Rowena stared down at the drop. Four pink pinpricks winked in the darkness. She dug her fingers into the Alchemist's sleeve.

"Ready?"

She nodded, still staring.

He bent his knees, back to the drop, and pushed out. Momentum hurled Rowena's gullet into her gorge, though the descent was over in only three bounds against the buttress arm. The Alchemist whipped the harness off them, then shooed her back toward the cover of the ornaments at his back. Then he turned the carbine toward the ambuscades set in the higher points of downspouts, peaks, and statuary. He moved the muzzle from one set of glittering, down-hanging eyes to another, lingering on each a threatening moment.

Rowena stared out from under an arch of sub-buttress, flat on her belly and wide-eyed. Off to her right, she heard the line zipping back up, grunts and voices, a shrill cry. She watched the aigamuxa.

One seemed to be picking a path to the clerestory roof, swinging steadily lower, gnawing at the Alchemist's patience.

Reverend Chalmers landed awkwardly, shaking like a teacup dog. He wriggled free of the harness and scuttled beside Rowena. The Alchemist's satchel, swollen with the heavy book and hundreds of leaf notes, lay cradled in his trembling arms.

The reverend noticed the aigamuxa swinging down from the scaffolding surrounding a half-restored tower. It was within one hundred feet of their position, about ten o' the clock.

Then ninety.

Eighty.

"Shouldn't, um," he wondered aloud, "shouldn't he be shooting the beast by now?"

The Alchemist whirled, cracking shots twice at another aigamuxa who had been prowling closer, utterly silent on its blind eye heels at his level. The one creeping in at ten o' the clock had been its distraction.

The shots kicked up sparks around the aigamuxa's heels, sending it scrabbling backward, bounding for higher ground. The Alchemist turned and fired at ten o' the clock for good measure. The bullet must have grazed the aiga as it closed fifty feet, for it howled, dangling awkwardly before it, too, fell back, swinging to a shared position with eleven o' the clock.

A shadow moved above the Alchemist, smaller than the aigamuxa's. Meteron pushed away from the buttress and dropped the last ten feet, landing in a crouch beside his partner's knees, the rappelling gear slung over his shoulders. He drew his pistol with his left hand, stood with his back to the Alchemist's, and checked the positions he'd neglected.

"They'll close as soon as we take up a position for the descent," he said.

The Alchemist grunted. "Then we'll need a better shot than me holding them off."

Meteron bucked the rig off his shoulders and kicked it out from under his feet. "I'll take the carbine and the girl."

The Alchemist shot into the dark, caroming sparks off another copper downspout. The silhouette of an aigamuxa flashed in the night. "Why the girl?"

"Reloading. Chalmers would shoot himself in the foot. He can set the lines with you."

The old man worked a mechanism below the carbine's trigger loop, some kind of lever action used to ready a round. He passed the gun to Meteron and grabbed the dropped rig. Then he ran in a crouch toward the north edge of the roof, calling back to the buttresses: "Stay on me, Doctor!"

Chalmers crawled out from his nook beside Rowena and scuttled after, throwing one arm protectively overhead, ready to fend off the missiles with which the aigamuxa were clearly not armed.

Rowena darted beside Meteron. He stalked backward, carbine tucked under his right arm and pistol held out with his left, working to keep the aigamuxa under its roving barrel.

"How many *are there*, Master Meteron?" she asked.

He chuckled. "Danger really should lead to intimacy, Miss Downshire. Let's dispense with formality. Call me Anselm."

"Um . . . *Anselm*, how many are there?"

"About a dozen."

They reached the end of the roof the Alchemist and Chalmers occupied. The two men crouched together, spooling up the rappelling lines.

"Aigamuxa *like* high places," Rowena complained. "Why come up all this way just to get back down again?"

"You choose your battles," Anselm answered. "The tunnels will be blocked off, and there are guards on the ground floor. They're men, and that means they can use guns. Aigamuxa are dangerous, but only when you let them in close. They can't see to fire a gun. And personally, I prefer killing monsters to men. Call it a peccadillo." He thrust the pistol into Rowena's hands, then unholstered its mate, dropping it at her feet. "Ever held a gun before?"

"No."

"That's a very nice one. Loads easily—there's a cylinder drops out to the side. Here are a dozen reloads in preset rings. Pointed end in, flat bit out. Close the cylinder and leave the safety hammer up when you pass it. The carbine loads the same way." Anselm winked down at her. "I'm afraid we're in direct violation of rule two."

Rowena smiled nervously. "Well—you're not actually in the middle of a firefight."

"Not yet." He shouldered the carbine and sighted along its snub barrel. "Whatever I put in front of you gets loaded. That's the new rule two."

For what seemed a long time, the aigamuxa didn't move, though Rowena could hear them calling back and forth under the wind's low song. Anselm watched. The Alchemist secured the lines, Chalmers jumping on his orders.

Nothing changed.

And then Anselm's lip curled. "God's balls. Bear!"

"What?"

"Nasrahiel isn't here."

The Alchemist looked up. He cursed around the docking pin held in his teeth. "You're certain?"

"Of course I'm certain!" Anselm snapped. "He's the only goddamned aiga I'd pick out of a crowd. He's *not here*."

"The hell he isn't," growled the Alchemist, driving the pin into the mortar at his feet. "Ambush."

He stood and put a hand to Chalmers's chest, shoving the younger man down onto the tiled roof. He drew the weaponette from its holster.

A clawed hand reached up over from the ledge behind him, its four-jointed fingers closing around the crenellation's edge.

There were three aigamuxa. Two leapt up from the face of the Cathedral they'd just scaled, ready to crash into the Alchemist's flanks. The third was Nasrahiel. He perched on the roof's edge between the riggings, leering with shark-toothed certainty.

Rowena cried out a warning, but two barking shots from the carbine punched through her words. Her ears rang, her nose full of burning ash.

The aigamuxa in the high towers began swinging down, the night exploding with their whoops and bellows.

For a moment, the world moved slowly.

The Alchemist flicked his wrist. The weaponette's shaft sprang into a blade the length of his arm. His retreat turned into two dancing steps and a spin. He avoided the first aigamuxa's lunge and sliced at the face of the other. The sword carved a bloody line across the creature's nose. It bellowed in rage—but that was all. The cut would have blinded a man. An aigamuxa was another matter.

"Rowena! Switch!"

She felt the stock of the carbine butting her shoulder. Anselm glared down at her, hands out for the pistols. She cursed and passed them up to him, almost fumbling the one for his right.

Anselm lacked a trigger finger on his right hand, but that didn't keep him from firing. With his middle finger in the loop, he could haul off the shots, though few were true enough to do more than discourage an enemy's advance. With the left, Anselm winged the fast-moving aigamuxa as they brachiated down to the clamoring chaos of the clerestory roof.

Rowena had time enough to reload the carbine. Then she felt the wind crushed from her lungs, a weight like a cart run wild plowing into her chest.

The sky spun. Rowena's feet left the ground, something long and sinewy curling around her throat.

Then there was only the hum of the copper roof falling still and the tinny whine of ringing ears.

Things had gone very quiet.

36.

"Surrender the doctor and the book," Nasrahiel called, "and I will not kill the girl."

The Alchemist put his back to Anselm's, standing at a right angle to the aigamuxa and his hostage. Rowena's feet stamped the air. She clawed the aigamuxa's hand, face purpling.

The Alchemist glanced at his partner. "Ann, I know you wanted to face him, but—"

"The stakes have changed," Anselm answered. He lowered his guns. "I'll explain later."

Chalmers scrambled to his feet. "He'll kill her anyway! That's what he wants. He must have figured it out when he studied the notations on my maps."

Rowena's kicking grew weaker. Her elfin face looked more gray than purple.

"Figured what out?" the Alchemist demanded.

"There's a *lot* to explain later," Anselm said apologetically. His left pistol snapped back up, leveled at the aigamuxa.

Two shots rang out. One came from behind Nasrahiel.

The aigamuxa doubled over when the machine pistol round took him in the shoulder. Anselm's shot, which would have drilled into the center of his skull, cut cold air instead, whanging off a gutter works in the darkness beyond.

Anselm and the Alchemist looked where the other shot had come from. Inspector Haadiyaa Gammon perched some fifty feet up, at the foot of the lower belfry tower.

Nasrahiel threw Rowena over his unwounded shoulder and staggered off, running a wide, blind path through Reverend Chalmers, the young man futilely barring the way. He crashed in a heap of elbows. The shadows of the aigamuxa, howling and bellowing, rushed onto the Cathedral's roof.

The Alchemist lunged after Nasrahiel, only to be spun around by a huge arm. A backhand blow swept him up off his feet and into a dark form, a red line scored in its face.

The two aigamuxa he'd fended off before closed with the Alchemist again. He moved his blade up, around, and between, ducking the blows he could and cutting to match the ones he was obliged to take. His head rang. His arm felt heavy. Somewhere far off, he heard Rowena scream.

Anselm emptied his left-hand pistol into the first two aigamuxa to rush forward. He heard the voice behind him call "Duck!" and obeyed in time to avoid the machine shot that would have cut through his back before punching into the stomach of the aigamuxa barreling up between its fallen comrades.

The creature took the shot full. It fell to the ground slack-jawed, its belly yawning viscera.

Anselm scowled at Gammon and the Alchemist's gift in her hands. "That," he noted tartly, "doesn't belong to you."

Gammon turned, shot at another aigamuxa, then shifted left. Anselm put his back to hers. She circled around, giving him cover to reload.

"True," Gammon said. "I'm also fairly sure it's illegal outside Vraska."

"And in Vraska." Anselm emptied his right-hand gun, scoring a line of dents in the roof as his target veered narrowly away. "Mind your nine, Haadi."

She did. The blunderbuss split the air with a sound like a hull breaching on the shallows.

The Alchemist spun left, driving the point of his sword into his assailant's swinging arm. It sank deep, biting the artery. Blood fanned from the wound, spraying across his face. The creature's knees buckled before he could tear the blade free.

The other aigamuxa dove in, ready to take the Alchemist with his blade bound.

He sidestepped, wrested the sword free, and brained the creature with the pommel as it sailed past. It landed on all fours, shaking its head and spitting curses.

He drove the sword's point into the small of its back and flicked the trigger to empty its charge between the aiga's twin spines. Crooked legs flailed out from under the creature, one last spasm, and then, at last, it stilled.

The Alchemist set the point of the blade in the ground and heaved for breath. There were stars out in the cloudy night—constellations he did not remember. He shook his throbbing head to clear the sky again.

Reverend Chalmers watched, stomach turning, as they died and they died. A lunatic impulse to check the book and see how it would record the bloodshed came to him. Though he squelched it with a very small effort, the absurdity still drove his hand down to his satchel, and he felt . . .

Nothing. The bag was gone, and with it the notes.

And the book.

Chalmers looked wildly around, trying to spy where the aigamuxa chieftain and his captive had gone. He saw Anselm Meteron and a strange woman with a very large pistol shooting down a ring of approaching aigamuxa. He saw the Alchemist struggling to keep his feet after his fray. There was blood running from his temple, and he looked dazed as another beast stalked nearer. Still, the old man saw the aiga and straightened in time to get his blade into a ready position.

And then Chalmers saw Nasrahiel's shadow swinging up the buttresses to the upper belfry tower. A moment later, the aigamuxa was running across the spine of the pitched roof and toward the inner buttresses and the square Gothic tower perched above the Cathedral's chancel. The girl's form was clamped tight to his and so was something else—something smaller, something bundled and square.

For the first time in his life, Phillip Chalmers set off at a run toward something decidedly unhealthy.

Haadiyaa Gammon raised the blunderbuss at the charging aigamuxa and pulled its trigger.

There was only a click.

"Damn it!"

Whatever the weapon was, she hadn't found extra munitions with it. She threw it aside, dropping to the roof, stabbing a hand into her coat for her constabulary issue.

"Anselm, get *down*."

Gammon's crouch saved her from the aigamuxa's leap. It also cleared the path for it to barrel into Anselm, flattening him against the copper roof. The rogue's left shoulder struck the tiles with a sickening crunch.

Anselm dropped his empty right-hand pistol and heard the left-hand clatter from his nerveless fingers. His knife sheath was pinned, his left side afire with pain, the creature's weight bearing down. The aigamuxa reared up to deal a hammer blow with its knotted fists.

Three shots, spaced by the clicks of a caplock hammer, shook the creature from behind. The last exited the aiga's mouth, raining blood and bone fragments as it toppled over Anselm. Groaning, he put his right hand to the roof and pushed. Then Gammon put a shoulder into the corpse and rolled its dead weight away.

She reached an arm around Anselm's back to lever him up. When Gammon touched the wounded shoulder, Anselm shoved her off with a curse, eyes watering.

"Dislocated," he gasped. "I think I'm done shooting for the night."

Gammon pulled him up by the right arm instead. "Just as well. It looks like the rest have gone."

Anselm looked for the Alchemist, blinking his vision clear. "Bear! Where the hell is Chalmers?"

The Alchemist pried his sword free of the last aigamuxa to have met it. He looked around.

And then, all three looked up.

Nasrahiel moved like a shadow across the moonlit roof between the chancel towers, grasping a kicking and clawing form. Picking a slow, slippery path up the gutter works of the upper belfry tower, the Reverend Phillip Chalmers followed after. He paused, kicking off his slick-soled dress shoes, and carried on in stocking feet, alternating between teetering in the skirling wind and clinging like an insect to the Cathedral's upper reaches.

The Alchemist flicked his wrist. The sword collapsed to its holster length.

"Can you catch up to them?" he called. And then he saw how Anselm leaned against Gammon, marked the droop in his shoulder. "Damn it all," he spat.

Gammon pointed to the south. "Look."

The hedgerows and larches of the Cathedral Commons were hazy shapes in the yellow fog far below, but all three could see a dozen or more constables and gendarmes spreading out to cover the grounds. One man carried a long, narrow case. He and two others disappeared into the Cathedral's front porch.

"They've sent a marksman," Gammon said. "He can take a shot at Nasrahiel from this level."

"Not while he has Rowena," the Alchemist barked.

"We might still get a clean shot. He's likely to—" The inspector stopped. She had been about to say "drop her."

Anselm shook his head. "It's a bad angle. The wind will take the shot off course. Bear, do you think—"

He turned, but the Alchemist was already gone.

Gammon frowned. "Where the hell is he?"

Anselm glared up at the gutter works leading to the upper belfry tower. "No," he whispered, then shouted, "You idiot bastard, *get down from there*!"

There was no telling if the Alchemist could hear his shouts, but Anselm knew he would have ignored them in any case. Bears were impossibly stubborn beasts, and they *could* climb—

The real ones, anyway.

Anselm watched the Alchemist's silhouette move across the gabled belfry roof, watched it pause and make a short leap to grasp the shoulders of a gargoyle leaning over the chancel roof. He had one of the rappelling rigs wrapped across his chest, flecks of mortar falling from the pin just torn from its moorings.

Gammon glanced between the Alchemist and Anselm. "Is he familiar with free climbing?"

"Familiar," Anselm said distantly, "is a relative concept. Get your marksman up here, Haadi. I'll get him into position."

37.

Reverend Chalmers wasn't one for high places—or low places, or risks, or pain, or anything that left him feeling cold and afraid. Yet somehow he'd ended up in the middle of all these things as he climbed his white-knuckled way after the aigamuxa chieftain.

Chalmers reached the last span of buttress connecting the upper reaches to the tower roof and there sank onto his belly, hugging the yard's width of stone with all his trembling strength. The wind was a deafening keen, running the staff between the tooth-grinding register that set dogs singing and the low, throbbing drones of a bagpipe.

Nasrahiel had started the climb well ahead of him, but Chalmers had had no captive, no satchel with notes and book to weigh him down, and the benefit of his eyes straight before him. The distance between them could be measured in yards now. The aigamuxa chieftain stood at the far end of the buttress, panting. Blood from the wound in his shoulder stained his side. He seemed at last to resent the weight he had carried all this while.

Nasrahiel clawed at Rowena's flailing form. Snarling, he peeled her off like a tick, then hurled her away.

Rowena struck the roof, rolled, and shot off its edge, her body skimming the buttress's face.

Chalmers opened his mouth to scream—

And Rowena's hands closed on a gargoyle's beak. She hooked an elbow around its stony head and struggled to get her feet up where they could dig for purchase.

Almost before he knew what his body was doing, Phillip Chalmers crawled toward her, worming across the buttress's span. The wind cut. Chalmers's hands ached. His eyes watered, tears frosting his lashes. He stopped to scrub the rime away and pulled himself along again.

And then she was there, just to his left, still holding on with one arm and one hand, her scabby fingers slick with sweat and dark with dried blood. Rowena saw him. Her eyes went wide.

"Can you reach my hand?" she shouted.

Phillip Chalmers stared at her. He had understood the words, but his eyes looked past her, down into the steep bluffs of ironwork and stone relief breaking the space between the buttress and the ground.

And then, he inched past her, eyes on Nasrahiel and the book. Chalmers gritted his teeth against the girl's shrill screams.

He was a scientist. There was an experiment underway. Experiments always had test subjects, control subjects, parameters, requirements. Often, the parameters were not gentle. That was why every good experiment had more than one subject at its center.

Chalmers believed in good experiments. He knew when to resign himself to their costs.

When his fingers touched the Cathedral's highest roof, he stood up, hugging his wind-whipped coat.

Ten steps away, Nasrahiel waited. His eyes flared triumphantly from their perches on his shoulders.

"I see I could have spared myself bringing two types of bait. I did not know I already had the kind you prefer."

At Chalmers's back, there was a strangled scream and a scrabbling sound. He winced but did not turn.

"The book is useless to you without an interpreter," he shouted.

"And you have been good enough to put one in my reach."

Chalmers's legs had been weak when he took to the roof. He nearly lost them at those words.

Phillip, you idiot. You've given yourself to him.

The wind staggered Chalmers. He threw out an arm to get his balance, then sank to a knee.

Unless, he considered grimly, *there are other options. . . .*

The tower roof was eighty or more feet above the clerestory level. To the right and left, very little of that lower level was visible over the eaves and overhangs. It wouldn't take much for a falling body to miss the clerestory altogether—to find its way to the cobblestones below.

The bones in Rowena Downshire's left hand were frozen, her fingers nerveless. They lost their grip of the ornament's beak for the second time. When she tightened her right biceps around its head, trying to swing the left arm back up and hug herself to safety, her shoulder jerked weakly in response. The stone bit into her arm. The pins and needles running through it promised it would give way soon.

The reverend's voice echoed nearby, tangled up with Nasrahiel's slithery rasp. All Rowena could see was the lip of the buttress sagging farther away as the strength drained from her fingers. She looked up, hoping to move her grip a little, and her arm slipped. Rowena yelped, dug her hands in, and kicked until her boots pressed the underside of the buttress.

You are going to die.

The thought came to her in a calm and practical voice, the sort of voice that would make a list of the day's chores. *The washing needs doing, and someone has to stop by the greengrocer's, and you are going to die, and things like this happen every day.*

Except they didn't. Three days ago, Rowena Downshire would not have been surprised to learn she'd die run over by a careless hackney driver, or falling on the charged rail of the lightning lines, or getting stuck up for her coin purse, or nicking a delivery surcharge and taking Ivor's hawthorn until he made a soup of her brains. Things like *that* happened every day. People did not fall from the tallest monument in Corma every day. Reason knew *she* didn't. Not after being duped and kidnapped and imprisoned and shot at and chased. Not after having her whole world turned arse over teakettle. Not after years of filth and flight and hunger and harassment, without even a bed for her mother that wasn't a holiday home for rats to show for it.

It was a bloody awful way to die. It had been a bloody awful way to live.

Knowing that only made her want to drive her thumb in fate's eye harder. She looked up again, reached with her half-numb arm. Her fingers were so close to a stone rose. They brushed the petals, but that was all. Rowena wanted to scream in frustration, but that might jostle her somehow, and it was such a long way down.

She stretched for the rose again. Something shadowed the face of the moon.

Hands. Arms. The Alchemist hooked her under the shoulders, hauling her up.

Rowena felt herself dragged to the far end of the buttress, away from the aigamuxa and the reverend and all their bookish troubles. She lay panting, staring up at the bright, full moon. The Alchemist was panting, too, but he perched on his heels, untying the rappelling rig wrapped over his chest. Dimly, Rowena saw the blood dried against his graying temple and the gashes torn in his sleeves where the aigas' claws had raked him. His shirt was starched bright red. Rowena was too exhausted to sit up. It dawned on her how tired the Alchemist must have been.

Rowena put a hand on his leg. He looked down at her hand, then her face, and smiled.

"You're all right, girl?"

"I think so."

He pulled her into a sitting position, working the harness over her head, fastening it under her shoulders, strapping it across her chest.

Rowena stared at his hands as they worked, brisk and automatic. It occurred to her this was not the way he had hooked the rig before. *Not* the way you fastened in a passenger.

She blinked. "You're coming, en't you?"

"Not yet," the Alchemist answered, frowning over a buckle. "Time for rule three. Stay with Ann. Do as he says." He cinched another strap.

The harness across Rowena's chest must have been too tight. Her breath wouldn't come.

"I en't leaving you."

The Alchemist's hands paused over the last buckle. He ran his fingers down the strap, shaking his head. "Rowena—"

"*No.* I won't."

The Alchemist took her head in his hands. His dark raptor eyes were close by, closer than they'd ever been. They were telling her something she didn't want to know.

He kissed her forehead gently. "I'll catch up."

And then he pushed her, and the rest was down, down, down, Rowena looking up as the Alchemist turned back toward the buttress and began crossing.

He'd set the braking wheel almost perfectly, her heels jouncing lightly against the clerestory roof. She bent her knees on reflex and sank onto her rear. There were hands grabbing the straps, pulling them loose. Rowena looked dully at two strange men stooping over her, each in constabulary blues. Behind them, Inspector Gammon pointed to different areas of the uppermost roof. Anselm flung curses at her. A young marksman stood by the argument with his rifle and bracing fork, waiting.

Rowena looked back up. She felt much colder than she had only a moment before, clinging to stone in the winter wind.

Chalmers considered the vertiginous fall, its path broken by the Cathedral's ancient ornaments.

Nasrahiel uncoiled himself, giving Chalmers a moment's advantage. The creature was effectively blind, and though he could still smell and hear his human quarry, Chalmers doubted he had a way of sensing what he intended to *do*.

He shuffled closer to the edge.

The wind banked off the tower. Chalmers's coat bloomed like a parachute, pulling him back. He staggered before wrestling himself free of its flailing hems.

As the coat whipped away, Chalmers saw his right foot was only a half step from the roof's edge.

He swallowed a bitter knot.

"You need the book *and* an interpreter," he shouted. "You're farther from having both than you know."

The aigamuxa tilted its head. Its clawed hands clamped the straining hems of the Alchemist's bag.

"This is a very inopportune time for you to develop principles, Doctor," Nasrahiel growled.

Chalmers laughed. He could almost see himself pitching over hysteria's edge. Then he felt a stockinged heel brush the roof's lip and froze. "I've always been a slow learner. I thrive on example. I'm surprised it took me this long to think of Nora again."

Nasrahiel edged closer, grasping.

"You wanted me to think you killed her. To keep me cowed," Chalmers continued. "But you wouldn't have risked losing her. She killed herself, didn't she?"

"You are making a terrible mistake, Doctor."

"I think," Chalmers shouted, "I am finally doing the *correct* thing."

And he lifted his foot.

"I'm going back up there," Rowena snapped. She broke free of Anselm's maimed hand with a twist. The left arm stayed tucked against his chest, limp. Useless.

"There's nothing you can do to help," he insisted. There was an edge of something in his voice—pleading? *He's not the kind who pleads with anybody.*

Rowena looked frantically around. Gammon's constables had taken their positions, sighting with monoculars and shouting things back to the city inspector. The marksman had bunkered in for his shot, Gammon hovering close. They wouldn't even see to stop Rowena if she made a break for the belfry again, and there was no way Anselm could make the climb up after her.

But she couldn't afford to go unprepared.

Rowena darted for one of Anselm's holsters, hoping to snatch a pistol and make a run for it. He saw it coming in time to swat her hand away and hook her legs from under her with a swipe of his heel.

The roof's copper ridges bit into Rowena's back. Her eyes welled with tears. She scrambled back to her knees, ready to pelt Anselm with curses—but he wasn't glaring at her anymore.

He squinted against the moonlight, eyeing the shadows moving on the high tower.

"*Ahead* of the target? Why?" he murmured.

Rowena stared at him. "Who are you talking—"

Anselm waved at her, shushing. His lip twisted. "I don't like it—and you may not have time. How many rounds do you have left?"

Rowena followed Anselm's gaze, and all at once, she understood.

Whatever answer the Alchemist sent, it earned a curse in response. Anselm turned on his heel, cradling his arm, and jogged back toward Gammon. Rowena looked back and forth, torn between the belfry tower and Anselm. She spied a third form crouched high above at the buttress's edge, hidden from the two on the roof.

"Stay with Ann," he'd said. *"Do as he says."*

"You'd better know what you're about, Old Bear," she murmured and ran after Anselm.

Gammon peered through her monocular, studying the scene above. "Five degrees left," she called.

The marksman shifted his rifle and sighted through its crosshairs. He curled a finger around the trigger, then uncurled.

"The EC collar's in the way."

"Scope it out a moment. Steady on."

Rowena arrived four strides behind Anselm, just in time to hear him bark, "*No!*"

He stopped close enough to Gammon the city inspector edged away, peeling like paint from his heat.

"Even if Chalmers moves," Anselm insisted, "the wind will take that shot clear past the target. The aiga will move forward. Shoot ahead of its position. Cut the angle to the right."

The marksman blinked at Gammon. "Ma'am, who is this bastard?"

"Anselm," Gammon said, reaching to turn his shoulder. "I think we have this."

"If you touch me with that hand, I'll break it," Meteron snapped. "Tell your man to take the shot my way, or it's wasted."

Gammon hesitated.

"There's a *reason* we learned enough to get here in the first place, Haadi. Trust me. Cut about ten degrees right, ahead of the target."

Reluctantly, the city inspector turned to the marksman. "Can you set it up?"

"I can't spot that angle from here, ma'am."

"Then get as close as you can," Anselm said. He stared up at the three forms nearly eclipsed by the glare of moonlight. "He can deal with close."

The Alchemist crouched at the buttress's edge, unseen by the aigamuxa and man only yards away. The wind scattered their words, but he could read the situation clear enough. At best, he had ten seconds. Experience told him things were unlikely to be at their best.

Chalmers stood nearer and to the right, about four o' the clock. Nasrahiel was at the one. The Alchemist hoped Anselm had accurately read the image of the scene he'd sent. He hoped, too, that his partner hadn't sensed he'd been lying about having three rounds left.

One. The Alchemist had one, and he knew exactly how to make the most of it—a plan much surer than his marksmanship had ever been.

He shifted his weight, keeping his knees bent and shoulders low. He was a big man, solid and perhaps even a little stronger than he looked. It had been years since his body had known so much use, yet it seemed to have remembered all the steps so far. It might have one last dance in it.

The aigamuxa lurched forward, moving toward the young reverend. Chalmers's hesitant foot passed the roof's edge.

The Alchemist raised his pistol and shot wide of Nasrahiel, letting the bullet sing off into the dark. He had never been even close to Anselm's equal with a gun. Fortunately, his plan didn't require accuracy.

It only required his enemy's attention.

The aigamuxa spun, aiming himself at the Alchemist. Snarling, Nasrahiel surged forward, ready to devour the bait.

The distraction had moved him ten degrees off his previous position, three paces forward.

The Alchemist heard the shot an eyeblink after it took Nasrahiel in the chest, just below the right shoulder. The aigamuxa howled and staggered back.

That was the moment's delay he'd needed.

As Nasrahiel whirled, reaching blindly for the reverend doctor at the edge of the roof, the Alchemist barreled into his back. He wrapped up the beast's bloodied flanks, pinning his arms.

At first, he felt only the *whuff* of the air rushing from his lungs as their bodies collided. Then came his sides and back smashing against the roof as they tumbled together, a tangle of mass and acceleration—

And then there was nothing—open air, the clutch of gravity, a whirling of shadow and stone, moonlight and limbs.

A sharp, cracking pain turned the world white.

Phillip Chalmers watched man and aigamuxa sail off the roof, forgetting how close he was to a similar end. Then he saw the satchel with the book and notes racing down the roof's planed edge, and he, too, leaped.

He landed on his belly with a whanging sound, his teeth snapping shut. The bag itself was just beyond reach. He snared the strap as it slid past his fingers. The sudden, braking inertia slingshot the satchel around in a graceful arc.

For a moment, Chalmers's heart danced at the sight of the Vautnek text and his notes spinning back toward him—but the book's mass carried it away, caroming after the falling figures. It disappeared into the dark, cover flapping like a wounded bird before pitching toward the ground. Momentum and the night wind played havoc with Chalmers's papers. He gaped as their remnants fell around him, mere snowflakes from the avalanche of evidence he'd compiled.

Below, he heard a leaden thud. There was a girl's scream, a woman shouting orders, then men's voices clamoring over one another. Suddenly, Chalmers remembered what had just happened.

He swept the last of his notes up, gathering them in a ragged bundle. Then he slid to the roof's edge and peered down.

Some eighty feet below, the Alchemist's body was the eye in a storm of movement.

38.

The fall from the upper towers began with man and aigamuxa locked in a grapple. And then they clipped the Cathedral's ornamented flanks, chests and shoulders and the back of the Alchemist's head dashing against downspouts and gargoyles and crenellation. He went limp. The bodies separated, his barreling down to the clerestory roof. The aigamuxa deflected against a rampart, its spidery form curling and flailing, plummeting past the sheer edge of the Old Cathedral's eastern wall into the hedgerows far below.

When the Alchemist met the clerestory roof, there was a boom like thunder, and a snap Anselm felt in his phantom finger. He grabbed his screaming left shoulder and ran, dropping to his knees and skidding the last few feet to the Alchemist's side.

A pool of blood spread at the nape of the Alchemist's neck, and his right leg bent at a sick angle below the knee. His chest rose and fell, the movement shallow. Anselm opened his mouth to shout for a physick, but a cloud of noisome vapors choked him back onto his heels. Dizzied by pain and rising panic, for a moment he couldn't think where it came from—

The coat.

Anselm reached for his knife, only to find a small hand snatching it from him. He knuckled his vision clear.

Rowena slit the buttons from the Alchemist's coat and threw it open. She tugged at its sleeves, trying to pull the stew of glass and chemicals away until a shrill cry froze her.

"*Don't move him!*"

Phillip Chalmers slid from the lower belfry tower's roof, skidding down its buttress arm. He landed in a heap and was running almost before he had his feet again. His coat bulged with half a stationer's shop of bedraggled notepaper.

"Don't move him," he panted, kneeling between Anselm and Rowena. "His neck could be broken, or his back . . . Might have a punctured lung . . . Where's that surgeon's kit?"

The reverend doctor froze, looking at Anselm in despair. Anselm shook his head.

"Get the girl away," Chalmers said. "There's no sense in her watching him d—" He stopped short. "I say, what on earth is wrong with her?"

The knife had fallen from Rowena's fingers. She knelt beside the Alchemist, a hand on his breastbone. Her eyes were lost in the space before her, as if studying a landscape unseen.

Chalmers grasped her shoulder, shook hard. The girl swayed.

Anselm had seen that look before. He doubted she knew they were there at all.

The library glows with wildfire, the air itself burning. All around, Rowena sees checkered tiles rise from the floor, drifting into an open sky far above. One by one, they disintegrate, and the air is choked with their ashes. Books fly off the long rows of shelves, the covers black, flapping wings, the spines splitting as they sail into the impossible distance, growing ever smaller.

Rowena spins round, staring. At the center of the library, the ground is a whirlpool, shelves swirling as if pulled down a drain.

There is a long staircase rising toward a gallery above, its halls lined with doors. She hears them slamming, hears panes of glass shattering.

"Minds are abstract things, girl," *the Alchemist had said.* "You can't walk into an abstraction, and so you enter the metaphor of it."

Rowena runs to the staircase, hurtles up its steps. For a moment, there is only her running and the sound of exploding glass. Then the whole structure ripples. She digs her heels in and sprints for the summit. The steps crumble under her feet. Rowena stumbles, snatches the balustrade, and leaps past the final gap, whole flights of the staircase plummeting into the yawning blackness below.

This, *she realizes,* must be what it was like going into Rare's mind. Everything falling apart, the mainspring unwinding.

Except the Alchemist en't dead yet. There's something left to save.

Rowena casts the doubt nipping at that thought into the darkness with the rest of the debris. Her whole life has been a foxhunt for uncatchable things—being free of the hawthorn, free of the debt, free with her mother, free to be unafraid. Life carved hope away, whittled her down, and no one noticed or cared or tried to change even the smallest thing.

But he *had noticed her. He had cared, though it would have been easier not to. He had done small things and impossible things, too—reached into minds and found the truth and spoken with the dead and acted with courage and risen from the dead and saved the girl another man had simply crawled past. It was all impossible. And yet it had happened, because he had willed it so.*

It was a lack of will that made things impossible.

Rowena Downshire has nothing but will.

The gallery is a maze of passages and doors. The knobs burn white-hot, running like wax, sealing the ways in.

She races down the corridors. Every passing moment, she knows less of where she is going or where she has been. The corridors curve and double back—rise into the air, or plunge like warehouse chutes, throwing her down in a heap. Every time, she leaps up and runs again, searching for the Alchemist.

One by one, the rooms seal themselves off, disintegrating. Burning. Some are fading away, turning into vague sketches, colorless and incomplete, then unwinding into threads of charcoal and ink, joining the gathering smog.

Rowena finds a cellar door, metal banded and unlatched. She avoids its white-hot ring and kicks at it, splintering the wood down the center. Inside, puddles of melted flesh and charring bone slide into one another like oil flowing in a skillet. Half a hand reaches from some ruined memory. A floating eyeball blinks within the crawling soup.

The girl staggers down the passage, gagging. She passes a door split open, growing vines and sprouting green shoots. It rends away its carpentry, the nails screaming free in iron curls.

The hallway turns a sharp right. It ends three paces later.

Rowena fights for breath, shoulders heaving. When she lifts her head for a gulp of air, she sees a woman at the dead end. She wears trousers patched with heavy pockets. Her tunic sleeves are pinned up with little leather garters, sets of hex wrenches tinkling from their buckles. A pair of welding goggles rings her neck, as lovely against her freckled collarbone as any jewelry. Her copper hair is cropped boyishly short, her keen gray eyes familiar.

Rowena stares at her. The moment seems to stretch on as she places the face and recognizes the eyes, the tapering chin, the crooked turn of her mouth.

There are things that make sense now, questions she didn't know to ask suddenly answered.

"I know why you're here," the woman says.

Her voice is sympathetic. It is not *hopeful.*

"So help me get him back," Rowena answers.

Leyah shakes her head. "It doesn't work that way."

"Then show me where to find him and I'll do it myself."

Leyah considers the girl. Her eyes are like scales taking Rowena's measure, but she seems to put her thumb on the balances before making her choice.

"Follow me."

The alchemical lamps leak gases that mingle and spark like aurorae in the air as they hurry past, turning back up the corridor and around a bend that was not there before, cutting deeper and deeper into the labyrinth of the Alchemist's mind. The passages coil tighter, all roads dwindling down into a horizon of sepia and tearing wind.

"If she finds us, you have to leave," Leyah shouts over the gale.

"If who *finds us?"*

The passage ends at a rough, clapboard door. Leyah paws around, as if searching for some hidden catch. "No," she cries, "this isn't supposed to be here! She changed the path, somehow."

"Who?"

The wind has shifted. It's heavy now, carrying the animal stench of butchering and some kind of woody perfume.

"I, of course."

Rowena freezes. She turns and faces Rare.

The white sheet from the morgue winds about her like a robe on a marble statue. The ragged wounds in her side wink through its cloth. One side of her face is still a ruin of bone and blood, and yet somehow, she's beautiful, the bow of her lips drawing a deadly smile.

Rare raises a hand, and the door at Rowena's back blasts open. She looks behind her. There is a green field, and a tree, and two figures on the hill beneath it, tangled up with one another.

And then, Rowena knows she has been here before.

"We have to find him, Rare," Leyah insists. If she is afraid of her daughter's revenant, she's wise enough not to let it show.

Rare's broken face twists in anguish. "You can't *go back there. I won't let you."*

"Darling, please—"

Somehow, the space all around them has bled into the grassy plain—or the hill has flowed down into the corridor. Rowena sees a pale, yellow light all around, feels the sun bloom against her skin.

"Stay here, Mother," Rare says. Her voice is honey, but under its sweetness, there is something else. A glittering edge. A wild, desperate fear. "This is a good place. You can't go back there again."

Rowena wonders where "there" is, but now it hardly matters. Only time matters. Time the Alchemist doesn't have.

"She has to go with me," Rowena snaps. "I need her to find him!"

And then, Rare turns. The pit of her ruined eye burns through the girl. "This is all your fault."

Fear turns Rowena's legs into stone. She tries to bend them, to move them, but can only stare into Rare's broken face.

"All I did was carry your letter," she whispers.

Rowena's feet come loose all at once, and she staggers back, looking wildly around the pale green valley. The ground has softened, turning into mire and moor. It sucks at her boots, pulls at her ankles, reaches for her knees—

Rare turns back to Leyah, as if Rowena has already been swallowed by the muck.

"Stay with me," she says, smiling. "With him. Here. We can fix it now. We'll have all the time in the world to make things right again."

Leyah ignores her daughter, scanning the horizons, looking for some way out. Rowena follows her gaze up the hill. The forms tangled there—two lovers, uncoiling from an embrace—are changing, the smaller twisting and shrinking, crawling atop its partner with long, dark claws raised.

Rowena looks back at Rare. Her pale skin shimmers in the air, steaming like a heat mirage. Her fingernails grow into shears, skimming against each other as she clenches her fists.

"I can *keep you here. If I must."*

Rowena reaches for her boots, starts tugging at her feet, trying to dislodge herself. The mire shudders her down further, brimming over her leather cuffs. Panic rings in her ears. She claws and tugs—digs against the slick mud.

Her fingers scrape the hilt of her boot knife. She looks up at the dark hill and its wild, rending creature. If she can make Rare let her go, make her come close enough—

"It won't work if I'm here," Rowena shouts.

Rare's eyes snap round, stinging like a lash.

"If you're all dead and together that's just jake. But then I'll be dead here, too." Rowena hauls against her boots again. The mud covers her fingers and the blade. Rare doesn't see her draw it free, buried in a muddy fist. "Anybody can see I'm his favorite." Rowena smirks. "That'll be a piss in your tea, eh? So much for the family reunion."

Rare stalks toward Rowena, claws scissoring. "Then get out.*"*

"I would,*" Rowena says, "except you've got me in a real jam here."*

The wind cuts across the plain again, spraying mud in Rowena's eyes . . . and then her feet are on hard ground. The mud is gone, even from her boots—and from her hands. The knife's edge glints in the sunlight.

Rare looms over her. She sees the blade. "Well. You're a clever little bird, aren't you?"

"Shit," Rowena whispers.

The claws swoop down, and she scrambles back, tripping on her own feet. Rare pounces. Rowena swipes with her blade, scraping clear the space between them. She stumbles, and the claws rake her, shoulder to hip.

This is a dream, *Rowena tells herself, scooting on her haunches. Her blouse falls in ribbons all around her.* This is a *dream.*

It still hurts.

Rowena searches for a place to run.

The tree on the hill is still there, the small, feral creature feasting from a ragged hole in the man's chest. The wind blows its hair like a golden banner.

You're a damned eejit, Rowena Downshire, *she thinks.*

She runs for the hill, anyway. If the child-thing is Rare, too, she knows it will still be hungry. It will always *be hungry.*

The revenant of Rare plunges after Rowena, claws scrabbling into the hillside.

At the crest of the hill, Rowena stops, skidding in the grass. The dead man's rib cage is a jagged nest of bone and guts. It must have been the Alchemist—but beneath that ruin, it might have been anybody. The child-Rare squats over her kill, her bare, flat chest smeared with blood.

The monster turns toward Rowena. Its eyes burn with hunger, and it lunges.

Rowena ducks, dropping to her knees with her hands over her head.

Rare's revenant reaches the crest in time to take the child-Rare's pounce full in the face.

The monstrous shades of the woman roll downhill, two broken pieces of what she'd been spraying blood and bone in their wake. The skies roll thunder. The lightning shivers with their screams.

Leyah waves wildly from the foot of the hill. Rowena stands to join her, but the ground rolls like seawater, pouring her down.

Somewhere amid her tumble down the hill, the plunging earth becomes steel, and the grass sloughs away. Rowena slams into something flat and tall and hard. She staggers to her feet and feels Leyah's hands steadying her.

The grassy plains are gone. They stand in another hallway, its lines charcoal dusted, faint, a badly rubbed image. Rowena stares at what stopped her fall: a bulkhead door with a great wheel at its center. Wordless, the women spin it open. A sucking sound crowds Rowena's ears.

The room is dim. It smells of blood and cinders and glycerin. All around the cargo hold, boxes and valises, ship's chests and satchels, are thrown aside or torn asunder. Bits of cloth and paper drift through the air.

At the center of a blasted circle of cargo lies a copy of the woman standing at Rowena's side, stretched out with her head in the Alchemist's lap.

It is worse than the ruin of a body beyond the cellar door, because this is not a metaphor.

This happened.

Leyah's right arm is a jagged length of bone and meat ending at the elbow. Her remaining hand twists in the gash of her belly, holding in a handful of the viscera that swells out with every rattling breath. Her eyes are fixed, her face pale. The rapid gasps parting her paper-white lips are the last signs of life. The Alchemist holds her head. He stares into her eyes. Rowena can feel him reaching into her, struggling to find something he can keep alive until help arrives.

But there could never be enough help for damage such as this.

"This is the place Rare was talking about," Rowena says.

Leyah nods. "Perhaps I could have come back from those wounds," she says, though her voice is doubtful. "Perhaps. But I couldn't face the pain."

The wounded Leyah's back arches. Her legs quake. The dying breaths come harder, deeper, rending her throat.

Rowena knows something of death. She has a dead father, and sister, and brother. She saw two of them breathe their last and thought she was done with illusions of death being pretty or easy. But she had always imagined living *must be better than the alternative—that light is better than darkness.*

The dying Leyah makes a heaving sound. Her body stills a moment before trembling in agony once more.

Rowena realizes the illusion she had left. Sometimes, the darkness is better. She had assumed that losing Leyah was the source of the Alchemist's pain. The truth was he hadn't given her up soon enough. And he knew it.

"What do I do?" Rowena asks.

The room shudders. The pressure in Rowena's ears becomes a tearing. The cargo hold's walls peel away, metal shrieking and curling. A howling wind sings through the gashes in the hull.

Leyah grabs a support strut. "If I knew, we wouldn't still be here!"

Rowena sacks her memory for something useful. The human mind is supposed to be a delicate, complex thing. But if there is a gesture that suits the Alchemist's metaphor, some key to his locks she's supposed to have, she can't waste time imagining it.

Rowena darts between the Alchemist and his dying wife. She shoves the woman out of his lap. When her hands come away from Leyah's clammy flesh, her palms burn with cold fire.

"You can't help her," *she shouts.*

The Alchemist wears a younger face, beardless and livid, distorted by grief. He glares through her. Rowena grabs his shoulders to shake him. He throws up an arm, buffets the girl aside, and reaches for Leyah again.

Rowena rebounds to her knees and throws a punch—a hard left, clean across the Alchemist's jaw. Her fist erupts with pain, an electric sting that turns instantly to pins and needles. For a moment, the Alchemist stares at the floor, hands propping himself up. Rowena pounces, shakes him and slaps him. Her heart feels full and burning, the secondhand memory too much to bear holding, too powerful to let go. She could not pry her hands from him if she wished it.

"Forget it!" Rowena cries. "It's done, it's over. Save yourself!"

She can't tell if he recognizes her—can't tell if she savages the Alchemist she knows or a ghost of his past or some knitting of the two. His dazed, dark eyes are lost in the middle distance. Over building wind and tearing metal, she barely hears his response.

"What for?"

"Because I *need you now!"*

The cargo hold opens like a flower, petals of scrap spinning away in the wind. The Alchemist's eyes widen at his first true sight of Rowena, the moment of recognition.

And everything goes suddenly, fiercely white.

39.

Dawn was a pink haze when Rowena Downshire finally stirred in the tangled bedsheets. She lay still a long time, not entirely certain where she was. Her body felt strangely distant, and so she tested it, lifting a hand before her eyes and bending the fingers, stretching one leg and then another under the coverlet. There was a long, white space in her mind where she knew *something* else should have been. She rubbed her arms, massaging life back into them. Her hands throbbed with a half-familiar ache. *A cold rush of air, blistering pain shooting up her arms, someone's eyes . . .* The scene, all scattered sensations, played in her memory. But its narrative was all gone.

When she breathed deeply and smelled chamomile and roses in the pillowcase, Rowena knew the bed, and the curtains around it, and the lace-collared nightgown she wore. She sat up, knuckling her eyes. A muzzle the color of rust and iron nuzzled her elbow.

"Hullo, Rabbit."

The dog wormed his way under her arm, whining and thumping his tail. Rowena ruffled his ragged velvet ears. Rabbit licked her face, his sweeping tail throwing open the curtains around the bed. Rowena spied a breakfast cart where several domed plates waited. Her stomach made noises very much like the dog.

Rowena was pushing her way past Rabbit's fervent kisses toward the edge of the bed and the promise of food when the door of Anselm Meteron's guest room opened.

Whoever it is can wait, her stomach commanded. She wheeled the trolley closer. A little cry of joy and dismay came from behind her. She knew without looking who must be there.

The Reverend Doctor Chalmers insisted on taking Rowena's pulse and peering into the pupils of her eyes, a ritual of medical attention that rather got in the way of tearing into two fried eggs, sausages, and a stack of griddle cakes. Rowena managed a good start in spite of him. Rabbit bounded off the bed, announcing himself loudly to anyone passing in the hall.

The young reverend sat back in the chair he'd dragged to the bedside. Slowly, he shook his head, ran his hands through his thinning hair with a look of wonder, and slipped a brass stethoscope into his ears.

"Like you've come up from a nap," he murmured. "Astounding."

Rowena let him fuss as long as he was of a mind. The food was good—not quite hot, but she didn't care. She had appetite enough for another cartload, and she meant to satisfy it.

"You seem very well," Chalmers pronounced at last. "Now what do you remember?"

Rowena chewed a forkful of eggs and considered. "We were on the roof of the Old Cathedral," she decided.

"And?"

"Is Master Meteron all right?"

Phillip Chalmers blinked. He tapped the stethoscope's end idly and flinched, reminded by the boom that it was still tucked into his ears. "Ah—ow! Well, yes. Dislocated left shoulder, some rather colorful bruises, but he's on the whole quite well. Give him two or three weeks in a sling and he'll be none the worse for wear. But don't you—"

"How did you know I'd be awake in time for breakfast?"

Again, the reverend doctor's face sorted through a look of utter perplexity, his features bending around a question of his own before finally bypassing it.

"Didn't. You've been out three days. We've had breakfast brought up each morning, and dinner, and supper, so it would be ready when you awoke. Nothing's gone to waste. Master Meteron's footman seems quite happy to claim the excess."

Rowena plowed through the last of the griddle cakes and poured as much tea as her cup would hold. Chalmers resumed his account, ticking items off on his fingers.

"God, what you've missed! Regenzi was found dead in the Old Cathedral. His manor has been cordoned off by the constabulary, but since City Inspector Gammon's resigned her post and gone missing, the investigation's in shambles. They found—the other constables found, I mean—Gammon's badge of office on her desk and a note in which she confessed her role in Smallduke Regenzi's conspiracy. Concealing Nora's actual disappearance by way of the murder at the ball, my kidnapping, so on. They sent a barrister and constable down to the prison hulks after the courtesan charged with Pierce's murder, but it seems the warden had already issued her a pardon. Nobody could say where the order first came from, and no one's been able to find her since. Master Meteron says that's just as well, since the new city inspector is a pet of the bishop of Corma. He doesn't think the EC will permit more details of Regenzi and Gammon's alliance to see the light of day. Probably there are scribes in the Court and Bar scrubbing the records even now." Chalmers pursed his lips, as if he might have forgotten something. "Let's see . . . Ah. Yes, of course. The constabulary searched the whole of the Cathedral campus and never found Nasrahiel's body. There was a nasty smashed row of hedges about where he ought to have come down and a blood trail coming off it. No sign of him or what's left of his particular tribe. The gendarmes have feelers out for him, much good may it do."

Chalmers began clearing Rowena's plates with all the fussiness of a governess. "We—I, rather—lost the Vautnek text. Fell from the roof. No sign of it, now, either." He wrinkled his nose in distaste as Rowena reached out at a departing plate, using a finger to swipe up the last of the sausage grease. "I can send for another round, if you—"

"Yes." Rowena looked up fervently. "That'd be jake."

The reverend found the Regency's concierge bellpull and speaking tube stationed nearby. Rowena looked around the room and scrubbed her eyes again, taking in details carefully. Now that the piercing hunger was more of a blunt ache, she realized the room looked off, its colors alternately livid and washed out. She felt curiously raw, as if she'd just risen from a hot bath, scrubbed hard and roughed down with a towel—exhausted and aware and somehow apart from herself. The window curtains were half-drawn, diffusing morning light that seemed to be growing steadily whiter.

She blinked at Corma's skyline.

"It's snowed."

Chalmers glanced at her. "Oh. Yes. It began yesterday evening—nearly five inches and still coming down. Hardly a surprise, after the dry summer and precipitous drop in autumn temperatures. Nature has a way of compensating." He paused and looked down at his shoes with painful self-consciousness. "Miss Downshire?"

"Hm?"

"You, ah . . ." He looked up, fingering the buttons of his waistcoat. His nervous hands wandered home to their pockets. "You haven't asked after the Alchemist."

Rowena put down her teacup and regarded Chalmers with perfect earnestness.

"I know what happened," she said. "He's already told me."

After his third attempt at the morning gazette, the Alchemist gave the early edition up for lost, spiking it into the waste bin at his bedside. The gesture earned a sharp, scolding pain from his bandaged ribs.

"It's useless," he said. "You're certain you didn't find them after the fall?"

Anselm Meteron stared icily over his wineglass's rim. "In the desperate search for whatever resources or persons might be secured to save your irascible, ungrateful life, no. I'm afraid looking for your bloody spectacles quite escaped me."

"You'd scarce believe the headache I get reading without them."

"That might also be owed to the skull fracture you're ignoring."

The Alchemist glared. "I suppose drinking before breakfast is doctor's orders?"

"*I* don't have the benefit of a rather generous dose of morphine. So I'm making do, thank you." Anselm shifted in his chair to prop his slung elbow against its arm and grimaced. "Although, since you insist on using only half your prescription, I'll happily take up the excess."

"I've no love of being doped into a stupor."

"And I've no love of your being a cantankerous arse. Why should we both suffer?"

The Alchemist rested his head against the wedge of pillows propping him at forty-five degrees. He closed his eyes. The throbbing pain in his skull eased, making way for his ribs and leg to call in accounts. Chalmers's skill in medicine was markedly less than his skills in the hard sciences, but he'd managed a competent splint for the leg and a solid line of bracers and bandages to keep the worst flexion from the Alchemist's rib cage. The medical corset made taking more than a half breath devilish hard, but there was no arguing with three broken ribs.

"I know you're worried about the leg," Anselm said. "I still keep in touch with Jane Ardai, if you're looking for . . . options."

"Little Jane from McManus's company?" The Alchemist snorted. "She's practically a child."

"Twenty years ago, perhaps. She does amazing work. These days, folks who get roughed up in the trade call her 'Resurrection Jane.'"

"I think I'll decline the assistance of anyone for whom resurrection is a requisite feature of medical practice."

Anselm shrugged his good shoulder. "Given the prognosis, you might consider what she does in brass."

"Let that be my affair," the Alchemist snapped. He considered Anselm's flat, patient look and sighed. "God, I really am a bear."

"A little more than usual."

"You're certain she isn't awake yet?"

"Chalmers would have told us."

Anselm drained his glass, glanced back at the guest room's nearly closed door, and dragged his chair closer to the bedside. He poured a second glass, an operation of several added steps done single-armed, and offered it to the Alchemist.

"I am an authority on wine before breakfast." He winked. "It's a white. That's allowed."

The Alchemist took the glass with a resigned smile. A moment later, Anselm refilled his glass and they clinked.

"Well, Old Bear, it seems you're going to live to fight another day, given your pet urchin's tender resuscitations."

"So it does." The Alchemist drank. The wine was still cool from the decanter, faintly sweet.

Anselm's expression darkened. "What exactly happened up there?"

"Exactly?" The Alchemist squinted at the ceiling. There was an ache in his head quite apart from the blow it had taken, a feeling that something had left him, and something else had taken its place. "I can't remember all. But she came for me. She held on."

"How?"

"No idea."

"Is it possible *both* of you—" Anselm paused, reaching for the right expression, "—are on the list, so to speak? Your mind tricks are the sort of extraordinary thing I would want to observe, if I were the Deity."

"They aren't," Phillip Chalmers interjected.

The Alchemist and Anselm looked to the door. The young doctor entered hastily, checking the hall for eavesdroppers that weren't there. Whining and wagging, Rabbit trotted through the closing door. He turned three circles in the space between Anselm and the Alchemist, thumping down on the rogue's feet.

Chalmers cleared his throat.

"Rather, he—or you—as it were, aren't 'on the list,'" he clarified. "Nothing in the Vautnek text ever pointed to you as one of the Nine." Chalmers glanced between the two men uncertainly. He knit his fingers behind his back like a schoolboy standing his headmasters' inspection. "The only subject in Corma is Rowena. I'm quite clear on that point. Whatever . . . thing . . . happened between you doesn't appear necessarily linked to her being of the Nine."

The young doctor realized what his patients had in their hands, eyebrows climbing.

"Good Lord, are you both *drinking*?"

"I blame Ann," the Alchemist said. "Bad influence."

Anselm smiled coaxingly. "Join us, Doctor—or do you prefer a red? I have that, as well."

"You are . . . the . . . the most . . . *appalling* patient I've ever had!"

"You're a physicist. It's a rather pale achievement to be both your most appalling patient and your second, all told."

Chalmers presented the Alchemist with his best scowl—really something more like a pout—and bustled up to check the old man's pulse. "*You* should know better."

"It appears I've outlived knowing better, Doctor."

The younger man met the Alchemist's eyes. He looked stricken. "It's shameful, really. I still haven't thanked you for—"

"Don't." The Alchemist passed his drink to the side table and lowered himself against his cushions with a hiss. Chalmers reached to help. He swatted the proffered hand aside. "Instead," he gasped, "tell us what you found out from the EC."

"In lieu of the keynote address, I've been asked to produce a long form of my conference paper." Chalmers noted the pointed look the other men exchanged. "It's not ready yet, quite. It will be something . . . expurgated." The reverend smiled manfully. "I doubt they'll think very much of my research again after they read it. That should help curb interest in the project."

The Alchemist studied Chalmers's tissue façade. He considered what to say to the scholar, but nothing properly conciliatory came to mind—nothing to suit the magnitude of his loss. In just a week, Phillip Chalmers had gone from his career's apex to its armpit, forced by hazard and conscience to substitute the work that would have earned him a place in history for some bowdlerized sham. The scandal of the Decadal Conference's spotlight stolen by a trumped-up piece of buggery would put an end to any meaningful appointments, projects, and funding for years to come—perhaps for the rest of his life. It was a kind of death for the young reverend, a suicide protecting what he'd put at risk. Perhaps the sacrifice was just. It would be no less painful for that.

"I told them I'll be taking sabbatical," Chalmers added suddenly. "Given everything that's happened, they could hardly deny me." The reverend searched about the room and, finding no second chair, perched himself on the window seat an awkward distance from his interlocutors. "I looked into who left Corma the night of Fourth-day, too, and early Fifth-day, as you suggested, Master Meteron. There were around six thousand members of the EC attending the Decadal. A little fewer than a hundred left during that time frame, most of them queerly early and without prior notice. Probably when Deacon Fredericks fled he spread word of trouble among his confederates and they scattered. In any event, it's too large a group to easily gather all the names, but I was able to track about two dozen down."

Anselm nodded. "You have some idea of whom to avoid now."

Chalmers's head bobbed rather too quickly. The Alchemist watched him wring his hands, dishwater eyes stubbornly avoiding Anselm.

"Doctor," the Alchemist pressed, "is there anything else?"

Another head bob, seeming to direct agreement at the reverend's shoes. "As near as I could determine, Bishop Professor Meteron and two of his deacons were the first to leave."

The Alchemist watched Anselm's face. He saw no change, but he felt the ripple of anger, watched him swallow it down with a sip of wine.

"Well," Anselm said quietly, "good to know the old man still keeps on his toes."

"It seems clear the plot had many EC allies," Chalmers added. "That would explain why the bishop of Corma moved so quickly to put one of his favorites in Gammon's place. It seems a few of his postdoctorals gave up the conference around the same time as our . . . um . . . exploits began. What I don't understand is why Bishop Meteron would be involved. He earned his reputation for repudiating Vautnek research. They teach his argument against Ruchell Bennington's theory to second-years in seminary. It's the third week of Meteronian Logic."

"I'm familiar," Anselm said.

Chalmers flushed. "I suppose you would be. Can you think why your father would have shifted positions, after all this time?"

"Because he's a scientist, Chalmers. He found evidence to justify reassessing his position."

The Alchemist raised an eyebrow. "What evidence, short of the book?"

"I'm not sure. He would not have relied on guesswork. The only guesswork we saw in this business was Regenzi's. He was a cat's paw, a way for His Grace to get hold of what he needed while distancing himself from its casualties. Once Regenzi had the book and Pierce in hand, my father could have stepped in to examine the matter personally. But that situation never materialized—never stabilized, with all the pieces in place." Anselm shook his head. "You were a poor substitute, Chalmers, ignorant of details. It was better for him to let Regenzi stay the visible agent, in case your work came to naught. If it bore fruit, though, he would act."

"And *how* would he act?" the Alchemist asked.

Anselm smirked at him. There was that peculiar light in his flinty eyes—the professional admiration of one ruthless strategist for the cunning of another.

"Abraham Regenzi wasn't so different from us, back in our campaigning days. He had ambitions, and so he took a job. He played at justifying kidnapping and murder, claiming that controlling a small number of people would ensure the safety of a larger one. Before all, he was eager to keep the power he had, and hungry for more—the influence my father could grant him. His Grace, on the other hand, is an actuary of human behavior, a pure and proper Utilitarian. He's written algorithms to predict almost every kind of social, political, or economic consequence that can arise from a given set of conditions, and they're damnably accurate. If Regenzi's tools were money, ambition, and heavy-handed strategies, Allister Meteron's are objective data, pragmatic philosophy, and the conviction that he can mathematically model the mind of God."

The Alchemist frowned. He had met Allister Meteron only once, in an encounter that had left an impression equal to Anselm's predictions. He knew his partner's wit and will were a family inheritance. Like most legacies, however impressive, it was only a small share of a much larger fortune.

Chalmers shifted in his seat uneasily. "So what do we do now?"

Anselm sighed. "Hope that wherever that damned book ended up, it will never find its way to my father. If it does, Rowena and the rest will be well and truly humped."

Chalmers shook his head. "That seems an alarmist interpretation. Bishop Professor Meteron . . . well. He *is* a bishop, sworn to act in the interests of Reason and his fellow man."

"Note," Anselm said, "that you listed 'Reason' first. So would he."

Chalmers jumped to his feet and paced between the fireplace and the window, moving with a caged animal's nerve.

"I had thought this was over," he said. "With the book gone, and only part of my notes left, and Regenzi dead . . ." He stopped and chewed his lip. "This will take more than a botch of a paper and a sabbatical to put to rest."

"Yes," the Alchemist agreed.

"So what can I do?"

"You'll have your sabbatical. You have the deposit box key Pierce intended for you," Anselm observed darkly. "Lives were lost putting it in your hands. I wouldn't let them go to waste."

Chalmers pursed his lips, nodding. "And what will *you* do?"

Anselm studied the ceiling. "Too many variables. Too little information. Until we know what's waiting in that box, we can't plan our next move."

"We know one thing," the Alchemist countered. "We know about Rowena."

Not long after he regained consciousness in the guest rooms of Regency Square, Anselm had told his partner what the book showed—Subject Six, the maps, the notes, the clear path of evidence stretching beyond coincidence. Anselm had described the whole business with a surreal humor, but beneath that feigned aplomb, the Alchemist felt an unspoken certainty of the truth—the deep, ineffable belief in what he'd seen. And somehow, that truth fitted with what the Alchemist knew of Rowena, the inscrutable details he'd seen in her mind. The thought of it weighed on him with every stabbing breath he'd taken since.

"It's safest to assume Nasrahiel is alive," the Alchemist continued, "however unlikely that seems. Or some lieutenant among his tribe might also know what he did of the Nine. If we're very unlucky, *they* have the book. Even an incomplete record of that truth is enough to put the girl in danger."

Chalmers shook his head. "I can't protect her."

"No one's asking you to."

Anselm put his glass down, a wincing caution coloring his voice. "*Bear*—"

"I'm responsible for her," the Alchemist insisted. "She came to me looking for help and found worse danger after."

"You saved her life up on that roof."

"Do you really think she didn't save mine, too?"

"But she *does* have family, yes?" Chalmers interrupted. "In . . . what, Oldtemple, is it? That was the indication in what's left of my notes on Subject Six. Surely if the debt were settled, her family could take her back."

"Clara Downshire is in a convalescent home for gentlewoman hysterics," Anselm answered. He resumed his wineglass and studied its emptiness with conspicuous interest. "Her debt has been satisfied by an anonymous benefactor."

Anselm must have felt the Alchemist's gaze. He waved his glass dismissively, setting it down again to pour. "It's some country manor a morning's ride out by lightning rail. You hear things about where ladies go when the fit is on them, if you attend the right sort of parties." He drank and tilted his chin thoughtfully. "Or the wrong sort. That stroke of good fortune notwithstanding, I'm afraid Mrs. Downshire is in no condition to see to her daughter's welfare at present. Some of the better medical minds in the area think she never will be."

Chalmers took his seat at the window, studying the Alchemist with evident doubt. "You're going to need two months, at minimum, before you're partly back on your feet, and at least a further month before the leg can bear regular weight. The break was patellar local, so—"

"Bone fragments," the Alchemist finished. "I know. I've done my turn in a surgery. I believe I have one last good job in me, Doctor. I think it should be her."

"You're quite sure you want this responsibility? A ninth of everything that matters in the world, something people are willing to kill over?"

"Not some*thing*, Doctor. Some*one*." Out of habit, the Alchemist reached to the jacket pocket he didn't have, searching for the pipe that wouldn't be there. He sighed. "To my mind, your discovery doesn't reveal that only nine people truly matter. That's not what makes it so staggering. It's the revelation that any soul could be chosen for some reason we will never know or understand and used as the litmus test of mankind entire. At any moment, there are only nine who play that role, but any person could be made one of them. You misunderstand me if you think I want to protect her because she's Subject Six. I owe her some kind of safety because she is *Rowena*."

Anselm applauded slowly against the leg of his trousers, his smile wolfish.

"Good show, Old Bear. A fine speech. But there's something to be said for keeping part of the bloody numerological universe from supporting herself by the industry of the streets, falling into utter criminality, and debasing the human image in the eyes of the godhead, no?"

"If that's the only rationale you'll accept. I see this as a matter of private conscience."

"There's one imperative," Chalmers stressed. "She *can't know* what she is. If she knew the weight she carries, think of how paralyzing, how stupefying—"

Anselm pinched the bridge of his nose, half-stifling a laugh. Reverend Doctor Chalmers's voice trailed, finally dying out. He looked to the Alchemist for help.

The Alchemist raised an eyebrow. "Problem, Ann?"

"Only marveling at the shadowy ex-mercenary and the degenerate spy shepherding the most dangerously impressionable girl the world has ever known. More precisely, at your suggesting it's a good idea."

"You have your life. I don't begrudge you going your own way."

"I've made an investment in what remains of the family Downshire," Anselm answered. "Quite literally. I prefer a hands-on approach to asset protection."

The Alchemist opened his mouth to speak, then frowned. He looked down at the shaggy hound snoring wetly on Anselm's feet.

"Useless beast," he murmured. "You might have told us."

Anselm blinked. "Told us what?"

There was a knock at the door.

Anselm glowered at Chalmers. The young reverend turned several shades of scarlet.

"Did I perchance mention," he wondered innocently, "that Miss Downshire is awake, and finishing breakfast, and intends to be down once she's attended to her toilet and dressed?"

"God's balls, Doctor—" moaned Anselm.

"Do you, ah, want me to . . . ?"

With an unceremonious jerk, Anselm pulled his feet from under Rabbit's chin and stalked to the door. The reverend scurried up in time to have Anselm's wineglass thrust into his hands. Anselm opened the door.

Rowena Downshire was small—not five feet nor a hundred pounds with her pockets full of rocks—but she looked much less like a child standing there in a gray woolen skirt and corseted blouse. The bruise around her left eye was a livid purple, and the cut slicing across her eyebrow promised to leave a scar. A wary readiness in her eyes showed the Cathedral might stay with her in other ways, too.

"Master Meteron." Rowena curtseyed. It was a wobbly gesture, a civility in its infancy.

Anselm honored it with the bow that was more of a nod. "Cricket."

Rowena touched his sling—a gold cravat unfolded and wrapped over plain hospital muslin. She smiled impishly. "It's, um . . . fetching."

"A little modification. The good doctor lacks something in the way of aesthetic impulse. I keep hoping the drink will help with that, but thus far, it's proven useless."

The Reverend Chalmers swept the hand bearing Anselm's wineglass behind his back with a flush. He edged his way around Rowena and out the door.

"I, ah, really must be . . . There's probably something—" He smiled abortively at the Alchemist. "Well, you need to talk."

And he scurried away with a haste that put the nimblest of pantry mice to shame.

Anselm swept his four-and-a-half-fingered hand toward the room. "I'll give you your privacy."

He was halfway through the door when Rowena put a hand on his slung elbow. She snatched it back at his wince.

"Sorry, I didn't mean to—"

"Quite all right," he said through gritted teeth.

Rowena glanced back into the room. She avoided the Alchemist's steady, silent gaze. "It's just there's something I wanted to say to both of you."

Anselm looked to the Alchemist, who nodded.

The thief sighed. "Since you'll manhandle me if I try to leave, I suppose I'm in your power."

He assumed Chalmers's place at the window seat and left the chair beside the Alchemist's bed to Rowena. She stood behind it, wringing its top rail in her hands.

"You left a . . . a feeling in my mind. That things were okay. That you were fine." There was an edge to Rowena's voice, as if she were accusing the Alchemist of something.

He attempted a smile—and wished, seeing her nose wrinkle skeptically, he had not.

"I've been worse off," he said quickly.

"The Hebrides back in fifty-four" Anselm agreed. "Two slugs in the belly. Leyah had to stop me putting a mercy dagger in him."

Rowena studied Anselm's face, searching. The Alchemist remembered only fragments of what had passed between them as he hurtled toward death. But he couldn't forget Leyah's face in his mind—how clearly it must have shown the girl what she couldn't have known before.

"You have the same eyes," Rowena announced. "Why didn't you tell me Leyah was your sister?"

Anselm smiled crookedly. That look, he shared with Leyah, too.

"It didn't seem important."

"But it explains a lot. Why she mattered to you. Why you two still have anything to do with each other." She marveled at the Alchemist. "You're brothers."

"In a manner of speaking."

A silence stretched on, long and fragile. Rowena sat, smoothing her skirts. There was a catch in her voice as she began.

"So, I had an idea. I thought of it while I was getting dressed, and—well, anyway, I took a long time doing it because I wasn't sure what I wanted to say, and then it came to me, like. I think maybe this has all happened a bit too fast, you know?" She looked up for confirmation. "I think it makes sense to start over."

The Alchemist frowned. "I'm not sure I follow you."

"I'll go first." Rowena straightened up, folded her hands, and announced in a voice a half step louder than normal, "Good day."

Anselm looked at the Alchemist doubtfully, then shrugged.

"Good day," he said.

The girl seemed to have found her footing. "My name is Rowena Downshire. I'm mostly an orphan, except for my mother, who's gone mad. I make my way delivering things and stealing stuff folk seem as they could do without. I've got a bit of a mouth, and I haven't much schooling, but I say what I mean and I'd really just like . . ." She paused, mustering herself. "I'd like to hang my hat somewhere for good, you know?"

Rowena looked from the Alchemist to Anselm and back again. Anselm cleared his throat.

"Good day." His expression suggested he found the exercise equal parts amusing and uncomfortable. "My name is Anselm Meteron, and I'm a villain with a penchant for self-aggrandizement and a portfolio of maladjusted habits. My elder sister married an exasperatingly moral mercenary whose conviction that I'm redeemable dogs my darker ambitions. Currently, I find myself nursing a wounded shoulder and a vendetta, which I prefer to acknowledging what I've lost."

Rowena smiled in relief. Two down.

The others looked expectantly at the Alchemist.

"How do *you* do?" Rowena prompted.

He furnished an incredulous stare. "Rather poorly, at present."

Anselm spread his four-and-a-half-fingered hand, waiting.

The Alchemist opened his mouth to protest, and Rowena's voice piped over him.

"You might start with your *name*, you know. It's sort of a thing people do, telling other folks what their name—"

"Pardon."

Rowena mustered her market voice. "*I—asked—about—your—name.*"

The Alchemist scowled. "I'm lamed, girl, not deaf. That is the name: Pardon. Erasmus Pardon."

Rowena bit her lip. "Oh . . . Well." She raised her eyebrows, expectant.

The Alchemist chewed his words a moment before beginning.

"I am Erasmus Pardon, widower and alchemist, reluctant tradesman, recluse, and reputed witch. I avoid the company of others because I come to know too much of them, by means of powers I shouldn't possess. I have driven away or destroyed most of those who have cared for me, with the exception of a very stubborn brother-in-law and a very stupid old dog." Pardon hesitated long enough it seemed he was done. And then, he gave the last. "I live in fear of being discovered for what I am—and of being alone."

The silence resumed. Anselm placed the stopper back over the wine carafe's nose, the grind of crystal far louder than it ought to have seemed. Rowena broke the stillness, first with a snigger, then a giggle, and finally a fully grown laugh. She buckled in on herself, turning pink. Pardon clenched his jaw to keep from chuckling. The very idea of laughter tore his splinted sides.

"You actually thought," Anselm marveled, "this would make things *less* awkward?"

Rowena wiped her eyes with the hem of her skirt. "It was a terrible idea." She looked at Pardon and took a slow breath, trying to discipline herself. "All right. How long do you need to mend?"

"Months—fewer of them if things go well."

"Then you're going to need some help around the Scales. I mean, no stock ladders and crate carrying for a while, I suppose?"

"Definitely not. Rowena—"

"I'm stronger than I look," she insisted.

Pardon raised an eyebrow. "A clerk needs to know her letters and figures."

"So I'll learn 'em. *One* of us is young yet, anyway. Plenty of time, yeah?"

"Rowena Downshire." He frowned. "Have you just hired yourself to me?"

"Way I see it, you need me." She stood and dusted her skirts with an air of finality. "And you were going to do it, anyhow. Just being slow about it. Come on, Rabbit. I've got the queerest headache. Let's have the doc see to it."

Rabbit zuffed and clambered to his feet, trotting out on Rowena's heels. The door swung to, the hound's skittering nails trailing away behind it.

Erasmus Pardon gazed up at the ceiling. His head ached, too, but not more than his heart. It must have been the bruise from the lead plate troubling him again. *It is*, he told himself, *the only reasonable explanation.* The pain lingered deep in his breastbone, a dull memory of something worse.

"Ann?"

A smirk colored Anselm's voice. "Yes, Bear?"

Pardon felt the ghost of a smile touch his lips. He exorcised it with a practiced scowl. "That damned girl just stole my dog."

AFTER

She did not have a name among her own kind, but, because humans seemed to require one for everything, she called herself Dor. Dor was not really a "she," either, but humans demanded a sense of *what* they looked at as much as a name to give it, and so she had trained her wooden flesh into a woman's shape, curved and mounded, her leaves spilling down over shapely, smooth-barked shoulders. It was merely an aesthetic exercise, though it pleased her that the long, curious stares Men gave her suggested she had done it well.

Dor combed the Cathedral campus for the third time since the Swinging People did battle with the Men. The first nights, her inspection had been hasty, disorganized. She'd brought two other treelings with her, and they had known so very little of how to bind their bodies into the soil and *feel* for answers. City-sprouted creatures. Cuttings of cuttings, planted in hothouses. Simpletons. They were nothing compared to Dor's copse clansmen, who lived in the wilds even in deepest winter. Her clan would have long since left the smoke-cloaked city, their autumn trading done, had the city not been home to such a gathering of Men. The conference ought to leave spoils behind, enough to make being snowbound, trapped through the silent season under plates of glass, worth her people's sufferance.

This morning, she brought only one other treeling: her copse mate, Lir, who had shaped as a man this season. Lir knew how to bind into the earth. He would be a good partner, and now, the Men soldiers and constables long since gone, they could work together and find whatever worthies remained.

There was *always* something.

Lir had crossed to the western side of the Cathedral and sunk himself in amid the hedgerows. Dor knelt at the east, hands dug into the deep bed of needles beneath a thicket of larches. Under the blanket of soil and gathering snow, she felt herself extending, thinning, reaching ever outward. She closed her eyes and listened with all her cells. She waited. In the distance, Dor felt Lir's body twining nearer, covering the ground between them. It was not a fast process. Feeling through the earth for the weight of something foreign upon it could take an hour or more, especially over so much territory. But Dor could not fail to notice something, if it was there. However well hidden to the eye, if there was a presence—the iron tang of a lost gun, the heft of a copper-heavy purse, even the feather touch of a broken necklace laced in among the grass—they would feel it, together.

Time passed.

And . . . nothing.

If Dor had had teeth, she'd have ground them to shavings. The treelings she had brought before would only come in the dark of night, such was their fear of the constables and their truncheons. Cowards. Idiots. Did they know nothing of their own nature? An ax or fire might fell a lanyani, but no city Man ever carried these. Still, Dor had yielded to their fear and put off a proper search until now. She had suffered their picking through the grasses, their bending and hunting hunchbacked, like fools. Like *Men*. She had suffered their ignorance, waited too long, and now, there would be nothing to show for it, the land already picked clean.

The last lengths of Dor's twiggings were sliding past the larches' roots when the shiver of recognition struck her.

What is it? Dor heard Lir's voice in her mind, not as words but as a pulse, a familiar pressing through the fibers of her senses.

Follow me and see, she replied.

Dor's twiggings did not have far to travel. They raced along the root path, Lir's distant stretched self closing in behind. Together, they wound up the arrow-straight trunk, and smelled sap, and felt the cold greenness, and the brush of needles like starched lace. Together, wedged against the larch's trunk and a center beam of branch, they found the burden of which the roots had whispered.

Lir's twiggings withdrew slowly, caressing the object's smooth, waxy surface. So perfect, even after days of snow and frost. Lir's twiggings scraped over Dor's as she told the distant part of herself to grasp the foreign thing and bring it close.

It came slowly, eased between the branches. Not a single snowflake shook free as her twiggings passed.

Dor watched her distant parts grow nearer, thicker, more *herself*. She stared at what they held.

Lir stirred in the earth beneath her, winding, wheedling.

What is it?

Dor hugged the object to her chest. The snow fell away from it, and yes, it *was* dry, somehow. She lifted it and stared at its black cover, its thick, unlovely spine.

Her heels rooted deep down, murmuring a reply.

A book. It must have fallen from somewhere. The Cathedral, perhaps.

Damaged?

Dor opened its cover. *No*, she answered. Pages fanned in the wind, settling slowly, like breath escaping a body.

A page of scrawl stared back at her. *So strange*, she hummed into the earth.

Why strange?

Come see, Lir.

The lines—the words—had begun moving, advancing like a parade of ants. Dor traced them with a slender finger.

Lir plunged through the earth, rooting his way to her in his eagerness. A burrow line like that of a giant vole traced his path back toward the western side of the Cathedral Commons. Lir unfurled from the snowy ground beside Dor, his limbs untangling and neck craning over her shoulder. The tips of his fingers twined around the hand that held their prize, his words humming into her heartwood.

Strange, indeed. Where do the words come from?

I don't know, Dor answered. *It is stranger still that they are written in our people's symbols.*

But it belonged to the Men.

Dor closed the book, her fingers stretching, braiding themselves around the cover, binding it shut. *Once. It belongs to us, now.*

ACKNOWLEDGMENTS

As far back as I can remember reading books, I remember turning to the acknowledgments page and daydreaming about the day I, too, would have the honor of crafting some beautiful statement in tribute to all those who supported my work. Never mind that I would have to have written a book first and found some way to get it published. All of that was quite secondary. The acknowledgments was the sacred space where I would, someday, emphatically demonstrate what it meant for me to be a writer.

Faced with the reality of writing these longed-for acknowledgments, I realize Past Tracy was something of an idiot. I've rarely felt so bereft of words. Yet I owe a great deal to the people who helped this work find its way into print and into your hands, and so, I will do my best despite. Any names omitted or favors done that I neglect to mention specifically are entirely my fault; the people I may slight will know how to find me and collect their due.

To Bridget Smith, my agent at Dunham Literary (one part Peggy Carter, one part the Morrigan) and Rene Sears, my editor at Pyr (story sister and geekmaven), thank you for investing hundreds of hours of hope, imagination, and talent in my words. It's an old but unfailingly true adage that the reward for doing your work well is more work. I aim to give you both a lot more work in the future and (hopefully) to prove worthy of it.

Many others at Pyr put their backs into the effort to see *The Nine* published, and I owe them each a debt. Special thanks go to Editorial Assistant Hanna Etu, who was a lighthouse of patience, clarity, and calm resolve (even when I lacked anything like these qualities, myself); to Senior Publicist Lisa Michalski, who gave me hope that my words would find their way into your hands; and to copyeditor extraordinaire Jeffrey

Curry, who made them worth reading, at the price of his sanity and a few Bon Jovi memes.

To my critique partners, Michelle Barry and Maura Jortner: here it is, at long last. There may be no humans alive who have read more versions of this manuscript or invested more time in e-mails and Twitter DMs and phone calls fretting over its future. I can't imagine surviving any of it without your unflagging enthusiasm and narrative savvy. You will always be first among the Unicorn Ninja Witches.

To my beta readers: each of you was the source of at least one critical idea without which this book could never have taken its final form. Joseph Maynen (high priest of the Church of Latter-Day Asimovians, the first and best hand seller of my writing), Leah Kind (courageous genre skeptic and eternal friend), Rachel Townsend (incisive as sister and critic, always), Hector Flores (crusher of nonsense and bringer of justice), and David Townsend (husband, coconspirator, knitter of plot holes, author of ambition), thank you a thousand times.

To my students and colleagues at the Illinois Mathematics and Science Academy: thank you for finding a new cliff, every day, to push me from. I've learned a great deal flapping my arms on the way down.

To my parents, Ned and Kathy Charlton: I sat down once to see if I could figure out the cost of my becoming a writer through my odd and aimless childhood. The notebooks, the sketchbooks, the summer camps, the computers, the college education. The endless library fines. The used book sales and study abroad. And yet, what must have cost the most was your believing in me, long before I ever believed in myself. Someday, I'll pay it all back, I swear.

And finally, because a single entry under beta reading could never say enough: to my husband, David, and also our children, Corwin and Deirdre. You've endured pitiful breakfasts, dirty laundry, unpaired socks, forgotten appointments, and lost paperwork these last several years. But now, we have a book to show for it.

I hope you can forgive me.

I loved you too much not to write it.

ABOUT THE AUTHOR

Photo by Jennifer Bronson

Tracy Townsend holds a master's degree in writing and rhetoric from DePaul University and a bachelor's degree in creative writing from DePauw University, a source of regular consternation when proofreading her credentials. She has served as chair of the English Department at the Illinois Mathematics and Science Academy, an elite public boarding school, where she currently teaches creative writing and science fiction and fantasy literature. She has been a martial arts instructor, a stage combat and accent coach, and a short-order cook for houses full of tired gamers. Now she lives in Bolingbrook, Illinois, with two bumptious hounds, two remarkable children, and one very patient husband.